SALMON CROQUETTES

SALMON CROQUETTES

GLODEAN CHAMPION

Black Muse Publishing

Black Muse Publishing
7052 Santa Teresa Blvd
San Jose, CA 95139

To request permissions, contact the publisher at publisher@blackmusepublishing.com

ISBN: 9780578767550 (Paperback)
ISBN: 9780578767567 (EPub)

First Black Muse Publishing trade paperback edition February 2021

Cover art by Design With Aim, Amy Balzer-Pemberton

Printed by IngramSprak in the USA

www.blackmusepublishing.com

In
loving
memory
of
Frances B. Champion
Without you, I never would have known all the
world had to offer or had the courage to explore
the possibilities until I found the ones waiting just
for me. I love you, Momma!
Your, Pootsie

"*Everybody's journey is individual. If you fall in love with a boy, you fall in love with a boy. The fact that many Americans consider it a disease says more about them than it does about homosexuality.*"
~ James Baldwin

Acknowledgments

I fell in love with writing in Mrs. Jones' creative writing class at Laney College (Oakland, CA) in 1993. Mrs. Jones was a sassy, sharp-tongued, witty powerhouse from the Caribbean. She didn't bullshit anyone and, if you were smart, you didn't bullshit her, especially in your writing. I did my best not to do that and avoid all the pitfalls of writing as she laid them out to us. When Mrs. Jones handed back my third short story submission, she'd written a note beneath her critique, "Glodean, you are a natural storyteller. That is a special gift that you would be best served not to waste."

I went home that night and danced around the living room because Mrs. Jones complimented me, and she never gave compliments. Halfway through the semester, just as I was finding my voice groove, I showed up to class one evening to find a substitute standing where Mrs. Jones should have been. He waited until we were all seated, then announced Mrs. Jones passed away over the weekend. We were all devasted, especially me, because by then, she'd become my mentor. The teacher who followed was the worst, and I gave up all hope and stopped writing until 2004 when I started at Mills College. During my time at Mills, I found my voice again and the inspiration for Zayla's story. Mills is where my gratitude begins.

To the LGBT sistas of Mills College (2004-2006) for your courage to live out loud and proud! YOU were the inspiration for this story because I saw Zayla in all of you. To Micheline Marcom, Cornelia Nixon, Sarah Pollock, and Elmaz Abinader (Mills College); Robin Marcus (Hurston/Wright Foundation Writers Week); Walter Mosley and Junot Diaz (VONA); Michelle Richmond, Anne Marino (deceased), Gloria Frym, and Opal Palmer Adisa (California College of the Arts) for teaching me the art of writing and the fearlessness and vulnerability required to do it right. Each of you contributed to the crafting of this novel, and I am forever grateful. And, special thanks to you, Opal, for being my kickass thesis advisor and insisting I continue writing Zayla's story (it took me a while, but better late than never, right?). Most of all, thank you for helping me find the spiritual relief I needed so I could stop grieving my mother's death and celebrate her life. Your love and support pulled me out of the dark into the light.

To Lorraine Thompson for supporting and encouraging me to keep writing! Thank you for reading and listening to every iteration of Zayla's journey and helping me push through in those times when I wanted to throw my hands up and walk away. To Tony Lindsay, Larry Redmond, Paris Smith, Nicole Bond, Delbert Tibbs (deceased), and Sam Greenlee (deceased) (the writers of The Perspectivists, Chicago) for giving it to me straight, no chaser. You made sure I got the Black experience and Chicago in the 60s spot on. Thank you! Thank you! Thank you! Y'all are the TRUTH! And, to Tjuan Smith for being right there by my side as I wrote to the end of the novel, and most of all, for naming "Evil Evie Sheffield" and Pastor Shuttlesworth!

To Anne Lynch and Stacy Johnson for being the "special sauce" I needed to get through the editing process! Stacy, thank you extra for saying, "Champ! It's fine just the way it is. Leave it alone!" until I listened. To Steve Farber for giving me that final kick in the pants I needed to get this book ready for the world and pushing through what felt like a decade-long OS!M! To Kwame Dawes for being such an honest and forthright editor. Thank you for helping me tighten the narrative so that I could once and for all introduce Zayla to the world and be proud of the story she unfolds. Your insight into the world of publishing inspired Black Muse Publishing. To Leslie Mc-Graw, my stalwart coach and supporter of all the crazy ideas I've had over the years. Your guidance through this process has been immeasurable. I'm sure by now I would have pulled my hair out trying to figure it out on my own. You know I have to give you a BIG SHOUT OUT for hooking me up with Janet Cannon (copy editor) and Designs With Aim (cover art) to pull me through the finish line! To Amy Balzer-Pemberton, Designs With Aim, for bringing my vision of the cover to reality! You didn't miss a single detail. From the black and white tiled floor, the circa 1960s décor, the gingham print tablecloth, Zayla, Frank, Zora...even down to the salmon croquettes, and red beans and rice. I am so impressed with your talent and grateful that I benefitted from it in such a meaningful way!

To Aunt Noonie and Uncle Sherman (deceased) for opening your home to me (and Maxx) so I had space and freedom to write every day. I valued every moment of it, and I still long for the day I will have six months of uninterrupted writing time again! I love you to the moon and back and around again!

Lastly, my eternal gratitude to my mother, Frances Champion! Words can't express how much I value your intentional parenting, undeniable leadership, and unparalleled courage while raising this "hellion." If it weren't for you, I wouldn't be the woman I am today. Thank you for reading to me every night and introducing me to the colorful, wondrous, fantastical worlds of Beatrix Potter, Richard Scarry, Maurice Sendak, and Judy Blume. And thank you for not killing me when I almost burned the house down, reading by nightlight under wool covers. My imagination is wild and my spirit free because you gave me the courage to shout unabashedly from the rooftops, which is proving to be quite useful in my craft. And, of course, I never would have known the truth about Watts had your car never turned off Central Avenue into the "Circle" and stopped in front of 10478 Pace Avenue. I love you so much, and while I still miss you like crazy, it doesn't hurt quite as much.

If I forgot to mention anyone, please blame it on my head and not my heart!

Much love to all of you,
Glodean

Part One

February 1965 – June 1965

I

U.S. Honors Men Who Died for Country
L.A. Times – Monday, May 31, 1965

> *& love is an evil word.*
> *Turn it backwards/see, see what I mean?*
> *An evol word. & besides*
> *who understands it?*
> *I certainly wouldn't like to go out on that kind of limb.*
> ~Amiri Baraka, "In Memory of Radio"

The first time I fell in love, I was in the sixth grade.

We lived in Watts, back then, a close-knit community of blue- and white-collar workers living side by side. "Good hardworking Negroes," as Daddy liked to say. Momma liked to say, "Those same 'hardworking Negroes' show up to Sunday service leaning sideways, smelling of sin," as if she'd never leaned with sin herself. Momma wanted me to believe she's always been a good God-fearing Christian, as if this knowledge would shame me into being the same. She wasn't fooling anyone. I knew she was a hellion in her days, B.Z. ("Before Zayla," that's me) because I saw pictures of her half naked, face full of make-up, hanging off different guys until those guys became one guy – my daddy, Frank Sylvester McKinney.

Daddy used to be a famous singer on the Chitlin' Circuit and was spitting distance from being the next Otis Redding, as he loved to say. Then, one night, he stepped into the narrow smoke-filled hallway of The Sanctuary, a blues club on 103rd Street, and collided into Zora Phillips. How they ever got beyond that first night was a mystery to me because Daddy was sunshine compared to Momma's thunderstorms. Yet, one year later, she traded in her BS degree from Loyola Marymount for an MRS degree. Nine months after that, baby makes three, as the saying goes. Daddy bought the brown stucco Craftsman in the middle of the block on Pace Avenue in "The Circle." Our close-knit neighborhood, where Daddy grew up, is just off Central Avenue and 104th Street.

For love, Daddy took a job at KGFJ, the most popular radio station in L.A., where he became one of the most popular deejays. When the owner of The Sanctuary retired, Daddy bought the nightclub to keep the nightlife going in Watts. Momma's claim to fame was loving Daddy and making my life miserable – and she was award-winning. I couldn't imagine giving up everything for love, although I didn't fully understand it. To me, love was winning a round of marbles and walking away with someone's favorite Shooter. So, when Kimberly Denise Mitchell moved into the house across the street the idea of love began to make more and more sense.

For three days, I watched, safely hidden behind the drapes, as she played jacks and hopscotch alone. My lack of confidence toward pretty girls prevented me from going over to introduce myself. She had this mass of auburn curls that reflected blonde highlights when the sun hit it just so, and deep dimples that could be seen from miles away. She was tall, but not so tall kids would call her "Gigantor." And she had just enough flesh on her bones so kids wouldn't call her "Bean Pole." Convinced I'd never get the courage to go over and meet her, I sent my best friend, Malik, instead. I had to bribe him with my fireball red Shooter to get him to agree.

I peeked through the curtains while they talked, wondering what he was telling her because she kept looking over at our house. After about ten minutes, he burst through our front door and flopped down on the sofa.

"Her name is Kimberly Denise Mitchell. Call her 'Dee-Dee' though 'cause she beat up the last person that called her Kimberly. Her and her mom...Sharon...can you believe she calls her mom by her first name? Anyway, they used to live in a fancy house in Hollywood with her mom's boyfriend, until he kicked them out. She don't know or care where her father is. She don't have no brothers and sisters. And, she wants to know how long you're gonna watch her out the window before you go introduce yourself."

"What did you say to her?" I asked.

So much for going unnoticed. How did she see me watching her? I wondered. Then punched Malik in his arm for being such a terrible spy.

"Owww. Nothin'. She told me you had two days and then she was comin' over here."

Just like Malik to not be helpful when I needed him.

"Thanks," I said, not meaning it.

Momma watched Ms. Mitchell come and go, too. Not from behind the curtains, either. Sometimes she stood on the porch watching, letting everyone see nosy in action. This is how Momma saw a white man drop Ms. Mitchell off at the corner instead of in front of her house. She almost broke her neck getting to the phone to call Aunt Evelyn (she wasn't my real aunt, she was Malik's mother and Momma's best friend, their lifelong friendship established around the coloring table in first grade). Momma was convinced Ms. Mitchell was a lady of the night. I thought that meant she worked the graveyard shift like the guys at the Long Beach docks. I found out later what it really meant.

"If she is trickin' at least she got her a rich white man. She could do a lot worse," Aunt Evelyn said.

Later that same day, Aunt Evelyn bumped into Ms. Mitchell and Dee-Dee while shopping at Giant Market on 103rd Street and she had a different opinion. Aunt Evelyn found Sharon fascinating, even called her "glamorous" and "shiny" with great big Diana Ross eyes. Dee-Dee, on the other hand, had the nerve to call Aunt Evelyn by her first name and quickly found herself on Aunt Evelyn's shit list. Children called close friends of the family "aunt" or "uncle," insert first name. Otherwise, they were "mister" or "missus," insert last name. Under no circumstances could we call an adult by their first name. No exceptions. Ever. Knowing Aunt Evelyn the way I did, I know she gave Dee-Dee a good dressing down because that's what adults did when we stepped out of line.

Obviously, it wasn't good enough because two days later, though, she showed up at our front door clad in a pink polka dot swimsuit, sporting fuchsia sunshades that took up most of her face, and did the same thing to Momma.

"Good morning!" she said in a sing-songy way when Momma opened the door. "My name is Kimberly Denise Mitchell, but you can call me Dee-Dee. We just moved in across the street, but you probably already know that, huh? You're Zora, right? And your daughter is Zayla?"

"Excuse me? To you, I'm Mrs. McKinney," Momma said. "How may I help you, young lady?"

"I'm sorry, Mrs. McKinney. I told Sharon you probably wouldn't like it if I called you by your first name, most adults don't. I know Malik's mom sure didn't. Sharon, I mean, my mother, makes me call her and all her friends by their first name. She says it makes her feel younger. Umm...I was wondering...if it's okay with you... can Zayla come out and play."

I waited for Momma to send her away.

"Zayla," Momma called, as if I wasn't sitting ten feet behind her on the sofa. "Put that book down and come out here and meet Kimberly."

"Dee-Dee," Dee-Dee corrected.

"Mmmm hmmm," Momma said, and walked off.

I threw my copy of *Charlie and The Chocolate Factory* on my bed and went to the door.

"Hi," I said, stepping onto the porch and closing the door behind me.

"Hi," she said and bounced to her feet. "Come on."

She grabbed my hand and pulled me across the street, talking non-stop as if we were old friends reacquainted.

"I'm so glad we moved to Watts to be around some other Negroes. White people are too much. Sharon hates being here, but my uncle owns the house and Sharon doesn't have a job and no one wants to take us in so here we are. Do you want something to drink?"

Before I could answer she told me to "have a seat" and disappeared into her house. She came back a few minutes later with two glasses of lemonade and handed one to me.

"Sharon's still unpacking, otherwise there would be cookies and sandwiches with the crusts cut off to go with this. Sometimes I think she wants to be June Cleaver. Funny, right? A Negro wanting to be a white woman."

I half-smiled, the other half of me was stuck on the fact that she called her mother by her first name. I didn't even have to wonder what Momma would do if I started calling her Zora. It would be the last word I uttered in life, that was for sure.

The front door opened and an old man, looking like a Negro Santa Claus in blue and white stripped overalls stepped onto the porch. He smelled of cigarettes, beer, and day-old funk, as Momma would say.

"Dee, you wanna play in the sprinklers? It's hot enough."

"Sure, Eddie. Thanks," Dee-Dee said.

I waited for her to introduce me. She didn't and Eddie acted like I wasn't there anyway. The curse of being the plain girl. People only notice the pretty girl, which is why people saw Momma before they ever noticed me. I was used to it.

Eddie left and came back holding a large box with "Garden" scrawled in black marker on all sides. He sat the box down and went back in the house. Dee-Dee rummaged around inside until she found the sprinkler head and water hose. I helped her pull the hose out. She grabbed one end, humming to herself as she assembled the two parts.

"Help me find the spigot," she demanded, jumping down all three steps into the grass.

She headed to the side of the house. I looked behind the shrubs out front because our spigot was under the front window. For some reason I had yet to understand, I wanted to be the first to find the spigot. I needed her to like me more than I'd ever wanted any girl to like me before.

"I found it," she called out.

Deflated, I dusted myself off and returned to my spot on the porch. The sprinkler head sputtered to life, shooting streams of water into the air. Dee-Dee tossed her sunshades in the direction of the porch and ran, screaming, through the water. I picked them up and sat them next to me.

"Aren't you gonna play in the water with me?" she asked.

"Nah. I don't wanna get my hair wet."

"Why not?"

"Because I hate the pressing comb," I said.

Dee-Dee shrugged. No surprise there. She had "good" hair. The kind of hair that could get wet and be straightened with the least amount of heat. My hair required a straightening comb, otherwise it was a nappy mess and Momma hated messes of any kind.

When Dee-Dee tired of the sprinklers, she came up on the porch, dripping water everywhere, and flopped down next to me. We watched the water go back and forth across the grass awhile. I searched for an excuse to leave, because as fascinated as I was, I was equally uncomfortable. Dee-Dee appeared to be completely comfortable in her skin, as if it was an extravagant evening gown designed by God Himself. She was one hundred percent girl. Polished fingernails and toenails. Matching swimsuit and sunshades. I was rough and tumble. My skin felt like a three-piece polyester suit four sizes too small – designer unknown.

Basically, I didn't care how I looked coming out of the house. I hated fingernail polish. Matching clothes. And anything frilly or ruffled. My experience with the girls in The Circle proved that "rough and tumble" and "girlie girls" didn't blend well. It probably didn't help that I took pleasure in decapitating dolls and breaking up tea sets. Momma said I did it out of meanness because I was jealous. Except I wasn't jealous. I just hated pretending to be a girlie girl when I had much more fun climbing trees and playing stickball.

All of sudden, as if she could hear inside my head, Dee-Dee turned to me and said, "We can't be friends if you play with Barbie dolls or have dress-up tea parties."

I grinned. "I hate Barbie dolls and I hate playing pretend even more."

We became fast friends. There wasn't a time you saw me that Dee-Dee wasn't nearby, and vice versa. We had sleepovers at her house, where Sharon let us turn the living room into our fortress. She'd serve us fancy meats and cheeses that had weird names and we'd drink apple juice out of champagne glasses. Aunt Evelyn was right. Sharon was glamorous with her smooth brown skin and gold stained lips. Her hair was different every day. Momma said she must have a closet full of wigs. I didn't have the heart to tell her it was only half a closet. At my house, Momma taught Dee-Dee how to make her famous salmon croquettes and we sat in the dining room and ate off Momma's fancy "show off" china.

The three of us, Malik, Dee-Dee, and I, would go up to Will Rogers Park on 103rd Street and play stickball. Or climb the tree behind First Baptist Street Church and talk about nothing and everything. Every morning we walked to school together playing "red light, green light" and "step on a crack, break your mother's back." I liked it when we all hung out together. I also liked having Dee-Dee all to myself. So I started avoiding Malik by lying about why I couldn't play with him. Then, one day he caught Dee-Dee and me coming out of Mr. Moskowitz's store after I'd told him I wasn't feeling well. He got so mad he called me Dee-Dee's lapdog and walked off in a huff. We didn't speak for a whole week after that. I spent that time trying to convince myself that he'd only said that because he was angry and hurt.

Sure, I was willing to do whatever it took to maintain my friendship with Dee-Dee. I carried her books to school. Helped her with her homework, sometimes doing it myself if she took too long. I often traded my red Jello for her green, knowing how much I loved red because I considered myself a good friend. But I most certainly wasn't Dee-Dee's lap dog. When I explained this to Malik, he laughed and said I acted like I was in love with her, and before long, the other kids were saying it, too. I realized, too late, that I shouldn't have given her such a big heart-shaped box of candy on Valentine's day. And that I should have refrained from signing the card, "All my love, Zayla." Even though I could tell it made her uncomfortable, we managed to remain best friends through it all. At least that's the lie I told myself knowing deep down inside we'd eventually go our separate ways as if never having met at all.

* * * * * *

"Zayla? Are you coming?" Dee-Dee asked, pulling me out of my head and back into the classroom.

"Huh?"

"Come on, slowpoke," she said.

I'd forgotten how it felt to have her rushing me to put my books up and telling me to "come on," like that. I was thrilled – so happy I could have danced right on down the hall behind her. I didn't, though. I acted like I had some couth. Momma would have been proud, not that I did it for Momma at all. I did it because I was tired of the kids whispering about me, which is why, I suspect, Dee-Dee started feeding me with a long-handled spoon in the first place.

I'd overheard most of the whispers. "Why does Zayla dress like a boy?" Or, "Zayla's so triflin', why does Dee-Dee even bother being her friend?" My favorite, mostly because it was so ridiculous, was, "Zayla acts like she wants to marry Dee-Dee." That thought had never even entered my mind.

The boys couldn't care less how I dressed. As long as I was around to play, that was good enough for them. The girls tormented me the most. I never could understand why they were so insistent on asking questions when they already had the answers. They'd known since kindergarten I hated wearing dresses. They knew I hated getting my hair pressed. And they knew the best way to piss me off was to accuse me of liking a boy. They'd all been just like me, until their first visit to the Montgomery Ward girl's section to get their training bras. My titties were still deliberating about what they wanted to do. After that, they dropped me and their stickball bats and picked up Barbie dolls and boy crushes. I told myself I didn't care because I still had Dee-Dee. Or so I thought.

I swallowed the smile I felt crawling up my cheeks and followed

Dee-Dee out to the playground. Malik was knuckled down in the marble pit. James and Tony perched on their knees a few feet behind the line on either side of Malik, who looked up as we passed and whistled. This had never bothered Dee-Dee before, but since she'd been hanging out with Melody and her poisonous snake friends, things they were a-changing.

Dee-Dee spun around and shouted, "Malik Edwards! Stop whistling at me. I am not a dog."

"Ain't nobody even whistlin' at you," he said, annoyed.

Dee-Dee rolled her eyes. Malik rolled his past her to me and twirled his yellow tiger's eye Shooter between his thumb and index finger. The Shooter was the coveted marble because it was the biggest in the set and was guaranteed to hit several marbles at once. We played for keeps. Over the years, we'd all owned each other's Shooters at one time or another. Malik currently owned my blue tiger's eye Shooter, which I'd been trying to win back for months. Today could be my lucky day, I thought. I hesitated and considered my options.

Dee-Dee grabbed my elbow and snatched me away in response. "She don't wanna play with you, Malik. We got other things to do."

"She got a mouth. Don't you, Zay?"

"Yeah. So?"

"You oughta try using it," he said.

"Shut up, Malik," I said.

Dee-Dee and I walked elbow in elbow across the playground. I felt so happy inside, my cheeks were beginning to hurt. Then I realized I must have been smiling super hard. I looked around to see who was watching. I always looked around to see who was watching because someone always was.

Next thing I know, Melody brought her scrawny behind over and whispered something in Dee-Dee's ear. As Melody slithered away, Dee-Dee released my elbow and scratched her head. I kept my hand stuffed in my pocket to make it easier for her to put it back where she'd had it, but when she finished scratching, she dropped her arm at her side and left it there.

"What did she say?" I asked.

"Nothing," Dee-Dee said.

"Ummm-hmmm," I said, trying hard not to nag. Momma got on Daddy's last nerve nagging him.

"I said it was nothing, okay?" Dee-Dee said for good measure.

She glanced over at Melody, then refocused her attention down to her shoes. It felt like she was ashamed to be hanging out with me. And since I wasn't forcing her to be there, I also couldn't understand why she was doing something she didn't want to do. That was so unlike her. I didn't think anyone could get Dee-Dee to do something she didn't want to do.

I was sure of one thing: I didn't trust Melody as far as I could throw her. Some days I wished I could throw her into the rat- and roach-infested Dumpster behind Giant Market. She was the kind of girl that would smile in your face and talk about you behind your back. And she had this way of looking down her nose at me, as if she was better than me. I had no idea why she couldn't stand me. Sure, I'd snatched the head off her brand-new Tressy doll, but she shouldn't have been shaking it in my face in the first place. That wasn't reason enough to hate me.

Dee-Dee grabbed my elbow and yanked me in the direction of the swings. Instead of getting on one so I could push her, she sat down in the grass just beyond. I looked at the swings and then down at Dee-Dee and reluctantly joined her. We didn't talk. I sat there waiting for her to say something, but she just snatched at one blade of grass after another. So, I lay back and locked my hands under my head. Thick white clouds drifted across the pale blue sky. An airplane with TWA painted on the back fin flew overhead, its wheels descending. In less than five minutes, it would touch down on the tarmac at LAX, ten miles away. I watched it until it flew out of view. I couldn't wait to take my first plane ride. Daddy said he was going to take me to New York City when I got old enough to enjoy it. When I asked him how long that was going to take, he said, "I don't know. Keep living."

"I'm bored," Dee-Dee announced. "Come on. Let's go behind the building. I wanna show you something."

Why did she want to go behind the building with me? I wondered. We'd never gone there before. Only fast girls went behind the building to let the boys feel them up. Is that what Melody whispered in Dee-Dee's ear? Were they going to get me back there to let some boy try to feel me up? Well, I wasn't about to let that happen. Nope, I decided. I'm not going.

Dee-Dee was halfway across the yard before she realized I wasn't behind her. She marched back over and planted her hands on her narrow hips.

"Now what's wrong?" she asked.

"Why do you want to go behind the building with me all of a sudden?"

She frowned. "Because I want to show you something."

"Why can't you show me right here?" I asked.

"Because I can't."

When I still didn't move, she added, "Come on, Zay. We're best friends, aren't we? Don't you trust me?"

Nope, I said to myself. "You promise you ain't up to something?"

"I swear!" she said, sticking her pinky out to prove it.

I watched her left eyebrow. It didn't move. Maybe she was telling the truth for a change.

"It doesn't feel like we're best friends," I said. "Especially now that you're friends with Melody."

"She's just a friend. Not like us. We're always gonna be best friends."

"All right," I said, giving in like I always did.

I folded my pinky in hers, and off we went across the yard to a path that led down the width of the school. To my left was the ivy-covered chain-link fence that separated us from Compton Avenue. To my right, the brick wall of the auditorium that protected us from prying eyes. Halfway down the path, Dee-Dee stopped. I shoved my hands in my pockets and waited. She stood there looking like she had no idea what to do next.

Finally, she licked her lips and said, "Have you kissed a boy yet?"

I stared dumbfounded. She knew damn well I hadn't kissed a boy.

"No," I said.

"Don't you want to?" she asked.

I held onto the dumbfounded look. "Nope."

"Listen, Zay. You need to come out of your shell. People are talking about you, and I'm getting tired of sticking up for you. You never talk to any of the boys, and none of the girls want to play with you because ..."

I waited for her to finish. When she didn't, I looked behind me to make sure I wasn't about to get ambushed by some boy. She was getting tired of sticking up for me? Who was she kidding? Best friends aren't supposed to get tired of sticking up for each other. Malik never got tired. And neither would I. I opened my mouth to say that but decided it wasn't worth it because she'd have an excuse. Instead, I asked, "Because what?" not sure I wanted to hear the answer.

"Nothing. It's not important. It's just that I would much rather play with you than Melody and her stuck-up friends. But we're getting older, and we gotta start acting our age. I'd probably still be acting like ... I mean, dressing like ... Well, I would have never known what was waiting for me if I hadn't kissed Kevin Monroe."

"What? What does that have to do with anything?"

I turned to leave.

"Zay, don't go." She gave me that begging puppy dog weepy eyed look, the one that made it impossible for me to say no even though I knew it was all an act.

"I think once you kiss a boy or have a boy give you some attention, you'll start wanting to be more like us. I mean, dress like us. And who better than your best friend to teach you how to kiss? Then I'm gonna help you get a boyfriend."

"Why do I need a boyfriend?"

And why was everyone so damned concerned about what I needed? I wondered. First Momma, then Nana, then Aunt Evelyn, and now Dee-Dee. It just didn't make any sense.

"Because you can't be a tomboy all your life," she responded as if that was answer enough.

I didn't feel like arguing. I also hoped she knew I had no intention of kissing any boys no matter how many lessons she gave me. I felt too much like one to ever consider kissing one, and I didn't see that changing anytime soon. On the other hand, the idea of kissing Dee-Dee wasn't so bad. So, I pretended to be the apt pupil and allowed her to pull me closer.

As I slowly inhaled the coconut oil in her hair and the Nivea lotion on her skin, a jumble of emotions shot through me. Happy. Anxious. Excited. Uncomfortable.

"God is always watching," I heard Momma say in my head.

The thought frightened me and should have been reason enough for me to push Dee-Dee away and run, but I didn't. Instead, I rubbed my palms against my pant leg and willed the stirring in my stomach to go away.

"Close your eyes," she instructed.

I looked at her one last time and pushed the frowning face of Jesus away as my eyes slipped shut. She leaned in, her breath warm on my face, and then pressed her lips gently against my own. Love shot through my body like a lightning bolt across a black sky. And right there, sandwiched between the brick wall of the school auditorium and the ivy-covered fence, I thought, this must be love.

I counted off the seconds our lips stayed mashed together. One. Two. Three. Four. Five. It was the sweetest five seconds of my misinformed, maladjusted life. I hoped Dee-Dee felt it, too, but when I opened my eyes, she was giving me a strange look.

"Why are you looking at me like that?" she asked.

I had no idea how I was looking, although I could have guessed. I tried to straighten my face out. Dee-Dee wiped her lips with the back of her hand and said, "You didn't like that, did you? You weren't supposed to like it! Ugghhh. That's nasty!"

Heartbroken and humiliated, I wiped my lips and said, "Who said I liked it?"

Dee-Dee mumbled something under her breath and stormed off.

* * * * * *

The warning bell rang. I stood there a moment, trying to compose myself before I hurried out from behind the building. The classes were lining up to go back in. Dee-Dee slipped in line behind Melody and looked around conspiratorially. She whispered something that caused Melody to giggle into her hand. I wasn't worried about them laughing at me. I knew Dee-Dee would never have admitted to kissing me. I giggled too, like I was in on the joke, and tried to slide in line behind Dee-Dee. Melody crowded me out.

"Dang, Zayla. Why you gotta keep following me around?" Dee-Dee said. "I'll see you in class."

"Yeah. Why don't you go to the end of the line where you belong?" Melody chimed in.

"Why don't you drop dead?" I responded.

I went to the end of the line, hurt and confused. Ten minutes earlier, we were kissing, and now I'm standing at the end of the line?

What had I done so wrong to deserve this? I never stood at the end of the line. Ever. I told her I didn't like the kiss. I even wiped it off my lips the same way she had, when I would have preferred not to. And what kind of way is that to treat your so-called best friend? I wanted to shout.

"What's wrong with you?" Malik asked, jumping in line behind me.

"Nothing," I said.

"Then why you at the end of the line looking like somebody killed your dog?"

"I don't have a dog."

"I know that, dummy! What happened? Who did it? Was it Dee-Dee? It's always Dee-Dee. Why are you even still friends with her? I wouldn't still be your friend if you treated me like that."

I sighed with relief when Mr. Bixby called Malik's class to go in. When Mrs. Fitzgerald called for our class, I kept my place at the end of the line. Daddy told me I could never play poker because I wore my feelings right on my face. Happy smile. Sad frown. Heartbroken cry. I wiped the tears away and followed my class inside.

2

When we got to our room, Evie Sheffield shoved past me.

"Watch out, Bulldagger!" she said, and laughed.

I ignored her just like Dr. King said I should. Mrs. Fitzgerald was always quoting Dr. King to us, and according to him, "The best thing to do with ignorant and conscientiously stupid people is to ignore them." So, I made my way to my seat without giving Evie a sideways glance. That didn't stop her, though. She kept on needling me even after we settled into our next lesson.

"Don't act like you don't hear me, bulldagger!" Evie shouted.

Mrs. Fitzgerald busied herself, writing the spelling words on the board, pretending not to hear us.

"Before we go over our spelling words, can anyone tell me what today is?" Mrs. Fitzgerald.

I was sick of being the "teacher's pet," so I refused to raise my hand. I decided if no one else raised their hand, then we'd be sitting there until the cows come home. Mrs. Fitzgerald waited, now and then glancing at me, her eyes pleading me to raise my hand. I couldn't do it even though I knew if she didn't get a response, she would stand there, making us feel uncomfortable until someone spoke up. She believed that as colored children, we needed to learn to speak up for ourselves so that we wouldn't be afraid to speak up as adults. We spent a lot of time talking about the racism going on down south and Fannie Lou Hammer, Dr. King, and the SLCC. And, before he was killed, we talked about Malcolm X when he became El Hajj Malik El Shabazz. Mrs. Fitzgerald said he became more like Dr. King after he went to Mecca.

I liked Mrs. Fitzgerald. She wasn't like the other white people. The ones down south seemed to be meaner than snakes. Daddy told me never to judge people by the actions of one or a few. So, I couldn't say all white people were mean. I only really knew two, Mrs. Fitzgerald, and Mr. Moskowitz, who owned the corner store on 103rd and Wilmington. There were plenty of other white people in our community. Most of them owned the stores, they just didn't live there. They pretty much ignored us unless we were spending money, and some of them were flat out mean. Like Mr. Crogan, who owned the store on Central Avenue, and most of the cops. Someone coughed. No one raised their hand. My stomach took over, and not wanting to miss lunchtime sitting in class, I raised my hand to end the torture.

"It's Memorial Day," I said.

"That's right, Zayla. And who would like to tell me what this day commemorates?"

"Men who died for our country."

"Very good, Michelle. And when did Memorial Day begin?"

"In 1868 by Major General John A. Logan, the commander in chief of the Grand Army of the Republic, for the annual decoration of war graves."

"Excellent, James."

"My father told me that freed slaves started the first Memorial Day," I added. "On May 1, 1865, in Charleston, South Carolina. They dug up the bodies of over two hundred Union Soldiers that were buried in a big grave and worked for two whole weeks to give all of them a decent burial."

"Why would they do something stupid like that?" Evie blurted out.

"Because, stupid, they were grateful that those soldiers fought for their freedom."

"That's a lie!" Evie shouted.

"Okay, everyone. Take out your spelling books. Zayla, will you start us off?"

I considered my options. I was proud to be Compton Elementary School's spelling bee champion six years running. I was also tired of being called the teacher's pet. I decided the last thing I wanted to do was start us off.

Evie shouted, in answer, "Yeah. Spell BULLDAGGER!"

She spat the word out like a loogey she'd coughed up from the deepest part of her lungs. For a twelve-year-old, there weren't many words I didn't know or couldn't figure out if I heard them used in a sentence. I'd never heard the word bulldagger. It sure was funny to me, though, so I laughed and said, "Oh, yeah? Well, I'd rather be a bulldagger than an old African booty scratcher."

The class erupted in laughter. The easiest way to get a roomful of twelve-year-old colored children laughing was to call someone an "African booty scratcher." For some reason, it got our imaginations running wild, as we pictured a bunch of Africans sitting in a hut scratching each other's naked rear ends. Daddy said if we knew our history, there wouldn't be a damn thing anyone could say about Africans that we would find funny. Sometimes Daddy didn't get it.

"Yo momma's an African booty scratcher," Evie fired back.

"Shut up, Evie! Ain't nobody talkin' to yo' black ass anyway!" Dee-Dee chimed in, surprising me.

"You shut up, mule-latto!"

"I got yo' mule-latto!"

"Yeah? Then why I see you and Zayla kissing behind the building?"

A dead silence followed by a thunderous chorus of "Oooooooooh!" reverberated around the room. I slid down in my seat and prayed for someone to pull the fire alarm. Dee-Dee sprang out of her seat.

"You ain't seen me and Zayla kissin' behind no building!"

I wanted to ignore the melee ensuing, until I heard the slap. I looked up at the picture of Sojourner Truth hanging between Harriet Tubman and Nat Turner and wondered what they would do in that moment. I pictured Ms. Truth and Ms. Tubman shaking their heads in shame. I saw Mr. Turner jump out of his frame and cheer Dee-Dee on for standing up for herself.

"Fight! Fight! Fight!" the class chanted.

I felt terrible for a moment and then found myself thankful that no one was thinking about Dee-Dee and me kissing behind the building anymore.

I pushed my way through the crowd. Dee-Dee had Evie in a headlock when all of a sudden Florence pushed through the crowd. The next thing I know, Florence had a handful of Dee-Dee's hair. Dee-Dee screamed and didn't let Evie go. I knew I shouldn't have gotten out of my seat. If I hadn't, I wouldn't have seen them trying to double-team Dee-Dee. Which means my hands never would have reached out and pushed Florence with all their might. Florence wouldn't have lost her balance and fallen backward over Evie's desk. And I wouldn't have been in the thick of my first real fight. If I'd stayed in my seat, Mrs. Fitzgerald never would have grabbed my arm with one hand and Dee-Dee's collar with the other and tossed us out into the hall like ragdolls. Evie and Florence wouldn't have come tumbling out behind us. And none of us would have had to see Mean Man Mulligan's face all day.

The door to the principal's office loomed in front of us. On the other side, typewriter keys click-clacked nonstop. Evie got to the door first and made no attempt to open it. She just stood there looking up at the chipped black letters as the rest of us made like a wall next to her. Mrs. Fitzgerald shoved us aside and flung the door open so hard, it slammed against the wall. Ms. Lucille stopped typing and looked up over her glasses as we stumbled in like inmates on the chain gang.

"Hi, Lucille. Is he in?" Mrs. Fitzgerald asked, pointing in the direction of Mean Man Mulligan's office.

Lucille nodded. Lucille Bradbury was the school secretary. I avoided looking at her because whenever she laid those sleepy eyes of hers on me, my words got all tangled up in my mouth. A cigarette dangled between her red, lacquered lips. She took one final drag and smashed it out in an ashtray overflowing with red-stained light brown butts. She pushed her glasses up on her nose and shook her head, 'umph, umph, umph'. Her eyes zeroed in on me. I focused my attention down at the gold-speckled linoleum floor.

"Zayla Lucille McKinney, I know that's not you I see."

I kept my eyes glued to the floor and mumbled, "No, ma'am."

"Well, it sho' looks like you. I don't know what you actin' like you shame fo'. You ain't gon' find the truth down there on that floor. Y'all sit down, and I bed' not hear a peep out of you."

Evie and Florence sat closest to the door. I sat one chair away from Florence. Dee-Dee sat one chair away from me. I couldn't understand why she behaved as if I'd done something to her. She wouldn't speak to me. She wouldn't even look at me. That's when two words entered my mind: Melody Armstrong. I would never have tossed Dee-Dee aside like that. Ever. So, I couldn't understand why she'd do it to me. Everyone's not like you, Daddy said in my head. The sooner you realize that, the better off you'll be.

Tears stung my eyes, and I focused my attention on the ceiling until they retreated. Ms. Lucille 'umph, umph, umphed' again and went back to her typing. Dee-Dee folded her arms across her chest and gazed out the window. It was as if I wasn't even sitting there, but the whole reason she'd gotten into a fight in the first place was because of me. If I'd known kissing her would create this mess, I would never have followed her behind the building.

Except for the click-clacking of the typewriter keys, the office was quiet. It made it easy for me to hear the familiar sound of high heels click-stomping down the hall. They paused on the other side of the door, the knob turned slowly, and with a whoosh the door swung open. I took a deep breath and exhaled as Queen Zora, otherwise known as my mother, barged in.

Trapped on the wrong side of the counter, I looked around for someplace to run and hide. Thankfully, Florence, Evie, and Dee-Dee put some distance between the door and me. Momma shot me a look that turned from anger to outrage. Suddenly, I remembered the dress I'd balled up and shoved in my desk that morning. At the same time, Mean Man Mulligan came barreling out of his office, holding the gnarled remains of a cigar between his lips. He dropped it on the pile of butts in Miss Lucille's ashtray, and red-stained butts bounced onto her desk. She brushed ashes off her lap and mumbled a few choice words under her breath as she dumped the ashtray in the garbage can.

"Good morning, Mrs. McKinney," Principal Mulligan said and stepped aside.

He and Momma exchanged pleasantries. She took a few steps, then turned and shot me another look. This time her eyes walked up my jeans, over my T-shirt, and back down to the Chuck Taylor All Star Converses laced on my feet. She closed her eyes in that "God give me strength, so I don't kill this child" kind of way before she walked off.

I sighed.

When Mulligan's door opened again, Momma stormed out and shot across the room past Evie, Florence, and Dee-Dee. I swallowed and looked up into her eyes. Without a word she grabbed me by the collar and snatched me out of my seat.

"If it wasn't for a shame, I'd beat your ass good right here in front of your friends. Kissing! And don't you dare lie and say Dee-Dee made you do it because I know damn well she would never do such a thing. Would you, Dee-Dee?"

Momma glared at Dee-Dee as if she dared her to disagree. I held my breath and waited for her to confess. She looked at me and back up at Momma, then shook her head and smiled her weasel smile.

"Of course not, Mrs. McKinney," she said, almost purring.

Momma turned her glare on me. "Come on here before I kill you!"

"She's lying!" I shouted.

Momma yanked me toward the door. I glared at Dee-Dee on the way out. She turned away. Evie and Florence looked away, too, more out of fear of Momma than of embarrassment for me. Momma stopped in the hall and snatched me up so close I could smell the coffee on her breath.

"Nobody would be calling you a damn bulldagger if you went to school dressing and behaving like a young lady!"

I stood there trying to figure out what, exactly, was a bulldagger. So much had happened, I'd forgotten all about that.

"Do you hear me talking to you?" Momma barked.

I nodded.

"Does your head make noise?"

"No," I mumbled.

"Then stop shaking it and answer me!"

"I'm sorry, Momma."

"All niggas are sorry!"

She raised her hand to slap me. My arm shot up reflexively. She knocked it away and squeezed my cheeks until they were almost touching.

"Fighting in class! Getting sent home! *Kissing a girl!* You make me sick!"

"Dee-Dee's lying, Momma! It was all her idea."

Momma grabbed a good chunk of skin from the inside of my upper arm and twisted it. I screamed as the pain pushed tears from my eyes.

"Shut your lying mouth," she whisper-shouted in my face and pulled the flesh of my upper arm in the same spot again. "I might not know much, but I know you!"

Momma pinched me again, and I screamed out louder. The classroom door closest to us opened. The teacher frowned down at me, then saw Momma. She smiled politely and closed the door. Momma could have killed me out there in the hall, and no one would have done anything until it was time to call the undertaker.

"I said shut up before I give you something to scream about. And why are you at school dressed like that? Where in the hell is the dress you had on this morning?"

She shoved my face away from her, spun around on her pink stilettos, and stomped off. Outside, I took running leaps on every crack in the sidewalk, landing hard and looking up to see which one would break her back.

3

Momma fast-walked me into the house. God forbid she have to explain why I'd been sent home midday. For kissing a girl, no less. She'd no sooner die.

"Go start dinner," she said on her way to her bedroom.

A moment later, she was giving Aunt Evelyn the rundown, embellishing on things she didn't know and didn't bother to ask me. It was okay for Aunt Evelyn to know I'd gotten in trouble again, because I was always getting in trouble. Aunt Evelyn was an Ann Landers of sorts for Momma, giving her advice she wouldn't take herself– because she had a boy, and you couldn't be too hard on them. Malik will have it hard enough in the world, she would explain. You got to stay on Zayla or she'll grow up weak, and we can't have that either.

I didn't want to start dinner. I wanted to know what a bulldagger was. As if I wasn't in enough trouble, I waited for her bedroom door to close, then tiptoed down the hall to the playroom. I grabbed the dictionary off the bookshelf and searched for bulldagger. I found bull and bulldog. I started back at the top and ran my finger down the page slower. I hadn't missed it. No bulldagger. I slammed the book shut and grabbed Volume 4 of the *Encyclopedia Britannica*. It wasn't in there either. Daddy said if it wasn't in the encyclopedia, it didn't exist. Except I knew bulldagger was real because it had gotten me in so much trouble. I stomped down the hall to Momma's room, determined to get an answer.

Momma told Aunt Evelyn she'd talk to her later and hung up. Her back was to me. I raised my hand to announce myself and put it down again. Instead, I watched her step out of her dress and hang it in the closet. She pulled the slip over her head, folded it, and placed it in its drawer. Her shoes went back in their designated box among the other hundred shoeboxes on the floor and along the back wall of the closet. She flipped through the hanging dresses, slacks, and blouses in search of something to wear. In or out of the house, Momma was a stickler about her appearance. We couldn't have been more different.

Standing there, I felt like a switch clicked on inside. For the first time in my life, I felt ashamed for not wanting to be more like her. I prayed almost daily for God to realize his terrible mistake and fix me. I needed my caterpillar self to bloom into a beautiful monarch. One day, I prayed. One day.

One day I will smell like rose petals and citrus instead of dust and dirt. I will hang up my shorts and T-shirts for dresses and Mary Janes.

One day Momma will smile instead of frown when she looks at me. We'll go shopping and pick out clothes for each other. We'll even go to dinner afterward and talk like old girlfriends, instead of fighting the entire way home. And she won't run for the straightening comb every time my hair naps up around the edges because I won't be ripping and running with Malik anymore, I thought.

One day she will notice how much I've become the daughter she's always dreamed of, and love me again. I will blossom into the little girl she's so desperate to have. She'll see. And then a frightening thought occurred to me. What if I didn't?

I sighed.

Momma spun around sharply, surprised to find me standing there. "Go get dinner started!" she yelled.

"Aren't you gonna tell me what a bulldagger is?" I asked.

"Yeah! They kiss other girls!"

She was on me in two long strides. Her hand flashed with sudden speed and struck me backhand across my face. I fell into the wall, hitting my head on the doorjamb. Red dots filled my eyes. I could only hear the ringing in my ears. I saw Momma's mouth moving and couldn't understand her. She slapped me again.

"Get out of my face and go do what I told you!"

She slapped me once more and shoved me out of her way. I stumbled down the hall and flung myself across my bed. It seemed she'd been storing all her anger up for that moment. There was no pleasing her. When I touched her, she cringed. When I tried to hug her, she pushed me away. How was I supposed to stop doing something if I didn't understand what it was I was doing? I thought. I shoved my face into my pillow and screamed until I was exhausted.

* * * * * *

"Come on, Zay. Let's get dinner started before Daddy gets home."

A new Momma shook me awake from the edge of my bed, the Momma preparing for Daddy's return home. The one who never let him see her treat me that way. The one who loved making everyone believe she had the perfect life. Dee-Dee's mom wasn't the only one who wanted to be a Negro June Cleaver, I thought. I drew away from Momma and curled into myself until she moved closer and rubbed my back the way she used to when I was younger and had a hard time falling asleep. As much as I wanted to continue pulling away, I couldn't. I was grateful for her touch.

I didn't move, barely breathed. I didn't want her snapping out of whatever nostalgic moment had her tangled up in tenderness. Before Evie called me a bulldagger. Before I kissed Dee-Dee.

I wanted her to stay in that place and time when her kisses were like sunshine. And she held me as if I were a precious gem. Back when I was her baby, and she couldn't stop loving on me. Before she learned to hate me.

"Dee-Dee made me kiss her. It wasn't my idea. She said I needed to get out of my shell. That I needed a boyfriend," I explained, all the words rushing from me at once.

Momma gave me a half-smile and my knee a gentle pat.

"Never mind about all that. Come on now. Let's go cook dinner for Daddy. I guess we'll have croquettes tonight," she said, as if nothing ever happened between us.

* * * * * *

Salmon croquettes were a household favorite. They were also Momma's way of apologizing without having to say the words "I'm sorry." I knew she was afraid I would tell Daddy that she'd hit me. I was just grateful she hadn't whipped me. The last time she'd whipped me, I was ten. She beat me so bad she left welts from the broomstick on my arms and legs. She tried to hide them from Daddy. He saw them anyway. When he asked what happened, I couldn't lie. The evidence was sticking out beneath my T-shirt and shorts.

Momma had left me at home that day to clean my room while she went to the store. I'd vacuumed, dusted, and even organized the clothes in my drawers. I hadn't made it to my bed by the time she came back. I could tell she was angry about something. She was always angry when she came home from Giant Market. I was folding the last of my clothes and putting them away when she stormed into my room.

"Why haven't you made your bed?" she demanded to know. "What have you been doing all this time? Laying around on your lazy ass?"

"I was cleaning, Momma. Look—"

"Don't lie to me," she shouted and walked out.

When she returned, she had the broom in her hand. Before I could say anything, the wood cracked against my leg. I collapsed to the ground. Momma snatched me up and threw me across the bed and swung that broom until she could barely lift her arm. Daddy inspected my wounds and told her she better not ever hit me like that again. She promised, and replaced beating me with pinches and slaps, anything that wouldn't leave evidence behind.

The scent of salmon croquettes lingered in the air on those nights, too.

I told myself Momma didn't mean it when she beat me. She thought it would help make me a better person. I convinced myself that she did it because it was the only way she knew to love me. So I accepted Momma's nonverbal apology and grabbed two cans of pink salmon off the shelf in the pantry. She placed two eggs in a small glass bowl, drained the water from the salmon, and placed the cans back on the table. I dumped the salmon into a mixing bowl while she cracked and beat the eggs.

We worked in silence. After a while she looked up at me and sighed, "What am I going to do with you?"

How was I supposed to know? I didn't know what I was going to do with me either.

She took a handful of salmon out of the bowl, studying me as she shaped into a small patty and dipped it on a plate of cornmeal. She sighed again and turned away. I sat quietly, poking holes in the tablecloth.

"Zayla! Stop poking holes in my good goddamn tablecloth!"

My finger traced a pattern of holes I'd poked over the years. Each one represented a time I'd questioned the mysteries of the world.

Why is the sky blue? *Because God made it that way.*

How do I know God exists if I can't see Him? *Well, you know the sun is still shining even if it's cloudy outside, right?* Yes. *Well, it's the same way with God. Even though you can't see Him, you know He's always there.*

How do I know God isn't a She? *Because He isn't.*

I dropped the knife and slumped back in the chair. Momma sighed again and shaped another patty.

"Momma?"

"Hmmm?"

"Do you think something is wrong with me?"

She placed the patties into the cast iron skillet until they were slightly touching and started humming. When Momma didn't want to deal with something, only God could get her to change her mind, and it wouldn't be easy, even for Him. The longer she stood there humming and tuning me out, the more I felt myself fuming inside. I wanted to shout everything I'd been feeling at the top of my lungs. "Stop treating me like a little kid. This is my goddamn life! If I'm old enough to cook, I'm old enough to speak for myself. I'm tired of being told how to think and feel! And Dee-Dee lied right to your face!"

The slap that followed stung the right side of my face.

"Don't you ever raise your voice like that in my house again! Do you hear me?" Momma shouted.

I hadn't even realized I'd spoken out loud.

"Yes, Momma," I mumbled.

"And, yes, I do think there is something wrong with you. I thought you'd outgrow it. But now it's in the Lord's hands. There's nothing that can't be fixed with a little help from the Lord. I don't care what your father says, that's precisely what you're going to get."

I knew what that meant—my days of loafing around the house with Daddy most Sundays, out of the Lord's grip, were over. I picked up the knife and started poking holes in the tablecloth again. "I don't need the Lord! There's nothing wrong with me!"

"Watch your tone. I'm not going to tell you again. And you do need the Lord. God knows you need the Lord!"

"But, Momma—"

"Don't 'But Momma' me! Girls your age shouldn't be hellbent on behaving and dressing like snot-nosed boys. Kissing other girls. You got the devil in you and I'm gonna make sure he gets out."

"I am not hellbent on doing anything, and I don't act like a boy." I am a boy! On the inside, I thought.

"What did you say?"

She stepped toward me. I didn't wait to see what she would do next. I ran to my room and slammed the door behind me.

"And stop slamming doors in my goddamn house!"

* * * * * *

I turned on the radio and flopped down on my bed. Out of all the things in my room, I loved my bed and desk the best. My bed was a light oak four-post canopy with sheer curtains. The curtains didn't last long. Malik and I always seemed to yank one or more from its support. Daddy got tired of rehanging them, and they never went up again. That's when Momma started buying lace or frilly comforters in soft shades to keep the "girlie" look going. I hated them, but loved my bed, which came with a light oak dresser, hutch, and desk, all with real brass handles. The Chatty Cathy doll Nana sent me for my eighth birthday sat alone on the top of the hutch.

On its shelves sat race cars, comic books, reading books, and the two empty Hellman's Mayonnaise jars that once held the paints and brushes I'd stopped using a year earlier. I'd dumped them in my bottom dresser drawer, where I kept all the other junk I didn't use and couldn't bear to throw away. The canvases, easel, and my inner artist got pushed to the back of my closet, to be forgotten forever. Maybe I should start painting again, I thought. Momma loved me when I painted for her. The bouquet of roses I gave her still hung above her side of the bed in her room. Then my portrait of a Black Jesus crossed my mind, reminding me why I'd put down my brushes in the first place. I'd have to think of another way to make Momma remember that she once loved me.

Daddy's voice drifted through the radio speakers. I at least had one parent who loved me. Sometimes it felt like he was trying to love me for both of them. I didn't have the heart to tell him that he was wasting his time. As much as I hated to admit it, I needed Momma's love almost more than I needed his.

There were two Negro radio stars in L.A. in the 60s, Daddy and the Magnificent Montague. Both had shows on KGFJ-AM, which was unheard of in other parts of the country.

The Magnificent Montague hit the scene in February, a short while before Malcolm X's assassination. It didn't take him any time at all to win us over. He was our rooster, calling reveille at sunrise and burning up the radio dial until he signed off at lunchtime.

Montague's show started every morning with three gospel singers, featuring Aretha Franklin, crooning, "Montague. The Magnificent."

Then Montague would say, "Put your hand on the radio and touch your heart," as the first song of the day began to spin. Throughout, Montague would scream, "Burn!" so we would know just how hot the song was. In between songs, Montague would take calls on the "Burn Line" from us kids. We could give our name, the school we went to, and then we could say, "Burn!" If we said anything more, he'd hang up on us.

I called in one morning, hands sweating, heart pounding in my ears. Malik crowded me on one side, Dee-Dee on the other. I had the handset pressed so tight to my ear I thought it might break. Montague picked up and said, "Who we got on the line?" and I froze. He asked again. I shouted, "Zayla Lucille McKinney. Compton Avenue Elementary School. Burn!" and slammed the phone down.

When I got to school, I expected all the kids to tease me for making a fool of myself. That thought never crossed their minds. All they could talk about was how I got to talk to Montague and say my name on the radio for everyone to hear.

As much as everyone loved Montague, the women loved Daddy a whole lot more, which drove Momma tee-totally insane, as Nana would say. I imagine it would have been a lot worse if Daddy hadn't walked away from his singing career. When I asked Daddy why he couldn't be a famous singer and have a family too, he said, "All money ain't good money, Ladybug. It has a way of making you forget who you are and what you believe in. Being away from home all the time wouldn't have been good for any of us. If I had to do it all over again, I would do the exact same thing."

Daddy's voice drifted through the speakers. "It's just about that time, folks. I want to leave you with this before I go..."

Violins filled the room, followed by the rest of the orchestra. I closed my eyes and let Sam Cooke's voice wrap itself around me. *I was born by the river* ...

"Zayla! Go to Crogan's and get me a head of cabbage," Momma shouted, interrupting my peace.

"Do I have to go to Crogan's? Can't I get it from Giant Market?" I shouted back.

"No. Now get your ass up and go do what I said before your father gets home and there's no coleslaw to go with his croquettes."

4

I hated going to Crogan's more than I hated chitterlings, cod liver oil, and rainy days.

Dusk settled in around the houses on the block. A cool breeze with a hint of seawater blew across my face. I pulled my jacket closed and zipped it. The scent of pork chops and something that smelled Italian, like spaghetti or lasagna, floated in the air. Dee-Dee stepped out on her front porch. I started to go ask why she stabbed me in the back until the scent of hog maws hit me in the face. My stomach turned. I covered my nose to mask the stench and added hog maws to the list of things I hated as much as Crogan's.

Cars moved up and down Central Avenue. An older man with stark white hair and a woman as round as she was tall, stood waiting for the bus. A light blue Lincoln Continental pulled up in front of them. Sharon Mitchell leaned over and kissed the white man behind the wheel right on the lips. Then climbed out of the car looking like Lola Falona in a pair of gold boots and an orange dress that just covered her unmentionables. She nodded to the man and woman at the bus stop and frowned down at the bus bench.

"Get up, nigga, and let these old folks take a load off," she shouted.

Ezel shot off the bench and hid behind it. Sharon laughed so hard she started to cough. She pulled a handkerchief out of her purse and wiped her eyes. As she put it back, she noticed me standing there.

"You better start looking for another friend, little girl. Dee-Dee's fast ass is gon' be on punishment 'til y'all graduate from high school."

She came closer.

"She ain't your friend, you know. Ain't neva been 'bout shit. Get that from her daddy," she said, more to herself. "And I bet it was her fast ass that kissed you wadn't it?"

I opened my mouth to answer and couldn't seem to find the words. I thought I had the only mother that could hate her only child. I almost felt sorry for Dee-Dee. Almost. Sharon didn't wait for me to answer.

"You're a nice girl. Too good for her, that's fa sho'. Cut your losses, chile, and move on down the road."

She kissed my cheek, smelling of cigarettes and alcohol with a faint hint of Jean Nate.

"Ok," I whispered to her back. "Bye."

The bus pulled up, the brakes squealing to a stop. The old man helped the woman up the steps and dropped his money in the change slot.

Ezel plopped back down on the bench and pulled a crumpled cigarette out of his pants pocket. He tried to straighten it between his fingers, then stuck it in his mouth. He reached in his shirt pockets and pulled out a wooden match. It stuck out between the third and fourth fingers of his right hand – he left the pinky and thumb in Vietnam.

"Hey, Ezel," I said, shaking Sharon out of my head.

"Whass happenin', baby girl?"

I started to tell him how I'd finally had my first fight when his eyes went out of focus and slid half-closed. His lower lip fell open. I'd gotten used to him drifting off like that, so I stood there and waited. It never lasted long. Just then two boys that went to Jordan

High with my neighbor Roger skulked across Central in the direction of Crogan's. They walked right in front of a car. The driver hit
the brakes and honked. Ezel's eyes flew open again. He remembered
the cigarette and snatched it out of his mouth. Then blew on it a few
times and put it back in his mouth.

Everyone loved Ezel before he'd found himself involuntarily
signed up to participate in a war he didn't start for a country that
didn't give a shit about him. He used to tell people he missed his
chance to go back to Africa with Marcus Garvey and them. In fact,
Vietnam would be as close as he would ever get to Africa. He returned less than a year later without that pinky and thumb. For his
trouble, he also earned a steel plate in his head that he said worked
like a movie screen, playing all his wartime experiences over and
over at will. No matter how much he drank or filled his veins with
horse, he could not escape those months in the rice paddies. He often spoke ghoulishly of intestines hanging out of walking corpses
and men running around with half their heads blown off. He said
it took a while, sometimes, for the body to collapse because the
brain didn't know it was dead yet. For almost a year after his return,
Ezel was often seen running down Central or 103rd Streets shouting
warnings about incoming rockets and exploding grenades, and div-
ing behind bus benches or parked cars for imaginary protection.

I felt sorry for Ezel. He'd become a shell of the cool, fun-loving
cat I'd once known. Before the war, he wouldn't be caught dead in
the same outfit twice. Daddy used to say Ezel was sharper than a
butcher's knife at suppertime, which never made sense to me. (Then
Malik explained what happened to pigs and chickens on his great-
grandfather's farm down South, and I didn't eat pork or chicken
again for over a month.) There wasn't a time I saw Ezel that he wasn't
skinning and grinning, ready with a fistful of candy for us kids. It
was nice to know some things hadn't changed. Ezel reached in his
jacket pocket with his good hand and handed me a few Nut Chews.

"Where you on your way to?" he asked.

"Crogan's for Momma."

"Then you best get a move on. It's gettin' dahk out and you don't want yo' fine-ass Momma gettin' worry lines 'cause of you."

"Thanks, Ezel."

I popped a Nut Chew in my mouth and ran across Central. I kept running until I got to Crogan's, and stopped dead outside the door to gather my thoughts. Get in. Get what you need and get out, I told myself. I took a deep breath and opened the door. Get the cabbage, put the money on the counter, and leave. That way Crogan can't say anything crazy to you.

I opened the door and stepped inside. The store smelled like stale beer and sawdust. The two boys I'd just seen on Central stood in front of the potato chip rack, arguing over which potato chips taste better with a bologna sandwich, plain or barbeque. They looked up when I came in. One was slightly taller and darker than the other, with an athlete's build. The other was thin and wiry with thick black-framed glasses over wide brown eyes. They were rumored to be members of the Farmers, a neighborhood gang. The athlete spoke to me. I smiled and made a beeline for the cabbage.

The vegetable section, such as it was, consisted of several heads of wilted and browning lettuce and colorless celery stalks with just a hint of green at the tips. Bruised apples. Questionable oranges. Overripe bananas. I scanned the rows in search of cabbage. I didn't want to have to ask for help. Mr. Crogan was especially nasty if you asked for help. He liked to use it as an opportunity to expound on the travesty of the *Brown v. Board of Education* verdict. According to him, the whole lot of us were wasting taxpayer dollars trying to get an education, knowing we weren't smart enough to learn. I spotted two baskets on the floor. One held onions, the other, cabbage. I grabbed one that was still white at the root, the way Momma taught me.

Crogan stood behind the register, eyeing the boys. They were still arguing about the potato chips. I could have told them to go with barbeque then thought it best I mind my own business. That's when the athlete announced they should go with the plain chips. Barbeque only goes with certain things. Plain chips go with everything, he reasoned.

I set the cabbage on the counter and waited. Mr. Crogan continued watching the boys and then shouted, "Hey! Make a decision or get your black asses out of my store."

The athlete turned to Crogan. His eyes darkened. I moved closer to the counter as if it could protect me.

"What did you say?"

"That'll be ten cents," Crogan said to me. To the athlete, he said, "Go on now. Get what you came for and leave. You've been in here long enough already."

"You know what, old man? You keep treatin' people this way and one day somebody gon' burn this mutha fucka to the ground."

I slid a dime on the counter, grabbed the cabbage up to my chest, and shot out the door. Once outside, I started running and didn't stop until I got home. I fast-walked into the kitchen and dropped the cabbage on the table. As I turned to leave, Momma grabbed my arm.

"What's wrong with you?" she asked.

"Nothing."

"Why are you crying?"

I snatched away. "I'm not!"

I could feel the tears rolling down my face and still refused to admit I was crying. So I stood mute until Momma pushed me away.

"Go on, then," she said. "Sometimes you make me so damn sick."

Only sometimes? I wondered.

I went to my room and climbed in bed. I lay there, curled in on myself with my eyes squeezed tight. I thought about how it would be for me once everyone found out I'd kissed Dee-Dee behind the building at school. I'm sure no sooner had we been sent home than the phone line started jumping. It would remain that way until the very last person got the news. I pushed the thought away. The idea of everyone in Watts hating me because of Dee-Dee was too much to bear. The thought of Crogan's store going up in flames was even more frightening because I believed if the latter happened, the athlete and the tall, wiry boy would come looking for me.

5

"I'm home!" Daddy called out like he did every night. "Where's the love of my life and the apple of my eye?"

I let the love of his life go to him first so they could get all the hugging and kissing out of the way. Sometimes I wondered if time for them went by in dog years. What felt like eight hours to me must have been like fifty-six years to them. They weren't perfect, by a long shot. But I know that most of the stuff between them had to do with me and Momma. And sometimes they argued when Momma couldn't contain her jealousy. I waited for Momma to go back into the kitchen, washed up for dinner, and ran to join them.

"... the produce is old when they ship it. I can't even get a good head of cabbage," Momma was saying as I came in.

Daddy was in his spot at the kitchen table flipping through the evening edition of The L.A. Sentinel newspaper. I sat in my spot, right next to him, and waited for a break in their conversation. He leaned over and kissed my cheek.

"Hi, Daddy," I whispered.

"How's my bug?" he whispered back. To Momma he said, "Baby, why don't you just go to Farmer's Market?"

"Farmer's Market!" Momma let out a loud snort. The way she was glaring at us, I couldn't tell if she was more disgusted with the idea of Farmer's Market or the reality of Daddy loving me in spite of her. Not to mention, according to her, the way the white women treated her.

"I will not drive all the way to Third and Fairfax to be insulted. Those silly-ass white women staring like they've never seen a Negro before or assuming every one of us cleans houses and raises their kids for them. 'Oh, hi. Don't you work for...' and that kind of shit. No, thank you."

She was exaggerating, of course. In truth, the times I went to Farmers Market with Momma those white women looked right through us. I think she just made up that other stuff so would Daddy feel sorry for her. It must have felt a lot better than having admit to being invisible altogether.

"Zayla, get up and start setting the table."

I kissed Daddy's cheek and did as I was told.

"I think it's time we get out of here before things get worse, Frank. It's not like we can't afford to move to Windsor Hills."

"I'm not so quick to leave Watts. My roots are here. I was born in this house, so let's not start talking about leaving until we have a good reason."

"But, Frank—"

"Listen, that kind of thinking is exactly why our community is falling apart. The minute one of us gets some money, we can't wait to move out and give our money to the white man. Live in his neighborhood. Shop at his stores. And for what? You don't see them crackers runnin' to Watts to do nothin' but listen to our music..." Daddy turned to me. "So, how was your day, Ladybug?"

I shrugged. "It was all right. Except for when Mrs. Fitzgerald said she'd never heard about slaves starting Memorial Day. She said you must be mistaken."

Daddy folded the newspaper and set it on the table. "I wouldn't expect her to know that. Most white folks don't know our history.

Hell, most of us don't even know our history. But that doesn't make it any less true."

Momma waved the dishtowel, dismissing the history lesson, and said, "Why don't you tell your father how you got sent home for fighting in class? Two girls from the projects, to boot!"

I stopped chewing and searched Daddy's face. "Fighting, huh?" he said.

I waited. He didn't speak, just sat there, chewing and nodding his head. And then I saw the hint of a smile tug at his lips. "Well, I hope you whupped their asses!"

"Frank!" Momma shouted.

"I did, Daddy! I whupped them real good." I jumped up and started dancing around the kitchen like Muhammad Ali, air boxing and ducking, grateful he wasn't disappointed in me. "Evie swung to punch me in the face and I ducked. Then I punched her in the stomach. I even punched her in the face and she didn't even see it coming. Just like you taught me."

"What does she mean, like you taught her?" Momma asked.

"That's my girl!" Daddy said, holding his hands out, palm up. I slapped him some skin. Momma frowned, causing Daddy to lean over and kiss her cheek. "Sorry, baby, but she was bound to have a fight one day."

"So, that's what you all have been doing out there behind the garage? I knew you were up to no good. Teaching her how to fight. Umph. Umph. Umph. How many times do I have to tell you she's not a boy, Frank?"

"Zora!"

Daddy hated when Momma said that in front of me. I hated it, too. Neither of us needed reminding that I was not a boy. That was clear. So, to keep from starting an argument, Daddy put on his "all jokes aside" father face.

"So, you want to tell me why you were fighting?" he asked.

"From the beginning?" I asked.

"From the beginning."

I told him almost everything that happened, except for the part about Dee-Dee and me kissing behind the building. When I got to the part about Evie saying she saw Dee-Dee and me kissing behind the building, he stopped me.

"Did she?" he asked, not looking up.

"Did she what?" I asked stupidly.

He answered with his eyes.

"I don't know. But it was Dee-Dee's idea. She said I needed to get out of my shell and kiss some boys."

"Why?"

I didn't get to play dumb a second time. "So I could get a boyfriend."

"I never did like that fast-tailed girl," Daddy said. "I give her a few more years before she's walking around here with her belly poked out and no idea which fella got it that way."

"Dee-Dee isn't like that," Momma said.

"How in the hell would you know?"

Momma shut up and went back to eating. Daddy asked me if there was more to the story. I shook my head.

"And that's why the girl called you a bulldagger?"

"I don't know ... I didn't even do nothin' to her—"

"Anything," Momma corrected.

"Anything ... Daddy?"

He raised his eyebrows in answer this time.

"What's a bulldagger?"

"It's an ugly word people use to describe something they don't understand."

This only further confused me.

"Like what?" I asked.

"Well, people who are that way," he said and twisted his hand from side to side.

"What way?"

"Homosexuals ... that way, when people of the same sex are attracted to one another."

"Then how come they call them bulldaggers?"

Daddy laughed. "I don't know. I guess because those kind of women dress and act like men."

I laughed this time. "That's stupid. Bulls are male, so why would they call women bulldaggers?"

"Good point, Ladybug. Now that I think about it, I don't even know where that name came from. When I was in high school, we suspected our English teacher was that way. She was too damn fine not to have a man at home.

"She made us read Claude McKay ... what was the book? Oh yeah, *Home to Harlem*. We saw the word for the first time in a song or a poem of something and went something like, 'And it's ashes to ashes and dust to dust, Can you show me a woman that a man can trust ... something, something and on like that, then ... And there's two things in Harlem I don't understand. It's a bulldykin' woman and faggoty man.'

"I wonder whatever happened to Miss Jordan. Last I heard, she'd stopped teaching high school and moved up to San Francisco to teach college. Man, we neva would have called her a bulldyke. She was a fox!"

Momma cleared her throat.

"Not as fine as you, though, baby."

"But you said 'bulldyke'," I corrected.

"Yeah ... that's what McKay said, but that was almost thirty years ago. I guess the word has evolved over the years. They have a way of doing that, you know. All I know for sure is bulldagger is an ugly word. I don't want you using it. You understand?"

I nodded, no longer interested in the word itself. I'd heard the word faggot before. It's what some of the boys up on 103rd Street called Ezel. They only said it to see how mad they could make him. He'd get some mad, and cuss them every way to Sunday, using combinations of words that made them laugh hysterically. I wondered if that was why Evie called me a bulldagger. Maybe she was making a joke at my expense. She couldn't think I really liked girls. I mean, sure, I liked Dee-Dee, and she was the only one. I didn't like other girls. I didn't like boys either. I didn't know what I liked. A thought occurred to me.

"I can't be a bulldagger anyway," I said. "I'm just a girl. Not a woman."

Daddy laughed so hard he almost choked.

"It's not funny, Frank," Momma said.

The phone rang. Momma snatched it from its perch on the side of the cabinet.

"McKinney residence," she cooed into the receiver. She glared at Daddy, then rolled her eyes and slammed the receiver down on the countertop. "For you," she said.

Daddy picked up the phone. "Hello? ... Uh-huh... Okay. I understand ... I'll be there in about an hour."

"The hell you will! She ain't got to call here every time—"

"Zora!" Daddy said, and slammed his hand on the table.

We jumped at the sharpness of his voice. Sometimes it felt like Daddy was raising both of us. Into the phone he repeated, "I'll be there in an hour," and hung up the phone.

"Why does she have to call you every time she needs something? She has friends. She has family. Why don't she call one of them?"

"You know why!" Daddy shouted again.

I asked if I could be excused and went back to my room, counting down the moments before the fight would begin.

* * * * * *

The "she" in question was Miss Evangeline, the neighborhood crazy lady.

Rumor had it that Miss Evangeline went crazy when her husband left her for another woman. She was so heartbroken, she hardly came out of the house. Some said she was too ashamed to show her face in public. Others said she was afraid what she might do to the woman who stole her husband if she ever saw her on the street.

Daddy owned the house that Miss Evangeline lived in, which is probably why he felt obligated to help her. Besides, my father had the biggest heart on the planet. There wasn't anything he wouldn't do for someone in need. He paid to have the lawn manicured and the trashcans moved to the curb every week. He did most of the plumbing and light maintenance. Sometimes the women in the neighborhood would do her grocery shopping. Everyone helped out except Momma, who said she'd die before she lifted a finger to help "that woman" in any kind of way.

The first time I saw Miss Evangeline was just before my eighth birthday. She'd been spotted running through the neighborhood in a sheer nightgown, her hair looking like she'd stuck her finger in an electrical socket. That day someone called Daddy and told him to go check on her. By the time Daddy stepped outside, Miss Evangeline was in our driveway, screaming unintelligible words into the night air. Daddy tried to calm her down, leaving Momma on the porch screaming, "No one cares anymore, Evangeline! Take that foolishness down to your own house."

"Go to hell, Zora, where you belong!" Evangeline shouted in reply.

A squad car pulled up in front of the house. Daddy whispered something to the officer and gently took Miss Evangeline by the

arm. She took two steps, then yanked away from the officer and
lifted up her nightgown.

"You want some of this pussy?" she shouted to the officer or
Daddy. I couldn't tell who she was talking to because their backs
were to me. "It used to be good enough for you once upon a time.
Lord knows, it ain't been touched in years."

Then her head fell back like a Pez dispenser, and out came a shrill
siren-like scream that went on long and loud. The officer called for
an ambulance. Daddy sat with her until it arrived, his arm draped
around her shoulder the way he would the sofa. Momma told Daddy
to come back in the house and stop giving the neighbors something
to talk about. Daddy politely asked Momma to go in the house if it
bothered her so damn much. Daddy rarely spoke to Momma disre-
spectfully. Sometimes he had to get her attention. She hesitated a
moment as if she was going to answer back, except something in his
voice told her he wasn't going to repeat himself. Momma slammed
the door behind her. I remained hidden behind the drapes. I thought
it odd how comfortable Miss Evangeline felt with Daddy, and decided it was just Daddy's way. He made everyone feel like they mattered.

We didn't see Miss Evangeline again for six months. Momma was
the happiest she'd ever been until Miss Evangeline called and asked
Daddy to come get her from the hospital. That day the argument
started before Daddy hung up the phone.

"You love her more than you love me, don't you, Frank?" she
shouted. "Just admit it. That's why you're always running to her.
Right?"

Daddy hung up the phone and tried to reason with Momma.

"Zora, calm down. You know I wouldn't turn my back on anyone
in this community."

Momma was too worked up to be reasoned with.

"She has people!" she shouted. "Why ain't she calling them?"

"Hasn't she been through enough? I don't know why she didn't call someone else, and I don't care. I'll tell you what, though, I'm getting tired of this argument, Zora. It's getting old."

Daddy stormed out of the kitchen. A little while later, the front door opened.

Momma shouted, "If you go, don't come back."

He went.

When he hadn't come home by midnight, Momma started calling around for him. After an hour she climbed in bed. Unable to tune out the pain-soaked wails coming through our shared wall, I climbed in bed with her. She still loved me back then, so pushing me away didn't occur to her. She cradled me in her arms and cried us to sleep.

* * * * * *

Daddy was only gone half an hour this time.

Later that night, as I was coming out of the bathroom, I heard him pleading with Momma. I crawled to their door and listened.

"Come on, baby. That's all over now."

"No, it isn't, Frank. And until you take this seriously, you can beg all you want."

"Awww ... come on, baby. I just want a little."

"Well, you can want in one hand and spit in the other. And you need to be paying attention to what's going on in your own g.d. house. Something has to be done about Zayla. I know you see it."

The bedsprings squeaked. Daddy's feet hit the floor with a thud. "What in the hell are you talking about? What do I see?"

Momma laid it out for him. I was changing clothes at school. My relationship with Dee-Dee was "unnatural." This probably wasn't the first time I'd kissed Dee-Dee. God only knows what we must have been doing when I was at Dee-Dee's house and her mother wasn't home. On and on she went. Daddy never opened his mouth until she said, "You should see the way she runs up behind Dee-Dee, just like a little snot-nosed boy!"

"That's ridiculous! Zay's a tomboy. She'll grow out of it."

"How can she? She spends all her time with you doing God knows what. Daughters are supposed to want to spend time with their mothers. They're supposed to want to be like their mothers. Not their fathers. You all need to quit playing basketball, and she doesn't need to be all up under you whenever Bill comes over. You have her thinking it's okay to behave that way."

"Zora," Daddy said in a real serious voice. "I think it's time for you to go to bed. You know damn well you were the exact same way with your father growing up, and don't you dare sit there and lie."

The bed squeaked again and the room went dark. The light clicked back on.

"I will not! I'm not your child, you know!"

"Then stop acting like one."

"If you're so convinced there's nothing wrong with her, then tell me why she was gawking at me while I undressed earlier today. I turned around and there she was staring at me, looking like she was enjoying it."

"Good night, Zora. I'm done with this conversation."

The light clicked off again and stayed off. I crawled back to my room and climbed in bed shocked that my own mother could even think a thing like that.

I hated them all. Two-faced Dee-Dee Mitchell. Evil Evie Sheffield. And Momma. As I turned over and tried to go to sleep, I began to hate God for making me a girl instead of a boy.

6

Mayor Re-elected
L.A. Times – Tuesday, June 1, 1965

> *There are so many roots to the tree of anger*
> *that sometimes the branches shatter*
> *before they bear.*
>> ~Audre Lorde, "Who Said It Was Simple"

Ordinarily, Momma had to drag me out of bed in the morning. That next morning, by the time she shouted for me to get up, I was already making my bed. As I smoothed out the sheets and folded down the top of my comforter, I suddenly understood what Nana always said about good Christians waking up every day with intention. I had, in fact, awakened with every intention of whupping somebody's ass, and the way I felt, it didn't really matter who that was.

"Zayla, I'm not gon' to call you all morning. Get –" Momma said from my doorway, then smiled. "Well, will wonders never cease?"

I pushed past her and disappeared behind the bathroom door.

As the sink filled with water, I inspected my face. Did I look like a bulldagger? I was obviously exhibiting signs of being "unnatural," except I had no idea what "unnatural" looked like.

I leaned closer to the mirror and turned my face from side to side, checking for signs. I stood sideways and studied my profile. If I was a bulldagger, I didn't see it. My almond-shaped eyes looked normal. My nose was average for a Negro nose. Not too wide and not pointy– not making people think I used it to look down on them. My ears stuck out enough to keep a hat on my head. My lips were full, yet not big enough to be considered liver-lipped, as Momma would say. As far as I could tell, I looked the way a girl my age should look.

I turned off the water and washed up as far as "possible," down as far as "possible," and then I washed "possible." It was a saying Momma often used to prevent her from having to say the real name for my private part.

I brushed my teeth next, taking in every aspect of my face. I leaned over to spit. When I raised my head again, I saw the culprits. There, above my eyes, looking like two caterpillars on my face. That had to be it. Up until then I hadn't paid much attention. Their only purpose was to register emotion. When I was surprised, they shot up in the middle, turning themselves upside down. When I was frustrated, they pulled themselves toward the bridge of my nose. When I laughed, they opened up and reached toward my hairline.

Momma hated them. She often reminded me just how much she wished I'd inherited her eyebrows instead of Daddy's. That had to be it. I had manbrows. The other girls had delicate, neat, well-shaped eyebrows, compared to the errant hairs sticking out and going every which way on mine. All bulldaggers must have big, bushy, untamable eyebrows, I reasoned.

I rinsed off my toothbrush and used it to brush them into some sort of order. Then I put a little Vaseline on my finger and spread it over them. Nothing helped. So, I reached under the sink and got

Daddy's shaving kit. Inside was everything I needed: Magic Shave, an old tablespoon and butter knife, a small Tupperware bowl, and Daddy's old pocket watch. I'd watched Daddy shave a million times. I knew what I had to do.

I pried the top off the can of Magic Shave and dumped two tablespoons into the Tupperware bowl. I added an equal amount of lukewarm water and mixed until it was smooth. Then I took the butter knife and dipped it in the shaving cream.

I stood in the mirror, making funny faces while my white eyebrows shot up and down. I watched the second hand on the pocket watch tick off five minutes and then used the butter knife to wipe away all faulty evidence that I was anything more than a tomboy who didn't like girls and especially didn't like boys. I also vowed that whatever feelings I thought I had for Dee-Dee had vanished when she ended our friendship.

"Zayla, what are you doing in there?"

"I'm coming."

"What's that I smell?"

"Nothing."

I quickly rinsed off my face until the white cream and black hair drained down the sink, then used the washcloth to make sure all evidence of my moment of insanity vanished for good. I looked at myself again in the mirror—and held the scream in my throat. The empty space above my eyes was more than noticeable. There was no way I was going to school looking like a circus freak. I panicked. If I didn't do something quickly, Momma was going to come charging in the bathroom. I looked down, and then there, sitting on the bottom shelf of the cabinet above the toilet, I found my salvation. Momma's makeup tray.

In it were the faces Momma used to wear back when she met Daddy and went to the nightclub almost every night. Back when she posed for the camera from Daddy's lap, her arms tight around his neck. In some pictures, his lips lingered on her cheek, back before she found the Lord. Now the frosted pink and varying shades of red lipsticks that she never wore sat collecting dust with the burgundy blushes— fake eyelashes and mascara. And stacks of blue and pale pink eye shadows. Next to all of it, in their own little cubby, were her eyebrow pencils. I grabbed the brown one, and, like a seasoned artist, I drew on new and improved eyebrows. I made sure to keep them close enough to my old caterpillars so Momma wouldn't be suspicious. I also wondered how long it would take my eyebrows to grow back.

It took almost ten minutes to get them just right. I was an artist, even though it was a long time since I'd held a paintbrush.

When I looked in the mirror, I was pleased with the face that looked back. I didn't look so bad, after all. Maybe no one would notice. I straightened up my mess and put Momma's eyebrow pencil and Daddy's shaving kit back where they belonged. The whole bathroom smelled like I'd dropped ten stink bombs.

I grabbed the Lysol off the back of the toilet and sprayed until I choked on the fumes. I took the long way to my room, through the living room, kitchen, back porch, and up the hall to my room. Momma sat on the edge of my bed with the comb, brush, and hair oil next to her. She glanced up and studied my face a while. Her eyes narrowed, and then she frowned like a detective inspecting a crime scene. I held my breath.

"What were you doing in there so long?" she asked suspiciously.

"Nothing," I said. "Just washing up."

"Then why does it smell like your father's shaving cream?"

"I don't know. When am I gonna be old enough to comb my own hair?" I asked.

Momma pointed at the floor in front of her with the comb. I gladly plopped down on the floor in front of her but refused to give up my fight for independence.

"I'm old enough, you know. I don't see why I can't."

"Watch your mouth, hussy. You can comb your hair when you're thirteen and not a day before," she said, making a part down the center of my head.

"Thirteen! That's almost a year away. Why can't I comb it now?" I whined.

"Because I said so."

"But, Momma. The last time I asked, you said I could comb it when I was twelve."

"And if you keep asking, it'll be fifteen."

I rolled my eyes and shut my trap.

Momma's hands moved swiftly, twisting and tugging on my head. Thirteen wasn't that far away, I told myself, unless the ponytails kill me first.

"I want you to come straight home from school today. No stopping for anyone or anything. Understand?"

"Yes, Momma."

She snapped the last barrette in place. I got up. On the bed behind lay the god-awful dress I was supposed to wear. It was light pink with ruffles around the sleeves and hems. There was a thick burgundy satin sash tied in a big bow at the waist. There was no way I was wearing that to school. I'd never hear the end of it. As soon as Momma was out of sight, I went looking for a pair of clean jeans and a T-shirt. I couldn't find them anywhere. My T-shirt drawer was empty along with my jean drawer. I ran to my closet and searched for my sneakers. My play clothes had vanished from every one of my hiding places.

"Zayla, what are you doing in there?"

"Nothing."

"Then hurry up and get dressed and get in here for breakfast."

Momma sat at the table, sipping coffee. She smiled smugly. I ignored her and sucked down my orange juice, slapped my bacon and eggs between two pieces of toast, and wrapped it all in a napkin. I walked out without even so much as a goodbye.

"Bye, sweetheart! Have a great day!" she called out behind me.

Malik was the only one waiting in the driveway when I came out. It felt odd seeing him there alone. The three of us had walked to school together since second grade. I pushed Dee-Dee out of my mind. When I got to the end of the driveway, Malik took one look at me and fell out laughing. I reached for the place where my eyebrows used to be then dropped my hand, afraid I'd smear them.

"Shut up!" I snapped.

Still laughing, Malik said, "Why are you in that getup? Ain't you gonna change?"

"I can't. Momma hid my clothes."

Malik laughed again, then his face turned serious.

"I tried to call you last night, but your phone was busy. Is it true? Was y'all kissin' behind the building, for real?"

"I don't want to talk about it."

"Okay, but you know everyone else is talking about it."

"I don't care. Can we please talk about something else?"

Malik shrugged and said, "Did you hear? Crogan's got robbed last night."

I stopped walking. "Did he say who did it?"

"Two guys from Jordan High, he thinks. He said they were in the store for a long time. He kicked them out, they came back when he was closing up and robbed him. Serves him right if you ask me."

I kept my opinion to myself. I figured if I didn't tell anyone what I saw, it would be like it never happened. And if it never happened, the athlete and the thin, wiry boy wouldn't have any reason to come looking for me.

The whole way to school I watched out to make sure neither of them jumped out.

7

I had the displeasure of seeing Evie as soon as I walked through the double doors. When she saw me coming down the hall, she took one look at my dress and laughed. The other kids laughed, too.

"You think just because you have on a dress today won't nobody think you ain't a bulldagger?" Evie said as she passed me.

"What did you say?" I demanded, more for the kids who'd laughed at me. I wanted them to know I was willing to make an example out of Evie if I had to. Evie didn't care who I was trying to impress. She was far from afraid of me, which is why she stopped walking and said, "You heard me. Did I stutter?"

A crowd began to circle us.

"What you lookin' at?" Evie asked. "If you feelin' froggy, you betta leap."

I planted my feet firmly beneath me and balled up my fist, prepared to pound away on Evie's head. Then I decided to walk away. As I turned to go, I heard Malcolm X say, "Turning the other cheek only gives the oppressor another cheek to kick." I was ready then. All I needed was for Evie to take the first punch. At least then I could say I was defending myself. And I had witnesses, although I wasn't so sure how reliable they'd be. Then I heard Momma whisper, "Good Christians know how to turn the other cheek. It is the sinner that allows themselves to be drawn in by evil." I also heard her say I'd be in a world of trouble if I had another fight at school. I decided I wasn't feeling so froggy after all and walked away.

"Yeah, you betta walk away. Bulldagger."

In my head, I stopped walking and turned around the way I'd seen John Wayne do at least a million times. I pulled my imaginary six-shooter out of its holster and fired. Evie hit the floor. I'd saved the school from the evil villain, and now I was the hero. Everyone cheered and told me I could kiss whoever I wanted. All was forgiven.

In reality, I did what any red-blooded non-thinking person would have done. I let my mouth write a check my ass couldn't cash. "You better apologize," I yelled.

"I ain't better do nothin' but stay Black and die!"

"Oh yeah," I shouted to her back. "Either you apologize or I'm gonna kick your ass after school."

"See you after school," she said.

* * * * * *

If ever there was a time for the minutes to fly by, that day was one of them. I tried to focus on our math lesson and doodled on my Pee-Chee folder instead.

"Zayla, will you read problem number five, please?" Mrs. Fitzgerald asked.

"By 2:30 p.m. on Monday, 25% of the classes at Valley Middle School had finished taking yearbook pictures. What fractional part of the classes had NOT yet taken yearbook pictures?"

"Thank you, Zayla. Does anyone know the correct answer?" Mrs. Fitzgerald asked.

I had a better question. If by 2:30 on Monday, 25% of the classes at Compton Elementary School knew I had threatened to kick Evie's ass after school, what fractional part of the classes hadn't heard yet?

When the bell rang for morning and afternoon recess, I stayed in and helped Mrs. Fitzgerald clean erasers and hand back homework assignments. After the lunch bell rang, I went to the nurse's office with a terrific stomachache that miraculously healed itself when it was time to return to class. By the time the bell rang at the end of the day, I was all out of options. Evie shook her fist at me on her way out of the room. I dropped my head on the desk. By the time I summoned my courage to go home, the hallway was empty, except for Malik, who'd been waiting at the foot of the stairs where we always met before walking home.

"What took you so long?" he asked and leaned closer. "And what happened to your eyebrows?"

I tried to move around him. He stepped in front of me, and then his eyebrows shot up.

"Why'd you do that?" he asked, pointing at my fake eyebrows.

I knocked his hand away. "Can we go home?"

"You know the whole school is waiting for you around the corner," he warned.

"Oh ..."

He reached down and took my hand, reminding me who my real best friend was. I couldn't think of a time when Malik and I weren't shoved into the back seat of the car, plopped into a grocery cart, or tucked into bed– together. Malik never would have lied to protect himself. Ever.

I gave him a crooked smile as we rounded the corner onto Compton Avenue, then stopped dead in my tracks. It looked like every kid at school was crowded around Evie, waiting for her to pull my head off and toss it into the middle of the street. I suddenly realized two things: one, we weren't on school grounds anymore, and two, anything could happen when there were no teachers to pull us apart. I was dead for sure. I decided, live or die, Evie wasn't going home without apologizing for calling me a bulldagger.

Malik grabbed me and pulled me in the opposite direction. "It's not too late to run," he whispered.

I started to go with him until someone shouted, "There she is!"

"Now it is," I said and turned back around.

Evie stood in the middle of the sidewalk, chomping on a huge wad of gum. I walked toward her until we were face to face. She blew a bubble and sucked it back in her mouth. She could barely swallow without having to push the wad into her cheek first, which made me want to slap that gum right down her throat. And then I stopped wishing and stepped forward, pulling up my courage like a pair of loose socks. Without a second thought, I swung. Once I punched her, I couldn't stop. I'd gotten the better of Evie and was holding my own. When I knocked her down, the kids cheered for me.

"Kick her ass, Zayla! Kick it good!" they chanted.

When Evie tried to get up, I pushed her back down and shouted, "Apologize."

"I ain't," she mumbled and rubbed the blood from the corner of her mouth.

I cocked my fist, ready to strike again. "Did you hear me? Apologize!"

A siren sounded. The kids looked toward the street and scattered.

"Zayla Lucille McKinney! I know that ain't you I see out here fighting on the street?"

I looked up to see Uncle Bill's squad car sitting in the middle of the street, the lights spinning overhead. This time when Evie tried to get up, I let her.

Uncle Bill made a U-turn and pulled up to the curb. Evie took off running. Malik and I climbed in the squad car. I caught a glimpse of Dee-Dee in the side mirror just as she disappeared around the corner with Melody Armstrong. I slumped back against the seat and wished I'd been strong enough to kick Dee-Dee's ass instead.

"What in the world has gotten into you?" Uncle Bill asked. "And Malik, why were you out here cheering her on?"

"Because Evie deserved it, Daddy," Malik explained. "That's the girl that called Zay a b-u-l-l-you-know-what."

"That bony thing?" he said. "Ain't that Charlotte Biggins' girl?"

I nodded. Malik gave Uncle Bill a blow-by-blow of the fight.

Uncle Bill asked, "Should I call you Ali or Liston?"

I laughed and thought of Evie laid out on the sidewalk with me standing over her. It might not have been the shortest fight in history, but I was definitely Ali to her Sonny Liston.

"Ali, of course."

"Of course you were Ali."

As we turned into "the Circle," Mr. Jones ran off his porch, arms flailing. Uncle Bill pulled to the curb, and Mr. Jones stumbled over to the passenger side. He leaned his elbows on the windowsill. Sweat trickled down his face and dripped onto his hairy arm in puddles.

"Bill, you gotta come right now!" he said, panting for breath. "Stan Thompson's over there on 105th getting his head cracked open."

It smelled like he'd been drinking. Malik and I slid away from the window and pinched our noses shut. If Mr. Jones noticed, he didn't let on.

"What? Who?" Uncle Bill asked, confused.

"Them cracker cops of yourn! They beatin' him! Right in front of his house!"

"Okay. Let me get these kids home and I'll be right there."

Mr. Jones stumbled away from the car. Uncle Bill sped off and hit the corner on two wheels. Malik and I clanged into each other like pinballs.

"Did you smell his breath?" Malik asked. "How come you didn't arrest him?"

"There's no law against drunk walking. Hell, I'd be drinking too if I just lost my job and had a family of five to feed."

We pulled up in front of the house behind Momma's car.

"Make sure Zayla gets in the house safely and then go on home," Uncle Bill told Malik.

I don't know what he expected to happen between the curb and our front door, but I let Malik walk me up anyway. I was more afraid of what would happen the minute I got in the house. Uncle Bill sped away from the curb and hit the siren as he turned onto 104th Street.

"What are you gonna tell Auntie Zora?" Malik asked while I fumbled for my key.

"I don't know. It's gonna be pretty hard to lie looking like this," I said, holding up my ripped belt.

I could feel my ponytails standing on top of my head. I fumbled at the tips of each. My barrettes were gone. And although I couldn't see for myself, I knew my eyebrows were brown smudges above my eyes.

"I'll come in and explain what happened. That way Auntie Zora won't be so mad."

Doubtful, I let him go in first anyway. He opened the front door cautiously and then waved me in. I peeked around the entryway into the dining room. Empty. The drapes were closed, and the house was dark and quiet. Momma must be out somewhere with Aunt Evelyn, I thought, and let out a sigh of relief. I allowed the belt to go slack in my hand as I closed the door.

I turned to make a beeline for my room and almost walked up Malik's back. Momma stood no less than two feet in front of him, her arms folded across her chest and fire in her eyes.

"Bye, Malik," she said, looking past him at me.

"Bye, Auntie Zora," he replied, hightailing it out of the house.

"Get over here, hussy!" Momma said to me.

I turned to run and she snatched my shoulder. I winced with

pain but dared not pull away. She grabbed my face and tilted it up toward her. "And what in the hell did you do to your eyebrows?"

* * * * * *

Momma made me take a bath and sent me to bed without supper.

"If you come out of that room for any reason before your father gets home, I swear to God I will kill you where you stand."

She needn't worry. I was so tired I couldn't see straight. I fell across my bed and drifted straight off to sleep. It was dark by the time I woke up. Daddy was in his practice room in the converted garage, running scales on his upright piano. Momma was in the living room watching *Peyton Place*. I climbed out of bed and lay on the floor by the living room door to watch along.

The phone rang.

I sat up, half hoping it was Dee-Dee calling to apologize.

"Girrlll, I know," Momma laughed into the receiver. "What am I going to do with that child? Can you imagine?"

It was Aunt Evelyn, Momma's only friend.

"I wonder who else saw that heathen out on the street fighting.... Truth be told, I'm glad Zayla whipped her ass. Have you seen the girl? Just as pitiful as they come ... You know who she reminds me of? That old black bitch Carla Johnson ... Yes! I know. The black ones always start shit. It's like they're pissed off God made them black and ugly and want to take it out on anyone that looks better, which ain't hard ... Lord, forgive me, but you know I'm telling the truth...

"What a sight Zayla was when she came home. Hair standing all over her head. That brand-new dress I bought her at I. Magnin earlier this year filthy dirty, belt ripped right off. Looking just like those ragamuffins at the Doolittle School. And she's standing there looking up at me with these streaks and smudges of brown above her eye where her g.d. eyebrows should have been."

That tickled Momma. She started laughing again. Aunt Evelyn said something that made her laugh even harder.

"Oh, Lord have mercy. I haven't thought about Cathy Little in years. Whatever happened to that girl? She was one to beat the band, wasn't she? It was bad enough she didn't have any g.d. eyebrows, walkin' around with that skull cap on her head all the time. Looked crazy as a Betsy bug."

Momma laughed on down memory lane with Aunt Evelyn until they were back in high school on the South Side of Chicago.

I felt a little better. Momma wasn't as mad as she pretended to be. And she didn't appear to hate me as much as I thought. For that, I was grateful.

Later, Daddy gave me a good long talking-to about using his things without permission. He had to cover his mouth at times to keep himself from laughing. I was quite a sight without my fuzzy caterpillars. He asked me what possessed me to shave them off. I didn't have the heart to tell him I'd been frantically trying to rid myself of a piece of him, so I played the "I don't know" card.

"Well, promise me you won't do anything like that again," he said and kissed the empty spaces above my eyes.

I promised. Only a fool would do something that stupid more than once.

"Now," he said, looking me directly. "About this fight you had. Your mother tells me it was the same girl who called you that ugly name."

I nodded.

"Well, why were you fighting this time?"

"Because I wanted her to apologize for calling me out of my name."

"Let me be the first to tell you. People are going to talk about you. You are a unique and divine creation of God, and as long as you stand in your uniqueness, you are going to make a whole lot of people uncomfortable and jealous. You can't fight everyone who calls you out of your name. The best thing you can do is keep on keepin' on. That gets 'em best. So, don't you go changin' on me. You hear me? And, I hate to tell you this, little Ali, but you are also on punishment for the next two weeks."

"Yes, Daddy."

Daddy laughed and gave me a few air body-blows. I returned an air uppercut, and we laughed and laughed until Momma came to see what was so funny. Then we were all laughing like crazy, which must have been the reason Momma leaned down and kissed me. Twice. One soft sweet kiss on each space where my eyebrows should have been. Daddy turned off the light. When they were gone, I slipped out of bed and knelt beside it.

Dear God. I don't really hate you. I just wished you would have made me look on the outside the way I feel on the inside. I'm not mad at you though because I'm so happy you made Momma love me today. Can you do it again tomorrow? And the next day? Thank you. Amen.

8

Yorty to Propose a New Anti-Poverty Program
L.A. Times – Wednesday, June 2, 1965

> *I want to go in the back yard now*
> *And maybe down the alley,*
> *To where the charity children play.*
> *I want a good time today.*
> > - Gwendolyn Brooks, "A Song in the Front Yard"

The next morning Momma laid out the ugliest dress I'd ever seen in my life. A green and gray plaid monstrosity with a white lace bib and green laces up the front. The blouse was white with a green ribbon around the collar and cuffs. It looked like something right out of Rodgers and Hammerstein's *Sound of Music*, my all-time favorite movie until that day. I slipped the god-awful thing over my head, confident I felt a terrible sickness coming on. There was no way I was going through another day of torture and humiliation dressed like the ghetto version of Louisa Von Trapp.

I wolfed down breakfast and contemplated a way to get out of going to school. As I got to the front door, the kernel of an idea began to form, take shape, and explode. Instead of grabbing my books,

I shoved my finger down my throat. The retching made a terrible sound. Once I started throwing up, I couldn't stop.

"What in the hell happened?" Momma screamed. "How many times have I told you to stop eating so goddamn fast? You just plow through your food without even chewing! That's what you get. One day you'll stop being so goddamn hardheaded."

I shouldn't have been surprised by her reaction, yet I stood there stupefied anyway. I decided to play to her sympathies.

"I'm sorry, Momma."

"All niggas are sorry."

I hated when she said that. For one, I was not a nigga. The retching started up again. Momma jumped back a second too late. Mostly orange juice and the few remaining fragments of breakfast covered her shoes and splashed on her legs. Having to stand in my vomit thoroughly pissed her off, and it served her right. I'm not a nigga. And I'm not sorry for throwing up all over you, I said to myself.

"God dammit! Come on here," she said and snatched me by the arm.

She kicked off her shoes and dragged me to my bedroom. I did my best not to bring up anything else. Momma snatched the dress up over my head and tossed it in the hall. She pulled the covers back, and I climbed in bed. She left and came back with a cold washcloth to mop my head and wipe my mouth. I had to admit, shoving my finger down my throat wasn't my finest hour, but it was good enough to get me out of going to school, and I wasn't going back.

At some point, between Momma going off about me ruining a perfectly good pair of shoes and cleaning up the mess I'd made on the living room carpet, I managed to doze off. When I woke up a few hours later, the house was quiet. I slipped out of bed to investigate.

Voices floated in from the backyard. I peered out as Momma pulled one of my T-shirts from the laundry basket and hung it on the line. Aunt Evelyn sat on the steps, sipping coffee and doing what she did best — telling other folks' business.

"... got her there just in time. The baby's fine. A beautiful little boy. Eleven pounds, three ounces."

"That's a big baby. What about Stan? He okay?"

"He's lucky to be alive. He's in the ICU until the swelling goes down on his brain. He's got a fractured arm, two broken ribs, and a sprained ankle. Thank God Bill showed up when he did."

"Did anyone say why they beat him?" Momma asked.

She pulled a pair of my shorts out of the laundry basket and inspected the frayed hem. She stuck her finger through a hole in the leg and then balled up the shorts and tossed them in the direction of the garbage can next to the garage. I made a mental note to rescue them as soon as I had the chance.

"Yeah. Get this," Aunt Evelyn said. "He double-parked to get Mildred to the car. The cop told him to move. Ain't that rich? Told him he was illegally parked in a residential zone. Stan's trying to explain his wife's in labor, Mildred's on the porch calling out to the officer, and he ain't paying attention to neither one of them. That's when Mildred tells Stan to move the car, but he won't listen because he starts telling the cop it is not illegal to double-park when loading and unloading a vehicle. The cop throws Stan to the ground. Mildred is screaming and hollering. Neighbors are coming out of the houses. The cop starts beating Stan with his blackjack. I mean, he's hitting him like he wants to see if Stan's head will pop open like a fucking watermelon or something."

"Damn, I hate to say this, but it's still better than shooting him to death."

"Yeah, I guess. It would be even better if they just left us the hell alone. They didn't want us in their communities, so we built our own and proved we didn't need they ass. What'd they do? Burned our shit down out of spite. Here we are all these years after our so-called freedom, and we're still begging the white man to give us our God-given human rights."

"We're not fighting for human rights, just our civil rights," Momma said.

"What planet are you living on? What's the damn difference? Civil rights. Human rights. Either way, it ain't for no white man to say whether or not we can have them. Shit."

"You see Yorty got reelected?"

"Yeah, I know. I don't know if we woulda been any better off if Roosevelt got in."

"I don't think Yorty's such a bad mayor. Did you see in the paper today? He's going to start an anti-poverty program."

Aunt Evelyn threw her head back and laughed. "What are you talking about? Yorty took the money before the idea of any program ever came up. He lied to Washington about it, and nobody even bothered to investigate."

"That's not true," Momma said.

"Shit if it ain't. You remember that big newspaper article in the paper a year or so ago. The first step in LBJ's war on poverty was to send money to communities all across the country. Yorty got our money, and he didn't do anything with it, for us. Then he said he earmarked it for something else. Then we never heard about it again. Ooooohh weee! Sometimes them crackers get on my last goddamn nerve!"

"Don't take the Lord's—"

"Shut up, Zora. I ain't in the fuckin' mood."

Momma pulled a pair of Daddy's pants out of the basket, shook them out, and pinned them to the clothesline. She hung one of his dress shirts next to it.

"What am I gonna do about Zayla?" she asked. "This is putting a strain on Frank."

She ran her hand down the buttons as if Daddy stood there in it.

"What are you talking about? That's you! Don't you dare put this on Frank."

"He is upset about it, you know."

"Yeah, he's upset that you're makin' a mountain out of a molehill. 'Cause you up here tryin' to fix somethin' that ain't broke."

"She is broke, Evelyn. You don't know like I know. I'm her mother. I've done everything I can. I can't beat it out of her. Lord knows I've tried…" Momma's voice trailed off.

"She's twelve. She'll outgrow it. And if she doesn't, well, she doesn't."

"Easy for you to say. I bet you wouldn't be so calm if someone called Malik a faggot."

"If they did, who gives a shit? Just because someone says it don't make it so."

"What? You know you would die. Especially Bill. That's the worst thing imaginable for a Black father. To know he somehow created a freak of nature. An abomination!"

"Zora, you know what your problem is? You spend too much goddamn time—"

"Stop taking the Lord's name in vain," Momma interrupted.

"You spend too much *goddamn* time worrying about what other people think. I could give less than a damn about what anybody thinks about me and mine. I keep telling you, the sooner you stop giving a shit, the happier you'll be. And, in case you have forgotten, my cousin Mark is one of those freaks of nature, as you so eloquently put it. You were there. You know the hell he went through when we were growing up. How they called him Missy Mark and tormented the shit out of him for playing with girls all the time. Then he had to deal with his own damn family treating him worse than that, as if them niggas was any better or less sinful. Give me a goddamn—"

"Evelyn!"

"Zora! I'm a grown-ass woman, so give me a goddamn break! You kill me stomping around here like you're holier than thou, because you can't deal with your own shit. Zayla is your daughter and if I'm not mistaken, the only one you have. You can play dumb all you want, but I remember how we used to play as kids."

"Yeah, so?"

"What in the hell do you mean, so? Hello, Pot. Meet Kettle. The only difference is you did all your roughhousing in a dress because that's what you preferred. Don't even act like you don't remember the time you chased Chester Robinson around the neighborhood because he stole a peek under your dress. You chased him right up that tree in front of Mr. Hall's house and then ran right up behind him. You didn't give a damn that half the neighborhood saw up your dress, just as long as it wasn't Chester."

"This is different."

"Umm-hmm. How?"

"Zayla's different. I can't quite put my finger on it, but she's different. Not just because she hates wearing dresses. It's inside her in a place I can't get to, no matter how much I try. I've noticed it for about a year now. It seems like the older she gets ... I don't know. She said she thought God made a mistake when he made her a girl instead of a boy. And you know the Lord don't make no mistakes."

"She was four. And you told Herbie you were going to marry him when you grew up."

"What's wrong with that? All little girls want to grow up and marry their fathers."

"You weren't hardly little. You were damn near sixteen years old."

"I was not! And stop trying to turn this back on me. My child needs help and I don't have the slightest idea what to do. I'm gonna ask Pastor Shuttlesworth to help."

"Oh my God! Pastor Shuttlesworth? What's he gonna do? Pour some holy water on her and cast her sins away? Who's casting his away with his blaspheming, lying ass? Goddamn! You just go from bad to worse!"

"I know you better stop using the Lord's name in vain."

Aunt Evelyn laughed. "People in glass houses shouldn't throw stones. God is always watching. Ain't that what you're always saying?"

"Go to hell, Evelyn. That wasn't my fault and you know it. That wasn't my fault!"

"Yeah, well. You put up with it for a long time after you found out, didn't you? Still are, aren't you?"

They sat in awkward silence for a while. Aunt Evelyn spoke first.

"Look, I'm not trying to throw your past in your face to hurt you. I just want you to think about Zayla. She hasn't even reached puberty. I'm sure the minute she gets her period and some titties, there'll be so many boys chasing her, it'll give you something else to complain about."

Aunt Evelyn stood up and I took off up the hall to my room. I jumped in bed and looked down at my flat chest. I hoped she was right. All the other girls at school already had their training bras and most of them had their periods. My titties were still missing in action and the only periods I saw came at the end of a sentence. I wondered if it was because I wasn't supposed to have them in the first place.

As young as four, I was all too aware that God made a mistake when he made me a girl instead of a boy. I'd never felt comfortable in my skin from that point on. If only I'd had the sense to keep my feelings to myself, I'd still have Momma's undying love. How was I supposed to know that being honest with Momma was the wrong thing to do?

I sat at the kitchen table reading "Little Black Sambo" for the umpteenth time. Feeling some sort of connection to Sambo, I innocently said, "Momma, I shoulda come out like Sambo. I think God made a mistake when he made me a girl."

I never saw her hand coming until it struck my face.

"God doesn't make mistakes. Don't you ever let me hear you say that again!"

I never did and that didn't stop me from feeling that way.

* * * * * *

Just around the time school let out, Momma led me out to the backyard for a little surprise. In the center of the grass, facing her rose garden, she'd set up a card table and a beach chair. A small vase held a short bouquet of white, yellow, and red roses. She brought out a bowl of homemade chicken noodle soup and a package of saltine crackers. I spent the rest of the afternoon reading *Stuart Little* and enjoying the sunshine and fresh air until Malik showed up and snatched the book out of my hand.

"How you feel, Buckethead?" he asked, not waiting for an answer. "Man, you better be glad you didn't go to school today. Evie was looking for you, talking about how she was going to teach you a lesson. I saw her show a group of kids a switchblade, and I went and told Mean Man Mulligan on her. When he called her into the office, Evie still had the switchblade on her. She got expelled. Can you believe it? Two weeks before summer and she gets kicked out of school!"

"Do you think she really would have stabbed me?" I asked.

"I don't know. Maybe."

"Was anyone else looking for me?"

I wondered about the athlete and the thin and wiry guy. The police were still looking for them.

"Like who?"

"I don't know. Anybody."

"No. Enough of that. Come on ..."

He dragged me around the side of the garage and plopped down cross-legged in the grass.

"Sit down," he commanded. "We're going to get to the bottom of this right now."

I didn't move, so he grabbed my shirttail and snatched me down next to him.

"What are you talking about?"

"Here," he said, tossing three *Playboy* magazines in my lap.

I pushed the magazines away. "Uh-uh. What do I want to see that for?"

"Quit playing. This is serious!"

He set the magazines back in my lap and flipped one open.

"What's wrong with you, boy? I don't want to see those things! Where'd you get 'em anyway?"

"In the bottom of my dad's drawer," he said, grinning. "He used to take them in the bathroom with him. I walked in on him one time and he was ... well, umm, never mind. I know if you look at these books and you get all hot and bothered, then we'll know for sure if you're a bulldagger or not."

"Malik Jerome Edwards, what in the hell are you tryin' to say?"

"Calm down, girl. Damn. I ain't tryin' to say nothin'. Don't you want to know if it's true or not?"

"Shut up, Malik! I already know."

"How do you know?"

Okay. So I didn't. I rolled my eyes and flopped back down on the grass. I snatched the first magazine and flipped through the pages, barely glancing at the photos. There was nothing to get all hot and bothered about. There was just page after page of white women in various stages of undress — big deal. I took the next book. Same thing. I'd almost gotten through the third book when I noticed the Playmate of the Month was a Negro.

"Malik, look!" I said, elbowing him and pointing.

"Are you hot and bothered?"

"No! Look at her! She's a Negro!"

He looked at the picture and shoved it back at me. "No, she ain't."

"Yes, she is. Look."

"That is not a Negro. She's probably Italian or something," he said, pressing his face closer. "Are you hot and bothered?"

The model's name was Jennifer Jackson and she was a dead ringer for Dorothy Dandridge. A white silk robe with red polka dots hung loosely off one of her shoulders. She smirked at the camera like a cat with her paw in the fish tank. Her left hand covered her "possible." I became very aware of her nakedness, her small breasts and the light brown pimply skin around her nipples. I ran my finger across her collarbone, down her arm, and across her stomach.

My insides began to move and stir the same way they had when Dee-Dee and I stood nose to nose behind the building. I didn't like the feeling. I wasn't hot, but I was certainly bothered.

"Well?" Malik asked. "How did it make you feel?"

"It didn't make me feel like nothin'!" I said, throwing the magazines at him.

"Why you gettin' so mad about it?"

"Because this whole thing is stupid and so are you!"

"You didn't feel nothin'?"

"No, Malik. I didn't feel nothin'! Now shut up talkin' to me."

"Don't be embarrassed," he said, putting his hand on my shoulder.

I jerked away. "I'm not!"

"Come on, Zay. You can tell me. How'd you really feel? You had to feel something. I saw how you were looking at her." He slid closer.

"Forget you, Malik."

I turned away from him and fought back the tears stinging my eyes. I didn't want to like girls. I didn't.

Malik draped his lanky arm around my shoulder.

"Look, girl. I'm gonna love you no matter what. You know, there is one way to know for sure. Do you wanna kiss me?" he asked.

"Why would I?"

"Because if you kiss me and you don't feel anything, then you will know for sure."

"And if I do feel something?"

"Then you do. Either way, you'll know."

Malik leaned forward and kissed me. At first it was just with our lips, then he stuck his tongue in my mouth. I gagged. He pulled back.

"Too much?" he asked.

"Do it again. I wasn't ready. No tongue."

Seven seconds it lasted. I kissed him the way I'd kissed Dee-Dee. When he pulled back, he had the same dreamy look I suspect I had, until Dee-Dee wiped my kiss away. I didn't want to hurt Malik's feelings, even though our kiss felt like a handshake with lips. It didn't mean I liked girls for sure. It just proved I didn't like kissing Malik.

"Did you like it?" he asked.

"Uh-huh," I lied. "Did you?"

"Yeah," he said, as a smile crawled across his face.

"I guess that means I'm not a bulldagger then, huh?"

"Guess so. Does this mean you're my girlfriend now?"

"Shut up, Malik," I said.

He shrugged and got up. I watched him climb the ladder up to the treehouse Uncle Bill and Daddy built for us. It wasn't a house. It was more like a big wooden crib with clear plastic lining around the sides and a green plastic roof to keep the elements out. The steps were wooden slats nailed into the trunk of the tree. You'd never see a treehouse like ours on *Leave It to Beaver* or *Daniel Boone*. We didn't care. It was ours and parents weren't allowed. And sometimes we went up there to be alone with our thoughts. I went back to *Stuart Little*, knowing that we were thinking about the same thing. All signs suggested I was a bulldagger. I couldn't fool Malik. He saw how I looked at Miss March, and he felt how little I enjoyed that kiss. He was just too good a friend to make me feel bad about it.

9

〇〰〰〰

Politics Pokes its Nose into War on Poverty
L.A. Times – Friday, June 4, 1965

> *Where we come from, sometimes, beauty*
> *floats around us like clouds*
> *the way leaves rustle in the breeze*
> *and cornbread and barbeque swing out the back door*
> *and tease all our senses as the sun goes down.*
> – Ntozake Shange, "People of Watts"

If our neighborhood had been an actual African village, Mr. and Mrs. Robinette would have been the village elders. Mr. Robinette was a deacon at 103rd Street Baptist Church. He administered prayer over the sick and ailing, and eulogized the dead. He counseled fathers and disciplined us kids when we got unruly. On Saturday mornings, while the colors of the sky emerged from black to burnt orange, Mr. Robinette would appear on their front porch. He would take his time watering the grass and washing the family car. After, he would go down the street and water Miss Judy's and Miss Ruthie's grass because they didn't have husbands of their own.

Mrs. Robinette cooked and cleaned for the church's sick and ailing until they got back on their feet. If they were called home to Glory, she helped make arrangements for the funeral and fed the grieving family. She had a habit of, as we say, putting both feet in everything she cooked, which is why no one ever said no when she volunteered to host Sunday dinner. On those rare occasions when someone else volunteered to host, Mrs. Robinette still showed up with pies or cakes and insisted on helping to cook. She also babysat for all of us when our parents went out on the town.

So, when the doorbell rang at a quarter to eight on Friday night, I ran to the door. Mrs. Robinette stood on the other side, out of breath and smelling of Watkins liniment and peppermint candy. In one plump brown hand she gripped her knitting bag with colorful balls of yarn stuffed inside. A pair of knitting needles peered out like antennae. Stuck down in the front pocket of the bag was a deck of playing cards and Policy Pete's Dream Book. Out of sight, beneath the yarn, was a pint of Jack Daniel's that she would sip on all night out of a teacup. By the time Momma and Daddy got back home, she would be good and tipsy and ready for bed.

In her other hand, still in its baking pan, was her famous lemon pound cake with powdered sugar frosting, my personal favorite. She handed it to me, and before I could put it down safely, she swallowed me up in her arms. I disappeared into her ample bosom and the folds of her housedress. I held the cake away from us to keep it from becoming part of the carpet. Although, truth be told, I would have eaten it anyway.

"Hi, Mrs. Robinette," I said, giggling.

She released me and gave my forehead a wet kiss, then frowned at the place where my eyebrows should have been. Reading the embarrassment on my face, she chuckled and didn't even bother asking.

"How's my baby girl?" she asked instead, digging around in the pocket of her housedress. She popped a peppermint into her mouth and handed one to me.

"I'm okay," I said, taking it.

She studied my face a second. "You sure?"

"Yep."

"Well, if you okay, I'm okay. Now help an old lady into the house, would you?"

I ran and put the cake on the dining room table, then took her by the elbow and helped her step up into the house. Still in her house slippers, she shuffled over to the sofa and plopped down. Her ankles and feet looked like fat sausages. She took her slippers off, plopped her feet up on the coffee table, and leaned back. I flipped on the television so she could watch *Hogan's Heroes*, then flopped down on the sofa next to her. Ten minutes later Malik showed up.

"What you doing here, little snot-nosed boy?" Mrs. Robinette asked.

"You're stuck with me for the night," he said.

He ran over and gave Mrs. Robinette a hug, then sniffed the air and looked around to see what she'd baked for us. When he spotted the lemon pound cake on the dining room table, he made a beeline for the kitchen and came back with a knife and saucer.

"Boy, you better go wash your grubby hands," Mrs. Robinette said.

"Yes, ma'am."

"And when you finish, go get two more saucers and cut us all some cake."

"Yes, ma'am."

When we finished our cake, Mrs. Robinette had Malik get her playing cards and poker chips out of her bag. We cleared the *Ebony* and *Good Housekeeping* magazines off the coffee table. Malik and I sat cross-legged on the floor in front of it. I had started dividing up the poker chips when Malik said, "I don't want to play for plastic. I wanna play for real."

"Real what, child?" Mrs. Robinette asked.

"Money. Bread. Moooo-lah!"

Malik slapped the back of one hand into the palm of the other. Mrs. Robinette shook her head and laughed.

"Well, okay then. Put your money where your mouth is."

Malik reached in his pocket and laid two dollar bills and seven quarters on the table. Mrs. Robinette reached into her bra and pulled out a coin purse. She gave Malik eight quarters for his two dollars, then counted out fifteen quarters for herself and placed them on the table. I folded my arms across my chest and watched.

"Come on, cheap chippy. Ante up," Mrs. Robinette persuaded.

"No, thank you. I'll keep my allowance right where it belongs. In my piggy bank," I said.

Mrs. Robinette was right. I was as cheap as they come, especially when it came to giving my money away. I'd learned about gambling listening to Daddy talk about losing his shirt playing poker. I'd just as soon spend my last cent on penny candy than give it away.

"Suit yourself," she said.

Mrs. Robinette shuffled the cards and started to deal them out. I might have been cheap, but I didn't like being left out either. I jumped up, ran to my room, and counted out fifteen quarters from my piggy bank. Mrs. Robinette waited for me to ante up and dealt the cards. In less than twenty minutes she'd separated us from our money and talked trash about the piss-poor job we must be doing in school because we couldn't add worth a damn.

"If y'all counted a lot faster in your heads instead of using your fingers like they're some kinda abacus, you mighta been able to stay in the game a little longer. The game is called twenty-one, which means you oughta be able to count that high and be quick about it."

"I counted fast," Malik said.

"Not fast enough, youngblood. If you had, I wouldn't be sitting here with all your candy money, now would I?"

"Let's play again," he demanded, hitting the table with his palm.

Mrs. Robinette laughed. "With what? You ain't got no mo' money and this bank don't extend no kinda credit to Negroes."

Malik yanked off his shoe and pulled out two dollar bills and two quarters from his sock. Mrs. Robinette made change and looked at me. This time I said no and meant it.

In the middle of their game the doorbell rang. I answered it.

"Hey, Roger," I said.

Roger was Mrs. Robinette's son. By all appearances, he looked and sometimes behaved like a street thug. In reality, he was a senior at Verbum Dei High, the all-boys high school a few blocks down Central, and he was on the honor roll. Very few people outside of "The Circle knew he had a scholarship to USC waiting for him after graduation. He liked it that way. The less people who knew how smart he was, the better. He had two things working against him. He was Negro and male, which made him a walking target. According to Roger, girls didn't have to worry about such things because we didn't pose as much of a threat to the white world. So, Roger pretended to be a hardhead to his peers, and to everyone else he attempted to be viewed as just another kid from the neighborhood. Sometimes the lines blurred.

"What's happenin', Lil Ali?" Roger asked.

He threw a few air punches my way. Man, the rumor mill never sleeps in "The Circle," I thought.

"You remember my cousin Marquette?" Roger asked me.

"Is Marquette out there?" Mrs. Robinette asked. "Boy, you better get in here and give your auntie some suga."

Marquette rolled his eyes and shook his head. A slight smile tugged at his lips.

Marquette Frye's intense brown eyes and serious demeanor made him frightening when he wasn't smiling, which was most of the time. On those rare occasions when he allowed his face to relax, he was a very good-looking guy. I often wondered if he didn't smile so

he always looked tough, or if he was just trying to hide the space between his front teeth.

"Hey," Marquette said, nudging me with his elbow. "How come
you always watching me out of the corner of your eye? You scared of
me or something?"

"No," I said, looking down at my feet.

He laughed. "I ain't scary, little girl. Just quiet. When you're quiet
you can hear better," he said and winked at me. "And people don't
remember you was ever there. I prefer it that way, ya dig?"

I nodded and smiled. "Got it."

"When's Ronald coming home?" Mrs. Robinette asked.

"In August," Marquette said.

"Praise God. I'm gon' pray every night don't nothin' happen to
him before he get a chance to come home. You know they say most
of them boys get killed days before they s'posed to come home."

"Ain't nothin' gon' happen to him, Aunt Vonelle. He made it this
far. He gon' make it home, too," Marquette said.

Mrs. Robinette reached for her coin purse again and pulled out
a small stack of bills. She handed a dollar to Roger and took a peek
inside Policy Pete's Dream Book.

"Put this on 865 because I dreamed about my poor cousin
Cordelia last night. I'm gon' have to call her and see if she's doin'
okay," Mrs. Robinette said. "And, hey! Y'all hurry up and get over
there. The cutoff is seven o'clock. Be just my luck y'all get to lollygag-
ging around and my damn numbers come in. Oooh, you betta hope
that don't happen 'cause imma whup both your asses if it does. Go
on now," she said, shooing them out the door with her hand.

"Come on, man," Roger said, then leaned over and kissed his
mother on the cheek. "Bye, Momma."

Marquette nodded and turned to me. "Miss Zayla, good to see
you again. Next time don't be 'fraid to speak to a nigga." He turned

to Malik next. "Malik, my man, I'll catch you on the down stroke. Stay cool, youngblood."

I closed the door behind them. Malik and I went to the window to watch them pull off. Marquette drove a fire-engine-red Plymouth Barracuda. It was long and boxy and made a world of noise when he revved the engine. I don't know why it made us so happy, we cheered every time he did it. Marquette started up the car, lit a cigarette, and pumped the accelerator twice. Vroomm! Vroomm! went the engine, rattling the front window, and then they were gone. Malik and I cheered like Marquette had just hit the winning point for the Lakers in a tied game at the buzzer.

"Oh Lord! That car's gon' be the death of that boy," Mrs. Robinette said. "Well, get on back over here. We got a game to play and I got money to win."

We flopped back down at the table. Mrs. Robinette shuffled the cards and dealt them. Both she and Malik had two aces showing. She peeked at her other card and placed it back on the table. Malik looked at his other card and flipped it over. The ace of spades and the ace of diamonds lay side by side.

"Double down," he said, adding another quarter to his ante.

Mrs. Robinette smiled slyly.

"Hit me," Malik demanded.

Mrs. Robinette placed a card face up on the table in front of him. It was the seven of clubs.

"Hit me again!"

She lay down another card. It was the three of diamonds.

"Hit me again!" he shouted.

"You sure 'bout that?" she asked.

"Yes!"

She flipped over the next card. It was the six of hearts. Malik demanded to be hit again. And again she slid another card off the top of the deck and shook her head at the five of spades. Malik threw his cards on the table.

"Blackjack! Blackjack, baby! Twenty-one ... count 'em and weep," he shouted.

"I think you better count 'em yourself ... and weep," Mrs. Robinette countered.

I looked down at the cards and frowned. It looked like twenty-one to me, too. Malik recounted the cards and demanded his money.

"Boy, hush up and pay attention. How much is this card worth?" she asked, pointing at the ace.

"One point."

"Or ..."

He looked at me as if the answer was written on my face, then said, "Eleven."

"Write that down. Matter of fact, write one and eleven in two columns."

She reached in her knitting bag and pulled out a small spiral-bound notepad and a pencil. She slid them over to Malik and he did as instructed. Mrs. Robinette picked up the seven.

"Write this under both numbers and add 'em up."

Malik had eight in one column and eighteen in the other. As he stared down at the two columns, it suddenly occurred to him what he'd done wrong. Embarrassed, he gave Mrs. Robinette the most pitiful face I'd ever seen.

"Umph. Umph. Umph. If you can't count no better than that it's no wonder your grades look the way they do. Speakin' of which, what's this business I hear 'bout you fightin' in class?" She turned to me.

"Evie called her a bulldagger," Malik answered for me.

"And?" she said.

"That's all."

"You mean to tell me you had a fight because of something some-body called you?"

I nodded, because Mrs. Robinette never asked me if my head made noise.

"So you plan on goin' through life beatin' up everybody who calls you out your name? Is that why you was out there fightin' on the street the other day?"

I shrugged my shoulders again. "I don't know. Evie's just plain evil."

"Well, listen here, I bed' not eva hear 'bout you fightin' at school or on the street or anywhere else. You hear me?"

"Yes, ma'am."

"And ... about that kissin' part. We ain't even gon' talk about it. You just bed' not eva 'low no one to talk you into doin' somethin' that's against God's wishes. All sinners fall out of God's graces, and He don't care that you was sinnin' because someone else told you to."

"Yes, ma'am," I said.

"Why is it a sin to kiss another girl?" Malik asked.

Mrs. Robinette looked down at her watch and slapped both hands against her thighs.

"Okay. Well, that's enough of that. Let's get you two in bed so I can watch Johnny Carson."

Mrs. Robinette waited for us to put on our pjs and get in bed. Then she turned off the light and went back in the living room. I waited until Ed McMahon said, "Heeerrrree's Johnny" before I said anything.

"Why do you think it's a sin to kiss another girl?" I asked Malik.

"I don't know."

"Seems stupid if you ask me. And if it's such a big deal, how come won't nobody explain it to me. Do you believe in God?" I asked.

"I don't know. Do you?" Malik asked.

"I don't know either. He seems pretty scary if you ask me."

"Not as scary as the Devil."

"I ain't afraid of the Devil. He ain't that scary."

"He is, too. Why you think women don't put their purses on the floor?"

"They don't want to get them dirty," I said.

Malik laughed. Mrs. Robinette told us to be quiet and go to sleep. I elbowed Malik.

"No," he whispered. "Because the Devil will steal their money."

"That's dumb. And what's he supposed to do with the money?"

"I don't know. But did you know when you sleep on your back, the Devil crawls inside you."

I laughed this time, then threw my hand over my mouth.

"Where'd you hear that?" I asked. "That's even dumber. The Devil could crawl inside anyone anytime he wanted to."

"Oh, yeah. Huh?" Malik said, surprised the thought hadn't occurred to him first.

I waited until he dozed off and turned over on my side.

* * * * * *

Momma and Daddy came home loud and boisterous, dancing on the edges of drunkenness. I sat up in bed. Malik didn't move. I shoved him until he stirred.

"What? Is it my turn?" he asked. He looked around the room for Mrs. Robinette.

"Shhh. Listen," I said.

"Well, if you hadn't been all up in her face ..." Momma shouted.

"Zora! Keep your voice down."

"Don't you tell me what to do!"

Daddy shushed her again. She said something I couldn't make out and then I couldn't hear them at all. I got up and pressed my ear against the wall. Malik lay back down and pulled the covers up over his head.

"You sure were generous, tonight, weren't you? Attentive, too!" Momma said.

"You didn't seem to have a problem when all that attention and generosity was on you and Evelyn," Daddy said.

Momma laughed. "Yeah, history has a funny way of repeating itself, doesn't it?"

"You can keep living your life waiting for the other shoe to drop. I'm not. And I'm getting sick and tired of you and your goddamn guilt trips and insecurities. It's been eight years. When are you going to accept that you didn't do anything wrong and get back to the woman I met and fell in love with?"

"Don't you dare use the Lord's name—"

"Give me a fuckin' break! You and this holier than thou bullshit. The Lord! Ha! You didn't know the Lord all those years ago. Mighty convenient you found him when you did, ain't it?"

"You don't love me anymore? Is that what it is? Time to move on? I can feel it. Coming home late, smelling of cheap perfume. Whispering on the phone. You're not foolin' anyone, Frank!"

"What are you talking about? Zora, I love you. I changed my whole goddamn life for you. You've got to let it go."

"Ha! Yeah, you changed your life. If your little precious Zayla hadn't been born, you wouldn't have. Don't lie!"

"What do you want from me? When is it enough? I'm with you! I chose you! I chose you from the very beginning. You want me to be honest? Okay, here goes. I'm getting sick and tired of your bullshit, Zora. I'm a patient man and I've put up with a lot because I put you through a lot. I apologized for that. I've been apologizing. For eight goddamn years! When is enough enough?"

"When you make it right!" Momma screamed.

"It's as right as it's going to get for now. But speaking of making things right. You either stop judging Zayla or find a way to fake it until you make it."

"Don't make this about Zayla, Frank. This is about you."

"You heard what I said. Now I'm done talking about it. She's your goddamn daughter and you better start treating her like it, or I swear you'll wish you had."

"I'll make it right with Zayla as soon as you make it right with me! Soon as *you* make it right, I will, too," Momma said matter-of-factly.

Their bedroom door opened and slammed close. I jumped in bed. Daddy peeked his head in my room and I slammed my eyes shut. The scent of Old Spice and cigarettes lingered in my doorway a moment, then followed Daddy out the back door. I waited the time it would take for him to smoke a cigarette. When he didn't come back in after three cigarettes 'time, I got up and went looking for him. The light was on in the garage. I turned the knob on the back door.

"What are you doing out of your room?"

I screamed and spun around. Momma was standing in the doorway behind me. I took a couple steps back and walked into Daddy as he was coming in the back door.

"Get your ass back in bed," she whisper-shouted.

"Zora!" Daddy really shouted.

The light from the garage gave the small space an ominous feeling. It didn't help that Momma and Daddy stood there like giant gargoyles preparing to battle. The bookshelves and knickknacks along the back wall of the playroom seemed to lean in, as anxious as I was to see what would happen next. I tried to move around Momma, relatively sure she wouldn't hit me with Daddy standing there.

"You okay, ladybug?" Daddy asked.

"Uh-huh," I mumbled.

"Stop coddling that girl! It's well after midnight–"

"Zora," Daddy shouted again.

I jumped and took one step toward my room. I couldn't take being between them while they argued. Things must be really bad if it's come to this, I thought.

"That's enough," Daddy said, softer. To me, he said, "Go back to bed, bug. I'll see you in the morning."

"Yes, Daddy," I whispered.

He kissed my cheek and I made a beeline to my room and slid in bed, trying not to wake Malik.

"Don't worry," he said, to my surprise. "He told my dad he was gonna make it right. He said he's trapped between a rock and a hard place."

"Huh? How do you know?" I asked.

"I heard him and my dad talking the other day. Uncle Frank said something about Miss Evangeline and killin' her, but I couldn't hear that part."

"Killin' her? What do you mean, 'killin' her'?" I asked.

"I don't know. I don't know if that's what he said. I could barely hear them," Malik said.

"Why didn't you tell me?"

He didn't answer.

I heard Momma and Daddy whisper-shouting from their bedroom. Then Momma shouted, "Get out of the damn bed! Get out!"

I don't know what, if anything, Daddy said. The front door slammed shut next.

"Where's Uncle Frank goin'?" Malik asked stupidly.

"How am I supposed to know?" I whisper-shouted.

"Maybe he's going to see Miss Evangeline. He said all this is her fault," Malik said.

I knew he was trying to make me feel better. It wasn't working.

"Why?" I asked.

"I don't know. I told you I couldn't hear everything they were saying. Something about Miss Evangeline almost keeping them from getting together in the first place and almost losing you. Did you know Aunt Zora wouldn't let him see you till you was four?"

"That's *not* true!" I shouted.

"Zayla! Malik! Y'all shut up and go to sleep."

I could tell she was crying. Even though she was yelling at us, her voice was heavy and thick with snot the way my voice got when I tried to talk through my tears as if everything was okay.

"Sorry, Momma," I said and immediately regretted it.

To my surprise, she didn't respond. Malik rolled over and was softly snoring in no time. I tried to sleep except I wanted to know where Daddy went. Was Malik right? Had he gone to Miss Evangeline's house in the middle of the night? And if he did, when was he coming back? Did he go there to kill her? I wondered, and quickly pushed the thought away. I knew Daddy wasn't crazy. What did Miss Evangeline have to do with all this? I was certain Momma was the hard place Daddy referred to. I just wanted to know why Miss Evangeline was the rock. And, most of all, I wanted to know why I couldn't remember Daddy before my fourth birthday party. Hadn't he said earlier it had been eight years? That would mean Malik was telling the truth. Four plus eight equaled my exact age.

"You shoulda told me," I whisper-shouted to Malik's back.

I'd hoped to wake him up, and to my surprise he rolled over to face me.

"I am telling you. It just happened," he explained.

"When?"

"The other day."

"When, Malik?"

"The other day. Right after you got sent home for kissin' Dee-Dee."

"You've seen me a bunch of times since then! You shoulda told me. How hard is it to say, 'Zay, your mom and dad almost didn't get together 'cause of Miss Evangeline. You—"

Before I could finish my sentence, Momma's hand stung the side of my face. I hadn't even heard her come in the room. She leaned over right in my face.

"Didn't I tell you to shut your goddamn mouth and go to sleep? And stay out of grown folks' business!" she said. "You too, Malik. Now take your narrow behinds to sleep. Don't make me have to tell you again!"

I pulled the covers up over my head and said, "Yes, Momma." My voice was heavy with sadness and thick with snot.

Dear God, please fix Momma and Daddy so Momma won't hate me so much. I don't know if my heart can take much more. And, could you please fix me? I don't know if my heart can take much more of that either. I hope you heard me, I pleaded. *'Cause up till now you don't seem to be listening to me.*

10

Johnson Plans to Parlay to Aid Negro Equality

L.A. Times – Saturday, June 5, 1965

> *I can pray all day*
> *and God won't come.*
> *But if I call 911*
> *The Devil be here*
> *in a minute!*
> ~ Amiri Baraka, "Monday in B-flat"

There was something fundamentally wrong with being on punishment on a Saturday. That morning even the sun hung lazily in the sky. The breeze slowed down and caught its breath a little bit. Grown-ups got dressed in a rainbow of colors and patterns and went about their errands. Every kid in the neighborhood came outside to play. We invented games that took us right to the brink of death. By the time the streetlights flickered to life, we were grateful to have lived to tell about it. Somehow, the world just felt bigger on Saturday– especially when you viewed it through a plate-glass window.

"Zayla? You up?" Momma called from her room.

"Yes, Momma," I said through the door.

"Tell your father not to bother making breakfast for me."

"Okay ..."

Daddy made his famous bacon pancakes every Saturday morning. It was his day to take care of Momma, so she didn't have to roll out of bed until she got good and ready. Momma leaned back into the fluffed pillows and became more regal than Cleopatra. I never thought I would see the day she turned all that down. I knew then something terrible was happening between them. I went into the kitchen with Daddy.

"Aaah, good mornin', Sleeping Beauty."

"Mornin'."

Daddy filled my Mickey Mouse mug halfway with coffee and set it in front of me. I added milk until it was caramel brown, just a shade lighter than me. Sharing a cup of coffee with Daddy was one of my favorite things about Saturday morning. Momma didn't allow me to drink coffee. She said it would make me black, and according to her, the only thing a Negro man wanted black was his coffee. She said something else about a brown bag test and how I was barely passing it as it was. I scooped out three spoons of sugar and stirred, then leaned back in my chair.

"Thanks, Daddy."

"Anything for my ladybug."

I'd been Daddy's ladybug since I was four. It was one of my first real memories of him. We were out in the garden one Saturday picking roses for Momma's breakfast tray. The basket was full of yellow, red, and pink blooming buds when I saw a single white rose with red edges in the corner of the bush. I pulled it forward to smell its fragrance. Something crawled onto my nose. I screamed and ran around in circles, yelling for Daddy to get whatever it was off. He knelt and calmly placed his hands on my shoulders. "Be still," he said. Except I couldn't because whatever it was was still there, so my legs marched in place while the rest of me tried not to move. Daddy stuck his finger up to the tip of my nose. A ladybug crawled onto it.

"It's a girl," he announced.

I pulled his finger down to eye level, turning it in different angles so I could see underneath the ladybug the way you do when you're trying to figure out the sex of a dog.

"How do you know it's a she?" I asked.

"Because girl ladybugs are plain."

"Plain, just like me."

"Why do you think you're plain?" he asked.

"Because Momma said I am."

Daddy pulled me into his side and kissed the top of my head. Even though he said, "Well, I can tell you you're plain in the most beautiful way imaginable," I got the feeling he didn't like Momma's choice of words to describe me. After that, I became his ladybug.

I sipped my coffee while Daddy poured the pancake mix and half a cup of buttermilk into a bowl. He placed two eggs in a different bowl and slid them over to me. I cracked and whisked them. He poured the eggs into the batter, added in a little melted butter, and slid the bowl to me. I stirred slowly until all the lumps disappeared.

"Momma said she didn't want breakfast this morning."

Daddy nodded as though he expected it and turned back to the stove. "Well, then that means there's more for us."

He rubbed his chin, concentrating on his approach. Frying bacon was serious business. It required skill and patience to get it crispy all over, and Daddy was a pro. The key was to make sure the skillet was the right amount of hot. He ran his hand under the faucet and flicked a few drops of water into the skillet. It sizzled. Satisfied, he peeled off six slices of thick bacon and arranged them so that none of the sides touched.

"Daddy?"

"Hmmm?"

"Are you gonna leave us?"

The muscles in his shoulders twitched. The rest of him stood stock still. He stared out the window over the sink, watching a sparrow flitter around the branches of a tree.

"Where would you get an idea like that?"

"I heard you and Momma fighting last night."

He returned his attention to the bacon. I sat quietly and watched, wishing I'd kept my big mouth shut. He finished the bacon and lined each piece up on a plate. He turned off the fire under the skillet and sat down in front of me.

"Ladybug, me and your momma have been together a long time. That wasn't the first fight we've ever had, and it won't be the last. It's just a fact of life. Couples fight. They make up. Everything is good for a while. Maybe they fight again. Maybe they don't. But I know one thing for sure. I would never leave you because I can't live without you. Okay?"

I nodded. He gave my hands a gentle squeeze and went back to the stove. I wanted to leave it at that, I just couldn't.

"What did Momma mean when she said you have to make it right? What do you have to make right?"

There was another long silence. After a while, Daddy said, "Why don't you start the orange juice?" Whenever Daddy didn't answer a question, it was because he didn't want to lie. I respected him for that, so I did as I was told and decided to ask him something he would answer.

"Do you think Momma will ever love me?"

Daddy stopped drinking his juice and looked over the top of the glass at me.

"Why would you say a thing like that? Your mother loves you very much."

I shrugged. "It doesn't feel like it." I paused and looked up. "Most of the time it doesn't."

For some reason, I couldn't find the words to say how I really felt. I knew that no matter how hard Daddy tried to love me enough for both of them, it wasn't enough.

He knelt in front of me and brushed the tears from my eyes. The instant his arms folded around me, and the smell of his aftershave filled my nostrils, I found myself crying harder and harder until I could barely breathe. He just held me, rocking me side to side and rubbing my back.

"It's okay, baby. Let it out. It's okay."

I know it should have made me feel better. It didn't. I felt worse. Daddy pulled a handkerchief out of his back pocket and wiped my eyes and nose. His eyes were wet and full of sadness.

"Zayla ... your mother loves you very much."

"She hardly ever shows it," I said.

"Maybe not right now. She has high expectations, so when you disappoint her, she takes it personally."

"I'll do better, Daddy."

"You'll do what you do. You're twelve. Your mother will get over it. Just give her some time."

After breakfast, I tried reading, then decided to kill time in front of the television instead. In the middle of *Atom Ant*, the phone rang. Momma came in and stopped right in front of the TV.

"I'm going to the beauty shop," she said. "Your father's going down to the club when he's finished with the lawn. I don't want you going out of this house while we're gone. Do you understand me?"

"Yes, Momma," I said, peeking around her at Atom Ant.

Malik showed up a few minutes after Momma left. We were heading down the hall to my bedroom when he realized he'd forgotten something at home. I told him to hurry back.

"Come with me," he said.

"I told you I was on punishment."

"Your dad's here. He'll let you go."

"Momma told him not to let me go anywhere," I said.

"Yeah, but that's to have fun. We're only going to my house and coming right back. He'll let you go."

"Stay here," I said, pushing him down on my bed.

I asked Daddy if I could go. He told me to hurry back. Even though he put me on punishment, he usually let me off when Momma wasn't around because I was always on punishment for something, or getting yelled at for something else. It was like Momma sought out ways to throw water on any fun I tried to have. "Get off the floor before you get dirty," she was forever saying. Or "Get out of that tree before you fall and break your damn neck." I remember the time Roger spent an entire Saturday teaching us how to ride our bikes with no hands. I'd finally gotten the hang of it. As I sped past the house, I saw Momma standing on the porch. I shouted, "Look, Momma, no hands," and she yelled, "Put your hands back on those handlebars or you'll be hollering, 'Look, Momma, no teeth.'"

I slipped on my shoes and followed Malik out of the house.

"You're it," he said.

He tapped my shoulder and ran off. We ran neck and neck the whole way down the block. When I saw Aunt Evelyn's car in the driveway, I decided to wait on the porch until Malik came back out. Aunt Evelyn couldn't hold water, and Momma didn't need to know I'd disobeyed her orders. When Malik came back out, I tagged him and ran off toward home.

"Zayla and Malik, y'all stop runnin' up and down the street in all this heat 'fore one of you passes out around here," Mr. Robinette yelled as we passed his house.

"Yes, Mr. Robinette," we said, and slowed down.

It wasn't even hot outside, but we started walking anyway, then fast-walking until we were running again up my driveway, into the backyard, and up into the treehouse. Malik reached in his back pocket. I closed my eyes, thinking it was another dirty magazine.

"Look," he said, handing it to me.

I opened one eye. There was a medal on a blue ribbon in his hand. I opened the other eye to get a better look. There were thirteen little stars embroidered on the fabric, and a gold star dangled from the bottom. He told me to put it in our box.

"What is it?" I asked.

"It's my dad's Medal of Honor from when he was in the Navy."

"Why'd he give it to you?"

"I don't know. He just said he wanted me to have it. Something for me to always remember him by."

"Why? He goin' somewhere?" I asked.

"No. I don't know. Just put it in the box," he said.

I grabbed the old cigar box that held our baseball card collection, mostly of the L.A. Dodgers, but we also had a Hank Aaron, Ernie Banks, Willie Mays, and Bob Gibson. There was our marble collection, two rubber balls and nine jacks, and a handful of penny candy. There were the remains of insect carcasses that we'd tortured: two moths, a bunch of wingless flies, two giant spiders, and a fossilized green caterpillar with black spots. And a one-armed green plastic Army man, the only remaining survivor after we tossed a cherry bomb into the old coffee can where the rest of the platoon hid out, waiting to be rescued.

That's not to mention the head of Shirley Breedlove's favorite Barbie doll that I'd snatched off at her birthday party because she kept waving her in my face. Shirley was the first to get a Barbie doll on the block. I hated Barbie, with her big fake blue eyes and big titties. If Shirley hadn't snatched the pieces out of my hand, Barbie would have wound up in the barbeque pit and been roasted beneath the hamburgers her father was grilling. Shirley didn't speak to me for a week after that, and then her family moved back to Mississippi when her father got laid off from the shipyard. The thing is, I liked

Shirley, and I know she liked me. I felt terrible that I never got a chance to apologize.

I put the medal in the box and closed the lid. It didn't seem right, though, having something that special in our old box. Malik should have put it up somewhere safe in his bedroom. He believed the tree-house was safer than the house. According to him, if the house ever caught fire, the treehouse would be the last to go.

I looked up in time to catch to Malik staring at the box as if he could still see the medal through the lid.

"You still havin' them dreams?" I asked.

He had been spending many a restless night dreaming that Uncle Bill had died. Each time he would wake up unable to remember how he died. All he remembered was looking down at him, dead on the sidewalk in his police uniform, lying in a pool of blood. I could always tell he'd had one of those dreams, because he'd be moody and distant.

"I think I am a bulldagger," I said.

I hadn't planned on saying that. It just came out. Malik looked at me with concern. I looked down and began making figure eights on the floor with my finger.

"Why?"

"Because. How come I don't fit in with the other girls? How come I hate Barbie dolls when all the girls like them? How come I'd rather spend an afternoon with a bunch of boys instead of playing make-believe with a bunch of girls? And how come I feel like a boy on the inside?"

"What's that supposed to mean? What do boys feel like?"

"I don't know. I just mean I don't care about the same things as girls, and I don't think I ever will."

I braced myself for his reaction. He leaned forward and planted a wet kiss on my forehead.

"What'd you do that for?" I asked, wiping off my forehead with the back of my hand.

"Because I don't care if you like boys or girls."

"God cares," I said.

"Says who?"

"My mom. And Mrs. Robinette, remember?"

"Oh yeah. I asked my mom about that, and she said, 'God created you. So, however you feel inside must be the way you're supposed to feel.' And besides," he said as an afterthought, "how can somebody else tell you how God feels? Why you think can't nobody explain why it's a sin? Only God can do that, and He don't talk!"

This time I leaned over and kissed his cheek.

"What'd you do that for?"

"To make you feel better. Your dad's gonna be fine. Don't worry. Let's ask Mrs. Robinette to look up your dreams in Policy Pete's Dream Book. Maybe they don't mean anything. Maybe she'll win the big number and give us some of her winnings."

Malik gave me a crooked smile and said okay. Somehow I didn't get the feeling that he really wanted to know what his dreams meant.

* * * * * *

Later that afternoon, Momma came in from the beauty shop and sent Malik home. Daddy left for the club, and Momma disappeared behind their bedroom door. I was sprawled across my bed, reading, when something clinked against my window. I sat up, something clinked again. I went to the window and snatched the curtains apart.

"What's up?" I whispered.

"Mr. Moskowitz is giving away free ice cream," Malik replied.

"For real?"

"Zayla! What are you doing in there?" Momma shouted.

"Nothing."

"Who are you talking to?"

"Nobody. I'm listening to the radio."

"Come here."

Momma was in bed, drapes drawn, Thelonious Monk adding an additional depth of darkness to the already dark room.

"Didn't I tell you to keep it down?"

"Yes, Momma."

"Don't let me hear another peep out of you."

"Yes, Momma."

"Now get your ass out of my room."

It took all I had in me not to slam the door shut behind me. I went back to my room and turned down the radio. Malik came closer to the window.

"You want me to get you something?"

"No. I'm going with you."

I pushed the window up and climbed out.

We took the long way to Mr. Moskowitz's store. In the window, a sign read, "No ice cream today. Freezer on the fritz." We looked at each other in disbelief and groaned.

God is always watching.

A car, looking like it was held together by chewing gum and rubber bands, pulled up in front of the store. Roger climbed out. He pulled up on the handle and shoved the door closed with his shoulder. A pretty brown-skinned girl behind the wheel waved. He told her he'd catch her later. Malik stared at the girl in wide-eyed wonder. I turned and stared at the words Mr. Moskowitz had scrawled on a piece of cardboard.

"What y'all doing standing there starin' in the window?"

"We came all the way up here to get some free ice cream," I said.

Roger read the sign. "Then go get somethin' else."

"We ain't got no money."

Malik turned out his pockets. I followed suit.

"Come on, then. Let me see what I can do for ya."

We followed Roger into the store. Mr. Moskowitz was unpacking cartons of cigarettes and placing them in their designated slots in the wooden racks affixed to the wall. Benson and Hedges. Pall Mall. More. True. He looked up and slipped a stack of Pall Malls into their slot and came around the counter.

"Good morning! Good morning! How are you all doing today?" he asked.

"Good morning, Mr. M.," Roger said. "Looks like these two came all the way over here for free ice cream, but there ain't none."

Mr. Moskowitz glanced over at the sign in the window and chuckled. He told us to wait a moment and disappeared into the back of the store. When he came back, he was holding three Neopolitan ice cream sandwiches. My favorite. He handed one to each of us.

"For everyone else, there is no ice cream. For you, always, there's ice cream."

We thanked him. Malik and I tore into our sandwiches. Roger leaned against the counter and took his time opening his.

"You ready for school, Roger? It's almost time. UCLA. What a big deal, huh? And a full scholarship. Very impressive!" Mr. Moskowitz said, clapping Roger on the shoulder.

Roger licked the sides of the sandwich and took a bite.

"Yeah, I'll be glad to get out of here too."

"Aren't you gonna miss us?" I asked.

"Sure. But y'all ain't goin' nowhere I can't get to. I'm just tired of bein' here every day. This place is like death waiting. And now I got them dudes buggin' me about joinin' their gang."

I don't think Roger meant to say that last part out loud. He took another bite of his sandwich and gazed out the window. He seemed surprised his mouth had betrayed him.

"You're going to join a gang?" Malik asked.

"Hell no! But I ain't gon' tell them that. I don't want no trouble. I just gotta make it through the summer, and then I'll be on easy street," Roger explained.

Malik and I went back to our ice cream sandwiches.

"That's very smart, you know?" Mr. Moskowitz said. "I heard it was one of those gang boys that robbed Mr. Crogan. I just hope they don't come here. I'm not looking for trouble."

"Naw. They ain't gon' bother you, Mr. M. You cool with us. They gon' be cool with you. It's all them other crackers that need to be worried. Sorry. You know who I mean."

Mr. Moskowitz smiled. "I don't understand it. They come to the community, but they don't like the people in it. I come to the community, I move my family here. I'm not looking for trouble, but if someone comes in here looking for it, they're going to find it. I don't need the police to help me."

Roger finished his sandwich and dropped the wrapper in the trashcan behind the counter. Malik and I had long since devoured ours and were busy licking the remains from our fingers.

"All right, I'll catch y'all later," Roger said. "I gotta get to the crib. Thanks for the ice cream, Mr. M."

Roger took a step toward the door.

"Where do you think you're goin', boy?"

We all turned and stared at the two white cops standing there. One of them had flaming red hair and a white pasty face littered with red freckles. The nametag above his pocket read, Kreps. The other one wore a permanent scowl on his large round face. Dumbrowski. I glared at them, unblinking. They looked like regular human beings, yet I knew they were meaner than junkyard dogs. Everyone knew it. I wondered what could have happened in their lives to make them turn out that way. Arthur Kreps and Steve Dumbrowski were the most hated LAPD officers in Watts because they were the most hateful. Daddy said they were the perfect example of cops who joined the force specifically to take their racist frustrations out on colored people. Kreps grabbed Roger by the arm.

Roger tried to snatch free.

"Man, get your fuckin' hands off me. This ain't the South. I ain't do nothin'! I know my rights!"

Kreps and Dumbrowski looked at each other and laughed.

"Did you hear that, Art? This nigger knows his rights. I wonder what else he knows," Dumbrowski said. "Did you know we got a report that a boy looking just like you robbed Crogan's the other night?"

Kreps yanked Roger's arm up higher toward the back of his head until his fingertips almost touched the nape of his neck. Roger howled in pain. I ran toward Kreps to make him let Roger go, but Malik grabbed the back of my shirt and snatched me back.

"Are you crazy? You can't hit a cop. They can take you to jail for that!" he said.

"They can?" I asked and shut my trap, as Pompa would say. Although I couldn't really imagine the police arresting a twelve-year-old.

"Yes, we can," Dumbrowski said, taking a step toward me.

Kreps dragged Roger out to the sidewalk and slammed him against the plate-glass window. The side of Roger's face flattened against the glass. Malik jumped. I screamed and threw my hand over my mouth. Roger's eye focused on us like he was telling us to be brave. To not let these cracker cops scare us. I wanted to believe everything was going to be okay, and somehow I knew it wouldn't. Mr. Moskowitz must have been thinking the same thing because he started moving toward the door. Dumbrowski stepped in front of him and made like he was reaching for his gun.

"Oh my," Mr. Moskowitz said and retook his place beside us.

Kreps made Roger turn his pockets inside out with his free hand.

I held my breath and prayed Roger didn't have any reefers that might fall out. Roger refused to do as he was told.

"Fuck you! I ain't turnin' out shit. If you want to see what's in my pockets, then get a warrant. Otherwise, I'm gon' sue your racist asses for illegal search and seizure!"

"Oh. I do wish he wouldn't antagonize them. It's only going to make them angry," Mr. Moskowitz said.

He was right. Kreps shoved Roger against the store window again. Roger said something else that made Kreps' face turn red. I said a quiet prayer for Roger and tightened my grip on Malik's hand. Dumbrowski stomped away from the door and gave Roger a kidney blow. Roger dropped to the ground. Dumbrowski stood over him and shouted.

"Who do you think you are, nigger? You think you're better than us?"

Mr. Moskowitz tiptoed away from us and took the phone off the counter. He knelt down behind it and dialed "O".

"Yes, operator. I want to report a disturbance...a fight, ummm, two men are beating up one of my customers ... Yes, it's pretty bad ... they have weapons ...Your Corner Store, 1454 E. 103rd Street...Yes, there are children in the store. Please tell them to hurry. Can you send an ambulance, too, please? Thank you."

Mr. Moskowitz hung up and pleaded with us to come to get behind the counter with him until help arrived, except we couldn't move. We watched Kreps and Dumbrowski take turns punching Roger. Roger took the beating because he knew, as well as we did, doing anything to defend himself would only give them an excuse to kill him. So we stood there and watched two officers of the law beat Roger like he was a disobedient dog.

Dumbrowski peered in at us and grinned. It was as if he could smell our fear, and it energized him because he kicked Roger with all his might. Roger screamed. My stomach jumped.

"Stop it!" I shouted. "Stop it! You're gonna kill him."

This pleased Dumbrowski. He kicked Roger again and kept on kicking him. I cried and asked God to make them stop. "Please! Please, God, make them stop!" Malik and I locked fingers and cried silently. Mr. Moskowitz pushed us around the counter and told us not to budge. We barely breathed as we watched Roger take blow after blow. Kreps grabbed the neck of his shirt and yanked him off the ground. Dumbrowski worked Roger's sides the way a boxer would a punching bag, each blow landed with a muted thud.

"Please, officers, please stop! You're frightening the children!" Mr. Moskowitz shouted.

Kreps stopped first. Dumbrowski looked up and glared at us through the window. This time Malik glared back until Kreps unhitched his gun from its holster and pointed it at us. This made me cry because I believed if anyone could shoot a child without any remorse, it was Dumbrowski. Malik began shaking, and for a second I thought he would go after Dumbrowski anyway. Mr. Moskowitz must have felt so too because he yanked us down to the floor. Although we couldn't see anymore, we could hear the blows of their fists and blackjack as they cracked against Roger's body. I looked up at Mr. Moskowitz and begged him to go do something, he just stood there staring out the window. He was as helpless as the rest of us against the police.

A siren chirped outside. Tires screeched. Car doors slammed. The beating stopped. Loud voices asking if they should take Roger in. No. Leave this nigger right here. Give him some time to think about how smart he is, someone said. Car doors slammed again. Tires screeched. Then all was silent, except for Roger's moans.

Knowing that the ambulance would take its sweet time getting to them, Mr. Moskowitz went out and helped the barely conscious Roger to his feet. Malik and I helped Mr. Moskowitz half-carry, half-drag Roger through the store, to the office and lay him down on the sofa. Blood dripped from his nose and mouth. His right eyelid bulged, and the eye beneath was red and runny. The sight of the blood made me queasy. Roger leaned over and spit on the floor. One of his teeth came out with it. Mr. Moskowitz told Malik to grab a handful of paper towels from the bathroom. I grabbed the trashcan in case Roger needed to spit again.

"You kids hurry home. I'll make sure Roger gets taken care of."

Neither one of us moved toward the door. We just stood there crying and staring at Roger.

"Go on now. Go home," Mr. Moskowitz insisted.

I waited for Malik to move and then followed him out of the store. We took our time walking home.

"Is that what they gonna do to me?" he asked.

"No. They won't mess with you. You're Uncle Bill's son. That has to mean something."

I wasn't lying, I just wasn't so sure I was telling the truth either.

We were about three blocks from the house when a black and white turned the corner in front of us. We didn't look to see who was behind the wheel. We didn't release hands. We just took off running. We ran until we got to "The Circle" and we didn't stop until we reached the side of my house. We dropped to the grass and tried to catch our breath.

"You have to tell Uncle Bill what happened," I said.

"I can't. You'll get in trouble."

"You don't have to say I was there."

"What if he goes and talks to Mr. Moskowitz? He's gonna tell him what happened and your name's gonna come up. You're already on punishment. I don't want you to get in more trouble."

"I don't care if I get in more trouble. You need to tell Uncle Bill what happened to Roger."

"I don't want to."

"Why not?"

"Because I don't. Now leave me alone."

I did as instructed and climbed back into my bedroom. I landed on the floor with a thud and lay there frozen, waiting for Momma to scream at me. The house was quiet. I didn't bother going to see if anyone was home. I just climbed in bed, pulled the covers up over my head, and tried to blank out the past two hours.

Well, if you are watching, why did you let those cops beat Roger in the first place? What kind of God does that? I asked, ashamed of the question almost as quickly as it formed.

I thought about the posters the Followers of Islam made after Malcolm X died. They were large and had an image of Malcolm biting his lower lip and pointing into the camera. The quote to the right of the photo read, "Usually when people are sad, they don't do anything. They just cry over their condition. But when they get angry, they bring about change." Underneath, in large bold letters, a question had been posed to the people of the community. "**WHEN ARE WE GOING TO GET ANGRY ENOUGH TO BRING ABOUT CHANGE?**"

I'd seen it many times since that February, but it was the first time it really made any sense to me.

Roger suffered three cracked ribs, a black eye, and his arm was broken in two places. He spent the night in the ICU for observation with Mrs. Robinette at his side. She had an excuse to miss church the next morning.

I wasn't so lucky.

II

Many Doubtful of U.S. Success in Southeast Asia
L.A. Times – Sunday, June 6, 1965

> *Of evil to bend its knees, admitting its guilt, to implore the forgiveness of God,*
> *is the hardest thing in the world.*
> ~ Malcolm X, El-Hajj Malik El-Shabazz, Civil Rights Leader

"Get up! It's time to go Praise the Lord!" Momma shouted from my doorway.

The 103rd Street Baptist Church stood on the corner of 103rd Street and Wilmington Avenue like a giant Jesus watching over Watts from the ten-foot cross on its roof. On the first Sunday of the month the parking lot looked like a used car lot on clearance day. Momma made one loop around the lot, blaming me for making us late even though I'd been sitting in the car for ten minutes before she decided to join me. I listened quietly as she prattled on about my lazy, trifling ways and how the good old Lord was going to be my savior.

We made a second loop around the lot.

"But if we're all God's children and Jesus was God's son, doesn't that make us Jesus' brothers and sisters?" I asked.

Momma looked at me and slammed on the brakes. "Don't you dare question the Lord!"

She mashed down on the gas pedal. The car shot out of the lot, made a wide U-turn at the corner, and screeched to a halt in front of the Largo Theater, which was right across from the church. *A Fistful of Dollars* was spelled out in red letters on the marquee. The U hung upside down.

I would have given anything to spend my morning with Clint Eastwood than spend the next two hours praying for my salvation. I tugged at the hem of my dress and tried not to complain that my legs itched under the tights.

We hurried across the street and into the coolness of the vestibule. Momma stopped just long enough to smooth out her dress, then snatched me by the wrist and dragged me through the double doors into the belly of the beast. Hazy sunlight spilled through large ornate windows to my left and right. Twenty rows of rich burgundy upholstered pews flanked the center aisle, each with small bookracks affixed to the back that held a King James Bible and a cardboard fan with a wooden handle. Martin Luther King Jr. was on one side, Simon & Sons Funeral Home, on the other.

A deep red runner parted the gray carpet like a dragon's tongue, licking its way up to the steps to the pulpit. An enormous organ loomed to the left, its pipes affixed to the wall above it; to the right, a shiny black Steinway grand piano. Between them, the choir in their burgundy robes and gold sashes lay in wait to stir up the congregation. Ordinarily, just Brother Carter played the piano. On special occasions, like First Sunday, Sister Thompson joined him on the organ. When the two of them got going, the vibrations rocked through the congregation until they shook the Holy Ghost out from its hiding place in the rafters. It's unnerving to watch someone possessed with the Holy Ghost. I often wondered if they were faking just to get attention with all the gyrating and convulsing and speaking in tongues. Not to mention the flailing arms every which way and flopping around on the floor. I swallowed hard and closed my eyes. Momma tightened her grip on my wrist and pulled me through the crowd, faking pleasantries, as if she didn't talk about half of the women in the congregation behind their backs. We always sat in the third row on the left, because Momma liked to sit up front so she could be seen coming and going. I often wondered if those same women said a few choice words about Momma.

I pulled the Bible from its perch. I flipped through the pages for a few minutes, then put it back in its holder. The chatter in the sanctuary began to die down. I pulled out the fan and smiled down at Dr. King's smiling face. All over the country Negro communities loved Dr. King. For Watts, though, Malcolm X was the revered leader. For one, he'd come to visit several times, most memorably after one of his own Nation of Islam brothers, Ronald Stokes, was killed by the LAPD. A lot of the admiration for Brother Malcolm could be attributed to the fact that he was brave enough to call racist white folks on their shit, as Daddy would say. I also believe a lot of people liked Malcolm's trash talking and the fact that he loved calling white folks "crackers." Dr. King was too tame for their taste.

I fanned myself a couple times, stuck the fan back in its holder, and picked up the Bible again. Momma elbowed me. I put it back and turned toward the pulpit as Sister Randolph moved gingerly up the steps to read the week's Sick and Shut-in list. Time had reshaped her from an exclamation point to a question mark. Her voice shook and rattled so much, I stopped trying to understand her and turned my attention to all the women's hats in the congregation. I counted fifty-two in total, only twelve were of any interest.

Three had huge peacock feathers shooting out of the top. Four were small pillbox types with black veils hanging from the edge.

One was bright orange and flat like a plate. One was red with a silver bow around the base and sat up high like the Mad Hatter's. One was bright yellow with great big sunflowers on the front, and the woman beneath it wore a matching yellow dress with ruffles on the sleeves and collar. I laughed out loud. Momma's elbow to my side silenced me. I covered my mouth, but couldn't stop laughing. Momma pinched my arm for good measure. I flinched and frowned up at her.

Sister Randolph finished butchering the announcements and shuffled back to her seat. Deacon Brice came forward next. He was a dirty-looking brown-skinned man with sleepy bloodshot eyes and false upper teeth that frequently slipped out of place when he spoke. He fumbled around in the breast pocket of his suit jacket and pulled out several sheets of folded paper. He cleared his throat and smiled.

"Good mornin', brothers and sisters, I want to start today's service with a prayer for the Robinette family. Dear Lord. We come to you this morning asking that you give Deacon and Sister Robinette the strength to get through this most trying time. We ask that you heal Roger back to good as new before hatred and evil almost took his life. We ask that you keep him safe so he can go off to USC and be the great man you intended for him to be. And we ask you, Lord, to give every one of us the courage to hold our heads higher and find forgiveness in our hearts for the evil men who hide behind badges and guns. Amen."

"Amen," we said in unison.

The choir sang their selections, and to my relief, no one caught the Holy Ghost. Deacon read a few Bible passages and then turned it over to Pastor Shuttlesworth, who said, "Open your Bibles to 1st Corinthians 1:18."

He read, "For the preaching of the cross is to them that perish foolishness, but unto us which are saved, it is the power of God."

The congregation said another amen.

"By the grace of God and the Holy Spirit, I want to talk to you this morning about a good battery with a weak connection..."

I tried to make sense of the sermon. What did batteries and cars have to do with God? And for the life of me, I could never figure out who the Lord really was. Was it God or Jesus? I let my head fall back against the pew. No sooner had my eyes closed than Momma's elbow was in my rib cage again. I sat up and tried to pay attention.

"Yes, Lord. We got corrosion right here at 103rd Street Baptist Church. Corrosion in the form of jealousy. Corrosion in the form of hatred. Corrosion in the form of homosexuality."

That I understood. I looked up at Momma. She gave me her best shit-eating grin, as Nana would say. Pastor Shuttlesworth was telling the whole congregation how the Lord felt about homosexuals– and, by association, me. At least that's how it felt.

"There's a whole lot of folks out there talking a good game. Folks who claim to be saved. But I'm gon' tell you. They really don't know God. Let the church shout, Hallelujah. Because if they really knew God, they would understand that he burnt up Sodom and Gomorrah, Amen, and two other cities because of their immoral practices. God is not with you being a homosexual. God is not with you being jealous. God is not with you doing the will of Satan instead of the will of the Lord. All you're doing is making God mad. Every single day you're just making God mad, and He's mad. He's mad at you and your wicked ways.

"You cannot say, 'I was born this way!'" Pastor shouted. "I don't care what scientists say. You can be converted. You were not born that way. Let me pray with you. Let me tell you, don't be conformed to this world, but be ye transformed."

I drifted off for a while, only vaguely following his lesson about power and God, until his voice started shaking the rafters. "You've got to go to church even when you don't want to. Showing up on

Christmas, Easter, and Mother's Day ain't enough because God is looking for some dedicated Christians."

Momma looked down at me again. The congregation shouted out "Amen" and "Praise the Lord."

"If you're looking for a good power source, let me introduce you to God's original power source. Jesus was the original battery. They crucified Him on the cross. They buried him in a tomb. They tried to drain him of his power, but early Sunday morning..."

Pastor Shuttlesworth pulled the microphone from its stand and came down into the congregation.

"Early Sunday morning," he sang. "Early Sunday morning, he sat up. He rose up. Early Sunday morning, my power source rose up, and I don't know about you, but because I am connected to Him, I can say, 'I love all of you! The saved and the sinners.'"

He stopped at our pew. I dared not look at him. I imagined every eye was on us, and they were all thinking the same thing. Zayla is a bulldagger. A sinner. An abomination of God. I squeezed my eyes and prayed that God would reconnect me to my power source. I didn't want to go to hell.

When church ended the congregation lined up to greet Pastor Shuttlesworth. Arlene Armstrong was holding court with a group of church members near the exit. Momma saw her at the same time I saw Melody. Momma and Arlene hated each other as much as me and Melody. So, when Momma steered me toward the side door that led down a long, dark hallway toward the pastor's office I followed her. We sat on the only pew in the hall and waited.

"Pastor was really good today, wasn't he?" Momma asked.

I shrugged and said, "I guess."

"You guess? Did you understand the message?"

"We can't get disconnected from our power source."

"Do you know what that means?"

"No."

"It means the more you sin the further you get from the Lord and the further you get from the Lord the closer you get to hell. Do you understand that?'"

I nodded then said, "Yes."

"Go see if that old Arlene Armstrong is gone. I don't feel like being bothered with her messy behind today."

I went just to get away from her. I peeked into the vestibule and heard the bathroom door open behind me.

"You know God don't like bulldaggers," Melody said. "You better pray he don't pull your plug."

I said, "Yeah, well he doesn't like stuck-up snobs either."

I walked off pleased with myself, until I heard Daddy say, "Two wrongs don't make a right" in my head. I allowed myself to feel bad for a second, then smiled again. I told Momma Arlene Armstrong was still out there with Pastor. A few minutes later Pastor came lumbering down the hall, his robe swaying in judgment. I swallowed and slumped in my seat. Momma smiled and rose to greet him.

"Good afternoon, Pastor."

"Good afternoon, Sister Zora. Miss Zayla. How are two of God's most beautiful children doing today?"

"Just fine, Pastor. Just fine, thank you," Momma said.

I mumbled hello into the bib of my dress and didn't look up. I waited for him to usher me into his office. To my surprise, he continued down the hall.

"Ready to go?" Momma asked.

When I looked up, she was giving me that same shit-eating grin again.

12

Black Racism Is Wrong as White
L.A. Times – Monday, June 7, 1965

> *she cried as the child stood*
> *hesitant in the last clear sky*
> *he would ever see the last*
> *before the whirling blades the whirling smoke*
> *and sharp debris carried all clarity*
> *away.*
> ~Lucille Clifton, "Move"

"Zayla! Sit down, please," Mrs. Fitzgerald instructed.

"I can't."

"Why not?"

I looked around the room. Everyone pretended to be busy reading or all of a sudden engrossed in some problem. Everyone except Dee-Dee, who combed through her hair with her fingers, bouncing her left leg. I knew that move. I'd seen it a thousand times and always after she'd done something she had no business doing.

"Because Dee-Dee put chewing gum in my chair," I said.

I waited for Mrs. Fitzgerald to send Dee-Dee to Mean Man Mulligan's office for defiling school property, like she did the previous year when Mark Holloway stuck gum in Florence's chair.

Instead, she said, "Then go find another seat," as if I found wads of gum in my seat all the time. "Dee-Dee, next time you do something like that, you are going to be in big trouble, young lady," she threatened.

Next time? I sighed and looked around for another place to sit. Mrs. Fitzgerald told us to take out our history books. I opened my desk to get mine, and the room exploded in laughter. Inside was a page from the encyclopedia with a picture of a bull charging a matador. Someone had scrawled my name across the top of the page in red marker. They'd even taken the time to turn one of the "Ls" into the shape of a dagger. I would have been impressed by the artwork if the insult hadn't been so hurtful.

"Zayla, please take your seat," Mrs. Fitzgerald said again, like I was getting on her last nerve.

I marched up to Mrs. Fitzgerald's desk and slammed the page on her desk. She sucked in air, astonished.

"Who did this?" she demanded, thrusting the picture into the air. No one moved. She adjusted her dress and started again. "Now, children, we've discussed the consequences of damaging school property. Which one of you tore this page out of our brand-new set of Encyclopedia Britannica's?"

Was she serious? Who cares who tore it out? my inner voice yelled. Doesn't she want to know why someone would do such a thing to me? I wondered. This wasn't normal or kind behavior. Why wasn't she all up in arms about it? Ms. "Love your neighbor like you love God." Or, "Treat people the way you want to be treated."

The meanness was getting up around my neck. All of a sudden, I could relate to how Ruby Bridges felt trying to go to an all-white school after desegregation. My classmates turned on me as if I'd done something to each one of them personally. All this because people heard I kissed Dee-Dee? What I couldn't understand was why no one was ostracizing Dee-Dee. She's the one that kissed me! I never would have asked Dee-Dee to teach me how to kiss, much less dared to follow through. And the most aggravating part was that no one, other than Malik, even bothered asking me if we actually kissed. Not that I would have told them. They just took Evil Evie Sheffield's word for it.

"May I be excused?" I asked.

I didn't wait for an answer. I grabbed the long wooden spoon hanging on the hook near the door and headed to the girls bathroom. I chose the stall with the "Out of Order" sign for the third time that week. The same stall where Dee-Dee and I had smoked cigarettes once during lunch and blew the smoke out the window so we wouldn't get caught. Where, in the fourth grade, we stole the teacher's grade book and altered Dee-Dee's math grade from a D to an A. Where Dee-Dee told me I was beautiful and vowed we would be friends for the rest of our lives.

I blew my nose. I don't know how long I'd been in there when the lunch bell rang. The bathroom door opened and closed. I knew I couldn't come out—that would give them more to talk about. So I dropped the tissue in the commode and waited.

"Make sure no one's in here." a voice that sounded very much like Dee-Dee's said.

"No one's in here."

"Are you sure? You looked under all the stalls?"

"The bell just rang. Who else could be in here?"

"Wait a minute ..."

I pulled my feet up on the toilet seat and tried to make myself as small as possible. Dee-Dee pushed at the door. Thankfully, I'd had sense enough to lock it. Then those ten familiar pale pink fingertips pressed down on the tile just outside the stall. I thanked God for the puddle of dirty water between them and me. She got close, not close enough to peer under the door. When she stood up, I slowly allowed myself to breathe again.

"What are you doing down there?" asked a familiar voice. I still couldn't quite place it.

"Making sure we're alone. I thought Zayla might be in here hiding. She took the hall pass and never came back to class. I figured she was hiding out in here."

"Ugghh. Why would she hide in the bathroom? That's disgusting." I knew then the other voice was Melody's. "I don't see how you were ever friends with her in the first place. She's weird and she dresses funny."

I closed my eyes and leaned my head against the wall.

"I know. You were right, she is that way. The minute I told her I was gonna teach her how to kiss, she got all excited. I'm glad I didn't kiss her for real. She mighta fell in love."

They laughed.

"So, you didn't kiss her for real?"

"Hell naw! But when I saw how happy she got, I knew I had to tell her we couldn't be friends anymore. She was starting to make me feel funny. Like she had a crush on me. So I told her I was done with being friends."

The bathroom door opened again, and a stall door closed next.

"Is it true?" the girl in the stall asked. "Did Zayla really ask you to go with her?"

We all waited for Dee-Dee's answer.

"Yeah. She's been asking me since third grade. I always thought she was playing, but when she asked me to teach her how to kiss, I knew she was serious."

"Yeah. Who wants to kiss her anyway?" the girl in the stall said. "I bet she has bad breath."

More laughs. I wanted to jump out of the stall and bust Dee-Dee in her lie. See if she could lie right to my face. The only thing that stopped me was the fact that somehow my hiding in the bathroom would be worse. I slumped down farther on the toilet, wishing I could crawl in it and disappear.

"I would kick her ass if I was you," the girl in the stall added. "She coulda ruined your reputation."

The toilet flushed. "Melody and Dee-Dee, y'all better not stay in here too long, or everyone'll be talking about you next."

"See, I told you everyone was talking about y'all," Melody said when they were gone.

"Who cares? I have a boyfriend, so it's obvious I'm not the one who's a bulldagger. Have you ever seen a boy talking to Zayla? Other than Malik?"

"Well, you can't be associating with her anymore," Melody said. "Otherwise, we can't be friends."

"Don't worry. I won't," Dee-Dee said with finality.

"Good, 'cause I had to beg my mom to let me invite you to my graduation party after she heard what happened."

"I know. My mom was pretty pissed off, too. But after I explained what really happened, she said she wasn't surprised. She always knew there was something wrong with Zayla."

"Now I just gotta find a way to get Malik to the party," Melody said. "I know he won't come without her."

Malik? Why was she trying to invite Malik to the party? I wondered.

"Maybe you should tell him you wanna be alone with him. He'll drop Zayla like a bad habit. You know how boys are."

As they left, I felt like a fool crouched down over that rusted-out commode, crying quietly and feeling just as "Out of Order" as the stall that surrounded me. When was I going to finally accept the fact that although Dee-Dee said we'd be friends forever, she'd really meant, until I have no more use for you?

13

The next morning I woke up early and snuck down the hall to get the flashlight off the back porch. I held the light in my mouth until my tonsils were good and red. Then I went to find Momma. She called Dr. Green, our family doctor. He told her to get me into bed, give me lots of fluids, and two aspirin every four hours. Sounded like I had strep throat.

Malik came by after school, begging me to get better so I wouldn't miss graduation.

"Why didn't you tell me Melody invited you to her graduation party?" I asked.

"Because she didn't."

"That's not what I heard."

"Well, that's what I'm telling you, and even if she had, I wouldn't go. She'd probably only be inviting me to get back at you."

"I thought you liked her."

"I did before she started messing with you."

I smiled. "You're probably right. But I don't know when I can go back to school. Dr. Green said I have strep throat."

"You gotta come back to school. You're gonna miss graduation. And if you're worried about everyone messing with you, they've moved on to Todd Joseph. He's in my class. He's had B.O. since fourth grade, then someone decided to point it out the other day, and now all the kids are calling him "Smelly Todd."

I almost changed my mind about graduation, convinced it wouldn't be the end of the world if I missed it. I still had several graduations ahead of me. Junior high, high school, then college. I imagined someone shouting "bulldagger" when my name was called, and couldn't bear it. So I stuck my finger down my throat the night before, and remained in bed another week. I wondered what I could do to stay out of sight all through the summer, so everyone would forget all about me. Then I figured if all else failed, I could take a flying leap out of the treehouse. I was sure to break a leg. It seemed like a good idea until I realized I could also break my damn neck.

So I took it easy around the house for a couple days and even stopped pretending I couldn't talk. Momma left me alone for the most part. On Sunday, I expected her to drag me out of bed for church, but she told me I didn't have to go. I got up and went anyway. It was part of my plan to stay on the right path. After church, she dropped me back home and went down to Aunt Evelyn's.

I went into the house and dropped my keys on the table. There were a few kids from school at church, and they didn't seem to even know who I was. Malik said it was a phase. We all went through it. He hadn't been through it, nor had Dee-Dee, I reminded him. He told me not to worry. They'd get it soon enough. He hoped his came before we got to high school. We'd heard life could be brutal in high school with everyone walking around with their chests out, thinking they were grown already.

Daddy was in the playroom, listening to Miles Davis. I tiptoed to my room. A few minutes later, the music stopped. Daddy lumbered down the hall and knocked on my door.

"Can I come in?" he asked.

He walked over to the window and pulled a cigarette out of its case. He took out a wooden match, flicked it with his thumbnail, and lit his cigarette.

"You wanna hang with your old man today?"

"Yes!" I said. "What are we gonna do?"

"Let's flip a coin and see where it lands," he said, as he examined the ivy crawling along the fence outside my window.

"You sure you feel up to it? I wouldn't want you to have a relapse."

I knew then the jig was up. Daddy knew I'd been faking all along, and I was going to have to explain myself. Sooner or later.

We walked out of "The Circle," past Will Rogers Park, and into the heart of the business district of 103rd Street, which was bursting with activity in the late afternoon sun. Men and women strolled in and out of the shops, laughing easy and talking loudly. Cars cruised by, and every so often someone would shout out the window at a familiar passerby. A conversation would ensue, only to be ended by honking horns and shouts of profanity.

As we passed Mabel's Soul Food Kitchen, a group of older women sat in the window, showing off their Sunday dresses and fancy hats and enjoying a feast of fried chicken, waffles, scrambled eggs, sausage, grits, and ham steak with the bone in. One of the women tapped on the window. She lived next door to Miss Evangeline. Daddy smiled and waved. She said something to the other women, and they turned and smiled politely. Daddy took my hand and pulled me away from the window.

Mr. Plummer stood in the doorway of his pawnshop, smoking a cigar and watching the street as if it was a movie he'd seen a thousand times. Daddy stopped to talk to him for a little while. I heard raised voices coming from the clothing store next door and went to investigate.

"I ain't payin' you three dollars for this shit. I'll give you a dollar." A woman flung a pair of shorts around in the air above her head.

"Ma'am, you are free to take your business elsewhere," the white man at the register said calmly.

"This is bullshit! I'd fuck you up if I wasn't a God-fearin' woman!"

"Yes, ma'am. I'm sorry you feel that way," he said dryly. He came around the counter, gently removed the merchandise from her hand, and politely walked her to the front door.

She snatched her hand away and balled her fist. The thought of being arrested probably crossed her mind, because she let her hand relax and stomped off down the street instead, mumbling and cursing under her breath. Daddy and Mr. Plummer watched her go, shaking their heads.

"You know them boys was around here the other day. They told that man to stop disrespecting his customers if he knew what was good for him. Had him so scared, he closed up shop early. Then this morning he up and fired the only one of us he had working for him."

"He fired Angie?" Daddy asked. "Why?"

"He accused her of stealing. Made a public spectacle of her, too. Truth is, he got wind that she was related to one of the boys that robbed Crogan."

"So what? He thought she was gon' let them come rob him?" Daddy shook his head in disgust. "Seems to me he'd have been better off letting Angie keep her job. Now they really got a reason to come rob him. Nothing more motivating than revenge."

"It don't make no sense to me either. But what's an even bigger mystery is why these people so damn anxious to come to our community and sell us anything when it's obvious they don't like us," Mr. Plummer said.

"That's easy. Then that way we can't sell to each other. They'd much rather shut our businesses down so they can set up shop and keep us from profiting. They've been doing it for years. They'll probably be doing it years from now. It's a shame, you know. I remember a time when every shop owner on this street was one of us. Now look at it."

Daddy and Mr. Plummer scanned the street from left to right, counting and comparing memories and notes. In 1950, Negroes owned twenty-three of the thirty stores on 103rd Street between Avalon and Wilmington Avenues. In fifteen years, that number had decreased to six. The Largo Theater, the Malidy Hotel, Plummer's Pawn Shop, the Sanctuary, Pete's BBQ, and Mabel's Soul Kitchen managed to survive. But for how long? they wondered. The two furniture stores, three shoe stores, and the big department store in the center of it all generated the most revenue, and were all white-owned.

"It's a shame, really," Mr. Plummer said. "I'd be gone too if the bank could figure out a way to get me out of here. I own this place outright, and I ain't goin' nowhere till they carry me out in a pine box."

"Well, let's hope that won't be any time soon," Daddy said.

"Bedda not. I might own this rat trap, but I'm still payin' on that house. If I left Martha with the mortgage, she might wake me up and kill me again."

Daddy laughed. "I know that's right."

Mr. Plummer got serious then. "Seem like we take two steps forward and get pushed back four. Ever since that man opened up that high-ass store, he has been cussed out more times than I care to remember. If he ain't careful, somebody's gon' hurt him."

"Well, let's hope that don't happen either. Change is in the air, waiting for the right time to settle. I can smell it like rain."

Mr. Plummer took a few whiffs of the air and nodded in confirmation. "You know, I used to have an aunt could smell things. When my mother went into labor with me, she smelled bacon. When the floods of '52 came, she said the air smelled sweet all day. I don't know 'bout all that, but if change smells like Jack Daniel's, well then I smell it too."

"Well, we gotta get movin'. I got a date with the little lady here. Talk to you later, Alton."

"All right, Frank. You take it easy. Bye, Miss Zayla."

"Goodbye, Mr. Plummer."

Mr. Plummer slipped a few Mary Janes into my hand. I unwrapped and shoved them in my mouth before Daddy could stop me. Daddy shook his head and thanked Mr. Plummer.

"Don't mention it," he said, and went back to watching the street again.

Daddy and I kept moving up the block and passed Ezel asleep on the bus bench. Daddy took out a couple dollars and put them in Ezel's back pocket. He woke up and pulled out the bills, then looked around to see who'd blessed him with such generosity. When he saw Daddy and me standing there, he sat straight up.

"Hey, thanks, Frank, man. I sho' 'preciate it."

He looked down at me and said, "What's happenin', Lil Bit?"

"Hey, Ezel."

He held his hand out, and I slid him some skin. Then he reached in his other pocket, pulled out a couple Nut Chews, and handed them to me.

"This is all you get," Daddy said. "I think you're coming up on your candy quota for the day."

I took the Nut Chews out of Ezel's hand and thanked him.

"What else iz I'm gon' do wit' 'em?" he said.

Daddy took my hand, and we crossed in the middle of the block. On the other side, an old guy with wrinkled skin and bloodshot eyes stepped in front of us. He stuck his hand out and said, "Man, you bedda give me some money too."

Daddy stopped and looked at the man in disbelief. "Man," he

said. "I ain't bedda do nothin' but stay Black and die. You want something from me, you ask for it. I don't owe you shit, brotha."

"Sorry, man. I didn't mean nothin' by it," the man said.

"Ain't no thang, man. Ain't no thang. What's your name?"

"George. George Mullins."

"Well, Mr. Mullins. I'm Frank McKinney, and this is my daughter, Zayla."

Mr. Mullins tipped his imaginary hat to me and reached out to shake my hand. I extended my hand. He kissed the back of it, scratching my skin with his rough face. I was sure the stench of his breath would linger long after he released my hand to me. I didn't want to hurt his feelings by wiping my hand on my pants, so I shoved it in my pants pocket.

"It's nice to meet you, Miss Zayla."

"You too," I said.

Daddy handed Mr. Mullins a couple dollars. When he saw Mr. Mullins' feet, he asked what size shoe he wore.

"Thirteen, sir."

"Hey, Alton," Daddy called across the street to Mr. Plummer. "You got any size thirteens over there you think Mr. Mullins here could get some use out of?"

"I'm sure I got something."

Daddy sent Mr. Mullins over to the pawn shop and told him to stay out of trouble.

"Thanks, sir. Thank you very much."

We passed Mr. Landes' bookstore, where Daddy got most of my books. A CLOSED sign leaned against the large plate-glass window.

James Brown's *Papa's Got a Brand New Bag* roared from the Malidy Hotel across the street. A small, colorfully dressed group of men and women mingled out front. Most noticeable was a woman in a bright pink dress that clung to her curves. She stood in the doorway, moving her hips side to side along with the music. She was engrossed in conversation with a tall, dark-skinned man in a black suit, swirling her cigarette around as she spoke. The man nodded, seeming more interested in her hips than her lips, and fanned himself with his hat. Daddy gave me a nudge and told me to mind my business.

"You ready?" he asked.

I turned around and found myself standing right in front of Daddy's nightclub. The black leather door had a large brass handle with a deadbolt lock underneath. A neon sign hung overhead that read "The Sanctuary" in red letters. At night marching lights ran around the edge of the sign. Daddy fumbled through a large key ring and found the one that opened the door. I'd thought it would be years before I was able to step foot in Daddy's club.

The walls, tablecloths, and napkins were a deep red, and the booths and chairs were upholstered in black leather. Mirrors with gold flakes hung like diamonds on the velvet walls. Just to the right of the entryway was the coat check. I imagined a pretty girl working in there, with sparkly jewelry and a fancy dress.

To the left was a wood-paneled wall covered with black-and-white photos of people like Sam Cooke, Jimmy Jones, Fats Domino, Jackie Wilson, and Buster Brown. Other photos showed Daddy standing with comedians like Redd Foxx, Moms Mabley, and Flip Wilson. In the main room, four large booths flanked the walls on my left and right. Sandwiched in between were ten small tables and chairs. Against the farthest wall was a small stage, and in front of it an even smaller dance floor. The bar was behind me. I heard her before I saw her.

"Hey, Frank. That ain't who I thank it is, is it?"

The woman standing behind the bar was tall like Daddy, taller if I included the enormous blonde beehive she wore. Pin curls hugged her hairline, and huge gold teardrop earrings hung from her lobes. My eyes followed her every movement.

"Millie, what are you doing here? Shouldn't you be home cookin' Sunday dinner for yo' man?"

"Child, please. Don't talk to me about that man! Ever since he retired, he don't do nothin' but sit 'round the house thinkin' up ways to get on my damn nerves. If he don't watch out, I'm gon' be up in here lookin' for his replacement. Shiiit, I need a break eva now and then. 'Scuse my French, suga'," she said, smiling at me.

"Miss Millie," Daddy announced, taking off his hat and bowing. "This is my heart, Zayla. Zayla, this here is Miss Millie. She's somebody you always want to know."

"Well, it's nice to meet you, Miss Zayla," she said, waving the bar rag at me. "I've heard a lot about you. Come over here and let me fix you a drink." Daddy had to nudge me to get me moving. I couldn't believe he was allowing me to drink alcohol, but I ran over to the bar before he changed his mind.

"She's gon' have to get it to go. We have an appointment on the roof."

Miss Millie placed a tall glass on the bar and filled it with ice and 7-Up. She poured red liquid in and dropped two cherries on top.

"You sho' is the cutest little thang I've ever seen. Frank, how did you and Zora end up making such a beautiful child?" She laughed. "Lord knows, she don't get her looks from neither one of you. You can tell Zora I said so." She laughed even louder.

Miss Millie's lashes looked like a thousand spider legs waving at me above shiny 14k gold lips. Her skin was a smooth, warm dark brown, and she smelled like spiced fruit and chamomile. She handed me my drink.

"This here is what they call a Shirley Temple in them white clubs, but since that ain't where you are, we gon' call this a Skinny McKinney, after your daddy."

"Thank you," I said, looking down into her cleavage.

She leaned over and said, "Don't worry, child. One day you gon' have a pair just like 'em, and your daddy's gon' need two shotguns and some bail money."

I smiled politely, not entirely understanding the reference, then self-consciously refocused my attention on the gold trim around her two front teeth.

"Come on, Zayla, before Miss Millie corrupts you."

"Nice to meet you, Miss Millie," I said. I put my free hand across my stomach and bowed, like Daddy had.

"Aw, ain't that cute," she said. "Ain't yo' mama teachin' you nothin' as refined as she likes to pretend to be? Little girls s'posed to curtsey. I'm surprised Zora ain't got you in one of them girls' club s'posed to teach you all that."

Daddy frowned. "Come on, Zayla. I'll let Zora know you asked about her, Millie."

"Don't do me no favors," she said.

Miss Millie curtsied to me and then leaned over and kissed my cheek. I wondered how long I could get away with not washing my face.

"I'm almost finished here. I'll lock up so y'all don't come down to no surprises. Night, Frank. Night, Miss Zayla."

14

There were two chairs on the roof. One had a telephone book duct-taped to it with a red velvet pillow on top. Daddy sat in the other chair next to the coffee can he used as an ashtray. I climbed up on a velvet pillow and sat back.

"So, how's your Skinny McKinney?"

"It's good."

"Look over there," he said, pointing just a bit to his right.

The sun was slowly slipping below the horizon. Rose blush, crimson, and yellow began the slow process of blending until they'd produce a rich navy blue.

I looked out among all the rooftops in Watts. A pigeon landed on the ledge, considered us for a moment, then took flight. It soared above the white stucco and red brick facade of 103rd Street Baptist Church. It dipped down and flew in front of the Largo Theater and the furniture store down the street. It headed in the direction of the Giant Market, then shot straight up in the air and leveled out over Martina's, the corner store on 105th and Wilmington, where we lined up on warm summer afternoons for sour pickles and peppermint sticks. It soared between the colorful mosaic structures, seventeen in total, of the Watts Towers and then breezed past Simon and Sons Funeral Home. It sailed over the playground of Compton

Elementary School, with its monkey bars and jungle gym, where an old clothesline we used as a double-Dutch rope lay abandoned in the grass. Then it glided over the Safeway down on Imperial Highway and over the Nickerson Garden Housing Projects before it flew out of sight.

"Daddy, can I tell you something?"

"Sure, Ladybug. You know you can tell me anything."

"You promise you won't be mad?"

"I'm not going to promise that, but I will promise to listen."

I told him what Kreps and Dumbrowski did to Roger. Daddy smoked his cigarette and stared out over the rooftops. I shifted in my seat and prepared myself for his disappointment, biting down on the insides of my cheeks to keep from crying. He took a slow drag on his cigarette. The smoke billowed around his face. He took another and held the smoke in a bit longer before exhaling. Some of the smoke came out of his nose, creating small curled vapors that vanished as quickly as they formed.

"How did you get out of the house without your mother seeing you?"

"I climbed out of my window."

"And why? What was so important that you risked getting in more trouble to go do?"

"Mr. Moskowitz was supposed to be giving away ice cream. But when we got to the store, we found out he wasn't."

"So you and Malik were the children in the store when Mr. Moskowitz called for the police?"

I nodded. "Why do some white people treat us the way they do?"

"Because they can. They make the laws. They control the money. They make the rules and change them when we become hip to them. They own the guns. And worse, *we* believe they have all the power."

"Don't they?"

"Power doesn't come from how much a man possesses. Power

comes from inside. You can have anything you want in this whole wide world; you just have to want it and then believe you deserve it."

"That's it?" I asked. "I thought I had to pray for it and wait for God to bless me."

Daddy laughed. "That's the problem. There's a whole lot of God-fearing Christians sitting around waiting for the Lord to bless them, but that ain't how it works."

"Does that mean it's always going to be this way?"

"Not necessarily. One day we will get our equality. But the only way it's going to work to our benefit is if we get it on our own terms. Malcolm X always said the worst thing to ever happen to the so-called Negro was desegregation. If we still had our own communities and banks and didn't need white folks for anything, like it was back during the Reconstruction Era, we would have been much better off."

"What do you think is gonna happen to those cops?"

"Probably nothing. But they'll get theirs. Eventually. People like that always do."

"Do you believe in God?" I asked.

"Of course I do."

"How come you don't come to church with us?"

"Because I don't believe in all that whoopin' and hollerin' and judgment and whatnot."

"Then how come I have to go to church?"

"When you get older, you can make your own decisions. But for right now, you gotta do what your mother wants, to keep the peace. Don't you believe in God?"

"I guess. He seems pretty complicated, though. And sometimes he's not so nice. It's confusing."

Daddy laughed and shook his head. "What am I going to do with you?"

"I don't know."

We sat there silently for a while before I said, "Daddy, I'm gonna do better. I'm gonna do whatever I have to do so the devil will get out of me, and I can be normal, even though I don't know how the devil got in me in the first place. I just want to make sure I can give you what you've always dreamed of."

The frown on Daddy's face deepened. He looked confused.

"And what have I always dreamed of?"

"For me to get married."

He took one more drag off his cigarette and used the toe of his shoe to stub it out. He picked up the butt and dropped it in the coffee can.

"Your mother tell you that, did she?"

Smoke billowed around his head.

"Yes."

"Hmmm," he said, nodding his head.

"I'm not a bulldagger, Daddy."

"What did I tell you about that word?"

"Well, I don't like girls."

"It wouldn't matter if you did," Daddy said, to my surprise. "Right now you don't know who you are. You've gotta figure it all out, and there's plenty of time for that."

He studied me a moment. I looked down at my shoes and reached over to retie them.

"You wanna tell me why you been faking sick to get out of going to school?" he finally asked. "You know your mother was disappointed that you missed graduation."

"You knew I was faking all that time?"

"Not at first, but I eventually figured it out. So, you want to tell me why you deprived yourself and your mother of your first graduation?"

"Because everyone at school said I'm weird and that I dress and act like a boy. They made fun of me because Dee-Dee told all these lies about me wanting to kiss her and that I asked her to go with me. Then they stuck gum in my chair, and they were all talking about me behind my back. And laughing at me. And Momma said I have the devil in me, and I want him to get out."

He shook his head and cleared his throat. A piece of phlegm came up. He spit it over the side of the building.

"Your mother's got that religion thing sewed up tight in her head and can't think straight."

"Why?"

"It's a long story, and more than you need to know right now. Just know this. God made you the way you are, and He don't make no mistakes. So, do me a favor. For now, focus on your books and try to stay out of trouble. I know it's hard for you. Trouble seems to follow you around like a lost puppy. Can you manage that?"

"Yes, Daddy."

"Good."

"Daddy?"

"Umm-hmm."

"Why did God make us if He hates us so much?"

Daddy laughed. "Got that from your mother, too?"

"No. I've just been thinking. It seems to me God is mean. If we don't act right, he'll punish us, even kill us. He says we shouldn't kill, but then He says, 'An eye for an eye.' That doesn't seem like love to me. Like the time He made that whale swallow Jonah for being disobedient. And He turned Lot's wife into a pillar of salt. And, why are we all born sinners if He doesn't like sinners? It doesn't make sense. Why would He make us broken on purpose? Just to give Him a reason to hate us?"

The more I talked, the louder Daddy laughed.

"God doesn't hate anything or anyone. He made us in His image and likeness," he explained.

"How do we know God's not a she?"

"That's just it. We don't. God can be whoever and whatever you want Him or Her to be."

"And when bad things happen, does it mean God is punishing us?" I asked.

"No, Ladybug. Bad things are the result of karma paying its respects."

"What's karma?"

"It's what happens to people who intentionally do bad things to others. It's what I like to call people getting their comeuppance."

"Because God is always watching."

"Yeah. Something like that."

* * * * * *

Three days later, a letter came in the mail addressed to "My Grand Baby." It was from Nana. I snatched it open and unwrapped the classified ad section of the *Chicago Defender*. Inside was a round-trip ticket to Chicago. On a small piece of paper inside the ticket jacket was a note from Nana that simply said, "Your cousin Suzanne is going to be here with you the whole time."

I cheered.

Momma snatched the paper from me and scowled. Suzanne was the daughter of Maxine, Momma's only sister, and they couldn't stand each other. I'd never met Suzanne, but I'd heard a lot about her from Nana, who kept up with both of us. Undoubtedly, Suzanne knew as much about me as I knew about her.

Here's what I knew: she made sixteen in March. She'd just graduated from high school. New York University gave her a full ride so she could study engineering. Her hobbies included acting, writing, and boys, although I believe Nana took liberties with that last part. She took a placement exam in third grade intended to prove the Negro students weren't prepared to advance to the next grade. Turned out, Suzanne wasn't ready for third grade. Or fourth. Fifth. Or sixth. More like the ninth. Aunt Maxine didn't want Suzanne that far ahead of the rest of the kids her age. So, the next school year, Suzanne skipped fourth and fifth grade and landed in the sixth.

Momma said the reason I'd never met Suzanne was because she lived "all the way" in New York. The truth had more to do with the fact that Momma and Aunt Maxine couldn't be in the same space for more than ten minutes. If Momma said the sky was blue, Aunt Maxine saw purple. If Aunt Maxine said it was nice out, Momma said it was unusually cold. I wondered how they managed to grow up in the same house without killing each other.

The first and only time I'd ever seen Aunt Maxine was when she came for my fifth birthday.

The first few days Aunt Maxine and Momma tiptoed around each other. They were well behaved at my birthday party. Then Aunt Maxine emerged from the bathroom with light blue eye shadow above her large round eyes. Momma commented on how nice the shade of blue looked on someone "like her." The fight was on.

It ended when Aunt Maxine said, "At least my man made an honest woman out of me ..."

"Get out of my house, you old ungrateful hussy," Momma screamed.

"Ain't no skin off my black ass," Aunt Maxine said.

She packed her bag and dragged them into the living room. She made a phone call and then kissed my forehead and cheek.

"Bye, my beautiful niece. When you get old enough to make your own money, come see your auntie in New York. Okay? My door is always open."

A few minutes later, a horn sounded outside. Aunt Maxine dropped her suitcase on the front porch and headed to the cab. The driver popped the trunk and ran to retrieve her bag. She looked up at the house as she lit a cigarette and, for a moment, almost looked remorseful. Then Momma stepped outside. Aunt Maxine cranked down the window and, in a voice loud enough for anyone within a two-block radius to hear, told Momma it would be a cold day in hell before she ever darkened our doorstep again.

"Good!" Momma shouted back. "And even then it'll be too soon."

And that was that. They hadn't spoken since.

I'd always believed that I would never get the chance to meet Suzanne until I was old enough to buy my own ticket. Now, thanks to Nana, I would be spending an entire summer with Suzanne, and I couldn't wait to leave. But at the same time I didn't want to go. I'd never been away from Daddy for more than a night or two. I'd also never been on an airplane by myself.

I read the letter once more and then threw it over my head. I danced around the living room, punching the air with the airline ticket clutched in my fist.

"I can't wait to leave," I screamed.

I pretended not to notice the look Momma gave me before she walked out of the room.

* * * * * *

A week later, I was sandwiched between Momma and Daddy in the front seat of the car. Momma rattled off a laundry list of instructions on how I was to behave and what I was to do, so as not to appear as though I had no home training.

"Brush your teeth at night," she instructed. "Don't go off with any strangers. Make sure Nana or Pompa know where you are at all times. Drink your milk. Wash under your arms often—I don't want you walking around funking up the house. Nana's going to put you in my old room, and I want you to take care of it, you hear me? Just because you're on vacation doesn't mean you're on vacation from your chores. Be sure you make up your bed every morning and clean up after yourself."

If I didn't know any better, it felt like Momma was actually going to miss me. Every now and then Daddy would reach over and give my hand a squeeze or look down at me and smile sadly. I knew he would miss me.

"I'll be back before you know it," I said, trying to cheer him up.

"I know. But what am I going to do all that time without my Ladybug?" he asked and stuck out his bottom lip out in a pout.

"Get some peace and quiet," Momma said.

"I'll miss you, too," I said sarcastically, and rested my head on Daddy's shoulder.

Momma shifted in her seat and gazed out the window. The squat houses and dense boulevards of Watts merged seamlessly into the rest of Los Angeles. We passed dirt lots with realtor signs that promised the coming of a new high-rise building. Oil pumps that looked like giant praying mantes bobbed up and down. One- and two-story homes with immaculate lawns and fancy cars parked in the driveway. The smell of ocean water lingered in the air. And then the rows of hotels that were always a sign we were close to Los Angeles Airport.

"You don't think I'm going to miss my baby?" she said, still watching the landscape. "Of course I am."

At the gate, Momma knelt down in front of me and started in again.

"Now, don't forget to brush your teeth in the morning and at night before you go to bed. Don't eat candy all day long, and be sure to have at least two glasses of milk a day. If you need anything, be sure to let Nana or Pompa know. Okay?"

"Yes, Momma," I said.

Tears pooled in her eyes as she grabbed me up close. After she'd squeezed all the air out of me, she released me and kissed both cheeks. She pushed me back by the shoulders so she could get another good look at me, and then grabbed me up again. She kissed me one last time and went over to the window. She pulled a hand-kerchief from her purse and dabbed at her eyes.

Daddy leaned over and whispered in my ear, "See, I told you she loves you. I bet she misses you already."

He reached in his pocket and handed me a twenty-dollar bill.

"Here's a little walking-around money. Don't spend it all in one place. And, if you can remember, buy your mother something nice to let her know you were thinking about her while you were away. Okay?"

"Okay, Daddy. Thank you."

"If you need any more, don't call me," he said.

He gave me a big hug, and I kissed his cheek.

"I'm gonna miss you, Daddy," I said. I stuck my nose in his neck and took a deep inhale. I tried to fill my lungs with enough of his aftershave and hair pomade to hold me until I returned home.

"I'm gonna miss you more," he said. "But maybe this is good for everyone. The distance might be good for you and your mother. You know what I mean?"

"Yeah," I said.

I took his hand, and we walked to the gate. A stewardess stood at the entrance waiting for me. She knelt down and pinned a pair of wings on my shirt. She introduced herself as Kathleen.

"Tell Miss Kathleen it is nice to meet her," Momma said, nudging me.

I stretched my arm to her and said, "Nice to meet you, Miss Kathleen."

We shook hands. I started to bow, and Momma grabbed the back of my shirt to straighten me up. Miss Kathleen chuckled. Daddy gave her instructions, and number one was to take extra good care of me. Even though she was a white lady, she didn't seem to mind at all that we were Negro. Her skin was deeply tanned. A mass of curly short jet-black hair hung just above her shoulders. She smelled like a rose garden. I knew the minute she took my hand that she intended to take good care of me just like she'd promised. Before we could walk away, Momma grabbed me and hugged me one final time.

"I love you," she whispered in my ear.

I hesitated. I felt my throat close, and tears sting my eyes. When I found my voice, I said, "I love you too, Momma."

"Bye, Ladybug," Daddy said.

I followed Miss Kathleen down the gateway. I waited until I'd fastened my seatbelt and couldn't see Momma and Daddy standing in the window anymore before I allowed the tears to come.

Part Two

June 1965 – June 1966

15

Negroes Treated as Outcasts Hope for Normal, Happy Life
Chicago Defender – Saturday, June 26, 1965

> *When you set out for Afrika*
> *you did not know you were going.*
> *Because you did not know you were Afrika.*
> *You did not know the Black continent*
> *that had to be reached*
> *was you.*
> ~Gwendolyn Brooks, "To the Diaspora"

Nana's round brown face and Pompa's scraggly gray beard were the first things I saw getting off the plane.

"There she is, Herbie! There's our grandbaby," Nana shrieked.

Miss Kathleen and I said our goodbyes, and she handed me off to Nana, who grabbed my face and covered it with kisses. Pompa gave my back a good clap.

"Hi, Pompa. How you feel?" I asked.

"With my hands," he said, then turned and walked off.

I giggled. I always asked Pompa how he felt just so he could say, "With my hands." It was nice to see some things would never change. Nana draped an arm around my shoulder, and I wrapped mine around her waist. We followed Pompa through the terminal to the baggage claim. I pointed out the pink-paisley suitcase Momma insisted on buying– instead of the solid green one that didn't draw attention to me. Pompa grabbed it with one hand and yanked me away from Nana by my shirt with the other.

We stepped out of the terminal at O'Hare International, and the heat socked me in the face like one of those clown fists. The humidity lay heavy on my skin. I could feel my hair napping up with every step.

"Hot enough for you?" Pompa asked.

"Uh-huh," I said.

"Welcome to Chicago, kiddo."

* * * * * *

The Woodlawn community on the South Side was a larger version of Watts—with a few exceptions. Trains, known as the L, ran on tracks high above the streets, and the wheels click-clacked along, adding percussion to the ensemble of horns blowing beneath. Most of the stores were Negro-owned. There was even a Negro-owned bank. And everything in between was owned, operated, or managed by Negroes.

Pompa turned onto St. Lawrence in West Woodlawn and slowed to let a group of kids about my age get out of the middle of the street. The sun made its way west overhead and a cool breeze pushed through the humidity. On the sidewalk, a group of older girls jumped double-Dutch. Nana's eyes scanned the crowd, and then widened in horror. She screamed so loud, I jumped. Pompa shook his head and told her to keep it down.

"The hell I will," Nana said and cranked the window down so I fast I thought the handle would break off. Nana gave Pompa's shoulder a shove.

"Herbie, will you take a look at your granddaughter? How many times have I told her not to come out of the house with half her behind showing?"

Pompa didn't even bother turning his head. He pulled up in front of a large gray brownstone and killed the engine. Nana sprung out of the car and shouted toward the group of girls, "Suzanne Elizabeth Nelson! Get your fast-tail behind in the house. What in the hell are you doing outside dressed like that?"

Out the back window, I scanned the group of girls. The two on either end of the rope wore ordinary shorts. The one jumping wore a jumper suit. Of the two remaining girls, one wore a sundress and looked like the last thing she planned on doing was jumping rope. The remaining girl couldn't have jumped if she wanted to. Her tight pink cotton dress stopped just a few inches below her unmentionables. That had to be Suzanne, I thought.

Suzanne sauntered across the street, in blatant defiance of Nana. When she got to my door, she screamed, "Cousin Zayla!"

I slid down in my seat, peered at her over the windowsill, and smiled like a fool. She pulled her sunglasses down on her nose and gazed back at me. Nana was still yelling and making her way up the steps into the house. When I didn't open the door, Suzanne yanked it open, and I spilled out onto the sidewalk in front of her. My hands sizzled the instant they touched the concrete. I looked up to see if Suzanne was laughing at me and caught a glimpse of her lilac undies. I looked away and scrambled to my feet. Nana continued fussing about the length of Suzanne's dress. Suzanne gave Nana a dismissive wave.

"Hi, Suzanne," I beamed. "It's nice to meet you."

Pompa went into the house with my suitcase. Nana stood on the porch, waiting impatiently for us to come inside. I kept my eyes locked on Suzanne as I walked into the coolest collector's museum in the world. The living room overflowed with antique artifacts and large, well-worn furniture. Colorful paintings covered every inch of wall space. Along with an antique paisley-print loveseat and a sofa covered with a large shiny piece of bright fabric, was a blue chaise longue that looked so comfortable I couldn't wait to climb up in it to watch television. None of the furniture matched, mostly because upholstery was one of Nana's latest hobbies, so whenever the mood hit her, she would re-upholster whatever piece of furniture struck her fancy. I loved Nana and Pompa's home almost as much as I loved them, and that was saying a lot.

On a tall wooden table that butted up against the back of the sofa was Nana's car collection. She'd been collecting antique model cars for as long as I'd been alive. Several of them she'd assembled herself. The console television Daddy bought them for their fortieth anniversary sat against the wall across from the sofa. On top were all sorts of knickknacks: a brass candleholder and two brass flower vases, an old telephone, a stack of random books, picture frames with black-and-white photos of Momma and Aunt Maxine as children, an old camera, and two large rocks. The two end tables on either side of the television were also filled with knickknacks.

I walked around the perimeter of the room like an art enthusiast at a New York gallery. Each one of the paintings portrayed a beautiful Negro woman, most of them as naked as the day they were born. In one, a naked woman walked into what looked like a door of light. Next to it, an old woman with a scarf tied high above her head scowled at something only visible on her side of the canvas. On the wall closest to the stair landing, a naked woman played a bright yellow cello on a shoreline. The moon glistened in the blue water below her feet, its reflection dancing on the surface. Next to her, a woman in an orange evening gown sat casually on a lilac chaise. If I had to give it a name, it would have been called "Waiting," because the woman sat there like she'd wait all night if she had to. All around the living and dining room area, paintings of women in various stages of undress took up most of the wall space.

"I can't wait to get you in my studio," Nana said. "I'm working on something I think you would like."

"I'm not sure I like painting anymore," I said.

"Why not?" she asked, genuinely concerned.

I didn't plan to tell her, except she looked like she had no intention of moving until I answered her question. So I did.

The first time I'd ever held a paintbrush, I was in third grade. Some things in life are preordained. For me, it was painting. The first time I dipped a brush into paint, I felt at ease. Comfortable. I was a natural. Blending colors. Sketching images, by sight or memory, all of it as natural as blinking. For a while, it kept me out of trees, or ripping and running up and down the street. Momma was happy, so Daddy kept me stocked with paint supplies. I used to paint pictures all the time and take them to school for show and tell.

Then one day Mrs. Nichols, our fifth-grade teacher, gave us an art project: to paint someone we admired. The best one would hang in the hallway for the rest of the school year. I chose Jesus because He wasn't around to complain about the end result. Since all the pictures I'd ever seen of Jesus depicted Him as a white man, I imagined how a Negro Jesus might look, and lost myself in the details.

I painted creamy mahogany skin with golden highlights along the forehead and cheekbones. Since the Bible said His hair was like wool, I painted a two-inch Afro that framed His face evenly and I made His nose and forehead strong and broad, like Daddy's. I gave him Momma's brown eyes and added Daddy's thick black mustache for good measure.

When my name was called the next day in class, I walked to the front of the room with my chest out and head held high. I slowly pulled off the brown bag and turned the painting around for everyone to see.

At first, they just sat there staring as if I'd pulled out a Martian for display. I squirmed in my shoes, prepared to run straight home when, almost all at once, they cheered. I straightened up and held my Jesus higher. Mrs. Nichols came around the desk. I gazed up at her, searching her face for admiration. I just knew she would take one look at my masterpiece and announce my painting would hang in the hallway. I imagined an assembly where all the ministers, bishops, and priests would be called from all parts of Los Angeles to view my Jesus. What I found instead was utter disgust. I couldn't believe my Black Jesus offended her. She snatched the canvas out of my hand and stomped out of the room.

Principal Mulligan told Momma that the son of God was a white man and that I had a lot of audacity to paint a Negro Jesus. Momma threatened to go to the NAACP, and they hung my painting in the hall for one day. The next day it was gone. I never saw it again.

"I decided if sharing my art was going to cause all that trouble, I didn't want to paint anymore," I added.

"Aww, suga," Nana said, pulling me into her. "You can't let other people dictate how you live your life. You have a God-given talent. Don't you allow no one to steal that away from you. You understand me?"

And just like that, I was crying and feeling like a big baby. Mostly, I cried because it felt so good to know Nana cared about me the way Momma should have. In some weird way, I'd also convinced myself that Nana's love was an extension of Momma's, so for as long as I was in Chicago, I would soak it up and even pack some up for the trip home.

"You and me got a date in my studio before you go home, okay?"

I nodded.

"Does your head make noise, little girl?" Nana asked. "Answer me."

I couldn't help laughing. At least I knew Momma got it honestly. "No, ma'am," I replied.

"Come on, Zayla. It's too hot to be dawdling," Suzanne shouted from the top of the stairs. "We need every second we got! We're talking about sixteen years of catching up!"

"It's not going to take me that long," I mumbled. "I haven't done anything."

"Humph, you'll be lucky if you get past the first grade before she cuts you off," Nana said. "That girl will talk your damn ear off. But you listen to me." She lowered her voice conspiratorially. "Suzanne is sixteen years old, and there's things she has been allowed to do that you cannot do. Don't do just anything she tells you. You hear me?"

"Yes, Nana," I lied and shot up the stairs, taking them two at a time.

Of course I heard her, but I had no intention of obeying. In fact, I'd already decided that if Suzanne told me to tape feathers to my arms to see if I could fly, I would knock her over trying to get to the roof. Don't do anything she tells me. Yeah, right. Nana must have been crazy.

"And stop all that running in my house," Nana shouted to my back.

* * * * * *

Momma's room was frozen in time. Pale yellow curtains covered the long windows and matched the walls almost perfectly. The four-poster bed had a pale yellow floral print comforter and matching dust ruffle. The ornate bedroom set consisted of a dresser, hutch, and the bed, and took up most of the space in the room. And in the corner, completely out of place, an oscillating fan whirred and clanked, doing its best to move the hot air around.

Suzanne and I flopped down on the bed and began our catching-up session. Nana was wrong. I actually made it to second grade before Suzanne interrupted me to tell me about the time she went to the Empire State Building when she was in the second grade. She sort of took over after that. I listened for a while, and before I knew it, I was sound asleep. When I woke up again, it was dark out, and the house smelled like salmon. I jumped up and took off downstairs. Nana sat at the kitchen table and supervised as Suzanne shaped a croquette, rolled it in cornmeal, and gently placed it in the skillet. A bowl of coleslaw sat on the table. I licked my lips. Before I could sit down, Nana said, "Why don't you help your cousin with dinner? At the rate she's going, we'll be up all night waiting."

Pompa joined us at the kitchen table for the meal. He said a quick prayer and piled his plate with food, ignoring Nana's protests. Nana turned her attention to Suzanne.

"Don't think you're gonna be running the streets all summer without your cousin. She came all the way here to spend time with you, and that's what you're gonna do. Do you hear me?" Nana asked.

"Yes, Nana," Suzanne said. "But I still have school too, you know."

"I know that. And watch your mouth, young lady. You ain't too old for me to pop you."

Pompa wolfed down his food as if he sat alone at the table. When he cleaned his plate, he got up and left the room.

"Thanks for dinner, little girls," he said and returned to his place in front of the television.

I took my time eating my croquettes. Nana's recipe included crab meat and diced green peppers, and she made a dipping sauce out of mayo, spicy mustard, and a splash of honey. I ate so much I thought my stomach would pop, and when Nana brought out the pineapple upside-down cake, I forced down a piece of that, too.

"You're gonna make yourself sick, little girl," Nana warned.

I didn't care. I figured if it all came back up the way it went down, that would just mean I had more room to refill.

* * * * * *

Suzanne slept with me that night. I thought it would take us half the morning to untangle ourselves from each other and the bedsheets. But by the time I woke up, her side of the bed was cold. I slid out and made my way to the bathroom. Nana was in her sewing room down the hall, talking on the phone. When she finished, she came in and sat down on the edge of the tub. I snatched a Q-tip from the container on the back of the toilet and cleaned my ears before she told me to.

"That was your mother," she said.

"What'd she say?"

"Not a damn thing, except she wants me to comb your hair. I told her, and I'm gon' tell you. I am too damn old to be doin' heads. You are old enough to take care of yourself. That includes combing your hair. So, you might as well stop pretending to get the wax outta your ears and start practicing."

"Thanks, Nana," I said and dropped the Q-tip in the trashcan. I hugged her around her neck.

"You're welcome, baby. Your grandfather should be just about finished burning breakfast. Come on down when you're ready."

Pompa made breakfast of fried green tomatoes, Polish sausages sliced down the middle and browned on both sides, scrambled eggs, and applesauce. I ate until I almost popped. Then I went upstairs to fiddle around with my hair again.

It took an entire hour to get it smoothed back into an Afro puff and another hour trying to get the puff in the center of my head. No matter how many times I bent over and brushed my hair toward what I thought was the center of my head once I snapped the rubber band in place and checked myself out, I looked like a one-eared Mickey Mouse.

"You want some help with that?" Suzanne asked from the doorway.

I jumped a little. I hadn't heard her come in. "Sure."

She lifted her dress and sat on the toilet. I turned to leave.

"Where you going?" she asked.

"To give you some privacy?"

"For what? I'm just peeing."

"Yeah, but don't you care if I see your privates?"

"We got the same thing, don't we? Except mine has hair. Does yours have hair yet? Mine didn't get hair until I was fourteen. Doesn't Aunt Zora come in the bathroom when you're in there?"

"No."

"Umph. Aunt Zora is a trip. Come here so I can tame that hair of yours. You just gotta learn how to work with it."

Suzanne finished her business, washed her hands, and then wet a washcloth with hot water. I sat on the edge of the tub and watched her work through the mirror on the back of the bathroom door. She pressed the wet rag over my head, grabbed a handful of Royal Crown, and rubbed it in my hair. She brushed my hair back and up until it lay down smooth on my head, then snapped the rubber band in place. In less than five minutes, I had a nice round Afro puff, perfectly centered on the top of my head.

"Thanks," I said. I'd aged four years. Afro puffs beat ponytails any day.

"You're welcome. Why don't you throw on some clothes so we can get out of here?"

She went into her room to change and came out almost an hour later in a white mini skirt and peach tank top. She'd brushed her hair up into an Afro puff, too.

"All right. Let's go," she said.

I was downstairs watching television. I turned it off and stood up. Suzanne took one look at me and stopped short. Her gaze marched down to my feet, up to my shirt, and back down to my feet. I couldn't tell which piece was most disappointing: the dirt caked along the top and sides of my sneakers, the frayed edges along the bottom of my cut-off shorts, or the chocolate ice cream stain on my blouse.

"What's wrong?" I asked stupidly.

"Nothing we have time to fix, that's for sure. Are your ears pierced?"

I nodded. She took off upstairs and came back with a pair of gold stud earrings. I slipped them in my ears. She gave me another once-over.

"Better?" I asked.

She shook her head again and ran back upstairs. She came back with a colorful shirt and tossed it to me. I threw my stained shirt on the foot of the stairs and slipped the shirt over my head. It didn't look too bad with the rest of my outfit.

"Better?" I asked again.

"Not really, but it'll have to do for now. But I gotta tell you, little cousin, you gotta start caring about the way you look when you leave the house."

I'd had almost the exact same conversation with Momma every time I called myself dressed. Except with Momma, I didn't care if she didn't like my outfit. Suzanne's disapproval hurt my feelings. I offered to change, but she didn't want to wait. She said something about it being too damn hot outside. We had to go while she'd talked herself into getting back out in it. But she didn't seem pleased to be hanging out with me looking like what I presumed to be a raga-muffin in her eyes. I was grateful she didn't let it bother her, but my feelings were still hurt. I followed her down South Parkway, thankful for the sweat running down my face to hide the tears.

"Where are we going?" I asked.

"All over Chicago. We're gonna go as far as our feet and public transportation will take us. Cool?"

"Cool."

Suzanne didn't disappoint me. For three whole weeks, we did something new and exciting almost every single day. She had only two conditions: one, she had to approve of my outfit, and I had to try different styles for my hair because, as Suzanne not so eloquently put it, "just because you're out of ponytails doesn't mean you got to replace them with Afro puffs every day." I could have argued with her. After all, she wasn't my mother. And, she wasn't the boss of me. But she meant well, and that's all that really mattered. By the second week, she only had to send me back upstairs once. Apparently, I'd violated every fashion rule by wearing sneakers with a skirt.

We went to Maxwell Street, where vendors from all over the world sold everything from shoestrings to expensive clothes right off card tables or blankets or out of the back of a ratty pickup truck. I bought Momma a bright blue scarf and a colorful Chinese hand fan and watched Suzanne haggle the guy down off the price. I told her I had enough money to pay the asking price, but she said no one pays asking price on Maxwell Street. "Only fools and suckas, and you ain't neitha," she added.

We had hot dogs in poppy seed buns filled with mustard and onions, relish, pickles, and peppers so hot I thought my tongue would never stop burning.

We explored the tall buildings in the Loop, pretending we knew people who worked inside and marched into elevators like we had a right to be there. We got kicked out of some elevators, but not nearly as many as we got to ride.

We ate Garrett's popcorn until our fingers were covered with yellow cheese sauce and sticky with caramel.

We went to the Chicago Theater, where shiny red letters spelled out, *Annette Funicello and Dwayne Hickman in How to Stuff a Wild Bikini*. I found out Suzanne loved movies as much as I did, but we didn't have enough money to buy tickets. So Suzanne pretended she had to pee. She wore the attendant down until he let us in to use the bathroom. Then we snuck into the theater and watched the movie until almost the end when the attendant found us and sent us packing.

We ordered chocolate malts and cheeseburgers at the Woolworth's counter and waited for someone to ask us to leave. No one did.

We took the elevator to the observation deck of the Prudential Building and paid fifteen cents to look through the binoculars at the city below. The loogies we spit off into the streets far below were free.

We walked along South Shore beach, and sometimes we stopped and sat in comfortable silence with our feet buried in the sand, watching the kids splashing around in the water. Suzanne told me that Negro children once were only allowed to play on one side of the beach. And the one time a Negro boy floated over to the white side by accident, some white people killed him. The boy's father went home and got his shotgun and other men in the community, and they went looking for the people responsible. She said it was rumored to have started the Red Summer of 1919. I got the sense that Suzanne was trying to impress me with her knowledge of Chicago history. So, I didn't have the heart to tell her that Daddy's version was slightly different. He said the Red Summer of 1919 started because white folks got tired of watching us thrive in prosperous communities with our Black Wall Street. We had more rich Negroes than the law allowed. I had a feeling Daddy's version was more accurate because he was like the first edition of a walking Negro history book, and he was hellbent on making me the second.

We touched all four corners of the city, from the near north side to the far south side, and everything in between. When we weren't out terrorizing the town, as Nana liked to say, we were going through Suzanne's closet for hand-me-downs that I could wear. Or, I was held captive while Suzanne modeled her new outfits as I lay across her bed, trying to read.

On the few days when Suzanne was too busy with schoolwork to hang out with me, I spent my time with Nana. We spent several afternoons into the early evening in her studio, where she taught me to mix colors and create beautiful abstract images. On other days she took me to the DuSable Museum, which was in the large living room of Charles and Margaret Burroughs' house. The South Side Community Art Center was right across the street.

We went shopping downtown at Marshall Field's and Carson Pirie Scott.

We had a "girls' lunch" at Gladys', a soul food restaurant on 45th and Indiana, and afterward, we went to Nana's beauty shop, and she had one of the ladies do my hair. Another lady polished my nails even though I didn't want her to. I didn't want to hurt Nana's feelings, so I didn't say anything, but Suzanne saw them before I could take the polish off and made such a big deal about it I left it on.

In my alone time, I wrote letters to Malik giving him a blow by blow of everything I was doing. He only wrote back once. Six sentences in total.

"Glad you're having fun. I am too. Is it hot there? I won your yellow tiger eye Shooter from Lucius. Good luck getting it back. See you when you get home."

I couldn't hide my disappointment. Nana said I should be happy I got one letter. She told me how Pompa only wrote home three times in the year he was overseas during the second world war.

"Count your blessing, child. Men ain't got the sense God gave 'em."

Not all of them, I thought. Daddy wrote me every week.

16

1st Mars Close-Up Photo

Chicago Tribune – Friday, July 16, 1965

> *The free bird leaps on the back of the wind*
> *and floats downstream til the current ends*
> *and dips his wings in the orange sun rays*
> *and dares to claim the sky.*
> ~ Maya Angelou, "I Know Why the Caged Bird Sings"

My time with Nana, Pompa, and Suzanne flew by so fast, and I didn't want it to end. I'd never had so much fun in my life. With only four days left, I couldn't help thinking about all the things I was going to miss.

Like getting bottles of RC and Snicker bars for Pompa from the man on South Parkway who sold candy and pop from the back of his station wagon. And the watermelon man who pushed his cart through the alleys singing, "Water-melonnnn man! Come get your waaaatter-melon!" No matter what we were doing, everything stopped when the watermelon man came by.

Just after midnight, I'd finally managed to doze off. At close to three a.m. Suzanne comes climbing up in bed with me smelling of whiskey and stale cigarettes. I hadn't seen her all day. There was some party on the last day of her summer classes, and Nana let her go. I bet if she'd known Suzanne was going to come home smelling like a distillery, she would have chained her up in her room and thrown away the key.

"Zayla?" Suzanne whispered in my face. "Are you 'sleep?"

"Not anymore," I grumbled.

"Good. Guess what?" she asked, and before I could respond, she answered her own question. "I'm in love! His name is Sean. We met at the record shop on 53rd Street in Hyde Park this afternoon."

"I thought you were at some party for your class."

"What? Oh. That. No. That's what I told Nana, so she'd give me some breathing room."

I rolled away from her.

"Don't be mad, little cousin. I didn't plan to be gone so long. It just sort of happened."

She sighed and fell back against the headboard. That girl could have given Bette Davis a run for her money with all her theatrics. The only thing missing was the hand to the forehead gesture. I got out of bed and moved the fan closer. The smell coming from Suzanne in the stagnant air was making me a little nauseous.

"How can you be in love so fast? You just met him," I asked.

"So?"

"So, that's not how it works."

"How would you know?"

"Because I was in love once, and it took me a long time to feel that way."

"Well, then you weren't in love. Who were you in love with?" she asked and scooted closer to me.

I moved to the very edge of the bed. "Nobody. I don't want to talk about it."

"Was it that girl in your class?" she asked.

I sat straight up, forgetting there was no mattress on my right side. There was a great crash as I tumbled out of bed and onto the floor. Suzanne laughed. I wanted to be mad, but I'd made so much noise on the way down I couldn't help laughing, too. I'd knocked over the fan, put a dent in the top of the Scrabble box, and pulled the top sheet entirely off the bed. I picked up the fan, put the Scrabble box back where it belonged, and climbed back up. Suzanne helped me put the sheet back on the bed, and I decided to leave the theatrics to her.

When we finally stopped laughing, she said, "All I'm trying to tell you is when you fall in love, it happens all at once. It's like magic. I got mine. And you, little cousin, need some magic of your own. There's a skaters set tomorrow night, and we're going on a double date."

"I'm not supposed to date until I'm much older."

Suzanne looked at me in that way people do when they're trying to figure out if you're as dumb as you sound.

"Who's gonna know?" she asked. "I had one job this summer, and that was to help you. I don't feel like I've done a very good job."

"I don't need you to help me. There's nothing wrong with me."

"I didn't say there was. It's just that everyone's all worried about you being 'that way' because you haven't come into your own yet. But how could you with Aunt Zora around?"

I moved over in the bed, put both hands on the mattress, and sat up again. "You know about that?"

"It ain't much that happens in this family that I don't know about. Besides, Nana has a big mouth. You think us being here at the same time is an accident? So, tell me. How was it?"

"What?"

"Kissing a girl."

I felt like I should be upset with Suzanne. It seemed like everyone was going through a lot of trouble to help me, but no one even bothered to ask how they could help. If they had, I could have told them it didn't start from the outside. They could have given me all the silk purses in the world, and none of them would have replaced the sow's ear I felt growing inside. Something was wrong with me, all right. It just had very little to do with my choice of shoes.

"I don't want to talk about it, I said."

"Why not? I've kissed a girl before."

She had my attention. "You have?"

"Sure. Her name was Lola. We were best friends. Then, one day, out of sheer boredom, I decided we should kiss. So we did. Simple."

"Maybe for you. I got in a lot of trouble."

"All I'm saying is you can't tell anything from a kiss that has no feeling. I used to kiss Lola all the time. We played house. I was the husband, she was the wife. It wasn't like we were sticking our tongues down each other's throats. They were pecks. Did you kiss kiss or did you just touch lips? If you just touch lips, then you didn't really kiss."

"We just touched lips."

"See? It didn't mean anything."

It meant something to me. It would always mean something to me because I lost my best friend in the process.

"It just proves that everyone is making a big deal out of nothing. Just because you're a tomboy and kissed a girl doesn't make you 'that way.' Trust me, the minute you get a real kiss, you'll know. Okay? But really, how do you expect to get a boyfriend dressing like you do?"

I got boiling mad then. After all, who made the rule that girls had to wear dresses and frilly things? What, about how I looked, had anything to do with who I was? Did it make me any less smart? Or funny? Or me? Okay. So what, fashion wasn't my thing. Why couldn't someone just explain to me why that wasn't good enough?

"Who says I even want to be in a relationship?" I asked. "Daddy said I'm way too young."

"You may not now, but you will."

"What's wrong with the way I dress?"

"Nothing, if you were a dude."

"Just 'cause I don't dress like a Barbie doll—"

"Hey! Don't get all defensive with me."

"I'm not. I just don't dress to make other people happy," I said.

"You shouldn't. That's not what I'm saying. You think I dress for other people? Hell naw. I dress for myself! The first thing my mom taught me when she let me start picking out my own clothes was to dress for success. 'Suzanne,' she said, 'if you know you look good, you don't need someone else to tell you. Don't you want to feel good when you get dressed and look at yourself in the mirror?"

"I don't look at myself after I get dressed. I just put on my clothes and go."

"Yeah, I can tell. But not anymore! Tomorrow night you're going to look so good every boy in the room will be checking you out. Well, every boy except Sean."

"If you say so," I said.

"I do."

She kissed my forehead, yawned, and lay back down. I turned on my side and grinned into my pillow when Suzanne slid close and put her arm around my waist. I took a deep breath and slowly let it out. I wanted to move away from her before she melted into me, but I couldn't. I'd grown accustomed to the closeness Suzanne, and I shared. Before that, I'd never felt like I was missing out on anything. But it wouldn't have hurt to have a sister to look up to. Suzanne made me wish I had a Suzanne of my very own at home.

* * * * * *

The Savoy Ballroom was on 47th Street and South Parkway, adjacent to the Regal Theater. A line of well-dressed Negroes wrapped around the block. Pompa dropped us off in front and handed each of us a dollar bill.

"Don't spend it all in one place," he said.

We thanked him and waited at the curb until he was out of sight. Suzanne scanned the crowd for Sean. I didn't need her to point him out. Somehow, I just knew he was one of the two shiny pennies standing near the front of the line. I figured the other one was supposed to be for me. One looked like a young, squat Duke Ellington in a starched white shirt and dark blue slacks creased so hard they could have cut glass. His shirt was unbuttoned to reveal the hair not growing on his chest.

The other guy was a dead ringer for Nat King Cole, tall and muscular, except he had naturally curly hair shaped in an Afro. He wore a black shirt buttoned up to the collar, black slacks, and black shoes. Suzanne went over to the one who looked like Duke Ellington and gave him a kiss on the lips.

"Hi, baby," she said and then pulled me over to her. "Sean. Marcus. This is my cousin Zayla from California."

All summer Suzanne had been introducing me as her "cousin Zayla from California" as if it were my actual name, and California was a city like Chicago. Sean and Marcus exchanged impressed glances, as most people had when they found out I was from the Golden State. To them, California was exotic and exciting, and the only place that really mattered was Los Angeles. If they'd ever heard of Watts, I would have told them it wasn't any different from the South Side of Chicago. Instead, I represented the movie stars in Hollywood and the rich people that lived in the homes of Beverly Hills. I was "lucky" to get to live in such a beautiful place, they'd all said in one way or another. In a way, it was frustrating, but it was also nice, too.

Marcus extended his hand. "Nice to meet you."

"Hi," I said, looking down at the sidewalk.

He took my hand and raised it to his lips, planting a soft kiss on the back. I couldn't bring myself to look at him again, for fear I'd notice he had a wart on his nose or pimples all over his face. I'd never been so uncomfortable around a boy before. But, then again, I'd never been around such a handsome boy.

Marcus stepped closer and held his elbow out. We locked arms and made our way into the ballroom. Inside, the Savoy reminded me of the Largo Theater, only the Savoy was ten times larger. Most nights, it was a dance hall for adults. On Sundays, they opened it up to the younger crowd for skating. We found a booth to share in a corner close to the skaters. Suzanne and Sean cozied up on one side. Marcus and I sat at a respectable distance on the other. We'd only been seated a few minutes when he turned to me.

"You ever been to Watts?" he asked.

"Yeah. That's where I live."

"Sho' nuff? What's it like?"

"There's not a whole lot to tell. It's where most of the Negroes in Los Angeles live. But it's not a ghetto. We have nice houses. Just like here."

"Do you know Charles Mingus?"

I didn't know him personally, but Daddy did. I decided not to share that, and shook my head. "Do you?"

"Naw. But I wish I did. I'm gonna be playing the bass in our high school jazz band in the fall."

"You're in high school?" I asked, suddenly getting nervous.

"Yeah, but I'm only in the ninth grade."

"Oh."

I turned my attention to the rink and waited for Marcus to make up an excuse to get away from me. He didn't. To my surprise, it made me like him a little more. I had to admit I liked him almost from the start. Something about him reminded me of Daddy. I could have spent the entire evening telling him all the things Daddy taught me about music and our history, but I didn't want him to think I was a know-it-all. I also didn't want to bore him. And, truth be told, I couldn't stop watching the skaters. They were doing things on skates most people couldn't do in shoes.

Everyone in the place could skate, including Suzanne. There was none of that stumbling around the way we did in our wind-up skates back at home. No wheels getting caught on rocks and sending anyone sprawling to the floor. I mean, they could dance in their skates. Stomp and spin on one leg. Backward skate. Crisscross. Do the splits. Skate in formations of three and four all connected at the waist and not one of them missing a beat. You name it, they could do it. Just watching them made me tired.

"So, what do you do at home for fun?" Marcus asked.

All of a sudden my mind went blank. What was I supposed to tell him? I didn't want to tell him about climbing trees in Will Rogers Park, or playing stickball in the street, or shooting marbles, or anything that would make him think I was weird. I could have lied and told him I played with Barbie dolls and had tea parties with my friends, but I also didn't want to start off our friendship with a lie.

I told him about Malik and school and Mrs. Fitzgerald. I told him about Mrs. Robinette and Roger and how even after the police beat Roger up, he's still going to USC in the fall. I told him about Daddy and the Sanctuary and all the famous people I'd seen on the walls there. And I told him about Watts and how much I loved living there. Then he asked me about my boyfriend. It was the first time anyone had asked me that question or even considered me normal enough to have a boyfriend. So, I told him about Dennis, the imaginary ex-boyfriend I made up.

"Why'd you break up?" he asked.

"Because he started liking my friend Dee-Dee."

Suddenly I understood what Momma meant when she warned that lying begets more lies. That one flew out so smoothly I couldn't have stopped it if I wanted to. I decided it would be best if I shut my trap after that.

"That's a mean thing to do," he said.

"Yeah. Tell me about it. Do you have a girlfriend?"

"Nah. They all think I'm weird."

"Why?"

"I'm not cool like Sean. He's had all kinds of girlfriends since he was in sixth grade. At his high school graduation he had both of the girls he was dating show up. They actually got in a fistfight over him."

"Sean's already out of high school?"

"Yeah. He's in his second year at Tuskegee University."

College? Sean was in college? That meant he was at least nineteen or twenty. Nana was going to kill Suzanne if she ever found out. Suddenly I wished I hadn't heard any of that. I turned off my brain and just listened.

"I'm a musician," Marcus said. "I've been one since I was six years old. I live and breathe music. I've never really been interested in girls because I've never met a girl who didn't complain about my music. I listen to all kinds. Classical. Jazz. Rock. Blues. Even country. Every girl I'd ever played something for complained about it because she'd never heard the song before, or it was boring because it didn't have any words. I did have one girlfriend who liked to go to the movies, but then she'd talk the whole time. No offense, but you guys are really kinda crazy, if you ask me."

"No offense taken," I said, completely understanding.

"You wanna go skate?"

"Not really."

"Come on. I can't let you sit there watching all night."

He extended his hand, and I took it. We waited at the edge of the rink for a group of skaters to go by. The two on either end broke away and zipped to the front of the group. They locked wrists and spun around, so they were going backward again. The next set of two did the same. The last set used their brakes to stop them, and in one smooth move they jumped and spun around and followed the rest of their group around the rink. There was no way I was going out there to make a fool of myself.

"I don't know how to skate like that," I said.

"I can teach you."

He did a little spin and bowed. Why is he so nice to me? I wondered. Maybe Sean paid him to pretend to like me for the night so he could be out with Suzanne. I looked up at Marcus. He just stood there smiling at me the way Daddy looked at Momma sometimes. The way Malik used to ogle Melody. I imagine the same way I stared at Dee-Dee.

Maybe he really does like you, I said to myself. Yeah, perhaps he does. I might be scrawny compared to Suzanne, but I am just as smart. I'm not too hard on the eyes—in fact, Suzanne said I was beautiful and funny. And, thanks to her, I looked like a million bucks in my pedal pushers and halter top. That's when something shifted inside me, the way a transmission shifts from first to second gear. Why not? I asked myself. Why wouldn't someone like Marcus be interested in me?

I took his hand, and Marcus led me out onto the smooth hardwood floor. I felt like the most important girl in the entire room. He took his time teaching me a few moves, like how to cross one leg over the other when I came around a curve, which I found to be relatively easy. Then he taught me how to skate backward, which wasn't as easy, but I managed to catch on without killing anyone. Or myself. Or him. I only fell twice, which wasn't so bad, except that I pulled him down with me both times.

He landed on top of me, and for a second I thought he was going to kiss me. Our faces were so close I could feel the heat of his breath. He smelled a little like Daddy, too, which made me think about Daddy and what he would say if he saw me on the floor with a strange boy lying on top of me, which created instant panic. I pushed Marcus off and scrambled to get back on my feet.

We left the floor as the lights went down and the DJ called for a couples skate. Marcus put one arm around my waist and turned us around as Ray Charles sang, "I can't stop loving you . . ."

Side by side, we went around the rink, dance skating, with me feeling safe and special and not like a sister, the way I'd always felt with Malik. It was more than that. Larger somehow. I saw the way the other girls watched us, and I knew they all wished they could take my place. I thought about what Suzanne said about dressing for success. I looked good that night. I knew it, and everyone else knew it, too. Or, at least that's what I wanted to believe since Suzanne convinced me that was all it took. As the song ended, I looked up at Marcus and prayed he couldn't feel me trembling. Before I could even think about what might come next, he leaned down and kissed me.

For about a nanosecond my brain considered stopping him, but the rest of me thought nothing of the sort. I braced myself for a new experience, one that would prove once and for all that I was not a bulldagger.

Marcus' lips sent electricity through me. I inhaled softly, and my eyelids slid closed, and nothing else in the world mattered. And it was real. There was nothing wrong or sinful about what Marcus and I were doing. Although admittedly, I had no idea what I was doing, I wanted this new experience to take shape all of its own accord. I didn't think about anyone or anything. I just counted to five and waited for him to pull away, but instead, he parted my lips with his tongue and gently pushed it into my mouth. I exhaled around it and willed myself not to pass out. My legs scissored, and I had to grab his arms to keep myself from doing the splits. Through it all, I didn't pull away, and we didn't stop kissing.

His breath was hot and sweet. His tongue moved around in my mouth, slowly thrusting deeper, exploring. I kissed him back, confident that if I mimicked his moves, he would think I'd kissed a million guys before him. I must have been doing something right because he moaned into my mouth, sending vibrations into places I didn't even know existed. I completely forgot where we were or that I was even standing on my own two unstable feet.

Then I felt something hard press against my abdomen, which caused a soft moan to escape me that was so sensual I became hyperaware of my surroundings. My eyes flew open, and my mouth slammed shut. I looked up at Marcus, who suddenly seemed to be very amused by me, and I shuddered. I gave him a weak smile and bit down on my bottom lip.

"You're a good kisser," he said. I saw the dreamy look in his eyes and felt a sense of pride that I'd put it there. "But I haven't kissed a whole lot. So what do I know?"

"Thanks," I said. "I guess."

This time I looked him in the eye and didn't shy away. I felt my confidence growing with every passing moment. There was really nothing to it. In a way, kissing was like dancing. I followed his lead and hoped for the best. I presumed the result of "the best" was what caused the bulge in his jeans. I didn't understand what it all meant completely, but I understood enough. Kissing had power. My kissing had power. I didn't feel the way Suzanne felt about Sean, but I felt something, and that was all that mattered.

"Come on," he whispered.

He took my hand. I floated to the booth and landed across from Suzanne, who was grinning ear to ear. Marcus excused himself and skated off to the refreshment stand. Suzanne slid around closer to me.

"So ... how do you feel, little cousin?" she whispered.

I felt great and beautiful, and regular.

On that sultry Saturday night on the South Side of Chicago, I felt like a sophisticated woman trapped in a twelve-year-old body. I hoped it wouldn't be the last time I hung out with Suzanne because she helped the world make a whole lot more sense to me. She also helped me make a whole lot more sense to myself. I couldn't wait to get back to Watts, to the neighborhood, and I especially couldn't wait for school to start. There was a new and improved Zayla Lucille McKinney, and everybody better watch out.

Just when I thought I couldn't feel any better, Marcus leaned over and kissed me again. Shorter this time, but still lovely. He handed me a folded slip of paper on which he'd written his address and phone number. Underneath, he'd added, "Don't be a stranger."

I smiled and promised I wouldn't. But I lost the paper before I went home. It was probably for the best, though. Suzanne told me Marcus was killed in a car accident a few years later.

17

Alabama Negro Shot in Back, Dies in Hospital
Chicago Defender – Monday, July 19, 1965

> *My mama has made bread*
> *and grampaw has come*
> *and everybody is drunk*
> *and dancing in the kitchen*
> *and singing in the kitchen*
> *of these is good times.*
> ~Lucille Clifton, "Good Times"

I came down for breakfast the next morning to find Nana pouring cake batter into a Bundt cake pan. I was still wearing the previous night's smile and thinking about Marcus. Nana set the mixing bowl, cake beaters, and spoon on the table in front of me.

"Breakfast! Eat up," she said. "And wipe that silly smile off your face."

I grinned and ran my finger around the edge of the bowl. I'd never had cake batter for breakfast, but it was definitely the breakfast of champions.

"Did you wash your hands?" she asked.

I looked down at my hands. I'd just gotten out of bed. What did she think I'd been doing with my hands in my sleep? But I got up and did as I was told just as Pompa came in from the backyard. The smell of spiced meat and barbeque sauce drifted in behind him. He lumbered through the kitchen and into the living room. A few seconds later, the television came to life, and the springs in the sofa groaned under his weight.

"Willa," he called out.

"What it is, Herbie?"

"Bring me a Coke in a glass with some ice, would ya?"

Nana smirked toward the kitchen door. I got up to get Pompa's Coke. She shook her head and pointed me back to my seat.

"You must be out of your damn mind," Nana shouted back. "You better get your ass up and get your own damn Coke in a glass with some ice. What do you think I'm doing in here? Sitting on my damn thumbs?"

"Well, then send the girl in here with it."

"She's busy, too! Get on up, Herbie. You ain't got no maids in this house."

The sofa springs groaned again, and Pompa stomped into the room, pretending to be mad, even though he couldn't help smiling.

"I don't know what's wrong with you, woman! You standing right here in front of the damn refrigerator, and there ain't nothin' wrong with this child's legs. How hard would it have been for you to—"

"You want to finish cooking dinner?" Nana asked, throwing her hand on her hip.

Pompa sniffed the air and harrumphed. "I don't smell nothin' cookin' in here. Seem to me, all we gon' have is a bunch of meat. So you must be in here sittin' on your thumbs jaw-jackin' with this little girl."

"Go on now, Herbie, before you make me hurt you."

Nana picked up the butcher knife and winked at me. Pompa

bucked his eyes and threw his hands up in surrender. Then he got a bottle of Coke from the refrigerator and filled a glass with ice. On his way out the door, he turned to Nana and said, "One day I'm gon' be gone and you gon' wish you'd a got me that bottle of Coke."

When he left, Nana sat down at the table with me. "See what you have to look forward to? Forty-five years with that man and never a dull moment. I wouldn't have it any other way, though. When it's time for you to get married, remember you don't just have to love him, you have to like him a whole hell of a lot, too."

"If I ever get married," I mumbled into the batter spoon.

"Awww. Don't you worry. You'll get married someday. And listen, I don't care what your mother says. I see the truth. I've been watching you all summer. If you was that way, I woulda seen it and we'd be having an entirely different conversation. Lord knows, life is hard enough for us without making it more complicated by adding being a homo on top of it."

"Homo?" I asked.

"Homosexual. That's what they call them kinda people. It just don't make no kinda sense to me why some man would choose to be all up under another man. Girls licking on other girls and all that foolishness. God gon' make 'em pay, though. God gon' make 'em pay."

I wanted to ask Nana what she meant by girls licking on other girls. Like kissing licking? Or, actual licking? It seemed like a strange thing for anyone to want to do. But Nana was on a roll. I could tell she'd been wanting to get that all out since I got there. I was thrilled she waited to see for herself first. Momma could take a page from her book.

"Thank you, Nana," was all I could manage to say.

"For what?"

"For waiting to see for yourself."

"You think I pay attention to anything yo' momma says? She's as nutty as a fruitcake. You mark my words, granddaughter. You're going to look up one day, and the man of your dreams is going to be standing there, just like Herbie was for me. We've been through a lot, seen a lot, and we did it together. It don't get much better than that. So, you wanna tell me about the boy you met last night?"

I see Nana wasn't the only one with a big mouth. The silly smile struck again. "His name is Marcus. He was really nice. He even taught me how to skate."

"You didn't know how to skate?"

"Not like they do here."

Nana laughed. "You got that right. Don't nobody know how to skate like we do." She got up and turned the flame down on the collard greens. "Listen, I'm going to lay these old bones down for a little bit. When the timer goes off, take the cake out."

I cleaned off the table, counters, and wiped off the refrigerator, then swept the floor. When I finished, I washed and peeled the potatoes on the sink. I was cutting them up when I heard a familiar voice coming from the living room. I stopped and listened. The voice quieted, so I went back to the potatoes. Then I heard it again. It sounded just like Daddy. The next time I heard it, I was confident it was Daddy, even though he wasn't supposed to be here. He was supposed to be at the airport in Los Angeles when I got off the plane the next day. I threw the dishtowel on the table and went tearing into the living room.

"Girl, stop all that runnin' in my house," Nana shouted from her bedroom. "Gon' make my damn cake fall."

"Daddy's here! Daddy's here!" I yelled, still running.

I almost knocked Daddy over, jumping into his arms.

"Hey, Ladybug! How'd you know I was here?"

"I could hear you."

"So much for me tiptoeing in on you."

He covered my face in kisses. "I sho' missed you."

"Save some for me," Momma said, gently pushing Daddy aside.

Momma smelled of Jean Nate and Djer Kiss talcum powder. I inhaled her and sighed happily. I didn't know it until that very minute, hadn't even thought about it, but I actually missed her.

"Well, well. Look what the cat dragged in," Nana said behind me.

"Hi, Ma," Momma said.

Momma and Nana didn't hug or anything. Just sort of stood there looking at each other.

Nana said, "We could have picked y'all up from the airport, you know. Must have cost you a fortune getting a cab to bring you in all the way. Hell, you lucky somebody even picked you up."

"I know somebody who knows somebody," Daddy said to keep the fight from starting up.

"Hey, Frank, how you doin'?" Nana said.

"Better now. Come over here and give me some suga."

Daddy covered Nana's face in kisses. She giggled like a schoolgirl, then swatted his shoulder with the dishtowel.

"Go on now, Frank. You gon' get me in trouble with my huzband."

"I done told you 'bout comin' on to my wife, boy!" Pompa said, trying to sound tough, but not moving from his place on the sofa.

Momma pushed me back with both arms. Her smile widened. I was wearing the khaki shorts and print tank top Suzanne gave me, and the tan sandals Nana bought when we went to Carson's. She took each one of my hands in hers and shook her head slowly as she admired my frosted pink fingernails.

"Well, as I live and breathe," she said.

"You like my outfit, Momma?"

I twirled around for her.

"I do. But what in the world did you do to your hair?"

"I like it like this. Suzanne taught me how to make Afro puffs."

"Hmm," she said. "Well, we'll fix it as soon as we get home."

"You'll do no such thing," Nana said. "Leave that child's hair alone. She did a fine job. She's gotta grow up sometime, Zora."

Nana turned my face up to hers and whispered, loud enough for Momma to hear, "You call me if she starts in on you about your hair. Okay?"

"Yes, Nana."

She swatted me playfully with the dishtowel, a sign that my time in grown folks' conversation had come to an end. I went and flopped down on the sofa next to Pompa. Momma, Daddy, and Nana stood in the entryway talking until Pompa told them to either get what they came for and go or close his goddamn door.

"I ain't payin' to cool the outdoors. My bill's high enough as it is."

"Oh hush, Herbie. You so cheap, you squeak when you walk."

"Say what you want, woman. Just close my goddamn door."

Daddy flopped down on the sofa next to me. "Looks like my baby went and grew up while she was away."

Nana pulled the screen door to and shut the front door behind her. Momma set her purse down in the chair next to the door.

"It looks like something else grew while we were away," she said.

I looked between Pompa and Daddy and folded my arms across my chest, self-consciously. Daddy laughed and took my hand to stand me up in front of him. He twirled me around to get a better look at my outfit and laughed in that "I'm so proud of my baby," fatherly kind of way.

Momma said. "Where's my niece?"

"With her boyfriend," I said.

"Boyfriend? Umph. Figures Maxine's child would be fast as greased lightning."

"Zora, mind your business. The girl's sixteen. Now, you come with me. I could use a hand getting dinner together. You ain't been here five good minutes, and you're already starting in on some-damn-body. Last time I checked, your child is sitting right over there, still trying to figure out what she's gon' do with them little titties stickin' out on her chest. Wait till them things get bigger, and boys start payin' her some attention!"

Momma sort of grunted and then walked off toward the kitchen. I heard her say, "Did you have that talk?"

Nana said, "I did not, and I had no intention of doing so. Ain't nothing wrong with that child that wasn't wrong with you at that age."

I smiled and leaned against Daddy's shoulder. We watched the ballgame with Pompa until Nana called us into the dining room for dinner.

* * * * * *

Black Chicagoans take three things as serious as a heart attack—God, baseball, and barbeque. I wasn't sure which ranked the highest, I just knew nothing was better than Pompa's barbecue. Not Daddy's bacon pancakes, or Nana's meatloaf, or Mrs. Robinette's anything. Pompa's ribs slid off the bone and melted in my mouth, and the barbeque sauce had just the right amount of sweet and tangy. Momma had to tell me several times to slow down and chew my food, but when I looked around the table, I wasn't the only one elbow deep in a pile of rib bones and chicken carcass. Nana told Momma to leave me alone. I smiled and kept shoveling food into my mouth.

"It's getting late," Momma said, looking down at her watch. "Shouldn't Suzanne be home by now?"

"Give it a rest, Zora. The girl's fine," Nana said.

"Who is this boy?" Momma wanted to know.

"I don't know, Zora. His name is Sean Marshall. Look, he comes from a well-off, nice family. That's all I needed to know."

"Sean Marshall? Not Peg and William Marshall's boy?"

"Yes. I think that's him."

"That boy is twenty years old if he's a day. What is Suzanne doing hanging around with a grown man?"

Nana and Momma stared at each other. Nana placed her fork down and turned to me. I knew better than to look away.

"Zayla? How old is this Sean boy?"

"I don't know."

"What do you mean, you don't know?" Nana demanded. "Weren't you out with him and his brother the other night? How old is his brother? What's his name?"

"Marcus. And I don't know. It didn't come up. He's in the ninth grade, though."

"Well, we'll see about this. You just wait until that hussy gets back," Nana said.

Momma, not one to pass up an opportunity to make someone's life miserable, said, "We can get to the bottom of it right now. I think I have Peg's number in my phone book. I can call her and—"

"Why don't we just enjoy our dinner and deal with Suzanne and whoever this Sean boy is later? Or, better yet, stay out of it," Daddy said.

"That's right," Pompa chimed in. "Stay out of it, Nosey Rosie."

Pompa ran his tongue around the bottom of his mouth and then pulled his lower denture out and placed it on the table next to his plate. He pulled a thick metal file out of his back pocket and picked the denture back up. I stopped eating and watched. I never saw him without his teeth before, and he looked funny sucking on his bottom lip and filing along the bottom edge of the denture as if he was sitting in the backyard whittling wood.

Pompa's whittling got Nana's attention. For a second I thought she might faint, until she slammed her hand on the table. Everyone jumped, except Pompa, who pushed his glasses up on his face and filed a little more off his fake gums. He blew on the denture and stuck it back in his mouth.

"Herbie! How many times have I asked you not to do that at the dinner table?"

Pompa ran his tongue around the bottom of his mouth again, chomped down a few times, and then took the teeth right back out. Nana slammed the table again.

"Herbie! Stop it now!"

"Leave me alone, woman. They hurt."

"Ooooohhh! Sometimes you make me so mad."

"Only sometimes? I must be losin' it," Pompa said.

He put his dentures in again, chomped down a few more times, ran his tongue around the top and bottom of his mouth, and nodded in satisfaction. He put the file back in his pocket, picked up a rib, and said to Daddy, "So, how'd things turn out after the burglary?" as if he was asking about the weather.

I stopped chewing. "Who got robbed? Did someone break into our house? Did they take anything from my room?"

"No, baby," Momma said. "They broke into the Mitchells' house. I keep telling Frank we need to start looking for a new house in Windsor Hills. You know, Ray Charles is having one built there as we speak?"

Daddy cut his eyes at her but didn't say anything.

"I know you don't like it when I bring up moving, but things definitely aren't getting any better."

I tried to feel sorry for Dee-Dee and her mom, and couldn't. Serves them right, I thought. God is always watching. I took a bite of chicken and chewed slowly while I relished the thought of someone sneaking into Dee-Dee's bedroom and stealing everything that mattered to her. Maybe the burglar hated Barbie dolls as much as I did, and snatched their heads off while he was at it. Or maybe he cut all her hair off, and then for good measure, stomped his foot down and crushed Barbie's dream house. I had to stifle the giggle that bubbled up at the thought of it all.

"You got someone watching the house while you're here? What's to stop someone from climbing through one of your windows?" Pompa asked.

"I had burglar bars put on," Daddy said.

"Burglar bars! Bars?" I shrieked. "Like in jail? What if there's a fire?"

"There won't be a fire."

"What if there is? How are we supposed to get out of the house?" Or, more to the point, how was I supposed to climb out of the window again?

"If there is a fire, the firemen will get us out. We'll be fine," Daddy said.

Burglar bars on our house? What had things come to? I'd never actually seen burglar bars before, but I imagined they would be black and thick and look exactly like the bars on the jail cells. Not that I'd ever seen a jail cell either, for that matter.

"Frank, I don't blame you for not wanting to sell and move out of your own community. That's the place that helped you become a man," Pompa interjected. "Believe me, that day I left Lynchburg was one of the hardest days of my life. If I had to do it all over again, though, I wouldn't change a thing. I had Jim Crow breathing down my neck. I was either gon' kill one of them rednecks or die swinging from a tree. You don't have that to worry about, so you should stay right where you are. That jumping up and leaving where we come from is going to be our downfall. If Malcolm said it once, he said it a thousand times. Desegregation is the worst thing to happen to the so-called Negro."

"Dr. King doesn't see it that way," Momma said.

"Dr. King? Ha! Dr. King is one of the biggest Uncle Toms goin'!" Daddy said. "He might be fighting for our rights, but he ain't doing nothin' for our freedom. For our equality. They gave us so-called access to the same education as their children on paper, but in reality, what has changed? It's been eleven years, and not a goddamn thing has changed."

"Damn right," Pompa added, chuckling. "These Chicago Negroes love them some Dr. King, but my money was on Malcolm X from the very start. If he was still here, he'da turned this country upside down on its head."

"Don't start, Herbie!"

"I'm not startin' nothin'. I believe the reason they givin' the folks in Watts such a hard time is 'cause they don't support Dr. King. Y'all been staunch Malcolm X supporters for years, haven't you?"

"That ain't got nothin' to do with nothin'," Nana chimed in. "White folks is givin' Negroes all over a hard time because they can. It don't matter who we follow. Whether it's King or Malcolm X. Hell, we could worship J. Edgar's ass, and they'd still investigate us to find out why. It don't matter. Long as we have all this melanin, they gon' give us a hard time. Ain't that right, Frank?"

"Sho' nuff. But think about what would have happened if the two of them, King and Malcolm, had joined forces ... man! Whitey would be tucking his tail and running for the border. My father always used to say that even a steady flow of water across a boulder will wear it down. I believe the same can be said about people. It's only a matter of time. Leaving Watts would be running, and I'm not one for running."

Suzanne crawled in my bed a little after midnight. Again, smelling of whiskey and cigarettes. By the time I rolled over to give her a piece of my mind, she was knocked out and snoring softly into her pillow. Although I wished I could have spent my last night with Suzanne instead of listening to Momma complain about her the whole time, I was grateful to have her next to me one last time.

* * * * *

"Come on, Zay. We have to go," Daddy called up to me.

Suzanne and I skipped down the stairs, hand in hand, and climbed in the backseat of the car between Nana and Momma. I let Suzanne go first so I could sit next to Nana, who thought it was the cutest thing she'd ever seen, how close Suzanne and I had gotten. Momma had the nerve to give us that look that was one part suspicious and one part disapproving. We ignored her, talking nonstop about our adventures all summer and how we were going to miss each other and how we couldn't wait to see each other again. Momma gazed out the window, lost in her own thoughts. Pompa and Daddy spent the drive talking about baseball and who they pegged to win the World Series.

At the gate, Suzanne and I found a spot away from Momma. For a while we just sat there, holding hands, watching the planes take off and land. Suzanne spoke first.

"So. We never got a chance to talk about it. You liked Marcus, right?"

I nodded.

"Well, he liked you, too."

"It's a good thing I liked him. I don't know what I would have done if I hadn't. I guess that would have proved I was a bulldagger."

"Can you not call yourself that? It sounds so ugly! And if you hadn't liked him, then at least you wouldn't have had to wonder anymore. It's the wondering that's worse. And, who knows, maybe you get home and realize you like girls after all and that Marcus was just a blip on your radar. Who cares? At least you'll know. Then you can decide what to do about it."

"I like to know that I liked him because that means I will like other boys, and Momma will be happy."

"You know what your problem is? You listen to Aunt Zora's bull-

shit too much. You have to start making some of your own decisions. You're gonna be a teenager next year. She can't live her life and
yours, too."

"I love you, Suzanne. And I'm really glad I finally got to meet
you."

Tears pooled in her eyes. She smiled, and a few rolled out. "I love
you, too, Zayla. I just wish you didn't live all the way in California.
I'm gonna miss you so much. I'm really sorry I wasn't there with you
last night. I'm not good with goodbyes. I almost didn't come today,
but I would have hated myself if I hadn't."

The overhead speaker clicked to life to announce TWA Flight 281
to Los Angeles was now boarding at Gate 12.

"Come on, Zayla. Our flight is boarding," Momma said, as if I
couldn't hear.

"Just remember," Suzanne said. "Only you are in charge of your
destiny."

"Yeah. I am, huh? She can't tell me what to do anymore."

"That's right. She can't tell you what to do, but she can ask you to
do things. And if she asks, then you have to be respectful and do as
she asks. It's only fair."

We hugged, and this time I kissed her on the forehead. We joined
everyone at the gate. I gave Nana a great big hug and let her cover
my face in kisses.

Pompa clapped me on the back and said, "See ya later, kid. It was
kinda nice having you around. Next time, come with some money.
You eat too much."

I smiled and wrapped my arms around his waist. He leaned over
and kissed the top of my head, and that's when the waterworks
started. First, just Suzanne and I were crying, then Nana started up.

On the plane, I took the seat closest to the window. Momma sat
next to me, and Daddy took the aisle seat so he could have room to
stretch out. We were having a good time at first, me telling them

how much fun I had and all the things Suzanne and I experienced, but in usual Momma fashion, she started in on me. First, with my hair and how she didn't care what Nana said, I was her child, and she was raising me, and if she thought my hair looked better pressed, then that's how it was going to be. Ordinarily, Daddy would have jumped in and tried to help, but he didn't. I noticed something different between them since I'd been gone. She seemed more at peace, and he seemed relieved, but cautious.

"I like her hair like that," he said.

"I know you do, baby. But I think for now, she needs to keep getting it straightened. She'll be more acceptable."

Daddy went back to reading his book without another word. I turned away and stared out the window at the clouds, wondering how it might feel to be light enough to walk on them. Or float through them. Or, if I was lucky, I could just go sailing through them and plummet to the earth below. Anything was better than listening to Momma carry on, because when she finished with my hair, she started in on my clothes.

"I didn't say anything at the house because I didn't feel like arguing with your grandmother, but I will not allow to wear you these cheap chippy clothes. Soon as we get home, I've got to get you some of much better quality."

She reached over and rubbed the material of my pants and shirt between her fingers.

"Yeah, see. This material won't last no time. Two or three washings, and it'll be just as threadbare as you please. And since you are not sixteen, young lady, I have no intention of letting you wear whatever you want. You are going to dress your age. Do you hear me?"

Everyone on the plane heard her. I sighed and mumbled, "Yes, Momma."

Daddy didn't look up once.

The stewardess came over and asked if we wanted eggs, sausage, and toast or pancakes and sausage for breakfast. Daddy and I ordered the pancakes. Momma got the eggs. The stewardess leaned over and said, "You have a beautiful daughter."

Before I could even feel good about it, Momma said, "Just like her momma."

I looked over at the exit door and wondered what would happen if I opened it. Would it really suck everyone out of the plane, or maybe her? She elbowed me and said, "Don't you hear someone talking to you?"

I mumbled, "Thank you," to the back of the stewardess's head and refrained from telling Momma to mind her own damn business. Suzanne was right. I was tired of Momma trying to live my life for me, and I decided it was time she stopped. I told myself when I got home, I was going to be in control of my life and make my own decisions no matter what she said. If I wanted to wear Afro puffs, then that's exactly what I was going to do. And if I wanted to wear the clothes Nana and Suzanne gave me, I would do that, too. Even if it meant I had to go round for round with Momma every day, I wasn't giving up.

The stewardess pushed her cart up to our row and asked if we cared for anything to drink. Daddy declined and leaned back in his seat. Momma asked for a cup of coffee, and I asked for another glass of orange juice. As soon as the stewardess walked off, Momma started in on me again.

"I don't know what Maxine is teaching that fast-tail hussy, Suzanne, but whatever she taught you this summer, you better forget by the time this plane lands. I better not ever catch you sneaking around behind a nineteen-year-old. At that age, he's a man. The nerve of Suzanne! She better be glad your father stopped me because I would have called the police and had that boy arrested for statutory rape. One day Maxine is going to look up, and Suzanne's belly is going to be poked out, and the father will go on about his business because that's what they do. Momma's baby, Poppa's maybe. I won't stand for any of that in my house, do you hear me?"

"Make up your mind. You don't want me to like girls. Now you don't want me to like boys either?"

The words were out before I could stop them. I couldn't take them back. I wasn't so sure I wanted to. I bit my bottom lip and waited for all hell to break loose. Momma stared at me so hard I thought she might have an aneurysm. A smile tugged at the corners of Daddy's mouth. He closed his eyes and turned his head away from us. I waited for her to slap me.

"What did you say to me?" she asked.

"You heard me."

The air pressure in the cabin must have had something to do with my temporary insanity. Momma sort of harrumphed and told me to wait until we got home. She leaned over until we were nose to nose.

"You better be damn glad we're on this plane. If you ever talk to me like that again, I will slap you to sleep. Do you hear me?"

I didn't answer. Momma snatched my shirt and turned my face to her, but I refused to respond. She rolled her eyes and mumbled something under her breath. I'd won. Momma knew I wasn't afraid of her anymore. I wasn't so sure that was a good or a bad thing, but at that moment there wasn't much she could do about it. I took Daddy's cue and pretended to nod off. Pretty soon I was fast asleep.

18

U.S. Planes Attack Near Red China
L.A. Times – Friday, July 23, 1965

> *i have returned*
> *leaving behind me*
> *all those hide and*
> *seek faces peeling*
> *with Freudian dreams.*
> ~Sonia Sanchez, "homecoming"

It felt good to be back home until we turned into "The Circle." I could see the white burglar bars fused to the side windows of our house. Even the front door with the glass motif hid behind a white security door with vertical prison bars.

Daddy pulled in the driveway and said, "It's not so bad, right?"

I looked from him to the house and frowned. I couldn't say anything nice, so I didn't say anything at all.

"Can I go see Malik?" I asked.

I scrambled out of the car and ran all the way down to Malik's house and rang the bell. Evangeline was sitting on her front porch, in her usual disheveled and neglected state. Her tattered housecoat hung haphazardly off one shoulder. I was starting to get the feeling that whatever Momma, Daddy, or both had done to her might explain why she was so crazy. I just didn't appreciate that she took her frustration out on me whenever she could. The minute she saw me she stood up and shouted, "What are you starin' at you, little bastard?"

She went into her house and slammed the door behind her. At the same time, Aunt Evelyn opened the door and screamed. I jumped. She yanked me in the house, pulling and tugging me like an octopus. She wrapped her tentacles around me and almost squeezed the life out of me.

"Let me see them," she said, and pushed me back.

By the time I realized what she was talking about, she'd already snatched my sweater open. "Well, I'll be," she said, and laughed.

I buttoned my sweater. "Don't worry," Uncle Bill said from his favorite chair next to the television. "One day you'll have children of your own to embarrass. Welcome home!"

I promised myself I'd never embarrass my children. No matter what. Then wrapped my arms around Uncle Bill's neck and waited for the kisses that would follow. Aunt Evelyn told Malik to come out of his room. He came to the end of the hall and just stood there. Something looked different about him. The old moody Malik was still there but hidden in the shadows was something else. It wasn't the couple of inches he'd shot up in the past month. Or the fact that he was beginning to smell himself, as Aunt Evelyn would say. I'm sure it had a lot to do with the fuzz growing above his upper lip.

"Quit staring at me, big head!" I said.

"Man, you sure have changed. What happened to you?" His eyes walked down my chest and lingered there. "Nice outfit," he added.

He slipped his arm around my shoulder, something he'd done a thousand times before, right before putting me in a headlock of some sort. So, I braced myself for an armpit in the face or to have my air supply cut off until I screamed. But he didn't do any of that. He pulled me close and sighed. I relaxed into him. It really felt good to be home.

"Miss me?" he whispered.

"A little bit. You miss me?"

"Nope."

"Liar."

Aunt Evelyn ushered us out of the house. The Robinette's were having a birthday party for Marquette Frye, and everyone was invited. It should have been my coming-home party, but I chose not to make a fuss about it. All I cared about was getting some of Mrs. Robinette's good cooking. Malik and I raced off down the street.

"What's happenin', world traveler? Welcome home!" Roger said, opening the door for us.

He gave me a one-armed hug and walked off. Malik sauntered off with Roger without even a backward glance at me. I followed my nose to the kitchen and found Mrs. Robinette pouring macaroni from a colander into a pot of cheese sauce.

"Well, will you look at what the cat drug in? I haven't seen you in a month of Sundays. Come on over here so I can love up on you."

I inhaled the peppermint and Watkins liniment and smiled. She kissed the top of my head, then pushed me back.

"Look at your little nubs," she laughed. "Now, sit down right there and tell me all about your summer."

I told her all about Chicago, and Nana and Pompa, and their house. Periodically, she would interrupt me to hand her the salt, or crack a few eggs, or get something out of the fridge for her.

"What time does the party start?" I asked.

"As soon as the guest of honor arrives."

I couldn't wait. Mrs. Robinette had gone all out for Marquette's birthday. In addition to the macaroni and cheese and the potato salad, there was a peach cobbler, 7-Up cake, lemon pound cake, pork ribs, beef ribs, rib tips, fried chicken, collard greens, cabbage, black-eyed peas, and green beans with potatoes.

* * * * * *

We sat around for over an hour, waiting for the guest of honor to arrive. People started complaining about being hungry and begging Mr. Robinette to stop being so chintzy with the booze.

"If you ain't gon' feed us, the least you could do is give us a little taste."

"Ain't no sense in drankin' ever'thang up 'fore the party even gets started. You wanna get drunk, go get your own," he said, standing guard over the bar.

At eight o'clock, Marquette finally decided to grace us with his presence, along with his parents, Rena and Walter. The Fryes were quite a pair. Mrs. Rena was dark and intense-looking, like Marquette, but petite and sturdy with shiny shoulder-length hair. A pair of black-framed cat's-eye glasses rested on the bridge of her nose and slid down whenever she bent her head. Mr. Walter was a foot taller and filled out his brown polyester suit the way a sausage fills its skin. The patches of black hair along his jawline contradicted the thick, curly salt and pepper hair on his head.

Marquette sauntered into the living room and threw up his arms. On cue, Roger announced, "All right, y'all. Now the party can begin," and cranked up the music. Marvin Gaye blared through the speakers. "You are my pride . . ."

I went over and wished Marquette a happy birthday. He gave me a sideways hug and said, "Thanks, little girl."

He tipped my chin up and kissed my cheek.

"I told you I wasn't gon' bite you. I never said I wouldn't kiss you. And you look very nice, by the way."

He walked off to greet some of his other guests. Mr. and Mrs.

Frye worked the room like seasoned partygoers. He laughed and slapped hands with the men. She exchanged tidbits with the women on raising children and dealing with the demands of their husbands.

"Men! Girl, they're all the same. They just have different addresses," Mrs. Frye said.

"Ain't it the truth?" Mrs. Robinette said and laughed.

Mr. Walter glided over and took Mrs. Rena's hand. He pulled her close, and they did a little dance across the room. He whispered something in her ear. She threw her head back and laughed. They danced a while longer, and then he spun her away toward the kitchen. She came back a few seconds later with a beer for him and a glass of lemonade for herself.

I excused myself to the bathroom. When I came out, Dee-Dee was sitting in the living room talking to Malik. He looked like he'd swallowed something worse than castor oil. Dee-Dee looked like she'd taken pleasure spooning it up for him. My stomach dropped at the sight of her.

"Hi, Zayla! I like your outfit," she said.

I rolled my eyes and went outside. James and Lucius were kneeling in the dirt on the side of the house, playing marbles. I ran home to get my marbles, only to find the door locked. That never would have happened before the burglar bars. We always left the doors unlocked until it was time to go to sleep. I kicked the door and ran back across the street. Dee-Dee and Malik came out on the porch as I rejoined James and Lucius. James told me I could play as long as I promised to return every marble I won. I agreed, with my fingers crossed behind my back.

"Zayla, come here. I gotta talk to you," Malik said.

"Wait! I gotta get James' big Shooter first."

And just like that, I slipped right back into my regular self. I knew I wasn't supposed to be out in the grass in my new outfit, flipping marbles off my thumb. But I wasn't that prim and proper girl, and I never would be. You might as well quit pretending, I told my-self. I'm the girl that likes to play marbles and get dirty. And, thanks to Suzanne, I wanted to look good doing it. So, without a second thought, I kneeled down prepared to take James' big Shooter once and for all. I wasn't leaving the game without it. When it was my turn, I aimed with all my concentration. The marble flipped off my thumb and landed with a clink. I jumped up, screaming and dancing around.

"That's what you get for letting her play," Lucius said. "She always takes our Shooters."

"Shut up, Lucius," I said and reached down and snatched his Shooter just for good measure.

"Hey! Give that back!" he shouted.

"Make me."

He lunged. I didn't move out of the way fast enough. Before I could stop myself we'd tangled ourselves into a ball of arms and legs, and then we were laughing.

"Y'all cut out all that roughhousing and go wash your hands. It's time to eat."

Mrs. Robinette ushered us into the dining room. We formed a circle around the table and joined hands. Mr. Robinette stood at the head of the table and waited for everyone to settle down. Then he bowed his head. I bowed mine and closed one eye. The other eye searched the room for Malik. He was sandwiched between Daddy and Uncle Bill a few feet away. One of his eyes popped open, and he jerked his head in the direction of the bathroom. I nodded in re-sponse and caught Dee-Dee watching us out of the corner of my eye. I opened my other eye and frowned. She smiled smugly and closed her eyes as Mr. Robinette prayed his way to Amen.

"And thank you, Lord, for getting our baby girl Zayla home safely. In your name, we pray."

"Amen," we all said.

Roger cranked the music back up while Malik and I made a bee-line to the bathroom.

"What is it? And it better be good!" I demanded.

Malik sat down on the toilet and looked up at me. I leaned closer. He looked like he was about to cry. I asked him what was wrong, just as a tear fell from his eye. I knew then something terrible had happened. I started to pelt him with questions, but he told me to calm down and be quiet.

"What?"

"Sssshhh. Somebody'll hear us. I'm gonna tell you. Give me a minute. Damn!"

I counted to three and got up. He grabbed my pant leg, pulled me back down, and grabbed my shoulders.

"You better not kiss me!" I said, although I could tell he wasn't thinking about kissing me.

"Ain't nobody thinkin' about kissin'! That's what started all this in the first place.

"Started what?"

"I did it with Melody," he whispered.

"You did WHAT with Melody?" I asked, getting frustrated because I knew he couldn't be talking about having sex with Melody. There was no way he was stupid enough to do that with *her*.

Malik slammed his hand against my mouth. "Ssshh."

I shoved it away. "Is that why you didn't write me but once all summer?"

"Stop playing. This is serious."

"How? Where'd you do it? Why'd you do it with *her*?"

"Could you stop with all the questions for a minute? Did you even hear what I said? Melody might be pregnant. That means I might be a father. Do you know what my dad is gonna do to me when he finds out?"

I knew I wasn't hard of hearing, and I definitely hadn't heard him say she might be pregnant. He was right about one thing. Uncle Bill was going to kill him.

"How do you know she might be pregnant?"

"Dee-Dee just told me."

"You're going to believe her? She's a liar."

I stood up and pulled Malik to his feet.

"Come on. Let's go get some food and then we can figure out what to do. But I bet you Dee-Dee is lying. Don't worry about it, okay? Melody isn't hardly pregnant. She's too young. She probably hasn't even had her period yet."

Tears streamed down Malik's cheeks. I rinsed off a washcloth and handed it to him. He wiped his face and tried to smile. I told him everything was going to be okay, and hoped I was right. I didn't know if Melody had her period or not, but maybe she was a late bloomer. After all, I hadn't gotten mine yet and we were the same age. I would have asked God to make it okay, but I knew He didn't listen to me.

* * * * * *

The food was almost gone by the time we came out of the bathroom. Mrs. Robinette saw us staring at the nearly empty pan of macaroni and cheese and told us to come with her. We followed her into the kitchen, me fighting to hold back my own tears and Malik still teary-eyed, until she opened the oven and pulled out two plates of food and handed them to us.

"I don't know where y'all disappeared off to, but I knew you'd have a fit if you came back and all the food was gone. Eat up. There's more where that came from."

We thanked her and found a seat at the kids' table. Malik sat next to James and Lorraine, leaving the only other empty space between Dee-Dee and Lucius. Dee-Dee pulled the chair out for me. I took the chair over to Malik and told James and Lorraine to slide down to make room for me. Lucius pushed my plate to me, and everyone else didn't even try to conceal their shock at my blatant disregard for Dee-Dee. It felt so good to show them she didn't mean anything to me. The new Zayla was back.

"What was Chicago like?" Lorraine asked.

I shared my adventures with Suzanne, Nana, and Pompa. They wanted to know what it was like riding on an airplane. I pulled my wings out of my pocket and passed them around the table. Malik barely looked at them before he stuck them in his pocket. Ordinarily, I would have made him give them back to me, but I knew he had a lot on his mind with Melody maybe being pregnant and all.

Lucius said he was going to live in Kentucky when he grew up. He said he didn't know anyone there: "I just like the way Kentucky sounds." James shoved Lucius upside his head and told him to stop being stupid. James' mother just so happened to come in the room at that exact moment and told James to stop being so mannish or she was going to slap the snot out of him. We all cracked up, including James. The idea of being slapped so hard snot would come out your nose was pretty funny.

When James Brown came on, Daddy grabbed Momma by the hand and pulled her out to the center of the living room. Uncle Bill and Aunt Evelyn and Mr. and Mrs. Frye followed them. And to everyone's surprise, Mrs. Robinette grabbed Mr. Robinette. At first, he just sidestepped and pretended he was too embarrassed to dance in front of us.

"Oh, Walter. Quit pussy-footin' around and let your hair down for a change," Mrs. Robinette shouted over the music.

James Brown pleaded, "Please, honey. Please." The rest of us egged Mr. Robinette on shouting, "Cut the rug," "Let it loose," "Come on, let's see what you got," until he started wagging his hips from side to side. All of a sudden he kicked his leg out in James Brown fashion and spun around. The whole room went crazy. He grabbed Mrs. Robinette's hand and spun her around. He shimmied up to her and did it again. We were so busy watching the Robinette's, no one even noticed that Evangeline had entered the house until Mrs. Robinette let out a startled scream.

Evangeline hadn't bothered combing her hair, and she was still in that crazy-looking housecoat. She didn't speak. She just stood there staring, at no one in particular. Momma cut her eyes at Daddy and walked into the kitchen.

"Bitch!" Evangeline shouted to Momma's back.

James Brown screamed, "Honey, please!"

Roger jumped up and turned off the music. The air stopped moving. Daddy looked between the kitchen door and Evangeline as if he didn't know whom he should deal with first. Mr. Robinette whispered something in his ear, and Daddy went in the kitchen with Momma. Mrs. Robinette went over to Evangeline.

"I don't want no trouble," Evangeline said. "I just came to get what's mine."

"Don't nothing in here belong to you. This is my house," Mrs. Robinette said.

"I just want to talk to him. You know what happened wasn't right."

"Now is not the time for all that. You need to go on home."

"Please, Vonelle. Can I just sit with you and talk?"

"Zayla?" Momma called.

I didn't respond. She called again. On the third time, I got up and walked in the opposite direction.

"Zayla! Do you hear your mother calling you? Don't make her call you again," Mrs. Robinette said sternly.

"I need to use the bathroom," I said.

I didn't know what Momma wanted but I knew it wasn't to tell me anything I wanted to know.

"Well, when you're finished, get in there and see what your mother wants."

"Yes, ma'am."

I had no intentions of going to see what Momma wanted. Instead, I went down the hall to Roger's room and closed the door behind me. I snuck out the door leading to the backyard and tiptoed over to the back porch. I peeked through the window. Momma busied herself cleaning the dishes in the sink. Daddy sat at the table smoking a cigarette. After everyone was gone, Mrs. Robinette came in the kitchen and shooed Momma back to the table.

Daddy asked if everything was okay. Mrs. Robinette laughed.

"If everything was okay, we wouldn't have had any interruptions this evening. When someone you love hurts you, you have two choices: hold on to the anger and resentment, or forgive yourself, forgive them, and move on with your life. You were hurt, Zora. No one denies that. Any woman in your position may not have ever gotten over it. But you made a choice to stay, and by staying, you chose to forgive and move on. Except, you haven't actually done that now, have you?"

"I have forgiven him," Momma said. "If I hadn't, how could I have stayed with him all these years later? I just know I'll never forget what he did."

"If you can't forget it, baby, then you haven't forgiven him. You're just paying him lip service."

"It's okay, Vonelle. I'm gonna handle it," Daddy said.

"It's too late to handle anything. You need to fix it. What you did wasn't right, and you know I love you like my own child. You need to go down there and apologize, and you need to ask for forgiveness. And, Zora, you need to stop blaming yourself for something that wasn't your fault. Here you are acting like things are perfect in your home when you and everybody else knows they aren't.

"If you don't watch out, you're going to make that beautiful little girl of yours hate you. She's doing the best she can trying to find herself, and instead of you helping her, you too busy standing judge and jury over her, pushing her away, because you can't let go of the past. Your sins are not hers. You keep on and you're going to lose her. So stop expecting perfection. Ain't none of us perfect, so how in the hell can you expect her to be? Now, take that child home, and the two of you go deal with your shit and don't you ever let it come to my doorstep again. You got that?"

"Yes, ma'am," Momma and Daddy said.

I ran back in the house, down the hall, and dived onto the sofa. I pretended to be sleeping.

"Come on, bug. It's time to go," Daddy said, shaking me.

I rolled over and sat up.

"What was Miss Evangeline talking about?" I asked.

"I'll explain it to you when you're old enough to understand."

"When is that going to be?"

"I don't know. Keep living. I'll let you know when you get there."

19

Draft May Expand

L.A. Times – Saturday, July 24, 1965

> *If there be sorrow*
> *let it be*
> *for things undone...*
> *undreamed*
> *unrealized*
> *unattained*
> *to these add one;*
> *Love withheld...*
> *...restrained.*
> ~Mari Evans, "If There Be Sorrow"

"Come on, Zayla! Get up. We have someplace to be."

I flipped one eye open so it could read the clock. Seven a.m. What was so damn important that I had to bear witness at such a ridiculous summer hour? I wondered. Nothing, that's what. I decided I wasn't getting up. Plus, I was still upset about the night before. It was bad enough Miss Evangeline, Momma, and Daddy played out their drama like an episode of *General Hospital* in front of everyone. But on top of that, we went home before I got to enjoy dessert. Even though I hadn't quite put it all together, I knew that whatever was bothering Miss Evangeline, Momma was the cause of it.

Momma shouted for me to get up off and on for fifteen minutes. The next thing I knew she'd snatched the covers off, her eyes black with anger. I wondered if a person could literally blow a gasket and what it might look like. Then I figured I'd better get up or I'd find out. I started to pull the covers back just as she shouted:

"Get up! Now."

As much as I knew I should get up, I also knew I was tired of being told what to do.

"No!" I shouted.

I pulled the covers up over my head in defiance. My summer. My life. My choice.

"What did you say?" she asked, snatching the covers.

"No!" I shouted again. "Why do I have to get up?"

She snatched the covers again. I held on tight. She yanked my wrist toward her and twisted the skin between her hands. I yelled and held onto the covers even tighter, ignoring the burn she'd left on my skin.

"Well, I'll be goddamned," she mumbled under her breath.

"Don't use the Lord's name in vain. God can hear you, you know!" I shouted through my bedcovers.

"Frank! Come in here and deal with this heffa before I kill her!"

"Zora, we agreed you wouldn't talk like that," Daddy said quietly.

Momma harrumphed and stomped off. Daddy came in and sat on the edge of my bed.

"Will you please cut your mother some slack?"

I pulled the covers back and said, "I will the minute she does."

He seemed to be tickled by the new defiant me. He'd always told me to stand up for myself. I'm sure he meant with other people, but who better to get started on than Momma? I needed to be in control of my life.

"I'm tired of her telling me what to do. I'm old enough to do whatever I want," I added.

That's when the humor drained out of Daddy's face. I didn't wait for what would come next. I threw the covers off, hopped out of bed, and ran to the bathroom.

When I finished washing up, I went back to my room and ignored the pink pinafore lying on my bed. I slipped on a pair of shorts and one of the shirts Suzanne gave me instead. This one had red and blue flowers embroidered around the bottom. I knew Momma would hate it just because I chose it, which is why I marched into the living room and announced I was ready to go. Momma sent me back to my room to put on the dress she'd laid out for me. I reminded her that I was old enough to dress myself.

Daddy stepped out of the kitchen. He didn't smile or say a word. He just gave me that look that said I was letting my mouth write a check my ass couldn't cash. Tail tucked between my legs, I went to my room and didn't come back out.

"What's taking you so damn long?" Momma asked from my doorway a few minutes later.

When she saw that I hadn't changed, she threw the dress at me and told me to put it on. I threw it on the floor. She grabbed my arm and gave it a good squeeze. It hurt like hell, but I refused to react. She reached down and threw the dress at me. I grabbed a handful of the bottom half to stop her from throwing it at me again. She yanked and I yanked and we yanked, until the seams gave way at the bodice and the dress ripped in two. I threw my half on the floor and folded my arms across my chest. Momma stood there with her half in one hand as the other hand slowly curled into a fist. She screamed for Daddy to come deal with me. And, once again, Daddy appeared in my doorway.

"Look what she did! This is the only pink dress she has, and look at it." Momma screamed, shoving the dress in Daddy's chest.

I tried to push my half under the bed with my foot and gazed up at Daddy sheepishly. He shook his head and closed his eyes for a moment. Then he reached under my bed and got the other half.

"Is there a reason she has to wear *this* dress?" Daddy asked.

Momma looked at him like he had two heads.

"Yes!" she screamed. "I told you. She has to wear pink. She has to wear pink! It's what all the girls are wearing on the first day."

"I have a pink dress," I said. "My first day at what?"

"Where is it? Go get it," Daddy said, ignoring my question.

I went to my closet and dug through my suitcase.

"My first day at what?" I asked again.

I found the scarf and hand fan I bought for Momma on Maxwell Street, and shoved them behind a row of shoeboxes. At the rate she was going, she might never see these gifts. I dug around some more until I found the pink sundress Nana bought when we went to Marshall Field's. At the time it felt a little too frilly, with the big ruffle around the hem. Not to mention it was a shade or two lighter than a bottle of Pepto-Bismol. But the shoulder straps crisscrossed in the back and the cotton was soft against my skin. I also liked the way I looked in it. If I had to wear a pink dress, it would be one of my choosing. I opened my mouth to say so, and decided against it. I just held up the dress so they could see it. It was a little wrinkled, but not too bad that I couldn't wear it. Daddy nodded his head in approval. Momma snatched the dress out of my hand.

"It needs ironing," she growled.

Daddy peeled it from her grip and left the room with Momma screaming behind him, "Frank. Please. Don't waste your time ironing that sad sack of a dress. I'll find something else."

A few minutes later he returned and handed me the freshly ironed dress.

"Put it on," he said.

"It's not the right kind of dress, Frank. It's too casual," Momma whined.

"It's okay," he said to Momma. To me he said, "Put on the dress." Then he turned back to Momma and said, in the same voice he used when he had the patience to cajole me into something, "It'll be okay, baby. It's all she has right now, and you don't want to be late. It's her first day. I'm sure they'll understand."

"My first day to do what?" I asked again.

Momma shot me a look. Daddy gave her shoulder a little squeeze.

"My first day to what?" I demanded again, my voice a little louder.

They both looked at me then.

"Zayla. Please. Put. The. Dress. On. Okay? Don't ask any more questions," Daddy said.

"But where—"

Daddy put his finger up to his lips to quiet me. "Don't say another word. Put on the dress and go with your mother."

"Why?" I asked. "Where am I going?"

Daddy closed his eyes again and this time when he opened them, he looked like he was out of gas and I was two seconds from a good talking-to. Which always hurt me more than it hurt him. Daddy never spanked me. The slave masters beat the enslaved Africans as a control mechanism. He'd promised himself he'd never spank me as a result. He never did either. He just mastered the art of nonverbal communication until he was forced to verbally communicate.

"Ladybug, you can't get what you want acting like this. Not in this house."

"Why not? The whole summer I got dressed in whatever I felt like wearing, *and* I combed my own hair, *and* Nana didn't complain one time."

"That was Nana. Grandparents are funny that way. I'm sho' she let you do a lot of things she wouldn't have let your mother do at your age. And, this ain't Nana's house."

We didn't speak for a while after that. Before too long, I got up and slipped on the sundress. In the bathroom I parted my hair down the middle and made two ponytails. I twisted the hair and snapped two pink barrettes on each end. Ready and acceptable by Momma's standards, I got in the car. Daddy walked Momma to the door and gave her a long kiss. "I love you," he said.

Her back was to me. I'm sure she said, "I love you, too, with all my heart and every ounce of my being," in that whispered way I'd hear late at night when they thought I was sleeping. She'd be a fool not to love Daddy that much. I'd heard plenty women say Daddy was a "good" man. Some were bold enough to call into Daddy's show and say it on the air for everyone, including Momma, to hear. It used to drive Momma crazy because she often wondered if those women were speaking from experience. On those days, as soon as Daddy's key hit the lock, the fight was on. Daddy eventually grew tired of her accusations and told Momma if it bothered her that much, she should stop listening to the show. "If you choose to listen, then you deal with your hurt feelings on your own," he told her.

Momma was a lot of things, but stupid wasn't one of them. She knew she had a "good" man, and that's why she knew not to push Daddy too hard. I'd once overheard her and Aunt Evelyn talking about how Miss Evangeline pushed her "good" man away. I wondered, then, if Daddy was that "good" man. From the way they were talking the night before, it could have been. I just couldn't see Daddy with Miss Evangeline – ever. He didn't look at her the way he looked at Momma. He wouldn't buy Miss Evangeline beautiful gowns and jewelry the way he did for Momma. Or leave love notes around the house for her. No. There was something else going on between those three, and it didn't have anything to do with love, I told myself.

"Where are we going?" I asked Momma when she got in the car.

She reached over and turned on the radio.

"Where are we going?"

She turned it up and hummed along with Aretha Franklin.

"You can't keep treating me like a child forever!"

She clicked off the radio. "I swear to God. If you say One. More. Thing. If you even breathe too loud, I will pull this car over and beat the black off of you. Do you hear me?"

"God can hear you using His name in vain, you know," I said.

"You better watch yourself, little girl," she warned. "You better watch yourself!"

The light turned red and the car in front of us stopped short. Momma hit the brakes and threw her arm out across my chest to keep me from flying through the windshield. After that I decided to shut up, sit back, and enjoy the ride.

We took the Harbor Freeway to Slauson. I got a sinking feeling in the pit of my stomach when we turned on Angeles Vista. Welcome to Windsor Hills/View Park, the sign read to my right. We took Angeles Vista to Inadale and turned right again. Momma stopped in front of the second house on the left and parked. I took my time following her up the walk to the large double doors.

"Don't you do anything to embarrass me. Mind your manners and do as you are instructed to do. Do you hear me?"

"Yes, Momma," I said.

She smoothed out her dress, tucked a lock of hair behind her ear, and pressed the doorbell. The door opened and a thin light-skinned woman with piercing gray eyes and a spattering of freckles on her cheeks greeted us.

"Well," she said, clapping her hands together. "You must be Zayla! I'm Miss Viola."

She wore a pink frilly jumpsuit that I couldn't make heads or tails of. When she stood still, the bottom half looked like a long skirt, but when she moved it looked like pants. She took a look at me and almost blinded me with her smile. I smiled back politely.

Miss Viola had way too much energy for eight-thirty on a Saturday morning. She extended her hand and I bent to kiss the top of it, corrected myself, and gave Miss Viola a gentle handshake. I tried to curtsy without tripping over my own two feet. Momma seemed pleased. I took in a deep breath and let it out slowly.

"Zora, you didn't tell me your daughter was so beautiful! And that dress. You aren't going to believe this, but I almost bought that exact same dress at Bullock's Wilshire for Ava. They didn't have her size. And thank God, right? How would it have looked for you two to be sitting up here in the same identical dress?"

Momma forced a smile and said, "Her grandmother bought it for her at Marshall Field's in Chicago. Isn't it adorable?"

I groaned and gave Momma the "God is always watching" face. She pushed me into the house behind Miss Viola and gave the back of my dress a sharp tug. I gave her the "I'm sorry" face and promised myself I would do better. I looked around at the boxy suede furnishings that filled the immense living room. Pastel paintings of white people in various stages of rest and play hung on the walls. A large painting of a blond-haired, blue-eyed Jesus hung above the fireplace mantel. The cream carpet didn't have any of the wear and tear our carpet had.

To my right was a formal dining room with the same cream-colored carpet and a dark dining room table with ten chairs around it. In the center of the table, on a cream-colored placemat, was a huge vase with a bouquet of sunflowers, hydrangea, tall stocks of blue delphinium, red roses, pink and yellow carnations, and purple statice. Eight women of varying hues, none darker than a hazelnut shell, sat around the table talking excitedly. They stopped when they saw us. The women smiled broadly at Momma as if they couldn't wait to get to know her better. They smiled politely at me and refocused their attention on Momma.

Miss Viola turned to me and said, "Well, Miss Zayla. I am pleased to welcome you to Miss Viola's Charm School."

I almost fainted.

Charm school? I'd been forced out of bed at seven o'clock on a Saturday morning to go to charm school?

Miss Viola took my hand and walked me down a hallway that ran the length of the house. We passed a bathroom on the left and a room on the right. At the back of the house was the kitchen and across from it the family room. It was decorated with antique, un-comfortable-looking furniture. Seated around the room on that fur-niture were nine girls, also in varying hues, only one darker than a hazelnut shell. They all wore different styles of pink dresses. I thought about fainting for real. I would land on the carpet, and if I was lucky I'd choke on my tongue and they'd have to call the ambu-lance.

Miss Viola cleared her throat from the doorway. "Ladies, I'd like to introduce you to Miss Zayla Lucille McKinney."

Thus began the introductions, starting with the girl seated clos-est to us on the sofa. Ava Delacroix, Miss Viola's beloved child. She made sure to let me know their name was French Creole. I rolled my eyes to make sure she saw how little I cared. Ava was the lightest of all the girls, with wavy hair like her mother's that came down to the center of her back. Our dresses were the same shade of pink— a fact neither of us seemed too pleased about. I didn't even know her, and I didn't like her.

Next to Ava was Tanya Watson, the darkest of all the girls with jet-black, perm-straight hair that was in the same style and the same length as Ava's. Her dress was a few shades darker, but it was still a sickening shade of pink. Tanya made sure to let me know she and Ava had been friends since kindergarten and they were the first of

Miss Viola's charm school girls. I knew then that the only person I disliked more than Evie, Dee-Dee, and now Ava, was Tanya.

On an ottoman in front of one of the wingback chairs sat Eunice Williams, a few shades darker than Ava, but her mother had the decency to put her in a soft pink dress that was easy on the eyes. Her hair was done up in a mass of Shirley Temple curls that barely touched her shoulders. On the chair behind Eunice sat Bernice Johnson. Eunice and Bernice were the same shade, and both wore Shirley Temple curls and identical dresses.

Shirley and Sandra Breedlove shared the small loveseat next to a ficus plant that looked like it might swallow them whole. Shirley wore a pixie haircut. Sandra's hair hung straight past her shoulders. If not for their hair, I wouldn't have been able to tell them apart. In the other wingback chair sat Sam-Ella Bethune. She looked like the only reason she'd been invited to the party was her matching skin tone. Sam-Ella was the largest of all the girls and had a short, nappy Afro. She also appeared to be very aware that she didn't fit in with this crowd.

Next to Sam-Ella was Carnell White. Carnell, on the other hand, was very clear she belonged anywhere she wanted to be. She sat taller than the rest of the girls, or maybe it was because she was the tallest of the girls and the only one with the shape of a grown woman. Not so much to make her unlikeable, but just enough to notice the difference between her and the rest of us.

Next to Carnell, on what looked to be a footstool, was Cynthia. I had to lean in to make sure my eyes weren't playing tricks on me. Cynthia was in my class, and she'd sat in the back of the room, silent and unnoticed, all year long. She was new to the school and didn't go out of her way to make friends. She stayed to herself at recess and lunch, and was always the first one out of the door when the bell rang at the end of the day. No one knew anything about her– where she lived, what her parents did for a living, what she liked or didn't like. She was a ghost we could all see. I envied that about her.

A thought crossed my mind and my heart stopped momentarily. I wondered how long it would take for her to tell all the girls they called me a bulldagger at school. I didn't know her, but I decided not to like her either. I found a chair near the door and sat down.

Miss Viola's first lesson consisted of table manners and table-setting etiquette. We practiced setting an informal table, which included the standard silverware placement: fork to the left of the plate, knife and spoon to the right, and the water glass was positioned on the upper right edge of the plate. Then a formal table setting, which included the same as an informal setting with the addition of a salad fork to the left of the dinner fork. A steak knife replaced the butter knife, which should then be placed on the bread saucer. And a wine glass should be added next to the water glass.

"Why do we need to know this?" I asked.

"Because it will be important when you grow up," Miss Viola explained.

"Why? Everybody we know uses a knife and a fork at the table and that's it. Well, sometimes Daddy uses a spoon if he's having coffee."

"That's why you're learning proper table-setting etiquette. So you don't grow up thinking that's the only way to set a table. You never know whose house you may wind up in as you get older. You always want to set a good example. And, in case you've never heard it, knowledge is power. Whether you need this or not is irrelevant. Understand?"

I could tell I was getting on Miss Viola's nerves, but she was too refined to lose her cool. The rest of the girls sighed and rolled their eyes every time I said something, which only served to egg me on. Cynthia seemed to be amused by my behavior. I wasn't being unruly on purpose. I just didn't understand how learning table manners and table settings was going to improve my life in Watts. No one cared whether or not I knew how to set a dinner table, formal or otherwise.

"Yeah, but it's not like white people are going to invite any of us over to their houses for dinner," I said.

That did it. Miss Viola closed her eyes and said through pursed lips, "Do it because I told you to."

It was my fourth time interrupting the lesson to add my thoughts on the insanity of teaching a bunch of colored girls how to do things only white people could do in real life. Then a thought occurred to me. What if Miss Viola was teaching us how to do all this white people stuff so we would be prepared to be their maid one day?

Our next lesson was about the importance of social etiquette. Miss Viola told us to pick a partner. All the girls started talking at once and moving around to find their partner. I sat and watched, figuring I'd get whoever was left over, or if I was lucky, get to work by myself. I wasn't so lucky. The girls were still chattering and going on when Cynthia walked over and sat down next to me.

"Want to be my partner?" she asked.

I shrugged. "Sure."

We waited for our instructions.

"I want you to sit with your partner for ten minutes. For five minutes you will interview her. You will find out her likes and dislikes and anything you have in common. When the five minutes are up, I will ring this bell." Miss Viola held up a small gold bell that looked exactly like a butler's bell from the movies. "When you hear the bell, it will be time to switch. For the last five minutes the other partner will do the interviewing. Are there any questions?"

Miss Viola looked at me as if she dared me to raise my hand. I thought it best not to, although I wanted to know when we could eat. Or leave. Whichever came first was good enough for me. She rang the bell and told us to begin. Cynthia turned to face me.

"Do you want to go first?" she asked.

I shrugged again. "No, I think you should."

We interviewed each other and did more laughing than I would have imagined. Miss Viola had to shush us several times. When she threatened to separate us, we finally settled down. Cynthia was a nice girl and very outspoken. She reminded me a lot of myself, and I couldn't understand why her mother drove her all the way across town to come to Miss Viola's when she seemed perfectly normal. It wasn't the time or place to ask, so I made a mental note to ask later. At the end of the ten minutes Miss Viola rang the bell and asked for volunteers to go first.

I raised my hand. Miss Viola groaned and called on me anyway.

"This is Cynthia Harper. She likes to sleep in late on Saturday mornings, but can't because she has to come here. She likes reading books and singing. She doesn't like stuck-up or conceited girls. She doesn't like people who hate other people for no good reason because she doesn't think there's ever a reason to be hateful. We have a lot in common. We both believe that Negroes can be as mean to each other as white people. And as racist. We both like climbing trees and playing stickball. We both graduated from elementary school this year as A-students. And we both live in Watts."

I turned to Cynthia, who was giggling behind her hand, to make sure I didn't forget anything. She nodded her head. I turned back to the other girls, who were all looking at me like I had three heads.

Miss Viola groaned again and thanked me for volunteering to go first. When I sat down, Cynthia leaned over and whispered, "Good job."

"Thanks!"

Miss Viola gave the girls a chance to ask one question of each of us. Tanya raised her hand and asked the question everyone wanted to know.

"You live in Watts?" she said to me, her face all scrunched up like she smelled something foul.

Spending time with Suzanne had made me feel less like the "reason first, and if necessary, run" kind of girl. Tanya made me want to slap the taste out of her mouth, which made it very easy for me to say, "Yeah. So? You got a problem with that?" Then I leaned forward in my chair like I dared her to answer me. It worked. She shut her mouth and Miss Viola took that as a cut to move on to the next set of girls.

"But I didn't get to introduce Zayla," Cynthia said.

"It's okay. I think we've heard enough from Miss Zayla," Miss Viola said.

I didn't like her being so dismissive of me, but if that meant she wanted to toss me out on my ear, that was fine. Sure enough, at the end of class Miss Viola pulled Momma aside. I sat on the front porch and waited for Momma to come and tell me how disappointed she was that I'd been dismissed on my first day. As the other girls left, they all cooed, "Goodbye," and "It was nice to meet you, see you next week," as they passed, as though they meant it. When Cynthia passed, she handed me a note. I opened it. It read. *Zayla, you make me laugh. We should hang out. Call me. 213-732-1923. Cynthia.* Momma came out next. She walked right past me and got in the car.

"Am I kicked out?" I asked, hopeful, as I climbed in beside her.

"You'd like that, wouldn't you? No, you're not kicked out. Miss Viola just thinks you need a lot of work, so you will be working with her one-on-one two days a week, in addition to Saturday afternoons."

I slumped down in my seat. I'd done it again. My own mouth had written a check my ass couldn't cash.

"Cynthia and her mother also offered to help."

I remained slumped in my seat and groaned, but I was happy to hear I would get to hang out with Cynthia again. There was something about her I couldn't quite put my finger on, but I really liked her.

* * * * * *

Cynthia called me the next day.

"Hey, Zayla. This is Cynthia from Miss Viola's. I got your number from my mother. I hope that's okay. *Tarzan's* playing at the Largo. You wanna go?"

I asked if I could go. Momma was so happy that a girl like Cynthia wanted to bother with me that she invited her over for lunch. Cynthia accepted. We had tuna melts with a side of dill pickles on Momma's "show off" china. We sipped fresh squeezed lemonade from her "good and expensive" Waterford crystal glasses. We even sat at the dining room table to eat. I was so embarrassed, I didn't know what to do with myself.

"So, Cynthia. Is everything okay? Do you have enough to eat?"

"Yes, Mrs. McKinney. Everything is very nice."

"Thank you. Thank you. I hear you and Zayla both went to school together. Have you been there since kindergarten?"

"No, ma'am. I went to George Washington Carver Elementary until fifth grade. We moved out of the district last summer, so I had to change schools."

"Oh, that's too bad. You didn't get to graduate with all your classmates. Zayla has been at Compton Ave. since the very start. She got a chance to grow up with all those kids. They're like brothers and sisters."

Cynthia and I exchanged glances. We continued eating in silence until it become unbearable. I cleared my throat to say something, and Cynthia beat me to the punch.

"You have a very beautiful home, Mrs. McKinney. Mr. McKinney is a very lucky man."

"Thank you, Cynthia. I'm the lucky one," Momma said in a syrupy tone.

"We have to go," I said, thoroughly annoyed. "The movie is starting in a little while."

"Do you want me to take you?" Momma asked.

Who is this woman? I wondered. Usually, she was ushering us out of "her" house so we wouldn't tear anything up. She'd never invited anyone over for lunch before, other than Malik, and we always ate in the kitchen.

"No, thanks," I said. "We'll walk."

"Oh, come on. I'll take you. I have to go to the market anyway."

"I thought you hated Giant Market?"

"I think I'll go over to Farmer's Market today," Momma purred.

Momma had clearly gone tee-totally insane, as Nana would say.

20

The Largo was a well-worn movie theater built in 1923. It wasn't as large as Grauman's Chinese Theater in Hollywood, and people didn't come from all over to watch movies there. But as far as I was concerned it was every bit as elegant, with its glass-encased ticket booth and gold-leafed façade. The employees wore red uniform jackets with gold braided epaulets and buttons, tan slacks, and black shiny shoes. Black Betty, the ticket window clerk, stuck out like a bunion in orthopedic shoes. She never wore a uniform. Just a fake smile over a mouth that resembled a jack-o'-lantern with too many teeth. Whenever we showed up to buy a ticket, she acted like it was an enormous inconvenience for her.

Every blue moon a first-run movie would arrive at the Largo, and the lines would wrap around the corner. That day *Tarzan Goes to India* and *The Black Pirate* was closing in on a two-week run. Sometimes that's how it was. Some movies came and went in a week or two. Some stayed for months. Daddy said that's just how little we mattered to Hollywood. They didn't feature us in their movies, and they didn't care whether or not we saw them.

Cynthia followed me up to the ticket window and asked for two tickets. Black Betty slapped her *Ebony* magazine down on the counter and pushed her glasses down her nose.

"Ain't you kids s'posed to be in school?" she asked.

"It's summer," Cynthia said.

"Umph, well, hand over fifty cents," Black Betty snapped.

We each dropped fifty cents into her outstretched hand. She dropped the quarters into a coin purse lying on the counter and handed us our tickets. As we entered the theater, I glanced back at the ticket booth and wondered why Black Betty was so mean. Maybe it's because people called her Black Betty, I thought. I wouldn't like it if people called me black anything, so I could only imagine how she felt. I remembered the ad I once saw in a newspaper Daddy brought home from Alabama. There was a cartoon image of a young girl with jet black skin, wide eyes, and big, bright red exaggerated lips. She held a large slice of watermelon. It read, "Eat seeds 'n all! Picaninny Freeze 5 cent. A Pal for your Palate." It made me feel sorry for Black Betty in spite of her meanness.

"She's just mad because we're cute and we pass the brown paper bag test," Cynthia said, as if reading my mind.

"What's the brown paper bag test?" I asked.

"Where have you been? Everyone knows. "If you're light you're all right. If you're brown, stick around. And if you're black, get back!"

"Not everyone," I said. "But what's the test part? What kind of test is it?"

Cynthia sighed and picked up a box of Boston Baked Beans that lay on the counter. She looked around for help.

"If you're lighter than the bag, you're more acceptable," she continued to explain.

"What kind of bag?"

"A grocery bag," she said.

"From the store?" I asked stupidly. Cynthia answered me with her face.

"Acceptable to who?" I asked next, then heard Momma say, "to whom" in my head.

Cynthia gawked at me like I'd been sent to the corner with the dunce cap on my head. I thought it best not to prove her right. But the more I thought about it, this conversation wasn't making her look very smart either.

"To us and white people. To everyone," she explained proudly.

"Well, that's just dumb," I said, unable to keep my opinion to myself. "Who cares if we're acceptable to us? We're still Negro. What we think doesn't matter. White people don't like us no matter what shade our skin is. My daddy said when he was touring around the country, he had to go through the backdoor of the place just like Lena Horne and Smokey Robinson, and they're way lighter than him."

Someone cleared their throat behind us and said, "Is this your new girlfriend, bulldagger?"

I spun around to find Evie Sheffield standing there looking like Moms Mabley on cleaning day. Broom in one hand, dustpan in the other, looking ridiculous in a pair of dusty, tattered blue overalls. My fists clenched immediately and I braced myself for a fight. Before I could decide what to do, Cynthia spoke up for me.

"Yeah, I'm her girlfriend," she said. "What's it to you?"

Cynthia leaned over and kissed my cheek. I smiled. Evie's grin slid right off her face. I relaxed my hands and laughed then. Cynthia laughed too. Evie's eyes narrowed and searched our faces for the truth.

"And, quit calling her a bulldagger, darkie," Cynthia added for good measure. "She's too cute for that."

"Evie!" Mr. Charlie yelled. "Quit standing around bothering paying customers and get back to work. Those bathrooms ain't gon' clean themselves."

He closed the office door behind him and crossed the lobby to meet us on the other side of the concession stand.

"Yeah, Evie. Go clean them bathrooms," I said.

Cynthia removed her arm from my shoulder and took my hand. Mr. Charlie shouted at Evie again. She rolled her eyes and skulked off toward the women's restroom like a gangly scarecrow. Cynthia returned her attention to the concession stand. I studied her for a moment, wondering if I wanted to be friends with someone who thought it was okay to judge another Negro by the color of their skin. Wasn't that what Dr. King was preaching all around the country? To be judged by the content of our character and not the color of our skin? But then again, I reminded myself, she'd also stood up to Evie for me.

"Thanks," I mumbled.

"No problem. That's what friends are for. Get what you want. My treat," Cynthia said. "I'm your girlfriend, remember."

"Don't pay that Evie no attention, Miss Zayla. I done told her a thousand times to stop bothering the customers, but she don't listen. That gal's got a head like a brick," Mr. Charlie said.

"It's okay. I don't pay her any mind anyway."

He smiled and said, "Now, what can I get you young ladies?"

"I'll have a pack of candy cigarettes," I said.

I loved candy cigarettes, but Momma didn't like me having them because she thought they'd start a habit that I couldn't stop. Like I didn't have sense enough to know the difference between a cigarette that turned to gum and one that you had to light with a match. Mr. Charlie set the box of cigarettes on the counter. Cynthia placed the box of Boston Baked Beans next to it.

"On the house," he said to both of us.

We thanked him. Then, as if on second thought, Cynthia ordered a bag of popcorn and asked me if I wanted to share a bottle of Coca-Cola. I had enough money to buy my own, but I liked the idea of sharing one better. Maybe Cynthia wasn't so bad after all, I thought. Dee-Dee never offered to share anything with me, but she always had her hand out if I had something. Sometimes I would foolishly share whatever I had, and other times I would just give it to her flat-out. Some friend she turned out to be.

We made our way into the theater. I decided to let Cynthia pick the seats and crossed my fingers that she'd pick the ones in the center. They were the best ones in the house, and where Daddy and I always sat. Six rows down, seven seats over. Whenever I went with Dee-Dee we sat in the back, which I hated because that's where the older kids sat so they could make out. There was nothing worse than being stuck next to a couple of teenagers that couldn't keep their hands off each other. To my surprise, Cynthia turned into the sixth row and took the eighth seat, leaving the seventh one for me.

"Best seats in the house," she said.

I couldn't stop the smile from spreading across my face. I really liked Cynthia, even when I tried not to.

"Daddy says so, too," I said. "These are the exact seats we choose when we come to the movies. We get here super early to make sure we get them, too."

"You go to the movies with your dad?" she asked. "I never do anything like that with my dad 'cause he's always working."

"You're not close to your dad?" I asked, suddenly feeling sorry for her.

"Closer than I am to my mother. Way closer. We do some things together, like I go with him to the barbershop on Saturday afternoons and then we go to Blair's downtown for lunch. We sit at the counter and have sandwiches and chocolate malts. Momma would die if she knew. On Sundays we go for drives up the coast to see this lady Daddy works with. They go in another room and do their work, and I play with her son, Robert. We're usually there all day, so I get to swim and play basketball, and do whatever else Robert can think of until they're finished. Then on the way home, we take guesses on how long it'll take Momma to start a fight. She always starts a fight when we get home on Sunday nights."

"You don't have to go to church?" I asked.

"Not anymore," she explained. "Last year my dad said I could choose for myself. I'd been going to church every Sunday from the time I could walk, and I hated it. Not the people or anything like that. Just the fact that Momma was such a two-faced hypocrite. She was one way at home and another way around her church people. So I chose to stop going."

"She sounds like my mother," I said.

"Plus, they have all these rules about who's acceptable to God and who's not. I thought God accepted everyone. But *they* don't."

"But how is that any different from not accepting Negroes because their skin is too dark?" I asked.

Cynthia tossed a handful of Boston Baked Beans in her mouth and thought for a moment.

"I guess it's not," she said and shrugged. "It's kinda stupid now that I think about it."

"Yeah. Real stupid," I said.

"Can I ask you a question," she said, changing the subject.

I nodded and took a puff on my candy cigarette.

"Was it true?" she asked.

"What?"

"That Evie saw you and Dee-Dee kissing?"

"No!"

"You didn't kiss her or Evie didn't see you kiss her?" she asked.

"No and no."

"You can tell me. I mean, you might as well. By this time tomorrow everyone will know we were holding hands at the movies."

We laughed. I considered telling her the truth, except the trailers ended and the movie started.

"I'll tell you later," I whispered.

"Promise?"

I didn't like making promises I wasn't sure I could keep. I wasn't sure I really wanted to tell her later. I crossed my fingers and nodded. Cynthia smiled and shoved a handful of popcorn in her mouth. I grabbed a handful of my own and we sat back to enjoy the Black Pirate, who wasn't even a Negro.

* * * * * *

The following Saturday, Cynthia volunteered for more time at Miss Viola's and we got to spend almost every day together after that. Eventually, I told her the truth about me and Dee-Dee. To my surprise, she wasn't fazed. She said it wasn't a real kiss because Dee-Dee didn't mean it, so it didn't count. Cynthia's reaction made me like her more than I already did. The more we hung out, the more I realized how alike we were. Until Daddy took us to the Santa Monica Pier.

Cynthia had never been before and said for a long time she didn't think Negroes were allowed there. I'd only been once before. Daddy and I were the only Black faces around, which caused us to get a lot of stares. I always found it fascinating how white people would stare whenever they saw us, as if they'd never seen Negroes before. If they'd ever turned on a television or picked up a newspaper, I know they'd seen many Negro people. And I knew that most of the women cleaning their homes and caring for their children were Negro. I mentioned this last part to Cynthia.

"They stare because they're just as fascinated with us as we are with them," Daddy interjected. "Our job is to ignore it. If they can be here, so can we."

"That's right," Cynthia said. "My uncle says our money is green just like theirs, and that's all that matters."

Daddy held his hand out and Cynthia slid him some skin. "Your uncle is a wise man," he said. "I'm going to take my leave of you ladies. Meet me near the entrance at five o'clock."

We wouldn't let him leave until he promised to ride the Ferris wheel with us. That proved to be a big mistake. He waited until our car got to the very top and started rocking it back and forth. Cynthia and I screamed bloody murder, and the louder we screamed the more it tickled us. The more we screamed and laughed, the more he rocked the car. He finally stopped when Cynthia said she thought she was going to pee her pants. I don't think she meant to say it out loud, but then Daddy told her if she couldn't hold it, she better not get any on his shoes, which made her laugh more. By the time the ride came to a stop, Cynthia and I were dizzy and hungry. Daddy treated us to a hot dog on a stick and gave each of us a couple dollars.

"Have fun, you two. Don't eat too much and don't be late. We have to be home in time for dinner or we'll be in a world of trouble."

Things were going along fine, until Cynthia spotted a picture booth where we could get four poses for two cents. We ran over and plopped down on the small bench inside. We made funny faces into the screen mounted in the booth, and just before the last shutter clicked, Cynthia leaned over and kissed my cheek. I giggled, but inside I got that same warm feeling I'd gotten looking at Miss March. The same feeling I'd had when Marcus kissed me. In the span of a few seconds, I went from feeling good to red-hot anger.

"What did you do that for?" I demanded to know.

"I don't know. Because we're having fun," she said.

"So what! You're not supposed to kiss other girls."

She blushed, confused. "I'm sorry. You didn't seem to mind at the movie theater."

"That was different!"

When the strip of photos slid down the shoot, I grabbed it from the slot. Without looking, I folded it in half, shoved it in my back pocket, and stomped off.

"Hey! Don't I get to see them?"

"No! I don't like the way I look. We'll do it again another time," I said.

I knew I was behaving like a three year-old, but I couldn't control myself. I'd been feeling hot and cold all afternoon, wrestling with my feelings toward Cynthia. One minute I liked her as a friend; the next I was trying to figure out if I liked her as anything else. A couple times I even imagined she liked me. I sulked on the pier until it was time to leave. Cynthia sat next to me, swinging her legs over the edge, but left me alone. We met Daddy at five o'clock sharp. I climbed in the back seat and told her to ride up front.

"Everything okay, Ladybug?" Daddy asked.

I didn't want him thinking Cynthia had done something to upset me when I'd done a bang-up job of upsetting myself.

"Yeah, I just think I had too much fun for one day," I said.

He asked Cynthia how she was feeling.

"I'm okay, Mr. McKinney," she said. "I guess I'm kinda worn out on too much fun, too."

On the ride home Cynthia and Daddy made small talk. I lay face down on the back seat, fighting with myself. I couldn't accept the sad, unmistakable truth of who I might really be– a truth that was burning a hole in my back pocket.

God, I know you're not listening. You never do. But if you are listening now, please take these feelings I have inside away from me. I promise if you do I will never do anything bad again.

I'd dozed off by the time Daddy pulled up in front of Cynthia's house. The sound of the doors unlocking woke me. I didn't want Cynthia to leave thinking she'd done anything wrong, and the thought of her never wanting to see me again was even worse. I had to apologize. After all, it was just an innocent kiss on my cheek. She'd done the exact same thing at the Largo in front of Evie. It wasn't like she'd shoved her tongue down my throat or anything. It's not like she'd kissed me the way Marcus had. She'd also never said she liked me, so why was I acting like a fool? I wondered.

Cynthia got out and said goodbye. Daddy put the car in gear.

"Daddy, wait. I forgot to give Cynthia her part of the pictures we took."

I ran up the walk and caught her before she went in the house. Daddy watched a group of young men pass by. They were talking loud and drinking something hidden inside a brown paper bag. I took hold of Cynthia's pinky.

"I'm sorry," I said. "I get a little cranky when I'm tired."

"It's okay," she said. "I understand. I get like that sometimes too. Call me tomorrow?"

"Sure," I said.

* * * * * *

I waited until I got home to look at the pictures. Just as I'd feared, Cynthia's lips were pressed firmly to my cheek, her eyes toward the camera. My lids were closed and I had a big stupid grin across my face. I know I should have ripped the photo into shreds and flushed it down the toilet, but I couldn't. I pushed it between the mattress and box spring and got down on my knees.

God, please, I'm begging you. Can you please, please, pretty please, make me normal? I'll do whatever you want.

21

Trial of Three Klansmen Set
L.A. Times – Wednesday, August 11, 1965

> *and when we speak we are afraid*
> *our words will not be heard*
> *nor welcomed*
> *but when we are silent*
> *we are still afraid.*
> *So it is better to speak*
> *remembering*
> *we were never meant to survive.*
> ~Audre Lorde, "A Litany for Survival"

In the weeks that followed, it became clear to me that my so-called friendship with Dee-Dee had only existed in my head. The more time I spent with Cynthia, the more I realized that I never truly felt good inside when I was with Dee-Dee. Not really. Dee-Dee only cared about Dee-Dee. She wasn't very nice to me, and whenever we got together it was always on her terms. We did what she wanted, when she wanted, how she wanted. I was always "too" something for Dee-Dee. I talked too much, which was laughable since I hardly ever got a word in edgewise. I put too much food in my mouth. I took too long to roll the dice. I stared at her too much. I touched her too much. And once we got older, and our sleepovers moved from the living room to Dee-Dee's room, she said I smelled too bad to sleep in her bed. I promised myself as I lay there on the hardwood floor, wrapped only in a blanket, that I would never spend the night at her house again. I cried myself to sleep, and the very next day I made up an excuse for her meanness and forgave her.

Cynthia and I were two sides of the same coin. We liked the same things, laughed at the same things, enjoyed spending time together, and not one time was I too much anything for her. We told each other everything, and the best part of our friendship was the fact that she grew to love Malik almost as much as I did. For a minute, he had a crush on her and, with my permission, he opened up and told her how he felt. I was relieved when she told him she wasn't interested in him. After that, he was convinced she was interested in me. What other reason could she have not to like him, he reasoned. Of course, I couldn't believe that was true, so I told him to get over himself. He claimed not to care one way or the other. He was just glad I'd finally made friends with someone who genuinely liked me.

And Cynthia did like me. She really and truly liked me, and after a while, it didn't matter how she liked me. It got so that every morning when the phone rang, I knew it was her calling and ran to answer it before Momma could. Every morning she'd ask the same question.

"What are we gonna do today?"

I'd always say, "Let's flip a coin and see where it lands," because that's what Daddy always said when I asked him the same question. Every day we flipped that proverbial coin, and every day I came home feeling as though I'd just had the best day of my life.

We went to the Watts Towers – two days in a row. The first day we went so we could marvel at the chaotic beauty of the sculptures, born from scraps of pop bottles, seashells, mirrors, pieces of pottery, and tiles, most of which Mr. Rodia found along the train tracks on Wilmington Avenue. We went back the next day to inspect every detail of his work in an effort to understand why he was so hellbent on building these particular towers in Watts for what seemed to be no reason at all.

We spent an entire afternoon out on the roof of the Sanctuary. Most of the time we sat in a comfortable silence, lost in our own thoughts or enjoying the view as we sipped Skinny McKinneys. Then, as dusk settled around us, Miss Minnie came flying up the stairs, stumbled onto the roof, and politely sent us packing.

"All right now, get on home, you little urchins. I gotta get ready for my payin' customers," she said, ushering us down the stairs, through the club, and out onto 103rd Street.

We cracked up laughing and raced each other all the way back to my house, collapsing in a heap on the front porch. Cynthia sat up abruptly, threw her hand on her hip, and said, "All right now, get on home, you little urchins," in a voice almost identical to Miss Minnie's. We cracked up laughing all over again.

We got to go to work with Daddy at KGFJ one day. We spent most of the morning sitting in the window, watching Montague burn records and take calls from kids all over Los Angeles. We even got to meet him, up close and personal. He wasn't nearly as big as he seemed on the radio. In my mind I'd imagined he was as tall and broad as Paul Bunyan. In real life he was several inches shorter than Daddy's six-foot, two-inch frame and as thin as a rail, as Nana would say. The rest of the time we listened as women called in to make requests for love songs and dedicated them to Daddy.

We went to the Largo and saw *Mary Poppins* twice, because it was just that good. The next day we ventured off to the Loyola Theater in Westchester to see *The Incredible Mr. Limpet*. We didn't tell anyone where we were going or when we'd be back, mostly because the only person who might have asked was Momma, and she was so happy that I'd finally taken up with a respectable girl like Cynthia, she didn't care. So we hopped on the Central Avenue bus to Manchester, then took the Manchester bus all the way to the end of the line. We had hot dogs and shared a root beer soda during the show, something they never had at the Largo.

After the movie, we walked to the Loyola Marymount campus, where Momma went to college. We sat on the grass in front of the administration building, and I imagined what Momma must have been like when she was a student. I told Cynthia that sometimes I wondered if Momma ever regretted having me, and she told me Momma could never regret having me. I was her only daughter, her pride and joy. Cynthia said I should always remember that, because no matter how badly Momma behaved, I was the one thing she knew she did right.

"How do you know that?" I asked.

"Because that's how all mothers feel. I read it in my mother's *Good Housekeeping* magazine."

Back in those days, *Good Housekeeping* was like a missing book from the Bible. From cover to cover, every concept, idea, and opinion was worshipped and treasured by women all over. So if *Good Housekeeping* said it, it had to be true, I told myself. Cynthia had that way about her, getting me to believe the impossible until I had reason to believe otherwise. So when she asked me to spend the night at her house, I was elated. Then I thought about where I'd have to sleep. In fact, I couldn't stop thinking about it. I spent most of the morning and the car ride over to Cynthia's house, praying there was some place soft for me to sleep that night.

The song on the radio ended, and Montague's voice filled the car.

"You're burning with Montague on KGFJ. Speaking of burning, the heat wave continues another day. It's gonna be hotter than Haiti and cooler than hell today. Stay cool, L.A. Stay cool. Who we got on the line?"

"George Jackson, Jordan High School. Burn!" the caller screamed.

"Burn, baby! Burn," I shouted in unison with Montague.

"I wish that man would stop saying that. It's the most ignorant thing I've ever heard in my life!" Momma said, and clicked off the radio.

"Why? He doesn't mean anything by it."

"Well, if he doesn't mean anything, he shouldn't say it. Words have power!"

I gazed out the window. Two boys raced their bikes down Central, jumping off curbs and using the driveways to glide back up on the sidewalk. Old Man Crogan stood in front of his store shouting in their direction and waving his broom. I thought about the time he called us "little nigger rats" for riding our bikes in front of his store. Malik and James told him to go fuck himself. I pedaled home as fast as I could, crying all the way. For Malik and James the words meant nothing. For me, well, let's just say I suddenly knew how it must feel to have a fire hose turned on you for simply being a Negro. I'd never been called such an ugly thing before in my life. It was true words had power, except it also depended on how the words were used, how often, and the context. I was very doubtful anyone would be tempted to set something ablaze just because Montague said, "Burn." Everyone knew he was talking about records.

We pulled up in front of Cynthia's house. Mrs. Harper's royal blue Cadillac DeVille rested in the driveway, sparkling like it was on a showroom floor. Momma wasn't envious of much, but she'd give anything to have a DeVille just like it. Daddy, not one for pomp or circumstance when it came to cars, told her he'd buy her one when her Ford Fairlane gave up on her. Daddy felt the only reason people bought fancy cars was for other people to watch them drive. "The day I can see myself driving, I may change my mind," he'd always say.

"That sure is a beautiful car. I don't know what's wrong with your father. I should have one just like it," Momma said, and put the car in park.

I hopped out with my overnight bag and ran up to the door without a backward glance.

"Say hello to Mrs. Harper for me," Momma called. "And have a good time and mind your manners!"

I waved with one hand and knocked twice on the door with the other.

"It's open," Cynthia shouted.

"Zayla, is that you?" Mrs. Harper called from the kitchen.

"Hi, Mrs. Harper," I called back.

Cynthia was on her back in the middle of the living room floor, arms folded beneath her head. She had on a pair of blue jean shorts and a pink and blue paisley halter top. She looked beautiful, as usual. She leaned up on her elbows and smiled. Her hair was pulled into a bun, set perfectly in the center of her head. Gold hoop earrings dangled from her earlobes.

"Hi," I said, dropping my overnight bag on the sofa.

"Hi," she said and smiled. "You look nice."

We were dressed almost identically. I wore a blue and white paisley halter top, blue jean shorts, and blue sandals. I liked how she always took notice of what I was wearing. Not as an excuse to pass judgment, like someone else I knew. She honestly liked the way I "expressed my outer self." Her words, not mine. Actually, they were Miss Viola's words, but I liked them better when Cynthia said them.

"Thanks," I said. "You, too."

A portable radio tuned to KGFJ sat on the coffee table just above her head. An oscillating fan stood at her feet, blasting cool air over her. I flopped down next to her and folded my arms beneath my head, too. The caller hung up and we shouted, "Burn, baby, burn!" along with Montague.

"I wish you two would stop acting so niggerish!" Mrs. Harper said from the kitchen doorway.

"What's so niggerish? We're just listening to the radio," Cynthia said.

"You don't have to repeat everything that nigga Montague says. And he ought to stop saying that ignorant mess. What's he burning anyway?"

Mrs. Harper set a plate of peanut butter cookies on the coffee table next to the radio and waited for an answer.

"Records, Momma," Cynthia said, exasperated.

I giggled into my hands. I couldn't believe how much Mrs. Harper and Momma had in common.

"Humph. Well, you stop saying it!" Mrs. Harper barked, then clicked the radio off on her way back to the kitchen.

Cynthia rolled her eyes and said, "Can we go outside, please?"

"No, it's too hot."

"What are we supposed to do, then?" Cynthia demanded to know.

"I'm sure you'll figure something out."

Cynthia got up and said, "Come on before I say something and get in trouble."

I grabbed my overnight bag and followed her down a long hallway to the back of the house. In her room, I flopped down on her bed. She slammed the door behind me.

"She makes me so sick!" she said.

I felt a little sick too, as I took in Cynthia's room. It looked like a multi-hued pink bomb exploded and got on everything, even the carpet. The bedspread and dust ruffle around the box spring. The sheer curtains hanging from the windows. Large dolls with long blonde curls and glassy blue eyes stood on shelves along the wall and at the top of the bookcase, looking down on us. A jewelry box filled with costume jewelry sat on top of a bleached white six-drawer dresser, like a prop in a Joan Crawford movie. Her room looked exactly like someone decorated it to impersonate a girl's room. Nothing about Cynthia was reflected in the space. There were a few books on the shelves and two records next to the Mickey Mouse record player, but other than that just bland pinkness. She left and came back with the oscillating fan.

"I know it's terrible. Momma thought pink should be my favorite color, and now I hate it," she said, plugging the fan in behind the dresser. "I can't wait till I grow up and have a place of my own. It's why I haven't had you over . We're friends now, though, so you can't make fun of me."

"I can't?" I asked, and laughed.

I didn't know what else to say. I looked around for something interesting to comment on. Neatly arranged over Cynthia's bed were three large abstract collages full of rich, brilliant colors. I examined one with red, orange, green, purple, lilac, and white overlapping textured circles.

"I just finished that one," Cynthia said.

"You did this? How'd you do it? I like it."

"I used sand and grass and an old tie my father gave me. There's also some dirt from the backyard and a couple rose petals. I started it the day we came back from the pier. I'm surprised it came out so well. I was pretty mad that day."

"I'm sorry. I didn't mean to make you mad," I said.

"It's okay. I wasn't mad at you."

"You weren't?"

She shook her head. I waited for her to explain. When it was obvious she wasn't going to, I changed the subject.

"I didn't know you painted. I used to paint," I said. "But I stopped."

I told her the same story I'd told Nana, and she had the same reaction.

"And you just stopped. Just like that?" she asked.

"Yep," I said.

"Don't you know the most famous painters got famous because they made people uncomfortable with their work?"

"So, I don't want to be famous and I don't like people being mad at me."

"Then you're doomed," she said and gave me a pitying look. "You're gonna spend the rest of your life worried about what other people think."

"You must care, too. You spent the whole year sitting in the back of the classroom and didn't try to make one friend."

"That wasn't because I cared what anyone thought of me. I just didn't want any trouble. Momma told me if I got into any trouble at the new school, she was sending me down South with my grandma. That would have been a whole different hell. My grandma actually has real chickens and kills them for dinner. Have you ever seen a chicken get its head whacked off? They really do run around for a while before they die," she said. "So, do you want to paint with me?"

"I guess," I said. "How do you not care what people think of you?"

"Easy," she said, reaching under her bed and pulling out a box of acrylic paint. "You just don't. My grandma told me that what other people think about me ain't none of my damn business. 'Cynthia,' she said. 'You tell them folk to keep runnin' over the sides of their shoes and let you run yo' business.' So, that's what I do. Right now Momma lives my life and that's all right. She only has five more years. I plan on going to college far, far, far away from her, and when I graduate, I'm gonna make sure I have a job so I won't have to come back. Five years, three months, and eighty-five days, to be exact."

She retrieved two small canvases from her closet. I leaned against the wall beneath the window. She leaned against the bed and placed the box of paint on the floor between us. She reached under the bed again and pulled out a multicolored stack of construction paper. She handed a couple sheets to me and kept a couple for herself. I thought about Suzanne.

She and Cynthia had a lot in common, too. They were both strong and knew their own minds. They didn't care what other people thought of them, and they seemed to have their whole lives worked out. What happened to me? I wondered. I hadn't even thought about high school, much less college or leaving home, for that matter. Sure, I wanted to get away from Momma, but that also meant leaving Daddy, which is probably why I'd never given it much thought.

"Starting today, I'm not gonna care what anyone thinks of me anymore!" I proclaimed and pounded my fist against the carpet to prove I meant business.

"Good for you," Cynthia said, not looking up from her painting.

I wondered if she believed me, then decided I didn't care. She didn't need to believe me. I did.

We painted until Mrs. Harper interrupted us for lunch. She brought our sandwiches in on a tray and left them on the dresser. Cynthia was still salty, which I assumed is why she didn't bother thanking her mother. I said, "Thank you, Mrs. Harper" for both of us. Not because I cared what she thought. I did it because it was the courteous thing to do.

The sandwiches sat untouched for over an hour. We were so immersed in our art projects, food could wait. They were still there when Mrs. Harper came in some time later to tell us Mr. Harper was having car trouble and needed a ride home.

"I'll be back in a little while. Don't open the door for any reason and don't go outside."

"Yes, Mother," Cynthia said.

We took a break after Mrs. Harper left and ate our sandwiches on the living room floor in front of the television watching repeats of the *Jack Benny Program*. When we finished eating she said, "Come on. Let's go outside."

We sat in the chairs on the front porch and waited for a cool breeze that never showed. Some girls about our age jumped rope on the sidewalk in front of the apartment building across the street. On the stairs leading up to the second landing, two women sat like bookends, laughing about something so funny, one of them almost laughed herself down the stairs. She grabbed the banister and righted herself. On the grass in front of the house next door, a group of men about Daddy's age played cards and passed a bottle in a brown bag between them.

The light at 106th turned green. A police siren signaled a driver to pull over to the curb. The car that cruised to a stop just beyond Cynthia's driveway looked very much like Marquette's. A motorcycle cop in the familiar California Highway Patrol helmet and khaki uniform pulled up behind the car and got off his bike. He flipped the kickstand down with the toe of his boot and walked to the driver's side. He and the driver exchanged a few words, and then the men laughed. Cynthia and I gaped at one another. Usually, white cops were gruff and stone-faced when they interacted with us. This cop politely asked the driver to get out of the car. He did and staggered to the back of the car. It was Marquette.

"Heyyy. Whazzs happ'nin, y'all?"

"Hey, Marquette," we said.

"Did I tell you Ronald was home?" he announced as if we were at a social gathering.

Ronald stuck his head out the window in confirmation.

"What's happenin', Cynthia?" Ronald said.

She waved back. I'd heard a lot about Ronald, but we'd never actually met. Considering the circumstances, I didn't expect him to get out of the car to formally introduce himself, so I wasn't disappointed when he didn't.

The cop asked Marquette to stand with his feet together and hold his head back. There was no question Marquette was good and drunk. He put his feet together and held his head back like the cop asked. The rest of his body leaned over like a palm tree blowing in a hurricane and landed on the trunk with a thud. The officer stood him up and asked him to touch the tip of his nose with each finger. Marquette's left finger touched his left eyebrow. The right touched his cheek, just beneath his eye. An inch higher and he might have poked his eye out.

"Have a seat," the cop said as he folded his ticket book and walked over to his motorcycle. Marquette dropped down on the curb and leaned back on his elbows. The cop radioed for a tow truck and a squad car.

The men playing cards came over and gave Marquette grief about getting caught drinking and driving. Marquette corrected them.

"I wasn't drinking and driving. I was already drunk when I started driving," he said and laughed. The men laughed with him. Even Cynthia and I had to laugh.

The women who'd been sitting on the stairs got up and came over. Then the girls jumping rope ran across the street and sat down on the curb next to Marquette. Marquette turned around and asked Cynthia to go get him some water. She came back with a glass of water and a packet of saltine crackers. I asked her why she got the crackers, and she said they'd help settle his stomach.

"I do it for my dad all the time," she said.

I followed Cynthia off the porch. We waited as Marquette drank the water. He handed the glass back to Cynthia and ripped open the packet of crackers open and shoved both in his mouth. The small group of us stood around talking to Marquette until the tow truck arrived. When the squad car with Kreps and Dumbrowski arrived, I pulled Cynthia back to her porch.

Ronald got out of the car and went over to the tow truck driver.

He begged the guy to let him drive the car home because his mother had to work that night. I knew Mrs. Rena would be furious if she got fired from her job for missing a day. Missing work, I noticed, was a big thing for us. Daddy and almost everyone I knew that had a job rarely took a day off, even when they were sick. Daddy said that's how it was for us. They didn't have a problem hiring us, but God forbid tragedy should strike, like a death in the family, or an illness. All of a sudden we would find ourselves summarily dismissed.

"Look to me like yo' mammy ain't goin' to work tonight," Kreps said, and motioned to the tow truck driver to take the car away.

"Please. Just let me go get her. We live right around the corner," Ronald begged.

"You ain't got to come get me 'cause here I am," Mrs. Rena said, coming up the block.

By now it looked like everyone in the neighborhood was gathered in front of Cynthia's house. Mrs. Rena asked to be allowed to drive the car home. Dumbrowski told her she could pick it up in impound.

"Now get your black ass out of my face or I'll lock you up with your boy," Dumbrowski added.

Mrs. Rena mumbled something under her breath.

"What did you say, nigger?" Dumbrowski asked.

"You heard me, mutha fucka! You and that other racist cracker rollin' around here terrorizin' innocent hardworkin—"

Kreps slapped Mrs. Rena so hard, her head snapped to the right. Spit flew out of her mouth.

"You need to learn your place, nigger bitch!" Kreps yelled in her face.

He turned to Dumbrowski and Mrs. Rena took the opportunity, foolish as it was, to jump on Kreps' back.

"The next time you lay your hands on me, mutha fucka, you betta make sure my black ass is dead!" Mrs. Rena shouted.

The crowd cheered. Dumbrowski snatched Mrs. Rena off Kreps' back, and Kreps swung at her head with his billy stick like he was swinging at a baseball. There was a loud crack! Mrs. Rena screamed and grabbed her head. Ronald stepped toward his mother and Dumbrowski punched him in the face. Blood dripped down Ronald's face and onto his T-shirt. I thought about how they'd beaten Roger and wondered if they'd do the same to the Fryes.

Three more squad cars arrived along with two motorcycle cops. They all watched as Kreps pulled Mrs. Rena's arms behind her back with such force she hollered. My stomach flipped. I moved closer to Cynthia and grabbed her hand, prepared to snatch her back in the house. Kreps threw Mrs. Rena into the back of the squad car. Dumbrowski shoved Ronald in next. Followed by Marquette.

Suddenly someone screamed in the crowd. I turned just in time to see a woman in a black smock spit in a cop's face. Without a second thought he punched her. She fell back into the grass. Someone else shouted, "This mutha fucka hit a pregnant woman! Did y'all see that?" The crowd charged the officers, who were outnumbered but not outgunned. Several officers pulled their guns on the crowd. One fired into the air.

In an instant Cynthia and I were on our feet. Cynthia pulled me into the house and slammed the door behind us. We ran into her parents' bedroom and hid in their closet. Another gunshot rang out, followed by screams. I slid closer to Cynthia. We held onto each other as if our lives depended on it. The closet smelled of mothballs and remnants of Mrs. Harper's perfume.

"It'll be okay," Cynthia said. "This can't go on all night. They'll get tired and go home. You'll see."

"This happens all the time?" I asked.

"No. But it happens enough."

After several hours, they didn't get tired and they didn't go home. The phone rang three different times. Each time Cynthia would slide to the closet door and push it open just enough to see the phone on the nightstand beneath the window. I think she believed if she stared at it long enough, it would float across the room to us the way it did for Samantha on *Bewitched*. One thing was clear: that was the only way it would get answered.

Outside, the shouting escalated and with it came the sounds of breaking glass, screeching brakes, and tires burning across the asphalt. Cheers and applause followed. In the distance I could hear the faint cries of children and several barking dogs. A siren started up, like the cop was in pursuit of someone, but it never moved from in front of the house. Glass broke and something large hit the carpet in front of the closet with a thud. Cynthia and I screamed.

Someone shouted, "Get your ass outta here, honky cop!"

Then what sounded like a thousand rocks clanked against metal. Then more glass shattered and silenced the siren. Tires screeched again and more cheers and applause broke out. Cynthia and I remained huddled together through it all. Not talking. Barely breathing. All of a sudden a bright light broke through the darkness. Cynthia and I screamed again.

"What in the hell! What are you two doing in the goddamn closet? I've been calling you for the last two hours. You had me worried to death!" Mrs. Harper shouted down at us.

Mr. Harper took inventory of the window and the brick lying in the middle of the floor. He gently took Mrs. Harper by the arm and moved her out of the way.

"I'm sure they're scared to death, Marsha. You yelling at them ain't helpin' one bit."

He extended both hands to us and pulled us to our feet. Cynthia fell into his side, wrapped her arms around his waist, and began crying. I stood there feeling awkward, wishing for my own father.

"You must be Zayla," Mr. Harper said.

I nodded.

"I just got off the phone with your father. He wanted to come get you when he heard what's going on over here. I told him he'd be safer waiting till morning. We'll keep you safe till then. He'll be here first thing to get you. Okay?"

I nodded again, unable to find my voice. I didn't care that Mr. Harper wasn't Daddy. I fell into him and sobbed. He held us until we'd managed to compose ourselves. Then he asked what happened.

Cynthia regurgitated everything that happened after Marquette stumbled out of the car. Several times Mr. Harper had to tell her to slow down so he could understand what she was saying. I still hadn't found my voice and wasn't much interested in finding it. Mrs. Harper scolded us for disobeying her orders.

"If you hadda kept your fast-tail behinds in the house, you wouldn't have seen any of that!"

I followed Mr. Harper and Cynthia down the hall through the kitchen and into a room I hadn't known existed. It looked like a family room and had a large green plaid sofa and a console television. Almost every remaining inch of floor space was littered with different types of plants, mostly rubber and ferns. Several hung in the corners of the room from the ceiling. Mr. Harper led us to the sofa, where Cynthia and I sat down and clung to each other like magnets.

"It's okay. Everything is going to be okay," Mr. Harper said.

He left and promised he wouldn't be gone long. Mrs. Harper was on the phone in the kitchen, telling Momma how she found us in the closet. Momma must have stupidly asked what we were doing there, and Mrs. Harper stupidly answered that she had no earthly idea. I shouldn't have been surprised, though. Not one time since she found us had she bothered to ask if we were all right.

I understood something that night. God blessed girls like Cynthia and me with loving fathers to compensate for the lack of love we received from our mothers. I also knew for certain that a God who hated people like me would never do such a thing if he didn't really love me. And, as if He were listening, Mr. Harper came back and sat down between me and Cynthia. He wrapped an arm around each of us. A few minutes later, Mrs. Harper sat down on the other side of Cynthia. She kissed Cynthia's forehead and cheek.

"Don't worry," Mrs. Harper said, more to herself, "God protects His children. Everything is gonna be okay."

* * * * * *

The eleven o'clock news opened with late-breaking news from the Watts district in Southeast Los Angeles. A male reporter appeared on the screen.

"This is Hal Fishman reporting from the Los Angeles Police Department Command Center. At this hour the intersections of Imperial Highway and Avalon over to Central are under siege. Masses of spectators are cheering as passing cars carrying white motorists and white police officers are pelted with bricks and rocks. The police appear to be outnumbered fifty-to-one. We are told some Negro motorists, caught in the crossfire, have been assaulted as well.

"It seems they ... the Negroes," Fishman continued. "They, umm ... seem to be focusing their anger toward any white people passing through. We've been told that this incident started earlier this evening when a Black motorist, a 21-year-old Marquette Frye, was pulled over on suspicion of drunk driving. After Frye failed the sobriety test, his car was impounded and he was arrested. But for reasons unknown the crowd of bystanders who witnessed the arrest got into an altercation with officers who'd been called to the scene and things escalated from there. We'll have more as the story unfolds."

I stared at the television as Markie demanded more Maypo. As the commercial ended, I couldn't help wondering how many white kids experienced life the same way we did. Always in fear of something terrible happening. Always aware that their life could be taken for any reason. Then I considered Mrs. Harper's words. If God truly loved His children, why was this happening to us? Why was something like this always happening to us? Why not white people? Why were they excused from the terror of the Negro experience?

* * * * * *

It was well after midnight before things quieted down outside. Cynthia and I climbed into bed. Just as I dozed off, I heard the boom of an explosion. A few minutes later sirens sped past the house, red lights filled the room momentarily, and then it went black again. I scooted closer to Cynthia and hugged her as if she were a teddy bear. She didn't pull away.

"Zayla? Can I tell you something?" she whispered.

"Yes," I said.

"Promise you won't get mad at me?"

"Promise."

She was quiet for a long time, then she cleared her throat and said, "If we don't live through this ... I, um ... well, I wanted you to know that I love you."

I didn't think twice before I replied, "I love you, too."

I was relieved once I'd said the words and a little surprised. What happened next was even more surprising. Cynthia rolled over. We lay there nose to nose, staring at each other through the blackness. Then she kissed me. Not like Dee-Dee kissed me behind the building. The way Marcus kissed me that balmy night in Chicago. Except, unlike Marcus, I didn't pull away for what felt like an eternity.

"Does this mean you like girls?" I asked.

"Yes. Ever since fourth grade, when I realized I didn't like boys."

"Have you told anyone?"

"No. It's nobody's business," she said.

It wasn't anyone's business, was it? I told myself. Who I like isn't as important as how I treat people. If I was a child of God and He made me in His likeness, then I'm okay however I came out because that's the way He wanted me to be, I reasoned. Then it occurred to me that there was nothing wrong with me. I was perfect just the way I was. Not a bulldagger. Not an abomination of God. I was a girl who liked other girls, and I didn't see that changing.

Something else occurred to me. The first time I fell in love for real just happened to be the same day Marquette Frye turned Watts upside down.

22

1,000 Riot and Battle Police in Watts Area
L.A. Times – Thursday, August 12, 1965

> *To a degree, academic freedom is a reality today because Socrates practiced civil disobedience. In our own nation, the Boston Tea Party represented a massive act of civil disobedience.*
>
> - Martin Luther King, Jr., "Letter from a Birmingham Jail"

Cynthia and I lay like two spoons in a drawer. My right arm rested across her body, our fingers interlocked. I couldn't feel my left arm, but I felt safe holding onto Cynthia until our slumber was violently interrupted.

I hadn't heard her enter the room. I don't know how long she stood there watching us. But Mrs. Harper slapped Cynthia across the face so hard, I felt it. My eyes shot open. Cynthia opened her mouth to scream, and Mrs. Harper pressed her hand over Cynthia's mouth before much sound could escape.

"Shut your mouth! Shut up!" Mrs. Harper whisper-shouted in Cynthia's face. To me she said, "Get your hands off of her."

Cynthia gripped my hand so tight it hurt. I couldn't have freed myself if I'd wanted to, which I didn't because I thought I could protect her somehow. I glanced around the room for the clock. That's when I noticed it was still dark outside. Why was Mrs. Harper waking us up middle of the night? I wondered. Something must have happened to Daddy. Maybe he'd tried to come get me anyway and had an accident. Or maybe he got arrested. Or maybe he was ... I couldn't allow myself to consider Daddy dead for even a second. But why else would Mrs. Harper be waking us up in the middle of the night? Was the house on fire? I wondered. Almost in answer, Mrs. Harper slapped Cynthia again.

"I said, get your filthy hands off of my daughter," she whisper-shouted again, and slapped Cynthia once more since she couldn't slap me. Back then adults could chastise children without repercussions, unless they went too goddamn far. Mrs. Harper knew as well as I did, had she slapped me the way she'd slapped Cynthia, Momma would have given her an alley-ass whippin', as Pompa used to say.

Cynthia must have sensed something different, though, which is probably why she released my hand.

I gave her forearm a gentle squeeze as I slid out of bed. I didn't even bother dressing. I didn't know what was going on, but now that I was awake someone was taking me home. I grabbed my bag off the chair and sped out of the room. Mrs. Harper watched me like a crazed hawk. I was afraid that anything I did or even said would give her a justifiable reason, in her mind, to slap Cynthia again. I was afraid to even look in Cynthia's direction before I ran off down the hall. For a long time, after that day, I wished I had taken that last look. I'm sure I would have had I known that would be the last time I would ever see Cynthia again.

"Everything okay, Ladybug?" Daddy asked. He looked like he was heading toward Cynthia's room. I was glad I came out when I did. Daddy didn't believe a man should ever have a reason to hit a woman. I believe he might have reconsidered that and given Mrs. Harper an alley-ass whippin' himself if he'd seen how close she'd come to slapping me.

"Huh?" I said.

I looked up at Daddy in wide-eyed disbelief. Was he really standing there, or was this part of the nightmare that followed me out of Cynthia's room?

He shook my shoulders. "Zayla! Are you okay?" he asked.

"Huh?" I said again.

I looked back toward Cynthia's room. Mrs. Harper stepped into the hall and closed the door behind her. She scowled down at me for an instant, and then up at Daddy as her scowl reshaped itself into a smile.

"I startled the girls when I went in to wake Zayla. Cynthia sleeps like the dead, so I had to clap my hands a couple times to wake her up. It's easier than shaking her awake. That seems to startle her terribly," she said in that tone Momma used when she was so full of shit you could smell it on her breath.

What a liar, I thought. To Daddy I said, "I'm just trying to wake up. How come you came to get me in the middle of the night?"

"It's a little after six o'clock in the morning," Daddy said and chuckled.

"But it's so dark outside."

"She has no idea what six o'clock looks like. You'd think the child was a vampire," Daddy said to Mrs. Harper, and chuckled again.

"She's something, all right," Mrs. Harper said. "She was just as sound asleep as Cynthia. Two peas in a pod, huh?"

This time she chuckled too. I grabbed Daddy's hand and started pulling him toward the door.

"Thanks for letting me stay over, Mrs. Harper. Tell Cynthia I had a great time and can't wait till we do it again," I said.

Now who's full of shit? I asked myself.

Daddy and Mrs. Harper exchanged pleasantries. When we got in the car, Daddy said, "So, are you going to tell me what really happened?"

I considered it for a moment, then thought, he doesn't tell you everything. If he did, you'd know what was going on between him, Momma, and Miss Evangeline. I decided I wasn't going to tell him. I knew Mrs. Harper had no intention of telling anyone what she'd walked in on, and she knew her secret was safe with me. Why should I tell Daddy what happened anyway? So he could get mad at me and tell Momma so she would be mad at me? No, thank you.

"Nothing. I was just mad at the way Mrs. Harper woke us up. I would have preferred if she'd just shaken me awake."

Daddy stopped at the corner and turned to me. He didn't say anything, just studied my face for the truth. I hadn't lied and I know that's what he saw.

"See, I'm telling the truth," I said.

"Ummm-hmmm," Daddy said.

Ordinarily, it would have been important that Daddy believe me. It wasn't that morning. The only thing that mattered was Cynthia and what was going to happen to her now that I was gone. I felt like a coward for leaving her there like that. What could I have done, though? I wondered. Since I knew damn well I couldn't give Mrs. Harper an alley-ass whippin', there wasn't much I could do. Daddy let up off the brake and pulled out into the intersection a little. He waited for two cars to pass, then turned onto Imperial Highway as dawn pushed through the night sky.

We passed Mr. Tony's light tan Chrysler as it crawled down the street. Morning copies of the *L.A. Sentinel* flew out the passenger-side window and landed on almost every porch. In the next block, we came upon two overturned cars. The one closest to the curb looked as if it had just been flipped upside down. The other car blocked a lane of traffic and looked as if it had been tossed in the air before it landed. Two officers stood in the street directing traffic. One used his hands, the other the firing end of his shotgun. Daddy pulled me closer to him. He nodded at the officers as we passed.

In the next block, several men carried a large piece of plywood toward a huge hole in the front window of a house that looked a lot like ours. Debris littered the streets on both sides, and as we turned onto Central, I saw what was left of the Safeway market. Steel girders stood in a pool of water and rubble. The only thing remaining was the sign that towered over the parking lot, much like the Jesus on the top of 103rd Street Baptist Church.

"It's gonna be okay," Daddy said. "The worst is over."

"Are you sure?" I asked.

"No, bug. I can't say that I am."

When we got home, I went straight to my room and climbed in bed. To my surprise, Momma didn't come bother me. I don't know how long I slept. When I woke up, Marquette and Roger were standing at the foot of my bed. Blood dripped from Roger's temple down his face and onto my comforter. His right eye was swollen shut and his left hung out of its socket and rested on his cheek. Marquette stood stock still. His unfocused eyes stared in my direction as blood ran from his mouth like water from a spigot. He had this sardonic smile frozen on his face, and he smelled like rotting meat. Together they leaned forward and shook my bed, calling out to me.

"Zayla! Zayla!"

I tried to run, to get out of my bed, but it was like invisible hands held me in place. I tried to scream, but no sound came from my mouth. I didn't want to talk to them. I didn't want to play. I wanted them to go away. I'd seen enough. Please, God, leave me alone! Please! I'm sorry and I'll do whatever you want to make this stop. Please!

"Zayla!"

I screamed and tried to run, but they had my legs and they were shaking me. God! Please help me, I screamed, but my voice was mute. God! Please? Is that you? I asked. And all of a sudden I felt His strong hands on my shoulders. My head lobbed around like a ragdoll. Then He was smacking me, first one cheek, then the next. Then both cheeks. Then voices. Loud. Familiar.

"Zay! Wake up!"

My eyes shot open. It was Daddy shaking me. I looked around the room, disoriented.

"Where'd they go? What happened?"

"You were screaming in your sleep. Where'd who go?"

"Marquette and Roger."

Daddy grabbed me and held me tight. It was so forceful it made me begin to cry.

"Don't leave me, Daddy. Please. Don't leave. I'm scared."

I didn't know if the words actually came out or not. In my head I screamed them. Daddy looked confused for a moment, and I realized I was still mute. My eyes pleaded with him because my mouth couldn't.

"Zay! What's wrong with you? What happened at the Harpers that's got you so spooked?"

"Marquette happened!" I screamed. "Then the riots!"

Now I find my voice, I thought.

"Yeah, baby. I know," Daddy said. "But you saw on the way home that they're all over now. Something else happened. I don't know why you won't tell me. Or, maybe I'll just have to call Mrs. Harper and ask her myself."

"There's nothing to tell," I said. "She'll just tell you the same thing she did when she came out of Cynthia's room."

He shook his head and stood up from my bed. "I don't know what's gotten into you, but I don't have time to pull it out. There's a meeting at Athens Park. They want to talk about what happened last night," he said. "Come on, bug. Go wash up and put on some fresh clothes. We need to leave here in an hour."

* * * * * *

The organizers of the meeting at Athens Park were made up of a few Negro leaders in the community and several white men I'd never seen before. They came to assure the crowd that the worst was over. They had one agenda. The attendees had another. There was standing room only as throngs of Watts residents filled the space. Daddy found a spot on the side closest to the wall that allowed us to see the panel seated at the table in the front of the room, but was also far enough away from the TV cameras that lined the other side of the room and the one in the center aisle.

I scanned the crowd and saw many of the same faces I'd seen the previous night, but they looked a lot worse for wear. Many were bandaged, bruised, or had broken limbs. I moved behind Daddy, wrapped my arms around his waist, and pressed my face into his back. Momma moved closer and rested her hands on my shoulders. I decided hearing what was happening was good enough for me.

At first, people who'd witnessed the Fryes' arrest blamed the cops for what happened. Of course, the cops standing along the back wall voiced their opinions, in opposition of the truth. The panel tried to calm everyone down. A boy about Roger's age told them to get the cops out of there.

"If you really want to help, then you'd listen to us and let us have our say without any opinions from the peanut gallery back there."

The crowd chuckled and started chanting, "Make them leave. Make them leave."

The request fell on deaf ears, which seemed to incite the audience to speak their piece, regardless. They shared how the motorcycle cops drove on the sidewalk, putting the children in harm's way. They pointed out how a cop punched a pregnant woman in the face. Someone even pointed him out in the crowd. He was immediately removed from the building, but not before he said, "They're god-damn liars. She spit in my face. That's why I hit her. She spit in my goddamn face."

A woman screamed out, "Yeah! They've been fucking with us for years, and no one cares. No one did shit when one of them mutha fuckas raped me! No one! Not the doctors! Not the nurses! Not the fucking lawyers! He came in my house because I called for help, and how did he help me? He fucked me! That's how!"

"People, please," one of the men on the panel pleaded. "The worst is over. We have heard your complaints and we plan on doing some-thing about it. We are—"

"This ain't the end," a young male voice cried out. "We're taking this shit out of the ghetto and putting it right at rich whitey's doorstep."

As the room fell silent, I mustered up the courage to peek around Daddy. A television camera was pointed at a tall, lanky boy. Upon closer inspection, I realized it was the thin, wiry boy I'd seen that night at Crogan's. I looked around for the athlete. He was standing a few feet away, looking like he meant business. I closed my eyes and nestled my head even farther into the small of Daddy's back.

* * * * * *

By the time we got home, it was just about dark out. The story that led the five o'clock news was thin, wiry boy's warning to rich whitey. It was as if that was the only thing said during the entire meeting. Daddy said it was a scare tactic to shift everyone's atten-tion away from the real issue and further the stereotype that all Ne-groes are angry and will act violently whether provoked or not. I got up to use the bathroom.

Outside, I heard several loud popping sounds, like ten firecrackers bursting through the night's stillness. Adult voices screamed. More popping sounds. A police siren screeched and a voice blared out of a loudspeaker: "You niggers! Drop what you have and put your hands up!"

I crawled into the space between the bathtub and the toilet and curled into a ball.

"Frank, they're shooting outside!" Momma said.

"Zayla! Are you okay?" Daddy called from the living room.

I didn't answer. I heard him get off the sofa and run to my room. "She's not here."

Momma ran to the kitchen and reported the same. I wanted to call out to them to tell them I was okay and couldn't. Seconds later the bathroom door swung open and Momma shouted, "She's in here. I found her!"

She helped me to my feet and took me to bed.

Two sets of spinning lights and wailing sirens zoomed by outside. In the distance, several sirens screamed down Central, and then a large boom shook the house at its foundation. Another set of lights flashed through the house and the street went dark again. I started crying.

I'd never felt so helpless, so small and insignificant. I imagined the news reporting, when things were finally over, that all the Negroes in Watts had died. And they would be happy because we would all be dead. I wailed even louder. Momma held onto me. Daddy stood helplessly at the door. I know if he could have made it all stop, he would have. But this was bigger than all of us.

Even with my twelve-year-old understanding, I knew I was living in a city, surrounded by a country, filled with people who had a deep-seated hatred for me just because I was Black. And their hatred was far too strong for me to overpower. I'd slipped down the rabbit hole to discover that if I managed to live beyond fourteen years of age, it wouldn't matter how smart, or innovative, or talented, or how well I could set a dinner table, I would still be Black. Negro. Colored. A Nigger. And for a brief moment, I wished I'd never been born.

* * * * * *

Uncle Bill stopped by later that evening. "I heard the meeting didn't go so well."

"Not at all," Momma said.

"Those young punks started talking about burning down the white businesses. They ain't about to let them go burn down no white nothin'. So, what's left? This community. They'll burn it down and we'll have to spend the next fifty years rebuilding," Daddy added.

"I know. Ted Watkins and Pastor Price said that to Deputy Chief Murdock down at the station after the meeting. They thought it would help calm things down if Murdock pulled the white cops out of the area and replaced them with Black cops in civilian clothes and unmarked cars. That asshole Murdock said it wasn't a good idea because it would be difficult to see the Negro officers once night fell.

"I don't know what's going to happen now. We just have to wait and see. Murdock has the whole station out there thinking they're going to calm things down by just showing up, which really means shoot first and ask questions later. They're even deploying cops from other stations, but I think it's only going to make things worse. We need to be prepared. Zora, can you help me and Evelyn gather up the folks in the neighborhood and have them meet at our place in about half an hour?"

"They can come here," Momma said. "I'll put on some coffee and warm up some biscuits."

23

It was close to ten o'clock by the time they managed to round up almost the entire neighborhood. There was barely enough room to walk between the sweltering bodies that filled our living room. As usual, they sent us kids out of the room so the "grown folks" could talk. Determined not to miss anything, Malik, Dee-Dee, James, Lorraine, Lucius, and me pretended to go in my room. As soon as the hallway door closed, we crowded around it and listened.

"What's this all about, Bill?" someone asked.

"Whew, it sho' nuff is hot in here. Ain't you and Frank got a fan, rich as y'all are?"

"She ain't rich, just him," Aunt Evelyn said.

It was supposed to be a joke, except nobody laughed because it was more true than it was funny.

"Quit complaining, Mabel. Russell, get up and let Mabel sit over there by the window."

"I could get the fan, but I don't think it would be much help," Momma said. "I can get you a cool glass of water, though."

"Thank you, suga."

Uncle Bill cleared his throat and said, "If I could have everyone's attention." He waited until everyone settled down. "I called us all together because we have no idea how out of control this whole thing could become. We're already dealing with snipers shooting at the firemen so they can't do their job of putting out the fires. So far there haven't been that many, but I think it's only a matter of time. It looks like they're targeting white-owned businesses, but even with that, if we can't get a lock on the snipers, the firefighters will have no choice but to let the fires burn themselves out. Judging by the looks of things, we gotta protect our families, our homes, and our businesses.

"Right now, though. Our biggest problem is what that damn kid said during the meeting. He's got them white folks running to the gun shops and arming themselves. I later heard from Reverend Brookins that the kid said some white man told him to say that. Now it doesn't even matter if it's true or not. That's the message, and as you all know, white lives are always more valuable than ours."

Everyone started talking at once.

"Outta everything that was said at the meeting, that's all they heard?"

"No, that's all they want everyone else to hear," Aunt Evelyn said. "God forbid somebody find out we got a legitimate beef down here."

"That's right, Evelyn! Do you know I went to Giant the other day to buy some hamburger meat and it was browner than I am?"

Laughter picked up speed, then fell like cars going over a cliff.

"I think it's time to get on up out of here."

"Where in the hell we gon' go? They got it so you can't buy nothin', and you'd be lucky to find a cardboard box to rent anywhere outside of Watts."

"Yeah! When they ain't screwin' with the law to keep us down, they got the banks, and the social workers. They're the worst. They come up in your house and take inventory. If you look like you got too much, but you ain't working, then they wanna sit on the god-damn furniture you bought with your hard-earned money when you *was* working and look over their glasses at you like they're tryin' to decide whether or not you're lying. And the only thing that's stopping you from knocking their goddamn head off is that goddamn piddly-ass check they have the power to stop if they feel like it. And all you want to say to them is, 'Hell, if somebody would give me a goddamn job, I wouldn't still be lookin'."

"What you need to do is get a gun and go rob you a job!"

More laughter, then several sirens whirled up Central and the room quieted down.

"They say Dr. King is on his way here," Aunt Evelyn announced.

"For what? Don't nobody want to hear from that old liver-lipped Uncle Tom. What's he gon' do? Tell us how we need to love them damn crackas?"

"Yeah! Why don't he go talk to them crackas to get their damn boot off our necks? That's what Brother Malcolm would have done."

"Dr. King has done a lot for his people," Momma said. "I don't think it's right you guys sitting up here bad-mouthing him. I don't see any of you fighting to make things better for us."

"That's 'cause—"

"That's 'cause nothin'," Momma said, cutting them off. "I know most everyone loved Malcolm X. Lord knows I did. But did you ever wonder how Malcolm X and Dr. King got more friendly after Malcolm came back from Mecca?"

If I hadn't heard it with my own ears, I wouldn't have believed Momma said it. I figured everyone else was looking at Momma, mouth agape too, because that is a side of Momma we'd never seen before.

"That's right, baby," Daddy said. "You set that record straight."

There was the distant sound of people screaming and what sounded like another explosion, the fourth of the day. I'd been keeping count since I'd heard the first one. A scream leapt out Shirley's mouth before she caught it with her hand. Billy's eyes got big and his mouth made a giant O. Malik grabbed my hand on one side and

Lorraine moved closer on the other. I was so scared, I thought I'd peed my pants. I ran to the bathroom. I pulled my underpants down and saw blood on the crotch. I screamed too, fully convinced God really was out to get me.

Dee-Dee burst through the door as if all of a sudden we were friends again. I pulled my pants up around my knees.

"Get out of here," I shouted.

I sighed with relief when Momma gently took Dee-Dee by the shoulders and moved her out of the way, closing the door right in her face.

"What's the matter, baby?" Momma asked.

"I'm dying," I said.

I pulled my pants down and showed her my underpants. She sat on the side of the tub and chuckled.

"I thought someone was trying to kill you. This sure is a welcome relief with all the craziness going on. You're not dying, baby," she said, pride in her voice. "You're becoming a woman."

God sure had a weird sense of humor. The city was on fire and people were pelting the white people with rocks and bricks and the rest of the white people in Los Angeles were terrified that Black people were going to bring their fight into their communities so they were buying up all the guns—and God chose that very moment in my life to make me a woman? I looked down at my underpants and shook my head. I was too mad to cry.

"I'll be right back," Momma said, putting the stopper in the tub and turning on the water for a bath.

I got it. I didn't like it, but I got it. I was finally having my "men-stroo-ation," as Mrs. Wilkins, our health teacher, pronounced it. "Men-stroo-ation" was a girl's passage into womanhood. Our bodies were preparing us to become mothers. Then she showed us a chart of the female reproductive organs. Now I had womanhood to deal with. Great! And I knew Momma went back in the living room and announced the arrival of my period to the entire group. I could just hear her, "Zayla's just got her period," and making that pitiful face so everyone felt sorry for me.

"Zayla! What's goin' on in there? Are you okay?" Malik asked.

"Yeah, I'm fine. I'm on the toilet, do you mind?"

Dee-Dee pushed the door open again and whispered, "What happened? Did you get your period?"

I raised an eyebrow and gave her my best "Shut the hell up" face.

"Tell me all about it tomorrow," she said, ignoring me.

I wasn't telling her anything. And what was to tell anyway? It's not like I was getting a parade the next day. Or the key to the city. I'd spent my entire twelve years of life listening to women talking about the "curse." Naturally, I was curious because all I knew was that I was supposed to get it one day. But they didn't tell me what "it" was and now "it" was staining the middle of my underwear. This kinda thing deserves a little warning. I thought of all those ads in the magazines with the lady dressed in a white flowy gown, smiling at the camera. The caption beneath her reads, "Modess ... because." I'd always wondered what was supposed to come after the "because."

Now I know, I said to myself. Modess because you'd never guess the mess that's going on under this dress.

"Congratulations, Ladybug," Daddy said through the door. I mumbled thanks and heard him walk away chuckling.

Momma came back into the bathroom. She reached under the sink and pulled out a blue box that was familiar to me. The sanitary napkin was as long as my arm. Forget about guessing, there'd be no way to hide it! It came with a large V-shaped contraption. Momma told me to secure the pad to the belt. I had to wear it around all day because it was supposed to keep the pad in place. And suddenly, it made sense why they called it "the curse." I didn't care if the pad moved or not.

"How comfortable am I supposed to be with a phonebook strapped between my legs?" I asked.

Momma laughed. "That's just the way it is, baby. You'll get used to it."

She gathered up my clothes and reached over to turn off the faucet. She left again, closing the door behind her. I climbed in the tub and stuck my face in the water.

"Bye, Zayla," Malik called through the door. "Will you tell me what happened tomorrow? Dee-Dee said you probably just got your period. Did you?"

I pulled my face out of the water and shouted, "Shut up and leave me alone," and stuck my face back in the water.

Momma came back with my pajamas, and for the first time since I was nine years old, she knelt down on the floor and bathed me.

"I was your age when I got my period," she said, rubbing the washcloth over my back. "And I reacted just like you. I hid in the bathroom and wouldn't let anyone in. Your grandfather had to pick the lock. They found me crouched down in the corner behind the bathtub, crying like a fool. Ooh, you should have seen me. I wouldn't come out of my room for school the next day. I was so embarrassed. Maxine kept saying it wasn't the end of the world, but she always had a way of trying to make me feel stupid. I didn't want to hear anything she had to say. It took Evelyn to finally drag me out of the house to go outside. She said everyone would know if I always stayed in the house when it was that time."

Momma explained all the things I had to look forward to, like cramps, mood swings, cravings for junk food and sweets, and weight gain. I told her the cramps I could do without. Cravings for junk food and sweets I could live with. Momma laughed and finished up bathing me. She rinsed me off and wrapped one of Daddy's big brown towels around me.

"Now listen, you have to be sure to change your pads regularly.

You can't wear the same one all day long. No matter how little you might bleed into it."

She led me down the hall to her room. Daddy was sitting in front of the living room window with a shotgun that I didn't even know we had across his lap. Everyone else had gone home to do the same. I climbed up in their bed.

"My baby is a woman," Momma said. "Things will get better for you now. You just wait and see. That old tomboy inside of you is being evicted as we speak."

She kissed my forehead, then my cheek and tucked me in bed, leaving room for Daddy. I sank into the pillows and inhaled Daddy's spicy scent. Momma changed into her nightgown and robe.

"You wait right here," she said. "I'll be back with something special just for you."
I gazed at the ceiling and counted the brush strokes in the paint, pretty sure I knew what Momma had. I was a woman now. I could get pregnant, not that it mattered. I thought about Malik and Melody and grabbed the phone to call him. I decided to call Cynthia first. I hadn't heard from her all day and couldn't wait to tell her I'd become a woman since she'd last seen me. There was no answer at her house. I hung up and called Malik. Aunt Evelyn asked five million questions, wanting to know how I felt now that I was a woman. I told her it felt great, knowing I'd provided the only answer that would get me closer to talking to Malik.

"That's right," Aunt Evelyn sang-shouted into my ear. "You should feel great! You're going through your first rite of passage. Becoming a woman will be the first best thing to happen in your life. The second will come when you do it for the first time. And the next will be the moment you hold your newborn child."

I wasn't embarrassed anymore. "Thanks, Aunt Evelyn. I really do feel great!"

"Good, baby. That's good because I knew your mama wasn't gonna tell you shit that would make you feel good."

"That's okay. That's what I have you for. Momma's getting me ice cream right now. That's always the next best thing."

Aunt Evelyn laughed and called Malik to the phone.

"I'm a woman now," I announced.

"If you say so," he said. "How does it feel?"

"I feel great! Your mom said I'm going through a rite of passage. I've become part of a special tribe."

"Yeah, now you and every woman over twelve all have a period. So what?"

"We bring life into the world. Not that I'm gonna be making babies anytime soon. If ever."

"Yeah. You and Melody. Good-bye. See you tomorrow."

"What's that supposed to mean?" I asked, but he'd already hung up.

Momma came back with two bowls of vanilla ice cream, as expected. Salmon croquettes were her nonverbal apology. Ice cream was her way of saying, "I'm so proud of you," which she couldn't seem to say either for some odd reason. Maybe because you don't do much to make her proud, I told myself. Then reminded myself that I was a straight-A student, and that was it. There was nothing special about me. I'm just an average girl, now woman, who has no idea where her life should go. If I didn't remember anything Suzanne told me, I remember her saying, "You are the captain of your life ship. Don't let anyone else at the helm." I was a woman now.

Momma and I lay in bed eating our ice cream and talking about what it means to become a woman, without the details of sex or anything because according to Momma I wouldn't need to know about that for years and years to come. Somewhere right before my wedding day.

"I already know about sexual intercourse," I said.

Momma put the spoon back in the bowl and licked her lips. She chose her next words carefully.

"Who told you about sexual intercourse?" she asked.

"Mrs. Wilkins. The health teacher," I said.

There was no way I was going to tell her Suzanne told me. I knew I'd never hear the end of it. I also knew what I needed to know. Having premarital sex was a sin and I'd already sinned enough. I wasn't adding that to the list.

Without another word, Momma got up. I'd only had a few bits of ice cream before she took our bowls to the kitchen.

"Is Daddy coming to bed?" I asked, trying to show it didn't bother me.

"Go to bed, Zayla," Momma said. "Your father is protecting the house."

And just like that, my moment with Momma was over. At least I knew I was safe with Daddy protecting the house. I slipped out of bed and went to my room. Momma didn't try to stop me.

* * * * * *

As I returned to bed after my umpteenth trip to the bathroom, I caught Daddy as he was coming in from getting the paper off the front porch.

"What are you doing up?" he asked when he saw me.

"My womanhood makes it hard to sleep the whole night. I don't want to have an accident."

I knew Daddy knew what I was talking about. He sleeps with Momma during her time, and she gets up in the middle of the night, too. Besides, Momma might not have explained everything to me, but I had sense enough to know that if anything slipped past that sanitary napkin, I'd be scrubbing blood out of my sheets for days.

"Can I sit up with you?" I asked.

"It's almost four in the morning. You sure you want to be up?" he asked, and laughed.

He picked the movie section out of the paper and handed it to me. I busied myself looking for new movies coming to the Largo. In a week *For a Few Dollars More* would be on the marquee. I couldn't wait to tell Cynthia. I waited until eight o'clock and called. Mrs. Harper heard my voice and hung up the phone. When I called the number again, I got a busy signal. I got that annoying buzz in my ear off and on for over an hour. I finally gave up and decided to try again the next day.

"I haven't heard you talk about Cynthia since we left her house yesterday. You still want to tell me nothing's wrong?" Daddy asked.

"Something's wrong with her phone. I keep getting a busy signal."

"Maybe the phone's off the hook and they don't know. I'll take a drive over there in a little while to tell them."

"It's too dangerous out there, Daddy," I said. "I don't want you to go."

"I'll be okay. I'll go the back way and I'll be back before you know it."

As if in answer to my pleas, someone knocked on the door, the knob twisted, and in comes Uncle Bill.

"You know, you need to lock your doors. Anyone can get up in here, and now is not the time to be temptin' fate," Uncle Bill warned in his cop voice.

"I just came in with the paper, man. One second longer and it would have been locked and double-bolted," Daddy said.

"Good. I would hate to think my man is slippin'. I ain't gon' always be around to protect you."

"Where you goin'? I don't see you goin' nowhere no time soon. And, you know you ain't gon' ever catch me slippin'," Daddy said.

He locked and double-bolted the door. Then, for good measure, slid the chain into its slot across the door.

"What's goin' on, man? Have them fools given up and gone home? This ain't the fight we need right now."

"If not now, when?" Uncle Bill said, more to himself as an afterthought. "These white folks are puttin' all kinds of protection in place. And they have no intentions of making it any safer for us now that all this is happening. They are out there burning down our home, Frank. Our home. Where we grew up. Nothing will be the same after this. Nothing. I just hope I live to see it. Between the snipers and the trigger-happy boys in blue, ain't none of us safe."

I noticed that Uncle Bill referenced his untimely death twice in as many minutes. Daddy noticed it too.

"Seriously, what's gon' on, man?" Daddy asked, more seriously.

"I just can't believe what's being done to solve this problem. And ain't nobody taking it seriously. Yorty said he didn't want to disappoint the people in San Francisco about some damn speech he was gonna give, so he went. If Beverly Hills was on fire right now, them people in San Francisco would still be waiting for his ass. But when it comes to us, why should they care? They ain't trying to make it safe for us. That's the objective, right? Keep us in fear for our lives? I'm living it every day. Who's protecting me? Huh, who?"

I'd never heard Uncle Bill so angry.

"Yorty is steady sendin' messages through the media, telling white Los Angeles to stay out of the 'riot area.' We ain't even Watts no mo'. We've become the 'riot area.' He told them to keep their children at home. And not once has anyone asked about our children! There ain't no consolation or advice for us! You know, those of us living in the 'riot area' and ain't a goddamn one of them even bothered to ask. Then they lyin', telling people comin' in to LAX that the flights were rerouted because snipers were firing on the planes."

"Come on, man. Let's go for a ride. I need to go check on my club," Daddy said. "Make sure them niggas ain't burned down Zayla's college tuition. Come on. Ride with me. Zay, tell your mom where I am when she wakes up. I'll be back before you know it."

Uncle Bill got up and quietly followed Daddy out the door.

I went and climbed in bed with Momma. I waited for her to wake up and kick me out, but she didn't move. Before long I was sound asleep– until a siren roared by just outside the window. Momma's eyes flew open. She sat straight up and called out to Daddy.

"He's not here, Momma. He went to the club, but he said he'd be back soon."

She fell back against the pillow and put her arm over her eyes.

"What time is it?" she asked.

"Ten-thirty," I said.

I'd managed to sleep for over two hours. I didn't feel rested. I needed more sleep. I got up and pulled the blinds down and closed the curtains.

"What are you doing? It's time to get up, child."

"I didn't sleep good."

"Well. You didn't sleep well," she corrected.

I didn't sleep well," I said. "Can I go back to sleep, please?"

"Will I let you go back to sleep?"

"Yes, will you?" I said.

She was getting on my nerves with all that correcting my grammar, I thought. Thank God the phone rang before she could say another word. It was Daddy.

"Is everything okay?" I asked.

"Yes and no. Depending on who you ask."

"Who's that?" Momma asked.

"Daddy." I handed her the phone without being asked and ran to the living room to get on the extension.

"Everything okay?" Momma asked.

"Mr. Plummer spent half the night trying to keep his pawn shop from getting burned down, and just when he thought he was in the clear, they set fire to that clothing store next door. It wiped out almost the entire block.

"There's not much left of 103rd Street. The destruction came in waves," he said. "They had a process. One car would pull up and throw a brick through a store window. Another car, loaded with people, would come empty the store of as much of its contents as could be carried. Then a last car would toss a Molotov cocktail through the window. When the firemen got there, snipers hidden on the rooftops started shooting at them so they couldn't do their job. Word spread that Negro-owned businesses weren't the target, only the white ones. So, all the Black store owners made signs that read, "Owned by a Negro" and stuck them in the window to keep the Molotov cocktails away. I made a sign for the Landes' Bookstore to keep it safe as well. But the furniture store next to the Largo, the department store, the shoe store, and Moskowitz's store weren't so lucky."

I'd forgotten all about Mr. Moskowitz. I felt a pang of sadness. They shouldn't have burned his store down. He was nice to everyone. We didn't see a white man. We saw a nice man. A fair man.

"How could they have burned down Mr. Moskowitz's store?" I asked Daddy. "He'd never done anything to anyone. Not like Mr. Crogan."

"Well, from what I hear, Crogan didn't make out too well either. Not only did they burn his store, they burned his car, too. As far as Moskowitz is concerned, he was a casualty of circumstance. They hit the store next to him, and like Mr. Plummer, Mr. Moskowitz's store became collateral damage."

"Come home, Daddy. Please," I begged. "I don't want anything to happen to you."

"Nothing's going to happen, bug. I'm on my way."

I went to take a bath. Momma and I seemed to be hovering

around that euphoric state of my new womanhood. I would have done anything to keep it going. So, instead of picking out my own outfit, I asked her to choose one for me. She flipped through my closet and then went to my dresser. She pulled out a pair of jean shorts and a tank top and handed them to me. I looked down at the clothes and up at her.

"I've been running this part of your life long enough," she said. "I think it's about time you should be able to wear whatever you'd like. And comb your own hair. Wouldn't you agree?"

I was so happy I didn't know what to do. I wrapped my arms around Momma's waist and gave her a big hug. To my surprise, she didn't stiffen up. She hugged me back.

I dressed and helped Momma make breakfast. Before we sat down to eat, I ran to get the gifts I'd buried in the back of my closet. I handed them to her.

"What's this?" she asked.

"I got them for you when I was in Chicago," I said proudly.

I would have explained why it had taken so long for me to give them to her, but it didn't seem to matter. That I gave them to her at all made her smile.

"They're beautiful," she said and tied the scarf around her neck. She stuck the fan in her purse. "I don't know about that fan, though. Didn't they have one that wasn't so colorful?"

* * * * * *

Daddy came home and resumed his place in front of the window. Momma told him we were walking down to Aunt Evelyn's. As soon as we stepped onto the porch, the stench of sulfur burned my nostrils. I plugged my nose with my fingers and coughed. Black smoke hovered in the sky above the houses on Mrs. Robinette's side of the street. Ashes floated overhead like snowflakes in a winter storm.

There were no signs of life in our part of "The Circle," and it was quiet out on Central as well.

Aunt Evelyn and Malik were glued to the television. They made room for us on the sofa with them, and we all watched as a television camera panned over empty streets all over Watts. Officers in riot gear stood at attention on opposite corners. Squad cars blocked off all intersections coming into and out of Watts. They patrolled the streets with shotguns in one hand, looking for a reason to shoot first and ask questions second.

"What are they doing?" Malik asked.

Aunt Evelyn said, "Protecting what's left of 42nd and Broadway and all the stores the white people owned."

Signs at various intersections read, "Turn left or get shot." The shops on both sides of the street looked bombed out as if World War III just hit California. Several cars smoldered at the curb and in the middle of the street.

"In other parts of the city—" the news reporter was saying.

"Bill said it's crazy all over," Aunt Evelyn interrupted. "He's got to work late. I wish he'd just come home. He can't do anything to stop this. They just got him out there in harm's way for nothing."

"He'll be okay," Momma assured her. "He's got God on his side."

"Yeah," Aunt Evelyn mumbled.

She told us they were talking about bringing in the National Guard. The governor was in Spain and "unavailable for comment." And even though the news reporters were saying the local police had managed to get things under control, we all knew it was a lie. That was the same lie they'd told the night before.

Malik and I went to his room and sat on the floor in front of his radio. He was still in a foul mood.

"Have you talked to Melody yet?" I asked.

"Yeah. I talked to her."

I waited for him to finish. He didn't. "And?" I pushed.

"She's not pregnant."

He abruptly reached over and turned the radio on.

A high school kid called into Montague's show and said, "My name is Kathleen Johnson. I go to Jordan High School. I just want to say, "Burn, baby! Burn,'" mimicking Montague.

He said, "Burn, Baby!" in response.

"And Montague," she said. "Don't stop."

The Magnificent Montague took fifteen calls back to back. People called in and talked longer than their allowable Name, School, Burn Baby, Burn lines. Montague didn't cut them off. He let them tell what was really happening in Watts. How the police started the commotion the night of the 11th. How they pushed Marquette into resisting arrest because they attacked his mother. Some people talked about the living conditions in some areas. Some talked about the schools. But just about everyone talked about the police and their brutality. They talked about the racism and how it was about time we 'Get Whitey!'"

Montague would end each call with, "Burn, baby!"

A song started to spin and then the volume went down. We could hear Montague talking to someone. He was saying, "Hell, naw! I'm not gon' stop. If you make this a special situation with me, you're really going to create something. Not to mention you're gon' make me lose my credibility. And I ain't about to lose my credibility just 'cause I'm a Negro, just 'cause you think I'm their leader on the radio, and all they want to do is say, 'Burn, baby! Burn!' For me to stop is to say they're wrong and the Establishment is right. I'm not an Uncle Tom and I will not go along with this shit."

He was quiet for a stretch. Every once in a while he'd say, "umm-hmmm," or "uhh-uhh." Finally, he said, "You know, not one of the so-called parents that you claim told you to make me stop said a word to me. Let them tell me to stop to my face. Matter of fact, I'll put out a call-and-respond message, for only mothers and fathers, to call me for the next fifteen minutes. Let them tell me if they're in agreement. Then you call me back in a half hour and I'll let you know. Or, better yet! Listen to your own station, man! Ain't no use of you coming down here now to pull me off the air in your pajamas."

Aunt Evelyn shouted, "You tell 'em, Montague."

"Mothers and fathers out there in Watts," Montague said into the microphone. "Call me. If you want me to stop saying, 'Burn, baby! Burn!' you tell me. If you want me to say it, tell me. Tell me your name and your child's name and school. You only got thirty seconds with the music under you. Otherwise, I cut you off."

"I'm Estelle Johnson, my daughter attends John Muir Junior High School, her name is Betty. Keep on burnin', Montague!"

He took six calls like that and then he took a call from someone we knew.

"I'm Evelyn Edwards, my son and goddaughter attend Compton Elementary School. His name is Malik Edwards and her name is Zayla McKinney. You keep right on burnin', Montague! Burn, baby! Burn!"

Malik and I ran into the kitchen chanting, "Burn, baby! Burn!" Aunt Evelyn was screaming and cheering. Momma even joined in. We all danced around, joined at the elbows, do-si-do–ing around the room. "Burn, baby! Burn!" we screamed.

"Hey, listen," Malik said, grabbing my upper arm. I froze. Momma and Aunt Evelyn stopped, too.

Shotgun fire cracked the air, followed by rifles. Helicopters flew overhead. The thump, thump, thumping of the propellers made me think of all the stories Ezel told us about being in Vietnam. A car horn blared like someone was standing on the steering wheel. Aunt Evelyn shouted for us to get down and away from the windows. We hit the floor and crawled under the table.

Montague reported, "...Looters are cleaning out the Giant food store on 103rd Street. Some kids are down on Imperial and Avalon, throwing rocks at passing cars. Unfortunately, the only two arrests the police have made so far were two Negro girls between the ages of nine and twelve. That's proof, folks, that Johnny don't care who he nab, long as he nab somebody."

"Ain't that the truth?" Aunt Evelyn said.

2 4

Yorty Inspects Ravaged Area from Helicopter
L.A. Times – Sunday, August 15, 1965

> *The class is confronted with a question,*
> *and no one — not even the professor —*
> *is sure of the answer:*
> *"Will you please tell us whether or not it is true*
> *that negroes are not able to cry?"*
> *America needs a killing.*
> *America needs a killing.*
> Survivors will be human.
> ~Michael S. Harper, "Deathwatch"

Watts burned for five straight days.

Daddy only moved from his post at the front window to eat, pee, and walk me and Momma down to Aunt Evelyn's every afternoon. We got into a rhythm of having breakfast at home, and then Daddy would walk us down the street to Aunt Evelyn's around noon and return home to his post. We'd have lunch and dinner with Aunt Evelyn and Malik until Uncle Bill came home, and then Uncle Bill would walk us back up the street in time for bed. He and Daddy would sit in the living room and talk about the good old days and how much Watts had changed over the years. The next day we'd start the whole process over again.

For two days straight, Malik and I didn't say much to each other. He was still brooding about Melody, except he wouldn't tell me why. He'd said she wasn't pregnant, so I couldn't understand why he still had a bee in his bonnet about it all. I had a bee in my own bonnet. I hadn't heard from Cynthia since I left her house four days earlier. I'd called nine times since then, only to have the phone ring and ring with no answer. Or, I got the busy signal. Mrs. Harper picked up twice, heard my voice, and hung up in my face each time. I couldn't help wondering what she'd done to Cynthia. Had she beaten her? Sent her down south to live with her grandma? What could have happened to make her disappear on me like that?

"Why don't you just call her?" Malik said, as if we'd been in conversation.

"Call who?" I asked.

He just looked at me and returned his attention to the Etch a Sketch he'd been playing with for the last hour. I snatched the red screen out of his hand and gave it a good shake, then handed it back. To my surprise, he didn't protest.

"Fine, don't call her," he said and put the Etch a Sketch down and climbed up in the top bunk bed.

"Are you going to tell me what's wrong?" I asked.

He didn't answer.

"Fine, then don't tell me," I said and stomped out of the room.

I sat in the living room with Momma and Aunt Evelyn and pretended to be interested in the show they were watching. I help Momma cook dinner and helped Aunt Evelyn clean up. When we were all finished, I took the phone into the bathroom and called Cynthia again. Mr. Harper picked up.

"Hi, Mr. Harper. May I speak to Cynthia?" I asked politely.

"Is that you, Miss Zayla?"

"Yes, sir."

Mr. Harper called Cynthia to the phone. I couldn't believe how nice he was being. Then it occurred to me that he probably had no idea what happened between me and Cynthia. Not like anything really happened. It wasn't like Mrs. Harper caught us kissing. I'd think that would have given her a real good reason to be pissed off. She might have even gotten away with slapping both of us.

"Hello ... ummm ... Hi, Zayla," Cynthia whispered.

"Why are you whispering? What happened? Why haven't you called me?" I asked, my words crashing in to one another.

"I ... ummm ... I can't talk right now. Can I, um, call you tomorrow? I have to go," she said.

The phone line went dead. I pressed the receiver against my ear and willed her to pick up the phone again. She didn't. And she didn't call me the next day. On the evening of the third day I decided to try her again. I wasn't so lucky that time. Mrs. Harper picked up.

I started to hang up, then decided it was more important to let her know she didn't scare me.

"Zayla, is that you?" Mrs. Harper asked.

I felt like Gretel at that moment when she realized the witch had every intention of shoving her into the oven and having her for dinner. I held the receiver away from my mouth and cleared my throat.

Into the receiver I said, "Yes, ma'am. May I speak with Cynthia, please?" in as confident a voice as I could muster. I was prepared for whatever she threw at me.

"Oh, dear. Didn't she tell you? Cynthia's down South with her grandmother. We thought it was too dangerous for her to stay here and all."

I wasn't prepared for that.

"She's gone?" I said in a weak whisper.

Mrs. Harper had knocked the wind out of me and she knew it. I could almost hear her smiling on the other end of the line. I refused to let her win.

"Oh no," I exclaimed, "I thought she said she was leaving tomorrow. We went to Sea World to get away and just got back a little while ago. Will you let Cynthia know I called and that I'm sorry I missed her?"

My courage grew as I talked. As it turned out, I was pretty good at lying. I didn't like lying, but I didn't like bullies either, and Mrs. Harper was nothing more than a big bully. I smiled and hoped Mrs. Harper could feel it. She was quiet for a moment.

"Well, now that you know, please don't ever call here again," she said, in that same nasty voice I'd heard that morning.

"Don't worry. I don't ever want to talk to you again in my life," I said and slammed the receiver back on its cradle. I may have won that round, but in the end Mrs. Harper won the game.

When I looked up, Malik was standing there watching me.

"Why are you crying?" he asked.

I wiped my eyes with the backs of my hands. "Nothing. I don't want to talk about it. Why are you in here?" I asked.

"It's the bathroom. I have to pee."

I got up, taking the phone with me, and went back in his room. When he came back, I asked him how long he thought the riots were gonna go on.

"Stop calling it a riot. Daddy said it's an uprising. It's what people do when they've been pushed around and their backs are against the wall."

"Oh. Then how long do you think the uprisings are gonna go on?" I asked.

"How am I supposed to know? Do I look like Carnac the Magnificent?"

Carnac, played by Johnny Carson on *The Tonight Show*, was this psychic character always clad in a big poufy feather-plumed mystical hat and a black cape. He would put a sealed envelope up to his head and provide an answer to the unseen question inside. I knew Malik wasn't trying to be funny, but it was funny because Carnac could never just walk out on stage. He always tripped up the step to his seat, and Ed McMahon had to help him up.

"Now that you mention it, you kinda do look like him," I said.

Malik managed a smile. "Very funny."

A few minutes later a blood-curdling scream came from the living room. We ran down the hall and stopped dead in the living room doorway. Two white police officers, one tall like Daddy, the other short and squat, stood uncomfortably at the front door.

The short one was talking to Momma. "Like I said, ma'am. We tried to call ahead, but as you know, the power and telephone service is down because of the rioters."

"Well, what happened?"

The tall one spoke up. "It looks like he was caught in the crosshairs between the snipers and the people on the street shooting at anything passing by."

"What do you mean 'anything passing by'? He was in a police uniform. He's one of you! How in the hell did he get shot by accident?"

"'Cause he's a lyin' mutha fucka!" Aunt Evelyn screamed. "Get out of my house! Go! Get out!"

Aunt Evelyn dropped into a crouch, balled her nightgown up in her hands, and screamed into it. Tears streamed down Momma's face. All she knew to do was rub Aunt Evelyn's shoulders and cry. What else could she do?

The two cops watched the scene unfold with empty eyes. Aunt Evelyn popped up like one of those snakes in a can gag. She grabbed Malik and pulled him down with her as she crouched again. Confused, he stiffened and tried to get away. Her grip was too tight.

"Lord have mercy," she pleaded. "No. Nooooooo. Not Bill! Not my baby. Noooooooooooooooooooo . . ." The word trailed off and disappeared into Aunt Evelyn's wails.

The officers continued standing there staring as if Aunt Evelyn was an accident they couldn't look away from. The short one had a white-knuckled grip on the doorknob. He kept saying how sorry they, and everyone down at the 77th Street Station, were for Aunt Evelyn's loss.

"If you need anything, Mrs. Edwards. Anything at all. Please don't hesitate to call," the taller cop said, handing Aunt Evelyn a business card. Momma snatched it from him and then moved him out of the way and opened the door for them to leave. Aunt Evelyn looked up to the ceiling and cried out, "Why, God? Oh why?"

I could have told her it was because God was a mean, vengeful God, but it wouldn't have helped anything. Uncle Bill was dead. Nothing was going to bring him back. Suddenly, a terrifying thought occurred to me. Four days earlier I'd accepted myself for the first time, and now the world around me was in complete chaos. First the riot. Then my period. Then Cynthia. And now Uncle Bill. Was it true? Had I brought all this on by admitting I liked girls? Except why do Malik and Aunt Evelyn and all of Watts have to pay for my sins? I wondered. Why couldn't God just punish me and Momma?

Each time Aunt Evelyn screamed, a part of me crumbled. Over and over her screams chipped away at my soul and made me wish, for the second time in my life, that I'd never been born. Tears flooded her face, snot dripped down her nose into her mouth. Her face was contorted in anguish. She pulled at her nightgown and used it to make a cocoon around her.

"Why him, God? Why? I need him. Ohhhhh. I need him so baaaddd," she wailed.

Momma and I drifted toward each other and held on for dear life. Malik's eyes were locked on Uncle Bill's first-place bowling trophy that sat on top of the television. Aunt Evelyn jerked his shirt back and forth with her violent spasms. He finally broke free from her and walked to the trophy. He ran his fingers around the edges of the name plate attached to its base. Tears crawled down his face. One hand fingered the white bowling ball affixed to the top of a gold bowling pin, the other hung paralyzed at his side. I couldn't even begin to imagine what was going on in his head.

He traced each letter engraved in the gold name plate. William Jerome Edwards, it read. Engraved beneath that in smaller letters it read, Perfect Score of 300. He traced the sides of the trophy from top to bottom, across the gold bowling pin and took hold of the trophy by the white bowling ball. He hurled it across the room. It flew top over bottom and shattered in the corner between the dining and living rooms.

Aunt Evelyn stopped screaming, Momma pushed me away and ran to Malik. He returned his attention to the space where the trophy had been. Aunt Evelyn pushed Momma away and went to him. He snatched away from both of them and ran out the front door. Aunt Evelyn screamed after him.

"Malik! Don't go! I can't lose you too! It'll kill me. It will just kii-iiiiiiillll me."

Then she threw her head back and howled– a howl filled with what seemed like a lifetime of anguish. The pain of having to live the rest of her life without Uncle Bill. I couldn't take it anymore. I wanted some air and needed to make sure Malik was okay. I squeezed by Aunt Evelyn and barely made it through the front door before Momma grabbed the back of my shirt.

"Momma, let me go talk to him," I pleaded.

"It's dangerous out there, Zayla. Just let me call around and see if we can get some help to find him."

"The phones don't work, remember?"

"Malik! Malik! Malik! Where are you, baby! Please come home to me! Please!"

There was no sign of Malik on the street. Aunt Evelyn threw her arms up in the air and collapsed. Momma helped her back into the house. I took off after Malik.

* * * * * *

I knew exactly where to find him. I ran down the street to our house. I hesitated, wanting to go inside to tell Daddy about Uncle Bill. I couldn't stomach it. Someone else much stronger than me had to announce that his best friend in the whole world was dead. I crept along the side of the house, up the driveway, and scrambled into our tree house. I found Malik curled up in a ball in the corner, holding Uncle Bill's medal in his hand and crying. I crawled over to him and lay down. There was no need to ask what was wrong, and there was no need to try and talk him down. What he needed was for me to be there for him.

"I love you, Malik," I said.

I figured it was a lot better than "I'm so sorry." What else was I supposed to say? He'd just lost his father. He had a whole lot of life left, and someone just blew out a huge part of it. I remembered the dreams that had plagued Malik all year. I reached out and took his hand in mine. And he was grateful. He gripped my hand so tight, I thought he'd break my fingers, but I didn't care. I wasn't going to let him go. We fell asleep that way.

It was daylight when we woke, and only then did I try to convince him we needed to get back to his house before Aunt Evelyn lost her mind. He sat up and pinned Uncle Bill's medal to his chest. I crawled out of the tree house and climbed down the ladder. He followed me. We walked zombie-like down the driveway toward the street. Mrs. Robinette was standing on the porch.

"Zayla, you take Malik home right now. What's wrong with you two running off like that?" she fussed.

I looked toward the house and waited for Daddy to come flying out of the door. Malik took off running and I ran off behind him. When we walked into Aunt Evelyn's house, Daddy was sitting next to Momma, who was on the sofa wringing her hands. She looked up, relieved, but couldn't pull herself up. Daddy's eyes were wet and tears stained his cheeks. I went to them and felt guilty for still having a father when Malik had none. Daddy grabbed me and cried into the top of my head.

"He's gone, Ladybug. Bill is gone."

The truth of that made me start crying. Uncle Bill wasn't just gone the way someone would be if they left the room or went on vacation. He was dead.

Uncle Bill was dead.

The next day, a list of known dead from the uprisings appeared in the paper. I scanned the list. There were almost thirty names on it, men and women. There were two police officers and one firefighter. I underlined Uncle Bill's name, tore the article out of the paper, and stuck it between my mattress and box spring.

25

Causes of Riots Assessed by City
L.A. Times – Sunday, August 22, 1965

> *Youths are passed through schools that don't teach,*
> *Then forced to search for jobs that don't exist and*
> *Finally left stranded in the street to stare at the*
> *Glamorous lives advertised around them.*
> ~Huey Newton, co-founder of The Black Panther Party

There was standing room only at 103rd Street Baptist Church on the day of Uncle Bill's funeral. Aunt Evelyn said his death unearthed niggas from every dark hole in Watts. She'd barely spoken up to that day, but that morning she found her voice and stitched words together that cut right to the quick. She called Momma a "bitch" twice, once at breakfast when Momma accidentally spilled coffee in Aunt Evelyn's plate and again in the car on the way to the church when Daddy's cigarette ash blew into Aunt Evelyn's eye. Momma didn't say a word, but I could tell she was hurt by the way she flinched each time. I felt sorry for her. Daddy explained to me that sometimes people take their grief out on those closest to them. He told me to expect the worst from Aunt Evelyn and Malik, "and be surprised when you don't get it." By all estimation, Momma was getting it coming and going.

Malik, on the other hand, hadn't uttered a word in eight days. He was only capable of grunts. One grunt for yes. Two for no. He stopped speaking to Aunt Evelyn the day after Uncle Bill died because she said she didn't want to sleep alone. Said she couldn't stomach the idea of sleeping in an empty bed knowing Bill was never coming home again. Said she didn't know how she was going to make it all alone. Malik looked at her long and hard, then walked down the hall to his room and slammed the door behind him. He shut everyone out after that, except me. Then, the day before the funeral, he shut me out, too.

"Look at 'em," Aunt Evelyn said from our first-row pew. "I didn't even know there were this many niggas *in* Watts."

She glared around the church, her lip curled in disgust as if everyone had a hand in Uncle Bill's death. Momma gently patted Aunt Evelyn's thigh and looked around to see who was watching. "Bill helped a lot of people, Ev. They're just here to pay their respects."

"They got 'im killed. If he hadn't been helping all those people, he'd still be alive today!" she said, in a whisper. Then she shouted, "All these niggas got him killed!"

I slid down a little in my seat and peeked over the back of the pew. I was certain every ear in the sanctuary heard Aunt Evelyn. They all "blessed her heart" in unison. A couple folks said, "Po' child." An energy, soft as a whisper, eased between the pews.

Someone behind us prayed, "Lord, Father God, we don't know why you called Bill home now, and we ain't here to question you, Lord. You know what's best. But we ask you, we beggin' you to keep close watch over Evelyn and her boy, Malik. Carry them through this, Lord. They ain't gon' get through this without you. Carry all of us through this, Lord. We need you now more than ever before. In Jesus' name I pray. Amen."

The few of us that could hear him said, "Amen," in unison.

I looked over at the casket and waited. I don't know what I was expecting would happen. I knew death was final. It had called on enough people I knew from a distance. This was the first time it played a starring role in my life. Which made me question God's motives. If God really loved us, why would he send my period and take Uncle Bill in the same summer?

I was grateful Aunt Evelyn decided to have a closed casket. That way I'd always remember Uncle Bill in life. His wide smile. The rich brown of his skin. I was grateful he'd passed down his strong jaw-line and wide brown eyes to Malik. My mind shifted to the night-mares I'd been spared. I would have played Uncle Bill's death face over and over again in my waking mind, and at night the pasty skin and partial smile beneath eyes that had been glued shut would come to haunt me. Like the dreams I had after Emmitt Till's bloated, un-recognizable corpse was featured on the cover of *Jet* magazine.

Aunt Evelyn sat, trance-like, staring at the casket as if she was willing the top to open and Uncle Bill to step out. She didn't cry, not even when Daddy read the eulogy. Hers were the only dry eyes in the house. She remained in her trance through the sermon and the soul-shaking music. She didn't flinch when Sister Johnson caught the Holy Ghost and jerked and gyrated back and forth right in front of us. As soon as I saw her coming our way I slid closer to Daddy just in case that ghost jumped out of her and into me. I knew Daddy would know what to do. Momma might have let it happen, praying all along that it would "straighten" me out.

When it came the time for people to take their turn at the mike, sharing their favorite memory of Uncle Bill and expressing their heartfelt condolences to Aunt Evelyn and Malik, she just nodded her head. She only pulled her eyes away from the casket long enough for Mr. Robinette to say his piece, and when he stepped away from the mic, there, standing behind Mr. Robinette was Evangeline, looking like she'd slid right out of the fashion page in *Ebony* magazine.

I heard Aunt Evelyn say once that Evangeline was so fine, she'd have given Lena Horne a run for her money. I couldn't imagine it, because the Evangeline I always saw was the one I'd always seen. The one who walked around the neighborhood looking disheveled and lost. Uncle Bill said, on that same day, that Evangeline was the finest girl at Compton High School. "It's no wonder Frank fell—" he started to say, then looked over at me and, for some reason, swallowed the rest of the sentence.

Nervous chatter erupted around the sanctuary. I figured everyone was thinking the same thing I was. "Wow, she looks good!" then "Oh Lord, please don't embarrass yourself in the House of the Lord."

Judging by the immediate calm that followed, it must have been everyone's belief that even Evangeline wasn't so crazy she'd show out in the Lord's House. She'd gone to a lot of trouble to make herself presentable. I couldn't take my eyes off her. Who would have ever guessed she had the body of a Coke bottle under that dusty house coat she was always tramping around in? She'd even straightened her hair. It hung several inches below her shoulder. She looked like a model in her form-fitting black dress and stiletto heels.

Daddy shifted in his seat. Momma looked over at him, then down at me. Then, as if something urgent crossed her mind, she pushed me forward and whisper-shouted across me into Daddy's ear. No else heard her, but I certainly did.

"What in the hell is she doing up there?"

Daddy whisper-shouted back, "How in the hell am I supposed to know. Maybe she's paying her respects like everyone else."

Momma pulled me back by my shoulder and started fumbling around in her purse for only God knew what.

Evangeline cleared her throat and said, "May God be with you."

"And also with you," everyone, except Momma, said in return.

"I can't believe our Bill is gone. We've been friends since third grade, not long after his family moved next door to us. We've been neighbors ever since. So many years ago now I've lost track. I guess my favorite memory of Bill was the night he introduced me to Frank."

She looked over at Daddy. Momma looked at Daddy, too. So did I. Judging by the sound of people shifting in their seats, I suspected everyone else was looking at Daddy. I was just too embarrassed to turn around and see.

"Remember that night, Frank? Who would have thought you'd marry me and then toss me aside when you met that floozy," she said, pointing at Momma accusingly.

Pastor Shuttlesworth took hold of Evangeline's left arm. He tried to pull her away from the podium, she held on.

"You didn't even have the decency to divorce me. Did you? Like a coward, you just left in the night."

Deacon Jones took Evangeline's right arm. She snatched it away.

"You moved that floozy into what should have been *our* house. Why, Frank?"

In answer, Pastor Shuttlesworth gently took the mic from her hand and put it back on its stand. He walked her off the pulpit.

She shouted, "Why? Because I couldn't give you babies? Is that it? Is that it?"

Then she collapsed into tears. I wondered why she couldn't give Daddy babies and why she waited until now to ask. Didn't she care that Uncle Bill was dead? Everybody was here for him. Nobody cared that she couldn't have babies.

"Come on, Sister McKinney," Pastor Shuttlesworth said, taking her arm in his. "Let's get you back to your seat."

"Why, Pastor?" she asked, still crying. "You know I'm not lying. I'd never lie in the Lord's house."

"It's okay. I know. But this ..." Pastor Shuttlesworth moved out of earshot.

Chatter started up around us. Aunt Evelyn cut her eyes at Momma and shook her head. Momma shifted in her seat. Daddy moved closer to Momma and took her hand. She snatched it away.

"Zora, please don't make a scene. Just let it go," Daddy said.

Momma sat board straight, barely breathing. The chatter moved around the theater like a game of telephone. When Pastor Shuttlesworth's came back to the pulpit he cleared his throat and said, "Amen."

The chatter continued. Rising and falling as it worked its way back to the front of the sanctuary.

"Amen," Pastor said again, louder this time.

The room fell silent.

"Amen" we said, in return.

"Gossip is an ugly thing. So, let's leave this moment here in the church. We aren't here for that." He glanced over at Aunt Evelyn who still hadn't shed a tear. "Sister Edwards lost her husband. Malik, a father. And we lost the only Negro police officer who ever did anything to protect this community. He helped the Robinette's get some relief when those two officers beat their son. He was starting a program that would hold LAPD accountable for their racist actions. And, we lost him, but none of us will feel his absence the way his family will. Sister Edwards. Thank you for sharing Bill with us. He's with the Lord now. He's in a better place. Your family just got bigger. We are here with you. We're going to carry you through this."

"Amen," everyone said again.

Except me, because I couldn't stop crying.

* * * * * *

I followed Momma, Aunt Evelyn, and Malik to the limo waiting behind the hearse. It had a large back seat and two individual seats directly across with a walnut finished cabinet in between. Malik and I climbed in first, followed by Momma and Aunt Evelyn. Aunt Evelyn lit a cigarette and yelled for the limo driver to roll down the window. Moments later, hot air and smoke filled the cabin. Daddy sat up front with the driver. I focused my attention out the window, refusing to look in Momma's direction.

No one said a word as the limo weaved its way across Los Angeles. Past the charred remains of 103rd Street where the best parts of my childhood floated between the smoky ash and bombed out remains of restaurants and shops I'd never experience again. Mabel's Soul Kitchen's dollar pancakes and apple pie ala mode. The possibility of free ice cream from Mr. Moskowitz's store. Books from Mr. Landes' store and the lollipops I always found in the bottom of the bag. The handfuls of nut chews courtesy of Mr. Plummer. Watching pretty ladies dance in the doorway of The Malidy Hotel. Sitting on the roof of The Sanctuary sipping Skinny McKinneys and watching the sunset with Daddy. Saturday matinees at The Largo sipping Coke and smoking candy cigarettes. All of it– gone. Just about everything that made me proud to call Watts my home was gone.

We turned right onto Central Avenue. Two blocks up on the left, smoke swirled above the piles of brick and debris. The Ennis Family Medicine sign lay across what used to be the entrance to the building where three generations of Negro doctors managed the health and well-being of three generations of McKinneys. I wondered if that included Evangeline, and swallowed the tears that came up with the thought. At Manchester Avenue we turned left into a new reality. In stark contrast to Watts, pristine stores and homes sat unaffected because the inhabitants happened to have white skin. A makeshift sign that read "turn around or get shot" leaned against the light pole facing Central Avenue. Two military vehicles, one on either side of the street, were filled with National Guardsmen pre-pared to make good on the warning. Malik squeezed my hand so hard it hurt but I didn't let go.

By the time we turned into the winding driveway of Inglewood Cemetery I was crying all over again. Not because my hand hurt, but because I'd become painfully aware that no one cared about the destruction of my community or any of us that live there. The news and Mayor Yorty assessed the damage, yet only focused on the mil-lions of dollars lost in what they called an "unprovoked act of vio-lence by the Negroes of Watts." There was no talk of rebuilding and Daddy said not to hold our breath because there wouldn't be any. We would have to make do with whatever remained, which wasn't much.

We stepped out of the limo into the blinding afternoon sunlight. The birds and trees stood still, too hot to move. Daddy lit a cigarette and waited for the rest of the pallbearers to arrive. Aunt Evelyn pulled Malik into her and, to our surprise, he didn't pull away. That left me and Momma standing there like gunfighters at the O.K. cor-ral. She reached for my hand. I hesitated at first and then allowed her to take it.

I tried to focus my attention on the names engraved on the head-stones, except I couldn't help wondering how different things might have been if Evangeline was my mother. She wouldn't have been hell-bent on making me just like her. She would have been so happy to have a family that she would have accepted us just the way we were. I bet Evangeline was really nice before Momma stole the life she wanted for herself. And instead of Momma being nice to make up for it, she was extra mean to Evangeline every chance she got. If I stole someone's man, I would have had the decency not to rub their nose in it. I would have done anything I could to make up for it, even if it meant letting my man help out every once in a while. I snatched my hand away from Momma's.

At the gravesite, I sat down next to Malik and put my hand on the open seat next to me. For a second I thought Momma was going to make me move my hand. Instead, she kissed the top of my head and sat down, leaving the seat open for Daddy. I didn't want to be so mean to Momma, but I couldn't help myself. She deserved it. Everyone was always so nice to her and all she could do was talk about them behind their backs. It explained why Aunt Evelyn was her only friend.

Malik took my hand again. His hand was wet from the tears he'd wiped away. I wanted to hug him and couldn't seem to move. I felt like I was on the edge of breaking from pain and grief. I could only imagine how Malik felt. The emptiness he would never be able to fill now that he would live without his father. The thought that there would be nothing I could do to make him feel better made me cry. I knew, without knowing, that I'd lost two friends that summer—because Malik would never be the same.

There was a short service, and when the minister finished reading from the Bible, he turned his attention to the nine Black police officers in dress blues that stood a few feet back from the gravesite. One lifted a trumpet to his lips and began playing "Taps." Seven lifted their rifles with white-gloved hands and waited for the command.

"Fire," the remaining officer shouted.

In unison, the officers fired three times into the sky above our heads. Malik flinched at each gunshot.

Two officers lifted the American flag from the casket and folded it into the shape of a triangle. One walked over and handed it to Aunt Evelyn. As soon as it touched her hands, she began to shake. Malik, who hadn't stopped crying from the moment they carried the casket out of the limo, took the flag from her and held it on his lap. Aunt Evelyn stopped shaking and began rocking back and forth. Malik watched the flag as if he was receiving instructions. Then he got up and carried the flag to the edge of the gravesite. It all seemed to be happening in slow motion. I wondered if he was considering jumping or trying to stop the casket from entering. The answer came when he threw the flag into the open hole and walked calmly back to his seat next to Aunt Evelyn. Everyone was staring at Malik as if he'd lost his mind. The casket dangled above the open gravesite while the crane operator searched the faces in the crowd for further instruction. The minister looked at Aunt Evelyn, who was rocking and holding Malik. Daddy motioned for him to continue, and Uncle Bill's casket slowly descended into the ground. No one bothered to get the flag out first. It was understandable, suddenly, why the flag had to be buried with Uncle Bill. It was as loaded for us as Uncle Bill's lifeless, bullet-ridden body.

* * * * * *

Momma stayed with Aunt Evelyn until the last mourner expressed their condolences. Aunt Evelyn had yet to shed a tear and I was beginning to worry about her. Daddy said that sometimes people go crazy when they hold their emotions inside. I wondered if that's what happened with Evangeline. I didn't want that for Aunt Evelyn. I closed my eyes and asked God to give Aunt Evelyn a reason to cry and I hoped that this time He was actually listening.

A slight breeze moved between the trees. I wiped the sweat from my brow as I studied Daddy. He handed Malik a handful of flowers to take to the limo. He stuck the guest book under his arm and took a handful of flowers for himself. In all my wildest dreams, I never would have imagined that he was like all the men Momma and Aunt Evelyn called, "Dirty Dogs." Men who cheated on their wives, had children outside their marriage, had families outside their families. What if we were the family outside his family? Had he really left because Evangeline couldn't have children? Or had he left because Momma had diamonds between her legs? I'd overheard Mrs. Armstrong say that once and when I asked Momma what it meant she told me not to pay attention to a thing Mrs. Armstrong said. She'd said, "You can't trust nothing that heffa says. She's a lie and truth ain't in her." I turned my attention to Momma then. Mrs. Armstrong wasn't the only liar.

Daddy pulled me out of my thoughts.

"Ladybug, take this guest book to the car and wait with Malik. Your mother and Evelyn will be there in a moment. I'm going to the church with Mr. and Mrs. Robinette to help set up for the repast. I'll see you later, okay?"

I didn't answer. My eyes were still locked on Momma. He elbowed me, and after a moment I turned my focus to him. He knew what I was thinking. He always knew what I was thinking, even when I didn't want him to.

"We'll talk about all of it later, alright? I promise."

Tears burned my eyes. I tried to keep them in, but they rolled down my face anyway.

"When?"

"When all of this is over and Evelyn and Malik are feeling better."

That seemed like a long way off. When were they ever going to feel better? Probably never. There was no point in arguing about it. I knew we would talk about it when he was ready and not a minute sooner. I took the guest book, pressed it tight against my chest, and walked away.

By the time Momma and Aunt Evelyn joined us they were sweat-drenched and talking easy. Malik and I took our seats. Momma and Aunt Evelyn resumed their place on the back seat. As the car moved down the winding road toward Manchester Aunt Evelyn kicked off her shoes and curled up next to Momma. She lay her head across Momma's lap and sighed. Momma placed her hand on Aunt Evelyn's shoulder and gave it a gentle rub.

"I'm sorry, Z," Aunt Evelyn said, and pulled Momma's hand down and kissed it.

Momma smiled and said, "It's okay, Ev. I understand," and began to cry.

"You know I didn't mean any of it, right? I'm just...so...so...I...can't believe he's gone."

And, finally, Aunt Evelyn allowed herself to let it all go and wailed.

"I know. I know," Momma said, rocking Aunt Evelyn gently.

Malik kneeled before his mother and said. "It's okay, ma. I'm here. I'll take care of you."

His words made her wail even harder.

"Come here, baby," she said, and scooped him into her embrace.

It was nice to see that God did listen to me. Sometimes.

26

Riots Shift to Long Beach
L.A. Times – Monday, August 23, 1965

> *There is no better than adversity.*
> *Every defeat, every heartbreak,*
> *every loss, contains its own seed,*
> *its own lesson on how to improve*
> *your performance the next time.*
>   ~Malcolm X, El-Hajj Malik El-Shabazz, Civil Rights
> Leader

I was determined to do something nice for Aunt Evelyn and Malik. The idea came to me that night at the repast. They'd barely eaten, even though there was enough food to feed all of Watts. Fried chicken, roast beef, rib tips, glazed ham, collard greens, green beans and potatoes, macaroni and cheese, candied yams, potato salad, coleslaw, and dinner rolls. Then there was Seven-Up cake, red velvet cake, pineapple upside-down cake, and a peach cobbler for dessert. I polished off two plates of food and Momma said I tried to eat my weight in peach cobbler. Malik, who usually eats ten times more than me, barely touched his food. Aunt Evelyn couldn't eat because every time she tried someone walked up to let her know how much they were going to miss Uncle Bill. So I decided before I went to sleep that I would get up early and make breakfast. I knew they would be good and hungry by then.

The next morning, I was up before the chickens, as Nana would say. Malik, after a long talk with Daddy, slept in the playroom with Aunt Evelyn, which made all of us happy – especially Aunt Evelyn. Although I missed having him there, I was glad to have my bed to myself without him kicking me half the night. As soon as the alarm went off at seven o'clock I bounced out of bed. I pulled on my robe, slipped my feet into my house slippers, and headed to the kitchen. To my surprise, Aunt Evelyn was sitting at the table drinking a cup of coffee. A cigarette burned in the ashtray. She took a long drag and blew it out slowly.

"Good morning, Sleeping Beauty. What are you doing up this early?" she asked.

"I'm gonna make breakfast," I blurted out proudly.

She chuckled and said, "You are, are you? Why? Does Zora have you in here this early trying to cook?"

"Nope. I'm doing it for you and Malik."

She looked up at me and smiled. Smoke swirled above her head. "That's nice. But you don't have to do that."

"I know. I want to. I want you and Malik to feel better and I want you to know how much I love you."

I hadn't intended on saying all that, but the truth was the truth. This made her laugh.

"Well, I can't promise you anything. Guess that depends on what you're gonna make. It better be good, too, 'cause I am hungry. I barely ate anything last night."

"I know. That's why I'm making salmon croquettes, eggs, and grits."

"Humph. That sounds like a good Zora style breakfast. Let me get out of your way."

She got up to leave. Before I knew she was there, I was prepared to cook alone. Having her there brought me a sense of comfort in case I needed help.

"Will you stay with me?" I asked.

"Of course," she said, and sat down. "You ain't gon' try to put me to work, are you?"

"No," I said, and laughed.

I started pulling the ingredients out for the croquettes. I chopped up half an onion, making sure to put a stalk of celery in my mouth so my eyes wouldn't water. Then I chopped up half a green pepper. I put the chopped peppers and onions in a skillet, added a little butter, and let it cook until the onions were translucent. I got two cans of salmon out of the pantry, removed the bones, and put the salmon in a mixing bowl. I cracked two eggs into the salmon and stirred until all the ingredients were blended together, just the way Nana taught me.

"Your grandmother taught us how to make salmon croquettes when we were your age. Did your mother ever tell you that?"

"No," I said, thinking off all the other things she never told me.

"I spent so much time at Zora's house they started calling me their third daughter. My father was a Pullman Porter and wasn't home much and my mother worked for a white family in Evanston. She got home late and was up and out early in the morning before the rooster crowed, as they used to say. My aunt stayed with me most of the time, but she wasn't good for much. She didn't have children of her own, she couldn't cook, so being left as my charge scared her to death. She was terrified she might break me. If it hadn't been for your mother I would have never been allowed outside. You better not let you mother see you cooking like this or you'll never be allowed outside either. She'll have you in here cooking every night."

We laughed. Mostly because we knew it wasn't true. Momma loved cooking, especially for Daddy, and if anyone was going to prepare his meals it was going to be her. For that I was grateful. I'd just started cooking and wasn't anywhere close to the chef Momma was. But I appreciated the compliment.

Aunt Evelyn helped me shape the salmon into patties and coat them in corn meal as she told me about growing up with Momma.

"I knew we were gonna be best friends the second she sauntered over to our table with a purse full of crayons that she brought from home. She introduced herself as Zora the Magnificent. Can you believe it? Yeah. I know you can. When she saw me outlining the image before I colored it in she asked me if I wanted to be friends. Lord knows we've been through hell and high water together since, but we've had more good times than bad. Don't get me wrong. She gets on my damn nerves sometimes, mostly because I know her better than she knows herself."

I pulled the cast iron skillet from its drawer under the oven and placed it on the stove. Aunt Evelyn handed me the oil can from the kitchen counter. I moved over so she could pour some into the skillet. I didn't trust that I wouldn't spill it all over the place.

"Can I ask you a question?" I said.

"Sure, baby. You know you can ask me anything."

I wasn't sure where to start. I also wasn't sure she'd answer me, but I had to ask. Last night I'd overheard Mrs. Armstrong talking about the night Momma and Daddy met. She was in the bathroom with another woman. I was just outside the door in the hall. I started to go in until I heard her say that she was there the night Momma met Daddy. She said Aunt Evelyn was there, too, and they told Momma that Daddy was already married, and Momma said, 'he is now, but not for long'. I didn't want to believe Momma could be that cold-hearted. That would mean I didn't know either one of my parents like I thought I did, which would also mean I wouldn't be able to trust either of them ever again. I told Aunt Evelyn what Mrs. Armstrong said. She laughed and told me to sit down.

"First of all, Arlene Armstrong is a lyin'-ass bitch. Pardon my French. She's so jealous of your mother she can't see straight. She's never been able to get over the fact that Frank chose Zora."

"But he was married."

"That ain't for me to get into. Your parents will talk to you about that when they're ready. What I want you to know until that time, no matter what you hear, is this...there was nothing funky about the way they came together. Do you hear me?"

I nodded even though I didn't fully understand what "funky" meant.

"Now, enough of grown folk's business. Come here and let me show you how to make my secret recipe grits. I won't even tell your momma how I make them, so take it to your grave."

I promised. Aunt Evelyn got a pot from the cabinet. She poured in half a cup of cold water and added an equal amount of milk. She told me to cut off half a stick of butter. I dropped the butter in the pot. She turned up the fire halfway and shook in a little salt.

"We're gonna wait for it to boil, then we'll mix in the grits. Let's get these croquettes cooking."

I placed the croquettes in the oil and cooked them on both sides. I wondered what the secret ingredient was, Momma made her grits with milk and butter, too. So did Nana. When the water began to boil, Aunt Evelyn took over with the croquettes and handed me a wooden spoon. She told me to stir slowly and pour the grits in even slower. I did as I was instructed.

"Now it's time for the secret ingredient."

She pulled a container of parmesan cheese out of the pantry. I frowned. Momma only put that on spaghetti. As if she was reading my mind, she said, "Trust me. You won't even taste it."

That made even less sense. If I couldn't taste it, why put it in there? Still laughing, she poured a handful into the pot.

"Here. Put this back," she said, stirring the cheese into the grits. "Now, we wait for it to boil again and then we'll turn the fire all the way down and let it simmer."

When continued cooking the croquettes. Then I got the eggs out of the refrigerator. Aunt Evelyn told me to go get everyone up for breakfast while she prepared to scramble the eggs.

* * * * * *

We sat at the dining room table eating off Momma's fine china. The good thing about that was that I wouldn't have to wash dishes. Daddy said grace and before she'd taken one bite, Momma started in on the croquettes.

"Did you put in the eggs?"

"Yes, Momma."

"Did you pick out the bones?"

"Yes, Momma."

"Ummph," she responded.

"Did you remember to cook the green peppers and onions first?"

"Yes, Momma."

Daddy took a forkful of croquette and chewed. "Mmmm, Ladybug! These are delicious."

"Humph, I'll be the judge of that," Momma said.

I couldn't tell if he really meant it or if he was saying it to shut Momma up. Aunt Evelyn rolled her eyes.

"Ignore her, baby. Everything is just fine. And the croquettes are perfect," she said.

"Thanks," I said, grinning.

Malik showed his appreciation by polishing off two croquettes and half his grits. I happily handed him the plate. We ate in silence for a while. Daddy said that's how you can tell the food is good. He said if folks are talking when they should be eating, you might want to find a better recipe. All of a sudden, Aunt Evelyn blurts out, "So y'all just gon' sit there eatin' and actin' like you don't have some shit to clean up?"

I almost fell out of my chair. Momma dropped her fork. Daddy, always cool under pressure, placed his fork on the edge of his plate and wiped his mouth. He considered Aunt Evelyn a moment and then looked across the table at Momma. I shifted in my seat. Aunt Evelyn sucked her teeth and opened her mouth to say something. Daddy cut her off.

"We're not doing this now, Ev," he said.

"Why not? If not now, when? Seems to me like everyone at this table knows the truth except Zay. And now folks are talking about it on the street. You want her to hear someone else's version of the truth? Or tell it yourself?"

Everyone, I thought. Including Malik? I looked over at him. He looked at me out of the corner of his eye.

"You knew?" I asked, for what felt like the hundredth time. I couldn't believe he'd lied to me all this time.

"Not everything."

"Ladybug," Daddy began. "Remember I told you I'd tell you about Miss Evangeline when you're old enough?"

I nodded. I was crying now.

Momma opened her mouth to protest, but Daddy cut his eyes in her direction. She closed her mouth and leaned back in her chair.

"While I don't think you're old enough to understand, Ev has a point. It's time you know the truth before–"

"Evelyn! You need to mind your own damned business. This ain't none of Zayla's business," Momma practically shouted.

"It's her business now. Thanks to you and your messy-ass friend, Arlene."

"Arlene and I are not friends!" Momma shouted, again.

"Not now, but she used to be. And if you had cut her ass off when I told you to, we wouldn't be here now."

Momma sighed in resignation. "Then let me tell her," she said. "Better she hear it from me."

"Can I be excused?" Malik asked. When no one answered, he excused himself anyway.

"Where you going?" I asked.

He didn't answer me. But when I heard the backdoor close, I knew I could find him in the treehouse when all this was over.

"Your father and I met on my twenty-second birthday," Momma said. "Evelyn and Arlene took me to the Sanctuary to celebrate. This was before your father owned it. Back then, he was still performing. It was between sets and I'd excused myself to the ladies' room. I was coming out as he was coming down the hall. We crashed right into each other and I remember looking at him and thinking, "this is the man I'm going to spend the rest of my life with." I can't explain it. I just knew we were gonna be together. I played hard to get, of course. But I knew. I think he knew, too."

"But he was married," I said.

"I didn't know that, at the time."

"Yes, you did! I heard Mrs. Armstrong say so last night."

Momma looked at Aunt Evelyn, who looked away and said, "I told you to drop that bitch that night. But you wouldn't listen."

"I didn't know he was married when we met in that narrow hallway. Did I, Frank?"

Daddy shook his head. And Momma continued.

"We had that kind of storybook romance. He proposed after only two months of courting."

"Three," Daddy interjected. "It took me three months to get up the courage. I was terrified she would say no."

Momma laughed and said, "There was no way that was happening. I was so in love with him, I couldn't see straight. But I was also in my senior year of college and had no intentions of getting married that soon. I'd come all the way to California to become a school teacher and eventually a school principal. So I told him he'd have to wait. About six months after graduation I found out I was pregnant with you. I was teaching at the time. First grade. I had my whole career ahead of me. But I knew I couldn't have a child out of wedlock, so I agreed to marry him. We planned a simple ceremony at City Hall. On the day of the wedding he didn't show. They called our name, no Frank. Evelyn and I waited and waited. I imagined the worst. Something must have happened to him. Just as we were headed out, here he comes. Not to get married, though. To tell me Evangeline wouldn't sign the divorce papers."

"Huh?" I turned to Daddy. "You were already married to Ms. Evangeline and you proposed to Momma?"

"Yes and no," Daddy said. "It wasn't that simple."

"Why not? If you were already married, you weren't supposed to want to marry someone else," I said.

"I'm really not ready to have this conversation."

"Get ready," Aunt Evelyn said. "There's no way around it. Arlene is making her rounds, telling her version of the story. Is that what you want Zayla to believe?"

Daddy sighed. "Look, Ladybug. My relationship with Evangeline goes all the way back to high school. We were in love once. Then we weren't. I'm not going into all the details. Let's just suffice it to say that she lied to me and tried to manipulate me so that I would stay with her. When I found out the truth, she lied some more and she got her whole family and mine in on the lie."

"What did she lie about?" I asked.

Momma said, "Tell her the whole story, Frank."

"No. I won't. I don't like talking about it."

"She lied and said she was pregnant," Aunt Evelyn blurted out.

"He was on tour back then. This was right at the beginning of his career. She didn't like him traveling all the time, so she called him one night and told him she was pregnant. When that didn't bring him home, she called a few weeks later and told him she was miscarrying. That did the trick. He came home and stayed for almost three months."

"Then something told me to make sure the hospital bill was paid before I went back out on the road," Daddy added. "When I called the doctor's office, they told me she didn't have a balance due. I couldn't believe she'd been in the hospital and there wasn't a bill, so I called the hospital. They said they'd never had anyone by the name 'Evangeline McKinney' admitted to the hospital. A little more digging and I found out she'd never been pregnant. You can just say that was the beginning of the end. I moved out two months later and had no intentions of moving back. And when I first asked for a divorce, she wouldn't sign the papers. So, I went on living as if we were divorced, and then I met your mother. When I asked Evangeline to sign the papers again, I figured she'd do it. Knowing I was moving on. But she fooled me. She still refused to sign. I couldn't believe it."

"I couldn't believe it either," Momma said, taking over. "He'd told me that it was all taken care of, and in truth, he had stopped living with her but she was so in love with him she didn't want to let him go. I guess long story short, I had a choice to make and I chose you.

"I told him I would give him time to get Evangeline to sign the divorce papers, and until then I would act as if we were already married. The idea of letting everyone know I was having you out of wedlock was too humiliating to bear. I would have never heard the end of it from your grandparents. It was important that you bear his name and he take total responsibility for you. That was what mattered most to me. And he agreed. So, we went about the business of being man and wife without the benefit of clergy. And then you were born and shortly after that Evangeline tried to take her own life."

A million questions popped in my head, but the most important one fell out: "So when did you get married?"

"Well, hang on. I'm getting to that. You were about three months old when Frank received the phone call. Evangeline had taken a bottle of sleeping pills. Except she hadn't really meant to kill herself; she just wanted to get Frank's attention. He didn't come when he said he would and save her the way she'd planned, so she was forced to call 911. Oh, she put on quite the act for him, blaming him for her psychological problems. Telling him how disappointed her father would be in him if he were alive. Frank felt so guilty, he moved back home with her."

I looked over at Daddy. In a million years I never would have guessed he could do something so cruel. To Evangeline. To Momma. I turned back to Momma and tried to keep the tears in my eyes. She took my hand.

"I didn't like it at first, but I knew the kind of man Frank was. So, I put up with it. I loved him unconditionally and I knew he would make it right. At least I hoped he would. I mean...for a while he did, at least for appearance sake. The first four years of your life he was there for dinner and breakfast, and he spent every weekend with us. But right around your fifth birthday, Aunt Maxine came to visit. I felt like I was dying inside. I made the mistake of confiding the whole mess to her. Except, she wasn't as accepting as I thought she would be.

"When she saw Frank later on that day, she told him to either leave Evangeline or leave me alone. I don't know why this pissed me off so, but we fought viciously after that. I told her to stay out of my business and when she left she said she'd do me one better. It's been eight years and we haven't spoken.

"But she'd done me a favor. Her ultimatum forced Frank to think about what he'd lose if he went back to Evangeline permanently. He couldn't imagine leaving me or you. He also knew the only reason he'd chosen to stay with Evangeline was out of guilt. He made a choice. He chose me. He chose you. And he left her. And he stayed gone even after she made a second attempt on her life. After she'd been picked up for indecent exposure for walking around the neighborhood naked. Every attempt she made to pull him back to her only served to push him further away. After a while, we were able to go on with our lives.

"But as you got older the guilt began to eat at me. I believed I was the laughingstock of Watts. I only had one true friend, and that was Evelyn. Arlene Armstrong wanted Frank for herself. When he chose me that night, she started this vicious rumor that I'd plotted to take Frank from Evangeline. People believed her. Folks started whispering about me behind my back. Some of them were so mean I learned to be mean right with them. I was so busy worrying about me and how I looked that I never considered what was happening with you.

"If I could take it all back and do it differently, I would. Not that I would change my decision to stay with your father. That was a choice I will never regret. But I wouldn't have let a piece of paper dictate how I behaved, toward you, your father, and the people in this community. For a long time, I hated them all for making me feel like the outsider who came in and disrupted a happy home. Because they weren't happy. The demise of their relationship had everything to do with the fact that Evangeline lied to Frank about something that mattered so much to him. To find out he was having a child, then to go through losing the child, only to discover there was no child was more than he could handle. More than anyone could handle.

"No, we didn't get married. And I didn't regret it until you started walking around calling attention to yourself. Calling attention to me. Here I was trying to create this perfect family and you get caught kissing a girl at school, dressing like a little boy, and then questioning God as if He made a mistake when he made you. And that mistake, at least in mind, wasn't that God made you a girl instead of a boy, but that God was punishing me for loving Frank. My comeuppance for getting tangled up with a married man.

"The part I would do differently is being a better mother to you. I didn't want people talking about you the way they'd done me. I just wanted you to stop giving people something to talk about. I'm really sorry, Zay, and I hope you can forgive me one day."

I sat there speechless. I didn't know what to say.

* * * * * *

Several days after Uncle Bill's funeral, a letter came addressed to me. I recognized the handwriting right away. It was from Cynthia. The return address read, C. Harper, P.O. Box 256, Route 10, Fairhope, Alabama. I felt tears well in my eyes before I could even get it opened.

> *Hi Zayla,*
>
> *I hope you don't hate me. I wouldn't blame you if you did. I'm really sorry about how things turned out and that it's taken me so long to write. For a long time, I didn't know what I was supposed to say that would explain what happened. Then I was talking to my grandma the other day, and she said sometimes it's just easier to start at the beginning. So, here goes.*
>
> *My mother sent me to Christian camp to straighten me out. For six months I had to read Bible verses and listen to sermons about how wrong it was to like girls. And talk. We talked a lot! Then some psychiatrist came in and gave us shock treatments once a week. I knew I'd never go home until I admitted I was ready to lead a "normal" life.*

My father left my mother for sending me away. So, Momma sent me to live with my grandmother because she blamed me for Daddy leaving.

Life with Grandma wasn't easy at first, but I figured out that it was easier to be "normal" than to let anyone ever know the truth. I'll probably never go on a date until I'm old enough to leave here because as bad as Grandma is, the people down here are worse. It's bad enough I had to be born as a Negro.

I miss you a whole lot and wish we could go back to the day before everything went crazy. Maybe we could have done things differently so that we would never be separated. But my grandma says don't nothing good come to those who sit around wishing for things to be different than they are. Everything happens for a reason, and even though I don't understand the reason, I'm glad we were ever friends to begin with. And, if we're still friends somehow, I hope you write me back.

What I wish most for you is that you're happy. That you're okay with who you are and you're happy.

Your best friend for life,

Cynthia

p.s. – I still love you and I'm glad we met.

I read the letter three times before I folded it back into its envelope and tucked it between my mattress and box spring.

I thought we would be friends for life. Momma told me to get over it. People move on. Sometimes friends outgrow each other. Yeah. Sometimes they do. And sometimes they don't. I never believed Cynthia just moved on without me.

That summer taught me a lot about life's frailties. The uprisings proved that to me because after all their efforts, the only thing that came from them was death, destruction, and the loss of an entire community. 103rd Street became known as "Charcoal Alley." The L.A. city council redlined Watts shortly after the uprising, which was a sign that no government assistance would be given for rebuilding. Daddy was right. Insurance companies found loopholes to climb through, and we were left to fend for ourselves.

Where it was hard for some people before the uprising, it became next to impossible for everyone afterward. Mr. Moskowitz and Crogan were gone. The Giant supermarket and Safeway, also gone. To get groceries, Momma had to drive to South Gate or go north into L.A. The same was true for clothing or anything else we needed.

Aunt Evelyn and Malik went to Chicago shortly after the funeral to visit and decided to move back there. Aunt Evelyn said it was too hard to stay when everywhere she looked, she was reminded of Uncle Bill. Malik and I talked on the phone every once in a while, but he had become a shell of the brother I'd once had, and there was nothing I would ever be able to do to bring that part of him back. I let him know that I would always be there for him when he was ready to let me back in. I prayed that day would eventually come.

Daddy resigned from the radio station and took the insurance money for The Sanctuary and opened a new nightclub on Slauson, The Sanctuary East, in Windsor Hills. He also became partners with the owner of a nightclub downtown, that they renamed Sylvester's. Momma busied herself with decorating both nightclubs, which occupied most of her days and some evenings. Sometimes it felt as if I'd been abandoned by everyone I'd ever cared about, because I spent most days alone, lost in my thoughts.

I still had to go to Miss Viola's, which was gruesome without Cynthia, but the girls pretty much left me alone. Every once in a while, I'd look up and catch one of them staring at me with questions in their eyes. I knew they wanted to know what it was like. It's what everyone wanted to know once they found out I was from Watts and had somehow managed to survive the summer of '65. I decided I wouldn't tell anyone until I was good and ready. As it was, it took a long time to accept that I hadn't just survived the uprisings. I was there on the front line and lived to tell about it.

One good thing arose from the rubble. On my thirteenth birthday, Momma and Daddy went to City Hall and made their union official. Aunt Evelyn and Malik were there. Malik stood as Daddy's Best Man and Aunt Evelyn was Momma's Matron of Honor. We all celebrated their honeymoon together in Palm Springs. When Momma started getting ideas about how nice the homes were down there, Daddy told her to put those foolish thoughts out of her mind. On our last night during dinner, Daddy ordered champagne all around. Even Malik and I were allowed to indulge, even if it was just a sip.

"What's the good news?" Momma asked.

Daddy handed her a photograph of a two-story house with two columns on each side of the door and large windows that faced a wide tree-lined street.

"Welcome to your new Windsor Hills home," he said.

Momma screamed so loud everyone in the restaurant turned around to see if she was alright. Malik and I rolled our eyes and then couldn't help laughing. Then Momma, Daddy, and Aunt Evelyn started laughing, too.

Aunt Evelyn draped her arm around my shoulder and said, "Brace yourself, kid. You're about to have a Windsor Hills big house having, upper crust, champagne drinking, wanna be white, but can't shake the Negro off no matter how hard she tries, charm school momma. We thought she was bad before. Lord only knows what we're in for now."

We all laughed again, but inside I cringed at the reality of those words. Momma and I had been getting along famously for quite some while and I wanted to keep it that way. So, I tried to convince myself that I didn't like girls. It was easier to believe that I was going through an experimental phase. Except the experiment never ended.

Oh sure, I tried many times to turn my feelings to the "On" position when it came to boys. I went on dates, such as they were, with the boys Momma set me up with. I kissed a small few, but when I realized most of them wanted more than kisses, I got really good at saying, "I'm saving myself for marriage." It protected me from roaming hands and raging hormones. All the while, I continued pushing my feelings down. Then, two weeks before my sixteenth birthday, Cleopatra Anaya Ndegeocello walked into my tenth-grade English class and made my truth hard to ignore and impossible to hide.

But that's a story for another day.

Champ's Salmon Croquettes Recipe

Prep Time: 15 minutes ~ Fridge Time: 30 minutes ~ Cook Time:
15 minutes

Servings: 8-10 croquettes

Nutritional Information: Now why would I go
and ruin this experience by telling you that?

Ingredients
- 1 (14.75) **pink salmon can,** bones removed
- 1/2 cup fresh jumbo lump crab (optional)
- 1/4 cup yellow cornmeal (for inside croquette)
- 3/4 cup yellow cornmeal (set aside to roll patties in before cooking)
- 1/2 cup finely diced onion or 1 tbsp onion powder
- 1/4 cup finely diced bell pepper
- 3 cloves minced garlic
- 1 tbsp lemon juice
- 1 large egg
- 1 large egg, white only
- 1 tsp balsamic vinegar (I use Trader Griottos)

- 1/4 tsp sea salt
- 1/4 tsp black pepper
- 3/4 cup vegetable oil

Instructions

- In a small bowl, add 1/2 cornmeal and eggs. Mix thoroughly and place in the freezer while you mix the remaining ingredients (no more than 10-15 minutes).
- In a small skillet, add onion, bell pepper, minced garlic. Cook on medium-high for 2 minutes, keep it moving in the pan. Remove from heat, set aside.
- Drain salmon, remove bones, and squeeze as much of the water off the salmon as you can.
- In a large bowl, add salmon, crab (if you're using), cornmeal, and egg mixture. Next add onion, bell pepper, and garlic, balsamic vinegar, salt, and black pepper, and lemon and mix until well combined.
- Add remaining cornmeal (3/4 cup) to a plate and set aside.
- Shape mixture into small to medium-sized patties and roll, carefully, in cornmeal. Place in refrigerator for 30 minutes.
- Add oil to cast iron skillet and heat until oil reaches 375 (7-10 minutes, but use a thermometer to check at the 7-minute mark). Fry croquettes until golden brown on both sides, about 2-3 minutes on each side, and drain on paper towels then serve.

Enjoy!!

Love, Glodean

Glodean Champion can be best described as a "Renaissance Woman with Flair." In her professional world, she is a business transformation leader & L.O.V.E. coach. Her L.O.V.E. Method and Kaizen Your Life programs help people get out of their way so they can create achievable goals to build a life they love free from constraints.

In her creative life, she is a photographer, graphic artist, musician, and writer. Her writing has been published in Hip Mama Magazine, Exposure, The Womanist, The Word, and The Mills College Weekly. Her photography and graphic artwork have been shown in several Bay Area galleries as well as the Art of Living Black, San Francisco International Arts Festival, the San Francisco Black Film Festival, and as one of four featured artists in The Colors Within: The Inner Splendor of the Black Female.

Glodean received a B.A. from Mills College and an MFA from California College of the Arts. She's a VONA Voices and Hurston/Wright Foundation alum. Glodedan currently lives in Monterey, Calfornia with her adorable Tibetan Terrier, Tashi, and is working on the sequel to Salmon Croquettes and a memoir, "Tough Love: Sh*t My Momma Used to Say" based on her mother, Frances Champion, and "the amazing intentionality" her mother put into raising her.

CPSIA information can be obtained
at www.ICGtesting.com
Printed in the USA
FSHW021656260521
81860FS

9 780578 767550